The Sting of
Justice

Also by Cora Harrison

My Lady Judge
A Secret and Unlawful Killing

THE STING OF JUSTICE

A Mystery of Medieval Ireland

CORA HARRISON

Minotaur Books ✺ New York

THE STING OF JUSTICE. Copyright © 2009 by Cora Harrison. All rights reserved. Printed in the United States of America. For information, address St. Martin's Press, 175 Fifth Avenue, New York, N.Y. 10010.

www.minotaurbooks.com

Library of Congress Cataloging-in-Publication Data

Harrison, Cora.
 The sting of justice / Cora Harrison. — 1st U.S. ed.
     p. cm.
 ISBN 978-0-312-37269-9
 1. Women judges—Ireland—Burren—Fiction. 2. Silversmiths—Crimes against—Fiction. 3. Burren (Ireland)—History—Fiction.
4. Community life—Ireland—History—16th century—Fiction.
I. Title.
 PR6058.A6883S75 2009
 823'.914—dc22

                                                              2009033804

First published in Great Britain by Macmillan,
an imprint of Pan Macmillan Ltd

First U.S. Edition: December 2009

10 9 8 7 6 5 4 3 2 1

In memory of my father,
William D. Mockler
1896–1959

He was a lawyer who loved his profession and
appreciated all the intricacies of the law, whether
Roman Law, Common Law or Brehon Law, and it was
from him that I acquired the interest that culminated in
these stories of the ancient laws of Ireland

the sting of justice

PROLOGUE

There is something evocative about the words: *the west of Ireland.* The pictures rise swiftly to the mind: purple mountains softly veiled with mist; smoke-grey lakes strung like shining jewels all along the coastline; trees permanently bent sideways by the force of the constant west wind; grass everywhere, always an emerald green, moistened each day by gently falling rain.

But that is not the Burren.

Ten miles long and ten miles wide, *An Boirenn*, the stony place, in the Gaelic language, juts out in a promontory south of Galway Bay, flanked on one side by the rich luxuriance of Kerry and on the other by the dramatic purple mountains of Connemara. It is a bare place, loved by many, disliked by some, a stripped and barren territory, a lunar landscape, a terrain of grey stone, its bones swept clean by great sheets of ice which left the fields paved in huge clints of limestone and the mountains rounded into spiralling terraces.

The people of the Burren found wealth in this rocky land. The grass that grew in the grykes, between the great clints or slabs of stone, was sweet and rich and the three wide valleys, formed by long-vanished rivers, provided lush spring and summer grazing for their herds of cattle. When

I

the autumn rains arrived and the valleys flooded, the cattle were moved to the limestone land of the lower mountains where the rocks stored up the summer heat and the grass grew through the winter months.

These mountains which girded the kingdom, like the enclosing walls of their dwelling places, held treasure within the mineral-rich seams where ancient seas had piled whorl upon whorl to form their terraced heights and this treasure was washed to the surface after winter storms and floods. Men herding their cattle or their sheep picked out lumps of gold and silver from the streams that bubbled down the mountains.

These were taken as a gift from their gods and to honour these gods they formed things of great beauty with these metals. Torcs, brooches, intricately patterned collars of gold, silver bracelets were all made by them and worn at the four sacred festivals: *Imbolc, Bealtaine, Lughnasa* and *Samhain*.

But the mountain was not despoiled.

Until, in the year 1489, a silversmith, named Sorley Skerrett, from the nearby city of Galway, heard of these finds. He climbed the heights of Cappanabhaile Mountain in the north-west corner of the Burren, sat on a terrace near the summit and bent to drink from a spring that bubbled up from the mineral-rich joint between the layers of this wedding-cake-shaped mountain. What he saw in the stream was enough to fill him with excitement. He was back next day with some men carrying picks and shovels and what they found was evidence enough for him.

Telling his secret to no one, he bought, first a tower house and its farm from Ardal O'Lochlainn, the newly appointed *taoiseach* of his clan. Then two of the three small farms nearby were bought up. The third farmer, a man with a young son, refused to sell the farm, Lios Mac Sioda, that had belonged to his family for time out of mind, but Sorley now had enough land to start to dig his mine. A party of Welsh miners, experienced in this work, were brought over and a small village was built for them.

Year after year a vast fortune in silver was smashed, hammered and melted from the mountain. Sorley grew rich: the land laid waste, the Welsh miners more wretched.

Nine years later the mountain took its revenge. The timbers that propped up the roofs had become saturated with water and unable to bear the weight of the limestone. The limestone itself, unstable and friable, began to crumble. On the last day of September in the year of 1508, there was a great storm. Heavy purple clouds swept in from the Aran Islands, sheets of lightning turned the ink-dark ocean a luminous silver, the thunderstrokes split the heavens time after time until it seemed as if the earth itself must rip apart. The people of the Burren brought their animals to shelter and then shut their door and windows and cowered within their homes until morning came and the storm died away.

They never knew that the mine on Cappanabhaile Mountain had collapsed that night, leaving nine men dead and one so injured that his friends hoped for his sake that he would die. By now the miners knew that no compassion would come from their master, Sorley. The dead were hastily buried. A new party of men was brought from Wales. The mine was rebuilt. Once again the rocks were hacked from the mountain depths; once again, the poisons seeped down through the grasses.

Sorley Skerrett became one of the richest men in the west of Ireland.

And the cows on Lios Mac Sioda died miserably on the polluted land of the mountain.

·ONE

Notes and Fragments of Early Irish Law, or Brehon Law,
transcribed by Domhnall O'Davoren and his law-scholars,
in the mid-sixteenth century, at Cahermacnaghten law school
in the Barony of Burren, west of Ireland.

This account comes from the notes written in the autumn
of 1509, by Domhnall's grandmother, Mara O'Davoren,
Brehon of the Burren, in the reign of King Turlough Donn
O'Brien. They deal with the case of a secret and unlawful
killing at the time of the festival of Samhain in 1509.

&&

THE YEAR OF 1509 had brought a golden autumn
to the west of Ireland. In the kingdom of the Burren
the sun shone almost every day. The farmers, *bóaires* and

ócaires, took a second, and then a third crop of hay from the rich grasslands of the valleys on the Burren. The limestone mountains of Cappanabhaile and of Mullaghmore sparkled silver in the warm light, storing up the heat for the winter months, and the cows grew fat on lowland grass that was moistened by nightly mists and warmed by daily sunlight.

Sunrise had come to the Burren at half an hour after seven on the morning of 31 October, the feast of *Samhain*. First the rounded terraces of Mullaghmore showed blue against the pale gold of the sky. Then the low sun of an autumn dawn dyed the polished pavements with a saffron glow. The aromatic purple-grey smoke of peat fires rose lazily into the air and the cattle came swaying across the stony fields on their way to the milking cabins, their plaintive lowing forming a soft musical background to the early morning scene.

Mara, Brehon of the Burren and *ollamh*, professor, of the law school, stood in her garden and looked over towards the ancient enclosure of Cahermacnaghten. Her six law scholars were noisily awake to the world, energetically pumping water from the well, banging the door of the scholars' house, joking with Brigid in the kitchen house, carrying a basket of sods of turf into the schoolhouse, shouting, jostling each other, the young voices drowning the lonely *chack, chack* of the plump fieldfares overhead. Cumhal, Brigid's husband and Mara's farm manager, was chopping logs outside the house where he and Brigid lived and one of the farm workers was walking the cows into the milking parlour.

It was time for lessons, but Mara lingered for a few

precious moments in her garden, gazing with deep pleasure at the magenta cranesbill, the soft-blue harebells and the mauve pincushion flowers, each colour framed by a diamond shape of limestone strips and all still blooming as if it were late summer. It had been such a beautiful autumn with almost no frosts and even now, though the leaves had mostly fallen from the trees, the sunlight brought an aromatic scent from the sharp green needles of the two rosemary bushes that grew beside her gate. With a sigh she shook herself and started to walk towards the law school. Her life was a busy one and today promised to be even busier than usual. As Brehon of the Burren she was not only responsible for law and order in that stony kingdom but also had the added responsibility of her teaching duties at the law school.

'Brigid, I don't think that I will take the boys with me to Father David's burial service,' she said, putting her head in through the door of the kitchen house. 'They'll have to go to Mass tomorrow as it's the Feast of All Saints and then again on Sunday. I think three times a week is too much. Fachtnan can supervise them for an hour or two and then they can have a game of hurley and an early dinner if I'm delayed for any reason.'

Brigid, a small sandy-haired woman, was flying around the kitchen, clearing away the porridge bowls, and wiping spills of honey from the large wooden table. She smiled now, looking at the tall, slim figure with a world of affection in her light green eyes. Mara's mother had died when she was young and Brigid, housekeeper to Mara's father, Sémus O'Davoren, Brehon of the Burren, had been more than a mother to her.

'That's probably a good idea, Brehon,' Brigid nodded approval. 'Fachtnan is a great boy, he's very good with the younger ones and Cumhal will be chopping wood in the yard for the next few hours so if Moylan or Aidan give any trouble he'll pop in and sort them out. I'll get Seán to saddle your mare now and you can be on the way. Mass is at eight o'clock, isn't it?'

'What would I do without you and Cumhal?' Mara smiled back over her shoulder as she went out. It was amazing how Brigid always managed to do so many jobs at the same moment, vigorously swilling out the porridge pot, casting a quick appraising glance over Mara and nodding approval of the fur-lined mantle, the dark hair neatly braided over her head, the green gown over the snowy white *léine*; while shouting orders about the mare to Seán, checking the time by the candle clock on the shelf, throwing a few extra sods of turf on the kitchen fire and then rapping loudly on the open shutter at the window as a signal to the scholars that morning school was going to start.

They were all sitting very upright in their desks when she went into the schoolhouse. Ten-year-old Shane and twelve-year-old Hugh were on the front bench; behind them were the two fourteen-year-olds, Aidan and Moylan, and the two older ones were at the back. Enda was sixteen and Fachtnan, who also acted as her assistant, was eighteen; both were due to take their final examinations next summer.

'*Samhain* tonight, boys,' said Mara. 'You'll have to work hard for Fachtnan if you want to have time to get ready for your party and for the festival afterwards.'

'Will we have the afternoon off, Brehon?' asked Moylan eagerly.

'Sometimes we even have nearly the whole day off,' said Aidan eyeing her hopefully.

'I can't remember that,' said Mara drily. 'However, I will have to attend the burial of Father David from Rathborney now, so I suppose if everyone works very well for Fachtnan this morning, I might think of cancelling lessons for this afternoon.'

❉

The dawn sun, low in a pale yellow sky, was almost blinding as she walked her mare sedately down the steeply spiralling path leading to Rathborney valley. The air was very clear and she could see people converging on the church from all directions, some walking, some riding, all determined to pay their last respects to a popular and devout old man.

There were figures also on the path that led from Newtown Castle, home of a prosperous silversmith and mine owner. Mara narrowed her eyes and leaned forward. Yes, it was Sorley Skerrett, the silversmith himself and Rory the bard was beside him. Mara could hear a loud laugh; the pair seemed to be best of friends. Mara lingered. After what she had learned of him last night, she had no inclination to meet Sorley again. He would probably go in by the nearby gate and would be in the church before she arrived there herself.

The bell had not yet tolled by the time that Mara reached the bottom of the hill. To her annoyance Sorley was still at the gate, engaged in earnest conversation with Bishop Mauritius O'Brien, who, no doubt, had come to honour the dead priest. Mara watched with amusement as Sorley produced a beautiful communion cup from a leather satchel. So that was why he was here – not to pay his respects to the dead, but to sell to the living. They were talking earnestly and Mara did not wish to meet either so she continued up the lane towards Gleninagh mountain, and entered the churchyard by the gate near to the old church ruins. There was a cart, with a young man holding the reins of the patient donkey, a little way up the lane and as Mara tied her horse to a nearby tree, a sturdily built man, wearing a beekeeper's veil and heavy leather gloves, came out carrying a straw skep or hive and placed it on the cart. Several bees were buzzing angrily around his head, and around the head of the young man, but both ignored them. Mara went quickly through the gate and turned to go up to the west door of the new church.

'Giolla is taking his bees up to the mountain for a last feed of heather before the winter sets in,' said a familiar voice behind Mara.

'Toin, how good to see you.' Mara turned and then hesitated. The customary thing would be to follow this by saying: 'you're looking well', but no one could say that of the figure sitting on a wooden bench beside the path; his hand was pressed to his side and his eyes were black with pain. She had heard that Toin the *briuga*, or hospitaller, was unwell, but she had not expected to see this level of deterioration in a man whom she had last seen hosting a cheerful crowd of merchants from Galway.

'You're not well, Toin,' she said, going over to him. She was fond of Toin; they shared a love of gardening and in the early days of her garden he had given her many plants, but in her busy life she had not seen him for several months.

He looks a dying man, thought Mara, eyeing with concern the *briuga*'s grey face.

'It's good to see you, Brehon, come and sit by me for a minute.' His voice was still extraordinarily rich and full – a beautiful voice, Mara always thought – but his head was like a skull, the skin dry and bloodless and the brown eyes sunk deeply into their sockets. As always, he was richly dressed; but the clothes fluttered on his emaciated form like those on a scarecrow in a windswept field.

'Can I do anything for you, assist you home perhaps?' He had been a neighbour and a close friend of Father David, but he certainly didn't look well enough to stay for the burial service and the funeral. Her words had hardly been spoken when she heard another voice.

'Could you use a strong arm, Toin? I'm all finished here now; my son will take that lot up to the hills to feed from the heather and I'll just leave these last few skeps down here in the shelter of the wall. There aren't many bees in these ones and they will be best in the warmth.' The beekeeper Giolla approached, pulling off his hat with the veil still attached and placing his heavy gauntlets inside of it before he bowed courteously to Mara.

'This is my friend, Giolla. He gives me a pot of honey every year,' said Toin with a wry smile. He was obviously very ill, but the habit of courtesy was still there.

'Your guests must enjoy that.' Mara smiled at the old man, but she feared that the hospitaller would not entertain many more guests in this life.

'I give a pot to those of my neighbours who have gardens and a swarm if they have a farm,' said Giolla sitting

down on the other side of the old man and looking at him
with concern.

'Ah, recompense for bee trespass!' said Mara. 'My scholars always find this very amusing when they learn the laws
about it. They make up jokes about spotting Eoin Mac-
Namara's bees in my garden and then serving a writ upon
him. It always seems to amuse them and it's one thing that
they never forget from their studies. Does everyone welcome the swarm? I'm not a lover of honey so wouldn't care
for it myself.'

'I don't force it on anyone.' For some reason Giolla's
open, pleasant face had grown dark with anger.

'Giolla is upset because when he presented a swarm to
our neighbour over there a few weeks ago,' explained Toin
with a nod towards the figure of Sorley still earnestly talking
to the bishop, 'well, the man picked up a shovel and thrust
the skep into the fire in the courtyard.'

'What!' Mara was appalled.

'And every one of the bees was burned to death,' said
Giolla bitterly.

'But why did he do that?'

Giolla shrugged his shoulders. 'Well, I brought them
along to him as he owns three farms. And he started
screaming at me to take them away. He had a big party of
men there. They'd all been out hunting and they were
putting the hares on trestle tables in the courtyard when I
arrived. Most of them were pretty drunk; they were swallowing down flagons of hot mead. They all started to laugh
at him and he got furiously angry. He screamed at them
that bee stings were dangerous for him. I put the straw skep

on the table and he pushed it into the fire. Anyway, let's forget him. Can I do anything for you, Toin?'

'No, no, my servant has gone for my medicine. You should go, both of you. There's the first stroke of the bell. The church will be full today.'

'I'll just check on those last few skeps and make sure that the bees are settling down,' said Giolla bowing a fare-well to Mara as she hastened towards the church.

❋

The bees were everywhere that sunny autumn, thought Mara; even here in the church a few adventurous bees had flown through the open window shutters and landed briefly on the flower-bestrewn coffin in front of the altar. From her seat at the top of the church, Mara smiled. The deceased priest, Father David, had always been fond of the little creatures. It seemed fitting that the gentle old man should have had this fleeting visit in his last hour above the ground. She glanced around the church, wondering if anyone else had noticed the bees' swift descent, but heads were bent in prayer or whispering to a neighbour and no one met her smile. Most of the people were known to her, but she caught sight of a deformed man whom she had not seen before. She turned back to the altar; the bishop had finished his last prayer, six men of the parish came forward, shoul-dered the coffin, and walked slowly along the side aisle towards the south door. The sacristan scurried ahead, key in hand; this door, which led to the ruins of the earlier church of Rathborney, was always kept locked except when a coffin was carried through it towards the graveyard.

Mara glanced around again. The custom was that the dead person's relatives were the first to follow the coffin, but Father David had only the people of the parish to mourn him. Probably Sorley Skerrett, silversmith and owner of the nearby Newtown Castle, the most important person in the parish, should be first, but he did not appear to be in the church. This was odd; surely he had not gone home once he had finished talking to the bishop. Bishop Mauritius O'Brien, cousin to the king, had a quick eye that would immediately notice his absence from the service. Sorley's plain-faced daughter, Una, was there in the front bench, as was his apprentice, Daire, and their guest, Ulick Burke, Lord of Clanrickard in the county of Galway, but Sorley, himself, was nowhere to be seen.

Quietly Mara got to her feet. As the king's representative, responsible for law and order in the kingdom, there was no doubt that, although only present today because of her affection for Father David, she was the person of highest status in the church. As soon as she moved, others stood up also and began to form an orderly line behind her, filling the middle aisle of the little church.

The key grated in the lock of the south door and the coffin bearers bent their heads in preparation for stepping through its low arch. The sacristan lifted the latch and then there was a pause. No one moved. Mara peered around the bulky form of the bishop. The sacristan's face was red as he put his weight behind the door and endeavoured to push it. Mara concealed a smile. No doubt, no one had thought of checking that the ancient door, part of the old ruined church, was still in working order. Perhaps it had swollen, or more likely, since the weather had been very dry, a giant stone had fallen from the old arch above it and had blocked it.

'Excuse me, Brehon, excuse me, my lord,' Daire pushed his way past both of them and put his powerful shoulder to the door. It opened, slowly and gradually, with no sound of stone grating on stone. As soon as there was a gap large enough, Daire squeezed through and stepped into the ruins. The crowd in the church shuffled impatiently, whispers grew louder, but then stopped abruptly as Daire stepped back into the church, closing the door behind him. His face was white and his pale blue eyes wide with shock. He hesitated for a moment, passing his hand through his silver-blond hair, while he looked around the congregation and then his worried gaze found Mara. Her reactions were swift; she moved forward and joined him. He said nothing, just turned and she followed him, squeezing through the door and then stopped.

Now she could see what had blocked the door. A body lay there. A heavy body, fallen on his back with his face upturned to the open sky above the ruined church. Mara took in a deep breath, looking at the man on the ground with a feeling of sick dismay. The rich velvet tunic, the opulent, fur-lined cloak were just the same as she had seen them less than half an hour ago, but the face was almost unrecognizable: awful, congested, and blue, with a swollen, purple tongue and frightful staring eyes as green and protruding as boiled gooseberries.

Sorley Skerrett, silversmith and mine owner, one of the richest men in the kingdom, was lying dead on the flagstones of the ruined church.

✝ΩO

Maccshlechta (son sections)

There are seven categories of sons who are ineligible to inherit from their father:

1. The son who is conceived in the bushes

2. The son of a prostitute

3. The son of the road (given shelter, but not formally adopted)

4. The son of a woman having a sexual relationship with two men at the time of the conception

5. The proclaimed or outlawed son

6. The son who attacks his father

7. The impious son who neglects the care of an aged parent

⳾

THE NIGHT BEFORE THE death of Sorley Skerrett, his great hall had been perfumed with the sweet smell of honey. Over a hundred beeswax candles, yellow as butter, burned in stately silver candelabra, or from within the shelter of ruby-coloured Venetian glass goblets. Each polished surface, of silver or of oak, reflected back the tiny triangular orange flames; purple velvet cushions glowed in their light and the pale blue silk hangings shimmered on the walls.

Mara, Brehon and lawgiver of the kingdom of the Burren, had stood inside the doorway and looked around the hall while the servant went to fetch his master. It was an unusual room, placed at the top of Newtown Castle, its octagonal shape fitting snugly into the rounded walls of the exterior. It had two wide, stone-mullioned windows at the west and north-west sides of the room and, twenty feet above their heads, a wooden gallery ran around the wall. A woman was up there; she did not raise her head or show any interest in the guest below, but stayed bent over her embroidery frame, a heavy woman, middle-aged, thought Mara, wondering who she was – her host, Sorley, did not have a wife, as far as she knew.

'Brehon, you are very welcome. It's good of you to come.' Now Sorley Skerrett, native of Galway city, silversmith and mine owner, immensely fat, immensely rich and dressed in the most opulent silks and velvets, was bustling out of a small room at the side of the staircase, greeting her noisily. Mara inclined her head. Sorley had owned this castle on the north-western side of the kingdom of the Burren for over twenty years, but had spent little time in it, so Mara hardly knew him. Her smile broadened though when she saw the burly figure of King Turlough follow him out.

Turlough Donn had become king of Thomond, Corcomroe and Burren ten years ago, in the year 1499. He was a heavily built man – about fifty years old, with the brown hair, which had given him the nickname of 'Donn', just turning grey, light green eyes and a pleasant open face. A pair of huge moustaches curving down from either side of his mouth gave his face a warlike look, but his eyes showed the essential gentleness and amiability of the man. Mara was betrothed to him and they planned to be married at Christmas.

'Mara!' Turlough was not inhibited by the presence of Sorley and he gave her his usual hearty hug. She released herself after a minute and greeted Sorley with a pleasant coolness. She didn't like this silversmith. For Turlough's sake she would get this supper over and then there would be no more friendly visits, she resolved. What business did Turlough have with him, anyway, she wondered? Why had he urged her so strongly to come on this evening?

'Una,' called Sorley and the woman above put down her needle and slowly and heavily descended the gallery stairs and came through the open door to the landing outside. 'My daughter, Una.' Sorley made the introduction perfunctorily and Una barely acknowledged Mara's greeting. Sorley whispered in her ear and she went to have a quiet conversation with the servant before returning to them.

'We'll sit at the table, I think, and have a glass of wine while we are waiting for the others.' Sorley was busy indicating chairs. 'My lord, will you sit here between me and my daughter. Brehon, you sit opposite. Ulick Burke and Lawyer Bodkin from Galway will be here in a moment and they will keep you company.' Busily he ushered her to a space between two empty chairs.

'What a splendid room,' murmured Mara. 'You must be very proud of it.'

'I am, indeed,' he gazed around him with satisfaction and then his face took on a flicker of malice as the door opened and a small man in his middle forties entered quietly. 'See how I am honoured today,' continued Sorley with a chuckle. 'Not just a king to dine with me, but also Ulick Burke, Lord of Clanrickard! Ulick, you will entertain the Brehon on your side of the table and my daughter, Una, will entertain King Turlough on this side.' There was a heavy note of irony in his voice as he looked from his guest to his plain-faced, silent daughter.

Mara glanced across the table. Una's pale, heavy features were suffused with an ugly red flush and her eyes flashed. Turlough looked a little annoyed at not being seated beside his betrothed lady. She gave him a reassuring smile and turned to Ulick. Ulick, of course, was his usual imperturbable self as he greeted her warmly. Things could have been worse, Mara thought with an inner chuckle. She could have been placed beside her host and have had to endure his interminable stories of his latest triumph of salesmanship or sharp practice. Ulick, at least, whatever his reputation, was always fun. How many wives had he had, she wondered? He married and then divorced with dizzying rapidity. Was it four wives, or five? She surveyed him. He had become *taoiseach* over twenty-four years ago and must now be a man of fifty at least, but he didn't look it. His blond hair was slightly greying, but his skin was smooth and lightly tanned and his blue eyes seemed to caress her subtly as he raised his glass of mead, nibbled on an almond from the silver dish in front of them and smiled sweetly at her.

'How is your wife?' she asked politely. It should be safe to assume that he had some wife, or other, she thought, but he shook his head firmly.

'Still living in sin, Brehon,' he said loudly and merrily. 'I haven't the least notion of how any of my wives are and I have no intention of finding out.'

Turlough gave an amused bark of laughter, but then politely bent his head to examine a piece of silver that Sorley had brought over from the window ledge.

Mara raised an eyebrow. 'Still living with . . . ?' she queried.

'With the wife of the O'Kelly. Living in open adultery, as the O'Kelly keeps telling everyone,' said Ulick with relish. 'I must be getting old,' he added thoughtfully. 'We've been together now for four years, since the battle of Knock-doe, in fact. I suppose since her husband fought against me then, it has made me more inclined to hang on to her. Still, sometimes I wouldn't mind something younger, do you have any ideas?' He looked at her with a sweet smile, and then glanced across the table where on the right hand of the king, in the place of honour, sat Sorley's daughter.

Una glared at Ulick and then got up abruptly, leaving her drink untasted and walked towards the door.

'Oh, dear,' said Ulick imperturbably, though he lowered his voice. 'Do you think I've upset her? Would you think that she is a virgin? Probably. She has no chance, poor girl. Look at the father! Could you get a more ugly face than that? And the mother, too! Very, very plain, my dear Brehon.

Still this Una may be her father's heir – she seems to be an only child – and that would compensate, wouldn't it?'

'Is Una's mother dead?' asked Mara, keeping her voice low, but deciding that to discuss Una's mother was probably more suitable than discussing Ulick's amours.

'No, no, Brehon! Of course, you probably don't know them well. Sorley hasn't been here in the Burren too often in the last ten years or so. He spends most of his time in Kinvarra. No, the mother isn't dead. He divorced her about eight years ago. Toin the hospitaller told me that. Lucky woman, I suppose, to get away from him.'

'Shh,' murmured Mara with an eye towards Sorley.

'Oh, don't worry about him, Brehon; like all bullies, he's quite a coward. I've seen him turn to a quivering jelly when a few bees flew near to him. Though, to be fair, it appears that he swells up like a balloon if he gets stung. Anyway, you're right. I must keep him sweet. Who knows – he may be my father-in-law at some stage.'

'Indeed.' Mara took a sip of wine and sat back, wondering what to do with this man. In a moment, Ulick would be overheard by his host and that would lead to trouble. As Brehon of the Burren, she was responsible for maintaining law and order in the kingdom and she could not afford to gossip in public. 'Beautiful silver, isn't it?' she murmured holding up her goblet and admiring it by the light of the eight-branched candelabra in front of her.

To her relief, he followed her lead and called out noisily, 'We're admiring your silver goblets, Sorley. Beautiful, my dear fellow, beautiful.'

Sorley's fat face creased in a smile, and Ulick turned back to Mara.

'Well, that will keep him happy for a while, won't it? Now what shall we talk about? You're looking very, very attractive, you know. I love that green gown – it goes so well with your beautiful black hair and your lovely hazel eyes. You don't look a day over twenty.'

'Thank you,' said Mara sweetly, trying to conceal her amusement as his gaze subtly flattered her, sweeping from the top of her head, down over the sheen of expensive blue-green silk from her new gown. It had been made by an expert seamstress in Galway and fitted her like a glove, tightly laced at the bodice and flowing out from the waist. The long loose sleeves, laced to the gown at the shoulders, fell to her wrists in a cascade of shimmering pale green. She knew she looked well and she also knew that Ulick certainly didn't believe that she was twenty; he had been a friend of King Turlough from the days of their youth and had known Mara for at least ten years. However, she had no intention of bothering to inform him that she was thirty-six so she just returned his smile.

'And how thrilling to be getting married to the king! You must tell me all about your courtship. I hope you ask me to the wedding. I always enjoy other people's weddings. I have even enjoyed all of my own.'

'What time is dinner, I'm hungry?' asked Mara. Obviously dinner wasn't going to be served for some time; Una had gone back up to the gallery and had seated herself at her embroidery frame. Mara's eyes followed her and she saw a well-dressed young man come out of a door and seat himself beside her. She frowned with surprise.

'Is that Rory the bard?' she asked and Ulick nodded vigorously.

'Yes, he's been staying here. A neighbour of yours, is he not?' A slight frown creased his face as he added, 'He's the life and soul of the party here. Pity he can't play a little better.' The young bard had begun to strum a soulful love song on a zither, the silver plectrum flashing on his thumb, and Ulick's eyes flickered maliciously as he bent to whisper in Mara's ear.

'I suspect that the bard is making love to the daughter of the house. What do you think? Should I try to cut him out? She's plain, but think of the money!'

'As far as I know, Rory is in love with Aoife, the daughter of Muiris O'Heynes, a farmer at Poulnabrucky,' said Mara mildly. 'Anyway, he's a bit young for her.'

'She looks about fifty, of course, but she's probably only about twenty-seven or twenty-eight, and as for your farmers' daughters, which one of them would have the wealth of the silversmith's daughter? Sorley is immensely rich, you know. It's not just the silversmith business. He has that mine, worked by all those poor Welsh miners, on the slopes of the mountain above our heads,' he pointed towards the silver heights of Cappanabhaile that could be seen through the western window, before continuing. 'Yes, I think I'll cut the bard out. Do you think that Sorley would be happy for me to marry his daughter? It would bring a bit of the good blood of the de Burgos into the family, wouldn't it, my dear Brehon? And I don't suppose that I would have to see too much of her.'

'Mara,' called Turlough from across the table and she turned to him with relief. 'I was talking to this lawyer from Galway. I told him that you would be here. It will be interesting for you to meet him.'

'I've placed him next to you at table,' said Sorley, with an oily smile. 'I hope you both will help me to solve a little problem. There's a small dispute between myself and Cathal the sea captain.'

Mara bowed gravely and took another sip of wine to hide the flash of irritation that she knew would show in her eyes. So that was it. Sorley had been very insistent on Turlough bringing her to supper here this evening. Now he was going to get two legal opinions, one of Brehon law and one of English law. He had a reputation for using either law as it suited his purpose. If she had known about this she would not have come, but for Turlough's sake, she would not make a fuss now.

'Of course he usually uses the Brehon of Kinvarra,' whispered Ulick, as Sorley started to explain to Turlough about the boatload of silver that he had lost in a storm. 'What I would call a pliable man, my dear Brehon! Shame he died last week. A great loss to Sorley! He's wondering whether you are going to play ball, now. I can see it in his little piggy eyes. You know about Sorley and the Brehon of Kinvarra, of course?'

'I understand that Sorley's principal place of residence is the tower house of Dunguaire at Kinvarra so of course he would have consulted the local Brehon,' said Mara in a non-committal way, but she knew exactly what Ulick meant. There had been ugly, distasteful rumours of bribery attached to that particular Brehon. She turned her shoulder to Ulick and looked enquiringly across the table at Sorley who was leaning across the table towards her.

'But before Lawyer Bodkin arrives there is something I want to show you, Brehon.' Sorley left the room hastily.

'Sorley was telling me that he has sold Dunguaire at Kinvarra to my cousin, Mahon O'Brien,' remarked Turlough as the door closed behind their host and his assistant.

'So now he is going to be based at the Burren,' mused Ulick with a smile hovering around his lips. 'Well, it will be interesting to see what he is going to show you, Brehon. A little present, perhaps. A goblet . . .'

'Lawyer Bodkin, he must be from one of the merchant families of Galway,' said Mara, adroitly avoiding the subject. 'There are the Lynches, the Skerretts, the Bodkins, the Blakes, the Martins and the Joyces . . .'

'All newcomers, my dear Brehon, the de Burgos were there before any of them.'

'And the O'Connors and the O'Flahertys before the de Burgos.' But Turlough said it with a smile. He was fond of the little man and amused by him.

And then the door opened and in came Sorley's assistant, Daire, a handsome, tall, silver-blond young man – probably of Viking origin, Mara had often thought in the past. He was carrying a wide, shallow box. Sorley bustled past him, cleared a small, deeply carved table of its silver boxes of sugared comfits, and then placed the table beside Mara's chair.

With pride shining from his face, Daire carefully placed the box on the table and took off its lid. It was lined with heavy green velvet and the bottom was a chessboard of dark cherry-tree wood chequered with squares of ivory. Without saying a word, Daire took the white pieces from the carefully carved sections at the right-hand side of the box and set them one by one on the board. Each piece was moulded from shining silver. The castle was a perfect replica of

Sorley's Newtown Castle, the knight pranced on a horse which looked almost alive, its nostrils tiny specks of rubies and the engraved lines in the silver mimicking the white and grey shading of the Connemara ponies. The bishop came next – it was obviously Mauritius, Bishop of Kilfenora; the queen followed, dressed in the traditional *léine*, showing beneath her gown; and then the king, in the garb of a chieftain, with great wide bristling moustaches. Daire set each piece on its dark square of wood or white square of ivory with the loving care of a creator and then glancing at Mara with a smile touching the corners of his mouth, he produced the first pawn and Mara gave a start of surprise. The pawn was a tiny version of her wolfhound, Bran. There was no mistaking the pose; the little figure sat, head slightly cocked to one side, waiting for a command, just the way that Bran sat day after day at his mistress's feet. Turlough picked up the king and roared with laughter as he fingered the moustaches.

'You made these, Daire?' asked Turlough looking at the wolfhound pawn.

From behind there was a wheezing laugh. 'No, no,' said Sorley, 'Daire is a good apprentice, my lord, but he is not quite ready for work like this yet. He helped, of course, in fact he did quite a lot, but it needed the master-hand to get everything right. Anyway, you like the set? And you, Brehon? Put the rest of them out, boy, show them all to King Turlough and the Brehon.'

Mara glanced at Daire. All the light seemed to have gone out of his face, even the shining hair seemed to be dimmed, his mouth was set in a hard, straight line and his hand shook slightly as he took out the remainder of the pawns and set them in their row. Then he took the black pieces from the left-hand side and Mara saw that these were made of copper, obviously from the same mould as the silver pieces. Last of all, Daire took out the queen and held it for a moment before placing it on its dark, polished square and Mara smiled slightly to herself. She hadn't noticed the resemblance with the silver pieces, but now in the dark copper she could see that the queen was herself: the head crowned with coiled braids of dark hair and even, as she looked closely, a tiny scroll in one hand.

At the same moment, Turlough recognized the likeness. He took the little figure affectionately in his huge hand and held it up to the light.

'I've never seen anything so beautiful in my life!' The words exploded from him. Mara gave him an affectionate glance. Turlough was a man who never could keep his feelings secret. If Sorley had hoped to sell this set to the king, he could probably ask any price for it now.

Mara looked keenly at Daire; more than ever, she was certain that Daire had made this magnificent chess set, something which any king would be proud to own. She looked at the figures again; the set was obviously inspired by Daire's visit to Cahermacnaghten a year ago. He had come back with Fachtnan after the festivities of *Samhain*; she had persuaded him to stay the night in the scholars' house, as the evening had turned very foggy. Sorley had never seen her wolfhound, Bran, but Daire had; and Bran made great friends with the young silversmith that day. Only Daire could have copied Bran's characteristic pose with such exactitude. If it were true that Daire had made this chess set, then why was he still an apprentice? However, if the master said that he did not do the work, then matters could be difficult. Mara glanced back at Daire and saw him look covertly at Sorley. There was a look of black despair mingled with hatred in the young man's eyes.

'This is one of the most beautiful objects that I have ever seen,' she said with sincerity. 'The man who made this set is a real artist.'

The dark look on Daire's face lightened slightly and he smiled, his hand lightly touching the head of one of the little wolfhound pawns and then his face fell again as he shot another resentful glance at his master. 'Shall I put them away now before we eat?' he asked dully.

'No, no, leave them where they are.'

So that the king will continue to be tempted, thought Mara and then, as she saw the silversmith's eyes rest appraisingly on her, she changed her mind. I believe they are meant for a bribe for me, she thought, feeling more amused than annoyed.

'Lawyer Bodkin is ready now, Father.' Una appeared at the door, giving the chess set a quick look of comprehension and then turning back to Sorley.

'Bring him in, my dear,' he said, and Una left the room without a word returning a few minutes later with the lawyer. She made no effort to introduce him, Mara noticed, but allowed him to make his own way through the room.

Lawyer Bodkin was a tall, thin, distinguished-looking man, dressed in a black lawyer's gown. He had a small pointed beard tinged with grey and a pair of intelligent pale blue eyes. He greeted the king with respect and Mara with interest.

'I've heard of you,' he said with a smile. 'It's a great privilege to meet you.'

'And a privilege for me, also,' said Mara with sincerity as the food was carried into the hall and the servants moved around filling plates and replenishing wine from silver flagons. 'I'm going to pick your brains about English law. I'm ashamed I know so little about it.' She leaned towards him eagerly as he took his place beside her.

Ulick began to flirt with Una across the table. However, Una made no response and Ulick turned his attention towards Sorley. He met his match there, thought Mara keeping one amused ear open while listening to Lawyer Bodkin's long explanation about common law and Roman law and then telling him of her responsibilities for maintaining law and order on the Burren and educating her young law scholars. Sorley seemed to be taunting Ulick with his poverty and Ulick, she noticed, was beginning to lose his temper, clenching his fist and giving short replies.

'Excellent food!' Lawyer Bodkin placed his fork with mathematical precision in the centre of his empty plate and leaned back.

'And drink,' said Ulick. He quaffed another goblet, full of wine, saying to the lawyer, 'do you have any beautiful lady judges like this one in Galway?'

Too much wine, too much food, too much of everything. Mara sat back in her chair to allow Ulick to converse with the lawyer across her. Her eyes went to Rory who was drinking heavily; he had given up trying to talk to Una and was concentrating on swallowing as much as he could from every dish and every flagon. Obviously he was a visitor in the house; he had come out of one of the guest chambers on the top floor. If he had been merely employed as a bard, he would probably just have bedded down in the guardroom or in one of the many small cabins that lined the courtyard.

'If you're sure you won't have anything else to eat, I'd like to discuss this legal matter with you two learned people,' said Sorley with an unctuous smile across the table at Mara and Lawyer Bodkin. 'My apprentice has work to do and the young people can go up to the gallery.' He addressed Una and she got up immediately.

'You must mean me when you speak of young people,' said Ulick gaily. He got to his feet, seeming quite unaffected by the amount of wine that he had drunk, went around the table and seized Rory by the arm.

'Come on, Master Bard,' he said. 'Let me play the zither to you and teach you how it should be done.' He guided the scowling bard expertly through the door and Daire followed them with a quick bow in Mara's direction.

'I'll get the papers.' Sorley bustled out after them.

'Mara turned to Lawyer Bodkin. 'This is where we sing for our supper,' she said lightly.

'Indeed,' he murmured. 'It's going to be interesting to watch you at work.'

Then he took a seat on the long bench by the fire and said no more. He had a cautious look on his face and Mara approved of that. They were both going to be put into a difficult position by their host of the evening. She left her own seat and went to sit beside him.

'We neither of us want this to be a court, I should imagine.' She kept her tone low; Una, Rory and Ulick were above their heads in the wooden gallery.

He bowed, looking amused. 'Reconciliation?' he queried.

'And perhaps a little elucidation,' she suggested, inclining her head.

He bowed again. 'I shall follow your lead, my lady judge,' he said. 'Judicially speaking,' and here he tugged at his grey beard, 'you are the senior here.'

Mara eyed him curiously. A man with an excellent mind and a sharp wit; how could he believe in such a flawed and unjust legal system as English law, which dealt so savagely with people and punished with the gallows, or worse, minor crimes such as stealing. Over dinner, he had been unable to convince her of its rectitude and she had been unable to shake him in his prejudices against Brehon law. He had been appalled to learn that they had no prisons in these Gaelic kingdoms.

'We must meet again,' she said and turned as Sorley came back in holding a scroll in his hand.

'The case is quite simple,' said Sorley standing up before them, dominating the proceedings, thought Mara. 'This is the list of the valuable silver candlesticks, goblets, plates, brooches, that were lost when Cathal's boat sank in the storm in Drumcreehy Bay. He managed to get the boat righted, but my silver was left at the bottom of the ocean. I feel that he should pay me what it was worth.'

'And what does Cathal say?' enquired Mara cautiously.

'Oh, he has some story that his son might be able to recover the casks in midwinter when the tides are low.'

'And would you be happy to wait?'

'Certainly not! I want the value now.' Sorley shook his head vigorously.

'What does the sea captain say?' Lawyer Bodkin responded to Sorley's enquiring look after a minute.

'He's complaining that he will be ruined, but that's not my affair,' said Sorley impatiently.

'And you have always been satisfied about the arrangements that he made in the past? You were happy with the way that he packed it; with the position of the goods within his ship?' Mara looked keenly at Sorley. Now was the time for a little subtle pressure, a covert hint that things might not go his way if he brought this case to court. In her experience this often helped to make warring parties resolve their differences. Lawyer Bodkin gave a nod.

'He always delivered the goods safely before,' said Sorley harshly, 'I had no cause for complaint.'

'Just so,' returned Mara. 'However, the law, our law, would say that sending goods by a sea is a perilous undertaking and you would, naturally, be aware of the risks. Do you feel that Cathal could have predicted this wave?'

'That's his business, not mine.' Sorley was losing patience.

'Surely,' murmured Mara, 'but the question is would you be willing to wait until the tides are lower and his son can make another attempt to retrieve the box of silver?'

'Lawyer Bodkin, what have you to say?' asked Sorley, turning his head.

'I think,' said the lawyer speaking slowly and carefully, 'that everything I've heard so far makes excellent sense in both English and Brehon law. This case would not come under the jurisdiction of the Galway court as the goods were lost in the sea adjacent to the Burren and the two people concerned are both inhabitants of the Burren. However, since I am here I will give my advice and that would be to wait and see what the lower tides will reveal.' He smiled imperturbably into the silver merchant's angry face.

'I'll wait no longer,' said Sorley harshly. 'I want the value of that silver and I want it now.'

'In that case,' said Mara regretfully, 'this is a case that I must deal with at Poulnabrone in front of the people of the kingdom. Shall we appoint Saturday 16 November for the hearing? I would advise both to bring witnesses and this will give you time to find those witnesses. I will send my farm manager to see Cathal and to tell him that he will need to find someone who is expert in tides and sea voyages, and Sorley, you will need to find someone who will testify as to the value of the silver.'

'Easily done,' said Sorley, sitting down again. 'In fact, if anything I may have underestimated the value of the goods.' He smiled the smile of a fat man, his eyes almost disappearing into the mounds of flesh. No doubt, he was running through a mental list of silver merchants who would be happy to oblige him.

'And now, I think I must leave you,' murmured Mara rising to her feet. 'I have a busy day tomorrow and will have to rise early. She looked towards Turlough; he had to be back in Thomond that night, but they would ride home together.

'Daire will show you downstairs and make sure that your horse is ready, Brehon,' said Sorley ringing a silver bell with alacrity. 'My lord,' he turned to Turlough, 'there is just one more little piece of business that I must detain you with. He will be down instantly, Brehon.'

❄

'Daire, why are you still an apprentice? Haven't you served the full seven years?' This matter had been puzzling Mara through the evening, and while they waited by the fire in the gatehouse she thought she would bring it up. She knew enough about English law to know that there were strict rules about the length of an apprenticeship.

'I have served my seven years,' said Daire bitterly, 'but I can't become a silversmith until my master says that I am sufficiently skilled.'

'I see.' It's none of my business, thought Mara, and then instantly changed her mind. Injustice was her business. 'You made that chess set, didn't you?' She eyed him keenly by the light of the pitch torch and he nodded reluctantly.

'But he wants to retain you?' This would suit with what she knew of Sorley's character.

'That and . . .' Daire hesitated for a moment, his eyes on the doorway. '. . . he wanted me to marry his daughter.' The gatekeeper had gone across to the stableman and was admiring the horses; nevertheless, Daire sunk his voice to a low murmur.

'Why does . . .' Mara's astonished voice died away at the sound of an anguished yell.

The gates to the roadway had been opened in preparation for the king and Brehon's departure. A thin ragged figure had stolen in. He was dressed in a torn, stained *léine* and his hair was ragged and untrimmed and falling over his face. As he turned his face to hers she could see that he was not much more than a boy, about the same age as her eldest scholars, she reckoned or even younger. It looked as if tearstains had run down through the dirt on his cheeks, bristly with adolescent fluff.

'Cuan, it's no good.' Daire's words were compassionate, but the porter who had run over had no compunction.

'Get out of there! Stop hanging around here!' he said, aiming a kick at the boy.

'Stop!' the quiet authority in Mara's voice made the man step back.

'I'm only following orders, Brehon,' he muttered.

'Who is this?' asked Mara.

'This is my master's son, Brehon,' said Daire quietly. 'Sorley has banished him.'

'That's right, Brehon,' said the porter, eager to justify himself. 'I've been told to drive him away as soon as I see him.'

'I just want to see my father, I just want to talk to him.' The boy's voice was broken with sobs.

'How old is he?' asked Mara in an undertone to Daire.

'About seventeen, I think.' Daire replied in the same low voice, but there had been no necessity. It was even difficult for Mara to hear his words as now the boy had turned his face towards the windows of the tower house and was shrieking at the top of his voice: 'Father, I must see you; I must see you. I'm starving. I must see you; I'm your son.'

If he were over seventeen, then his father's legal obligation to care for him had ceased, thought Mara. Nevertheless, it was very harsh to banish your only son, especially for a man of such huge wealth.

35

'Where do you live, Cuan? I'll come and see you and we can talk.' Mara put a hand on the boy's arm, but he shook it off and with a final despairing cry he ran back into the dark shadows outside the gate. They all looked after him and then turned back to face the tower house. For a moment, Mara thought she saw a face in the upper window, but it vanished in a second leaving nothing but a welcoming yellow glow.

An impressive house, like a castle in one of those illuminated books, with its conical roof and regular battlements, a fairytale castle, she thought, but what of the man who owned it? Had he no ounce of compunction within him for his unfortunate son whom he had disowned?

THREE

BECHBRETHA (BEE JUDGEMENTS)

Congal Caech (Congal the Blind), King of Ulster, was stung in the eye by a bee and was blinded.

Evidence was given for Congal that the hives were placed beside a narrow pathway.

Evidence was given for the beekeeper that the path was on the south-west side of the hives so normally the bees flew in the opposite direction to it as they hate to fly against the wind.

Judgement was given against the beekeeper, King Domhnall of Tara, and he had to supply a hive in compensation.

杤×

AND NOW SORLEY WAS DEAD, mused Mara; she watched Malachy the physician, accompanied by his

37

fourteen-year-old daughter and apprentice, Nuala, squeeze his way through the door. He nodded to her and knelt down beside the body, putting his finger on the swollen wrist.

'What killed him, Malachy?' Mara voiced her thoughts aloud.

Malachy shrugged. He was a dark, sallow-faced man of about forty, a widower with an only child. He turned away from the body, took his medical bag from Nuala and began to riffle through its contents. He was a slow thinker and a slow talker and Mara knew she had to curb her questions until he was ready to give his verdict. She herself bent over the body and looked more carefully. There was a faint smell of something unexpected and she could not think what it was. And something was moving slightly under Sorley's hair. For a moment she was puzzled; then she realized that it was a dying bee. She could see more bees, all dead, trapped amongst Sorley's clothing and in his hair. Now Mara knew what the smell was. She had smelled it strongly less than an hour ago from Giolla; the beekeeper's veil, hat and gloves had that strong odour when he had removed them. What she smelled was venom. As she looked more carefully, she could see that the whole of Sorley's face was swollen with innumerable bee stings. In the centre of each lump was the dark thread of the sting. She gave a long sigh and straightened herself. Daire was at her side looking over her shoulder with an air of sick horror.

'What happened to him, Brehon?' he asked huskily.

'I don't know,' said Mara honestly. 'What do you think, Malachy?'

'It looks as if he were attacked by some bees and

perhaps died from a seizure.' There was a note of uncertainty in Malachy's voice as he joined her and leaned over the body. 'A terrible accident.'

'I suppose so,' said Mara, but within her there was a doubt. Her eyes went to the east wall of the ruins where the straw bee skeps were placed, each in a stone niche which had formerly housed the statue of a saint. There were ten niches there, but only nine of them showed the curved shape of the hive. The tenth was empty; the skep had been knocked on the ground and thousands of bees clustered over the honey that spilled out over the ancient slabs of stone. What was it that Ulick Burke had said to her the previous night when they dined at Newtown Castle? Something about Sorley and his terrible fear of bees, something about bee stings affecting him, that was it. Her eyes went again to the straw skep lying on the ground with the bees clustered over the sticky honey and then back to the events of the night before. She would have to see Giolla – but first Sorley's family would need to be told.

'Daire, would you go and get Una, Sorley's daughter,' she said quietly. 'Don't interrupt the burial service – just get her back through here as unobtrusively as you can. And see if the young son is here, also. I thought I saw him at the back of the church.'

'Sorley must have died from bee stings, mustn't he?' asked Nuala as Daire slipped out through the empty door archway and walked down the path towards the graveyard.

Malachy frowned. 'Yes, but if he were stung, wouldn't he have called out? It's more likely that he was gripped by a sudden seizure after the first few stings.'

'His throat is almost closed up!' exclaimed Nuala peering

around her father's elbow. 'He wouldn't have been able to call out. He couldn't draw breath with a throat like that. Surely that's enough to kill him. Look at the colour that he is – of course that is the poison from the bees' venom.'

Mara gave her a quick glance of appreciation – she had always thought that Nuala was brighter than her father – but she waited silently for a comment from him before asking her question:

'What did kill him then, in your opinion, Malachy?'

'Well, his neck is not broken, anyway. There is no sign of anything like that.'

'What could it have been, then?'

Malachy shook his head in a puzzled way. 'I'm not sure,' he said. 'It could have been bee stings. It is possible, you know. There are some people who swell up very badly after bee stings and he could have been one of them, his throat could have been swollen enough to stop his breathing, but it could also have been a seizure.'

'Did he ever have trouble with seizures?' asked Mara.

'I wouldn't know. He never came to me. He probably had a physician in Kinvarra or in Galway, As far as I know he wasn't here a lot, not during the last eight or ten years, anyway. Toin might know; he's known the family for a long time as they lived so close to each other.'

'I'd say that he died from bee stings,' said Nuala decisively.

'You may be right,' said Malachy indifferently. 'It doesn't make much difference one way or the other. The fact is that the man is dead. Go and see if the burial service has ended yet, Nuala, the bishop will probably wish to give him the last rites.'

Father David was being buried on the north side of the new church so Mara could hear enough to know that the burial service was not yet over. When it was she would have to post someone at the entrance to stop curious bystanders coming in. She regretted not having her six law school pupils with her. Perhaps when Daire came back he and Malachy could carry the body through into the church, or at least place it on the stone tomb near to the west doorway. Mara got to her feet and walked over to look at it. The stone slab on top was certainly large enough to hold the body, she thought and then a flash of silver caught her eye. She bent down to examine it. It was a silver stylus, its pointed edge gleaming in the sunshine and lying beside it was a set of wax tablets. She picked them up and saw a well-drawn sketch of a communion cup with the O'Brien arms as prominent as the figure of Christ. This explained why Sorley did not come into the church as the bell rang. The silversmith had probably delayed to make sure that he had a finished sketch of the communion cup to show the bishop after the Mass and burial of Father David was over. This also explained why he had come into the ruins; he was probably looking for a flat surface on which to lay his tablets.

'Here comes Daire and the daughter,' said Malachy. The noise of several footsteps sounded on the limestone flagstones outside. The first to appear was Una, closely followed by her maidservant; behind her was Daire, and then, to Mara's annoyance, came Ulick Burke, his small-featured face alight with curiosity. There was no sign of Cuan.

Una was the first to speak. 'He's really dead, then,' she stated. There was no emotion in her voice as she surveyed the body of her father on the ground.

'Yes,' said Mara simply. She made a consoling gesture, putting out her two hands towards the woman, but Una stepped back and turned her face towards the body. Mara did not know whether to offer comfort or to say nothing. Una just stood looking at her father. Perhaps she was in shock. Mara had seen violent death often enough to know that the nearest relations can often be numb with disbelief and will show no emotion while mere strangers weep. The woman's colour was unchanged so she was not about to faint. Mara wondered what she was thinking about as she looked down at her father's distorted face, but when Una spoke it was not to her, but to her maidservant.

'There will have to be a wake back at the castle tonight,' she said. 'We'd better get back and see to the food. Will you stay here, Daire, and see that the body is taken back to the house when the burial is over? There are plenty of our men here. I'll send a cart and some more men. We'd better go now; these things take longer than you think.'

Then she stopped and stood very still. Perhaps full realization that her father was dead had dawned, thought Mara, but Una's face bore a look of exasperated annoyance and when she spoke her tone was irritated. 'What am I thinking of,' she said. 'Of course, it's *Samhain* tonight. No one would come. They'll all be going to the bonfire. In any case, I'll have to send someone over to Galway to give the news to the silversmiths and silver merchants there. The wake will have to be tomorrow night.' Shaking her head at her own forgetfulness, she gave the corpse a glance of indifference and then turned to Malachy.

'So, it was the bees that killed him?' she queried and then as Malachy nodded hesitantly, she said reflectively, 'It was an accident, then.' There was a faint note of query in her voice and this time she looked straight at Mara.

'Perhaps,' said Mara, her tone non-committal.

'Well, that's something, anyway,' said Una. Her grey eyes explored Mara's shrewdly. There was a sharp intelligence in her gaze. 'When Daire told me that he was dead, then I was afraid that madman, Sheedy, had done what he threatened.' With that she made a signal to her maidservant, turned on her heel and strode back down the path and out of the doorway.

'Sheedy?' queried Mara with a lift of an eyebrow towards Daire, but it was Ulick who answered her.

'One of our late, lamented friend's admirers,' he said lightly. 'A farmer from Cappanabhaile Mountain: he appeared at the castle the other day ranting and raving about his cattle being poisoned by Sorley's mine. I must say that I was sorry for the fellow, but . . .' He stopped as if he had been about to say something, but decided to reconsider; his green eyes were shining with mischief as he watched to see what the effect of his words would be on her.

'Perhaps you three would carry the body into the church now,' suggested Mara. Daire and Malachy, both powerful men, could probably manage this on their own, but she wanted to get rid of Ulick for the moment. Nevertheless, he had given her some useful information. As the three men carried the body carefully into the church her eyes went to the silver heights of Cappanabhaile Mountain. Where exactly was Sheedy's farm, and why did the mine affect him? Mara narrowed her eyes, noting the scar on the mountain face, just above Newtown Castle and then looked back at the south doorway as brisk footsteps stopped there.

Standing at the entrance to the ruined church was Giolla. He gave an exclamation and hurried forward looking at the mess of honey and the angrily buzzing bees.

Mara looked at him keenly. It was obvious that Giolla was upset and angry, but from his face Mara could not tell whether the beekeeper realized what had happened to Sorley.

'I was coming to find you, Giolla,' she said quietly.

Giolla looked a little surprised. Either he did not know what had happened to Sorley, thought Mara, or else he was very good at hiding his feelings.

'That will be that young fool, Marcan, who did that,' said Giolla roughly. 'Do you know the lad? He is a big gawky-looking fellow. The son of Fionnuala, that rich widow who owns the land over there. His mother doesn't give him enough to do and he is forever poking around my bees and trying to annoy them. I am sure that it was he. How did he knock it over without being badly stung himself?' he muttered to himself and moved off abruptly.

A minute later, Mara saw his head above the ruins of the eastern wall of the little ruined church. 'Look, Brehon!' he called. 'Will you come out, come here and I'll show you.'

Mara followed out through the remains of the ancient south door and around the east side of the ruined church. She could see that no one walked there as a rule. The grasses and nettles were almost waist high, but through the middle of them a path was trampled, quite recently, judging by the smell of bruised nettles in the air, and in the wall there was a small space, a space from which a stone had been removed. It was obvious now what had happened. From behind the shelter of the wall, in that quiet secluded spot, someone had taken out a stone, thrust a stick through and knocked the hive to the ground, driving the bees to a frenzy of anger. But was it an accident, the mischievous trick of an idle boy, or was it a cold, clever, calculated murder? Mara did not know. Her intuition said 'murder' while her logical brain said 'not enough evidence, yet'.

She turned to Giolla. 'Have you heard what has happened? Did you hear that Sorley the silversmith is dead?'

Giolla nodded. 'The steward from Newtown Castle told me . . .' he began and then a look of horror crossed his face. 'You mean it was the bees were after him and made him drop dead from a seizure?' he asked, aghast.

'I'm not sure yet,' replied Mara. 'I think that the first thing we had better do is to see that young lad, what is his name? Marcan, is it? We'll have to find out first if he did anything. Was he at the burial service?'

'Yes, I saw him there with his mother. Look there he is, over there. Marcan, come over here. I want a word with you.'

Marcan did look uneasy as they approached, Mara noticed, but then he had probably had many an unpleasant encounter with Giolla in the past. His mother, too, looked defensive. He was quite a good-looking boy, about thirteen, Mara judged, dressed very richly, wearing a saffron tunic. Giolla addressed him harshly:

'Have you been meddling with my bees again?'

The boy's eyes widened with a look of innocence, though there was a spark of mischief in his virtuous gaze. 'No,' he said, 'I haven't been near them, not for a long time.'

'Well, someone has,' said Giolla. 'It must have been in

the last hour too. I looked at them just before the service, and all was well with them, then.'

'It wasn't Marcan, then,' said his mother decisively. 'I had to call and call to get him out of bed this morning and get him dressed in time for the service. You know what boys of that age are like,' she added, turning to Mara as a more sympathetic audience than Giolla. 'He was with me from the moment he dressed until this very minute, so don't you go accusing him of something that he could not have done, Giolla. You shouldn't have those bees so near the church anyway. Poor Marcan came home with quite a bad sting on his forehead one day. I don't know why Father David, Lord have mercy on him, gave you permission to keep those bees there.'

'The bees won't sting Marcan if he leaves them alone,' said Giolla shortly. 'Are you certain that you did not go near them, today, Marcan?'

'Certain,' said Marcan, with wide-eyed innocence. 'Why, what is wrong?'

'Sorley the silversmith has died from bee stings.' Giolla looked rather pale and worried-looking now. He ignored the exclamations of horror from Marcan's mother and went back into the ruined church. Mara followed him, looking at him keenly. The anger had faded out from his face and was replaced with a look of anxiety. He made no attempt to regret the death of Sorley, but it was obvious that he was concerned on his own behalf.

'You will be seeing me again, I suppose,' he said.

Mara nodded. 'I suppose I will,' she said. For a moment she hesitated. Her warm heart was moved by the obvious apprehension on his face. 'Don't worry too much,' she said as she left him.

She would not go straight back to the church, she decided. A quick walk around the graveyard and a few glances at those who were still standing chatting outside one or other of the gates would give her a fair idea of who was present. She kept her face preoccupied and her gaze aloof; no one would dare question her unless she spoke to them first. There was a very high respect in the kingdom of the Burren for the office of Brehon, and for her personally.

Yes, she thought, Cathal the sea captain was there. He was outside the Rathborney gate talking in a low tone to what looked, from the resemblance, like his son. He stopped when he saw her and looked keenly at her, but she did not respond. No doubt, Marcan and his mother had spread the news.

Where was Sheedy, she wondered? There seemed to be no sign of him in the graveyard and he was not amongst those outside the gates. She walked to the upper gate and gazed up the lane leading up the river valley between the two mountains. There were a couple of figures going up there, a middle-aged woman and a young man, perhaps the unfortunate banished son of Sorley's – it did look like him. Ahead of this couple was another man; he was climbing the steep path at a fast pace. He was too far away for her to see his face; in any case, she did not know Sheedy very well, but she guessed that it was he.

By the time she returned to church, Sorley's body was being carried out of the west door to a cart. It was just an ordinary farm cart with no attempt at softening it with branches of laurel or flowers, Mara noted with interest. The bishop was standing beside it, talking gravely to Malachy, and the remaining people lined the pathway. The sun was warm and everyone lingered. No one seemed to know what to do or say. No members of Sorley's family were present so there could be none of the usual condolences. The bishop began to recite the rosary and everyone responded with relief. The ritual murmuring of the phrases gave them an excuse to remain and perhaps hear more of this unexpected death.

The Welsh mineworkers began to arrive just as the rosary finished. Probably a message had been sent by the efficient Una and their overseer had sent them down as a mark of respect. Many of them were already there, dressed in their working clothes, still with picks or shovels in their hands, standing silently on either side of the cart that carried the remains of their dead master. As Mara raised her eyes to the grey heights of Cappanabhaile, she could see a long line of tiny figures straggling down its slopes. The deformed man whom she had earlier noticed briefly in the church was still there. Mara's eyes watched him with pity. He stood, as far as he was able to stand, amongst his former workmates and then just as the rosary finished and the order was given to move the cart, he struggled forward and placed his hand on the wheel of the cart and a strange sound came from him. For a moment, Mara thought it might be the start of a traditional keen, but then the man stepped back and Mara realized that the sound was a laugh, or a shout of triumph, almost a victory sound, a sound which celebrated the death not mourned it.

'What happened to that man?' asked Mara quietly as Malachy approached.

'I don't know.' Malachy surveyed the crippled man with a professional interest. One of the other Welsh mineworkers came up, spoke to him, took him by the arm and helped him away. Mara did not understand all of the miners' Welsh speech, but the repetition of the word, Anluan, made her guess that was the injured man's name. She turned back to Malachy.

'You mean you weren't called to treat him?' That was surprising. Malachy was the only physician in the kingdom of the Burren.

'His scars look fairly fresh,' observed Nuala. 'It must have been a mining accident. His leg and his whole right side were probably crushed by a boulder. It's the right side of his face that has been damaged, also.'

'Well, I wasn't called,' said Malachy shortly.

Sorley probably didn't want to waste any silver on paying a physician to treat one of his workers, surmised Mara.

'Toin was talking to me about that mine the other day,' went on Malachy. 'He was saying that it was a miracle that there hasn't been anyone killed up there – as far as we know, of course. Those Welsh miners keep their distance; they have their own village and they never mix with people on the Burren.'

'Shouldn't we visit Toin, now?' asked Nuala. 'He looked very ill when I saw him and he didn't come into the church.'

'I'm sorry that he tried to attend the service.' Malachy's voice was concerned. 'Yes, we'll go now if you have no further use for us, Brehon.'

'Come to supper today, Nuala,' said Mara. She would have liked to find out more about this Anluan, but it was probably none of her business. 'Will it be all right if she goes to the *Samhain* festival with us, Malachy? The O'Lochlainns and Mairéad are coming, and probably some other young people. Either Cumhal or Fachtnan will accompany her home.'

'I'd love that,' said Nuala, her eyes shining. 'Oh, I do hope it keeps fine for a few more hours!'

'Any invitation for me?' asked Ulick hopefully.

'It's just some boys and girls,' said Mara firmly. 'I don't think that you would enjoy it. Anyway, I presume that you will be off back to Galway now that your host is dead.'

'I don't think so,' said Ulick thoughtfully. 'I think that I'll enjoy seeing you at work, Brehon. I'll tell you one thing, if I may: if that skep of bees was deliberately upset in order to cause the death of Sorley the silversmith then there will be quite a choice of names for your killer.'

FOUR

There are seven nobles of the forest:
1. Dair (*oak*)
2. Coll (*hazel*)
3. Cuilenn (*holly*)
4. Ibar (*yew*)
5. Uinnius (*ash*)
6. Octach (*pine*)
7. Aball (*apple*)

If anyone injures one of these trees on another man's property he shall incur a penalty of five séts, or two-and-a-half ounces of silver, or three cows.

☙❧

'LORD BLESS US and save us, that was a terrible thing to
happen,' said Brigid with huge enjoyment as Mara rode
into the courtyard of the ancient enclosure which housed
Cahermacnaghten law school with its kitchen house, scholars' house, schoolhouse and farm manager's house.

'So you've heard the news!' No surprises there! Brigid
always did hear all of the news. Despite all of her worries,
Mara found herself smiling broadly.

'Cumhal was over repairing the wall in the Moher field
and he met Muiris O'Heynes on his way back from the
burial mass at Rathborney,' explained Brigid. 'Muiris told
him the whole story.'

'What did Muiris say?' enquired Mara, neatly jumping
from the mounting block and handing the mare's reins to
Seán, one of her farm workers. 'Give Brig a good rub down
and let her cool off before you give her a drink, Seán, that
hill is very steep and she's very hot. Yes, Brigid, so Muiris
told Cumhal all about Sorley, did he?'

'Someone tipped over a hive and he was stung to death,'
whispered Brigid with evident relish as Mara marvelled at
how rapidly news spread throughout the kingdom. Brigid
waited for a moment, eyeing Seán to make sure that he was
not dawdling in order to listen and then, when he had taken
the mare into the stables, she leaned forward so that her face
was quite near to Mara's shoulder and whispered, 'I'm not
one to gossip, as you know, Brehon.'

'No, of course not.' Mara hoped her tone held the right
mixture of curiosity and shocked denial.

'Well, between us both and that gatepost there, Muiris
told Cumhal that he knew who had done it.'

'Done what?' queried Mara.

'The murder, of course, the murder of the silversmith.'
She paused dramatically while Aidan retrieved a hurling ball
from in front of the kitchen house and waited until he had
vaulted the wall back into the field before hissing: 'Muiris
says that it was young Rory the bard that murdered the
man.'

'It may have been an accident,' said Mara blandly. 'It
appears as if a whole swarm of bees stung Sorley. He ran
away from them and collapsed at the church door. Malachy
thinks he might have had a seizure.'

'Hmm.' Brigid had a very expressive range of sniffs.
This one seemed to express doubts about Malachy's competence or, indeed, about his ability to come to a firm
decision about anything.

'Anyway, why on earth should Rory kill Sorley?' Mara
decided to move away from the subject of Malachy.

'Well, I swore to say nothing to nobody about this so
I'd only mention it to you, Brehon,' Brigid lowered her
voice even more, 'but do you know that young *bithlúnach*,'
Brigid always reverted to the old Gaelic of her grandmother's time when she wished to be emphatic. 'Well, that
young scoundrel has walked out on poor little Aoife, and is
paying court to the daughter of Sorley. Perhaps he got up
to his usual tricks with her – and he's no saint that one – we
all know that – and Sorley was going to throw him out so
Rory made the first move. It stands to reason that the
daughter will be easier to *plámás* than the father. Muiris
told Cumhal that Aoife is in a terrible state.'

'I wonder, Brigid, could I ask Aoife and her brothers to
the *Samhain* supper tonight – as well as the O'Lochlainns?'
The news about Aoife's grief was no surprise; she and Rory

had been almost inseparable for the last eighteen months. Mara was sorry for the girl and, in any case, the issuing of the invitation would give her an excuse to go across to Poulnabrucky and have a word with Muiris. 'Oh, and I've asked young Daire the apprentice silversmith, and Nuala and a few other young people. Is that all right, Brigid? I should ask you, I know, before I throw out all these invitations,' finished Mara, feeling a genuine penitence. What would I do without Brigid, she thought for the millionth time.

'Lord bless you, Brehon, don't you worry about that.' Brigid was immediately diverted from the question of Sorley's death. 'There's plenty for everyone. I expected a bit of a party tonight,' she called over her shoulder as with rapid, decisive steps she crossed the courtyard towards the storeroom. In a moment, she was out with a basket of turnips on her arm.

'Come on, lads,' she shouted across the wall. 'Put those hurleys away now. I want these turnips carved before a scrap of dinner is put on the table for anyone. I'll get the candle ends.'

Mara lingered for a while in the courtyard, watching the boys whittling the turnips into skulls with empty eye sockets and grinning teeth. When Seán emerged from the stables he was immediately dispatched to pick a basket of apples from the tree that grew sheltered from the west by a little hazel woodland. This tree was always the last to be picked and the apples were carefully guarded from marauding crows until the day for *Samhain*.

'I'll set up the tables in the schoolhouse, Brehon. That will be best. You don't want all these youngsters in your

house.' Brigid was flying in and out calling directions to Nessa, who helped in the kitchen, to Seán and to the boys. All would be perfectly arranged; Mara knew that. For once, there was nothing urgent for her to do. It would be an hour at least before the scholars had finished their dinner. Quietly she clicked her tongue at Bran, her wolfhound, who was looking at her hopefully; she would take him for a walk and sort out matters in her mind.

❋

There were two routes to Poulnabrucky where Muiris and his family lived and Mara decided to take the lower road which descended steeply into a hidden valley. It was one of the few places on the Burren where trees grew and the small woodland of alder and oak trees was Bran's favourite spot. The ground was thickly carpeted with crisp, golden-brown and yellow leaves, and the huge gnarled and looped grey tree roots, clinging to the stony ground beneath, formed homes for a large population of rabbits. While Bran chased happily after them, Mara paced the ground, crunching underfoot the empty, small, round calyxes of the acorns and thinking about the sudden death of Sorley that morning. The boy Marcan had seemed genuine in his denials and his mother, also, unless she was an amazingly fluent liar, had seemed to be speaking the truth. If these two were to be believed, then who had inserted that stick into the wall and tipped over the hive with its thousands of little furry inhabitants?

When Mara emerged from the wood shaking the last few tinder-dry leaves from her hair she saw that she did not need to go across to Poulnabrucky as Muiris was there in

front of her mending a stone wall. She stood and watch
him for a moment, a square undersized man of immens
strength and determination; a man to whom family was
everything. She would have to handle this matter carefully,
she thought as he called out a greeting to her.

'I was going across to your house and now I'm saved
the journey. I wondered if Aoife and her brothers would
like to join some other young people for supper and a few
games before going on to the bonfire?' As she spoke she
gazed admiringly at the wall, marvelling at the skill and
strength that could make these huge stones into such an
effective and beautifully constructed barrier without a trace
of mortar used in the construction.

'The lads will, I'm sure . . .' There was a shadow on his
face as he added, 'Aoife is a bit upset and I'm not sure that
she will want to come.'

'Oh, what's wrong?' It seemed as if the speculation
about Rory's involvement with Una was correct.

'Well, you know Aoife, always one to have the boys
running after her,' he said hesitatingly and Mara nodded.
Aoife was the only daughter of Muiris, and Mara often marvelled how such a plain-looking couple as Muiris and his
wife, Áine, could have produced a beauty like Aoife, with
her blue eyes, flaxen hair and her apple-blossom complexion.

'Well,' went on Muiris angrily, 'that young bard, Rory,
started hanging around her over a year ago now, and since
then she's had eyes for nobody but him. He's not what I
would have wanted for her; her elder brother has married
well and I would have liked a match like that for Aoife, but

she wanted Rory and you know what girls are like,' he finished helplessly.

Mara concealed a smile. Muiris, renowned for his toughness, was as pliable as damp straw in his pretty daughter's hands; Aoife would get her way.

'So you are going to agree to a betrothal and a marriage contract,' she said. Perhaps Rory was just pretending an interest in Una in order to force Muiris to agree to the betrothal.

'It's not like that at all,' he said, shaking his head. 'It's that the young fellow has walked off on her. He's moved into Newtown Castle.'

'Oh,' said Mara, innocently. 'But that was a good move, wasn't it? I suppose that Sorley the silversmith took him on as a bard, did he? That would have been better than all this hand-to-mouth business of singing at festivals and weddings, Muiris. You can't blame him for trying to better himself; he may even have hoped to earn enough to get married on,' she ended encouragingly, though she doubted her own words even as they echoed in her ears. She watched him narrowly trying to decide whether it was spite or fact behind his report of Rory's guilt.

'Aoife went over to see him,' continued Muiris, clenching his fist, his face full of anger and pain. 'I didn't want her to go, but she would do it. Rory hadn't been to see her for a few weeks and she went off to see what the matter was. She went to the castle and asked for him. He came down and, you wouldn't believe this, Brehon, he was furious. She told her mother that. He shouted at her to go away. He told her that he was sick of her following him around and that she wasn't to do it again. Him! Sick of her!' Muiris moved his boot restlessly and kicked one sod of turf into the embers and then stopped himself, staring moodily at the toecap of his heavy leather boot. 'That fellow has been hanging around the house caterwauling his miserable love songs week in and week out for over a year and now he tells her that he's tired of her!'

'I see,' said Mara sympathetically.

'She's at home crying now. She does nothing but cry. I don't know what to do about her. She won't eat; she doesn't sleep. I moved in with the lads to let her sleep with Áine, but she just cried all night. That's what Áine said in the morning.' Muiris sounded like a man at the end of his tether.

'Very hard for a father to bear,' said Mara gravely. She looked at him carefully. This was a self-made man, a man who had risen from nothing to become a prosperous *bóaire*; a man who adored his family and who could be moved to violence in defence of his beloved daughter. She felt some concern. She had no liking for Rory the bard, but she did not want Muiris to put himself in the wrong. 'I'm glad that you told me this,' she continued carefully.

'I felt like going over to Rathborney and giving him something to think about,' he said grimly and she had the impression that he was not listening to her words, 'but Áine persuaded me not to do it. It's just as well. I might kill him if I saw that smug face of his.'

'You were very wise not to do that,' said Mara. 'This is the trouble with having children, Muiris: when they are little, and they hurt themselves, you can pick them up and kiss them better, but when they grow up, sometimes you have to let them grieve in their own way and just be there for them when they turn to you. Aoife will get over this, you know. I would advise you to keep away from Rory and to say nothing to him.'

'I wondered could I do anything within the law?' His voice was hopeful as he looked up at her questioningly.

Mara shook her head. 'Not unless there was some sort of legal contract and there isn't. Muiris, I think she is just as well without him. It's hard on her now, but no doubt some other young man will come around and there will be a match made for her.' Busily her mind trawled through the number of eligible young men in the district. The trouble was that Muiris O'Heynes was an outsider; most people on the Burren belonged to one of the four clans: O'Brien, O'Lochlainn, MacNamara or O'Connor. Despite all Aoife's beauty and the evident prosperity of the family, fathers would not encourage their sons to think of her.

'Forget Rory,' she said decisively. 'That's my advice to you, Muiris, don't try to do any harm to him; you will only injure yourself if you do that.'

'Well, I'd better be getting back home,' said Muiris. 'Thanks for the invitation, Brehon. I'll try and persuade her to go.' He looked downhearted, but Mara could think of no further comfort to give him. There were no relations, as far as she knew, to whom Aoife could be sent; the poor girl would just have to swallow the disappointment and endure the pitying looks for a while.

And, she thought, as she turned to go back through the woodland, Muiris had said nothing about his accusation to Brigid about Rory being responsible for Sorley's death. She was glad of that. It sounded most improbable. At the moment it appeared as though Rory had far more to gain from Sorley alive than from Sorley dead.

❈

'So, do you think that this Sheedy has anything to do with the killing of Sorley the silversmith, Brehon?' asked Fachtnan. Mara looked around her schoolhouse. Ordinarily on the afternoon before the celebrations of *Samhain*, her six scholars would be in an excited, fidgety state, unable to concentrate on their studies, but now the excitement of this unexpected and unexplained death kept them alert and interested.

'And what about Giolla the beekeeper?' asked twelve-year-old Hugh.

'No one would murder a man because of a few bees, birdbrain,' said Aidan scornfully.

'It's possible, though unlikely,' said Mara. 'He is very attached to his bees – Aidan, don't keep using that silly expression, *birdbrain*. You're nearly fifteen now, so it's time for you to express yourself in a more grown-up way. However, let's go back to Fachtnan's question. I need to look at the map that we made a few years ago of everyone's holding on the Burren, but I think that Sheedy's land does not really come too near Sorley's silver mine. However it may be that some of the mountain is common land. Thank you, Enda, yes, spread the map out on my table. Stand around it, all of you.'

'There's Lios Mac Sioda, is that where he lives?' Ten-year-old Shane picked it out with lightning speed.

'That's right,' said Mara. 'And below that, on the lane

between the mountains, are two small farms: Lios na gCat and Lios Mac Taidhg.'

'Who owns these?' asked Fachtnan with a puzzled frown. 'I thought that just Sheedy lived up that lane.'

'I think that Sorley the silversmith bought them when he bought Newtown Castle,' said Mara.

'Lios Mac Sioda is nowhere near the silver mine, though, is it?' Moylan estimated distances with his finger and his thumb.

'I suspect that the land where the mine is situated is probably common land. No one seems to own these upper terraces. You remember when we did this map, don't you, Fachtnan?'

'I think I was about twelve then, Brehon – I don't remember too much about it. It was more Cormac and some of the others who were doing the drawing. We did a bit of measuring, but that was all.'

'We'd only have been about eight or nine, then,' said Moylan looking at his friend Aidan.

'I remember doing it,' said Enda thoughtfully. 'And I do remember that the farms around the mountain did have common grazing rights. I remember telling my father that and explaining to him why mountain grazing rights were so important for farmers on the Burren and how the grass keeps growing on the limestone through the winter and the cattle have dry feet as there is no mud. And, of course,' his voice rose with excitement, 'that is why Sorley bought these two farms as well as the land belonging to Newtown Castle: they gave him rights over the common land on the upper slopes of Cappanabhaile. Is the mine on the common land, Brehon?'

'I think,' said Mara, rolling up the map and placing it in her leather satchel, 'that we should go up there now and see for ourselves. It's a lovely day and we can ride as far as Rathborney. I'm sure that Toin the hospitaller would not mind if we left the horses in one of his fields. We'll take Bran, he'll enjoy the climb,' she smiled affectionately at the giant white wolfhound who lay stretched across the doorway.

'So Sheedy is our suspect, then, Brehon, is that right?' Aidan nodded wisely.

'I imagine,' said Mara thoughtfully, 'that Sheedy won't be the only suspect. A man like Sorley Skerrett makes many enemies.'

FIVE

BETHA IM FUILLEMA GELL
(PLEDGE-INTEREST JUDGEMENTS)

Silver is the basis for all fines and loans under Brehon Law. A sét (treasure) is valued as half an ounce of silver and one milch cow is valued as one ounce of silver.

A king must always be paid in silver, never with cows or other animals. Conversely, a man of low status, such as an ócaire must not be paid in silver as it may be of no use to him.

If defective silver is used to pay an obligation then the contract is cancelled when the defect is discovered, even if years have elapsed.

⊝⊙

'I'M LOOKING FORWARD to seeing this mine,' said Enda as they rode down the hill towards Rathborney. 'I was reading something in a judgement text about what happens when a mine pollutes the land. If Sorley's mine is a big one, then that might be the problem with Sheedy. Anyway, I'd like to see how it works. I think we should understand these things if we are going to see how the laws affect silver and copper mines.'

'Are you worried about this Sheedy, Brehon?' asked Fachtnan. 'Don't you think that we should visit him as well?'

'I'm not sure that we have the time to do both, Fachtnan. At this time of the year dusk comes early.' Mara pursed her lips in exasperation. It was a familiar wish of hers that the days, whether it was winter, summer, autumn or spring, had a few more hours in them.

❋

Toin's stableman was happy to accommodate the boys' ponies as well as Mara's Arab mare. Toin himself came out to point out the best route for the short, steep climb towards the mill.

'Have you heard about the death of your neighbour, Sorley Skerrett?' asked Mara. Toin looked a little better, she thought. As usual he was cheerful and seemed to enjoy the sight of Aidan running races across the field with Bran.

'Save your energy,' he called and then turned back to Mara. 'Yes, I have.' There was a certain reserve in his voice and, as she glanced at him, he added, 'A neighbour, but not a friend.'

'You didn't like him much.' Mara put a query into her

voice and he nodded a silent assent. 'I saw his son last night,' she continued. 'I hadn't even realized that there was a son. What happened to the mother, why did he divorce her? What was her name?'

'Her name is Deirdre,' Toin's voice was compassionate. 'As for why Sorley divorced her, well, she isn't what you could call a good-looking woman. She was only about sixteen when Sorley married her, so perhaps she had a certain bloom, then. I think that Sorley just got tired of her. He divorced her when the boy was about seven or eight. He said that she had a lover, swore it in front of the Brehon at Kinvarra; they were living most of the time at Kinvarra at that time, and he won the case. I don't know that anyone around here believed it. She didn't look like the kind of woman to have a secret lover. She spent a lot of time here at Newtown Castle while he was away in Galway, buying and selling, or even while he was at Kinvarra: she liked this place best of all. She was very religious and she was devoted to her children, especially the boy, and anyway there was no sign of a lover afterwards.'

'Did she go back to her own people then?'

'No,' said Toin. 'She's still living around here. She lives up the mountain, up there.'

'I see,' said Mara. 'I think I saw her walking away from the church with young Cuan after the burial Mass for Father David.'

'Yes,' said Toin. 'She was there. I remember noticing her going into the church in front of Cathal the sea captain.'

His voice was now quite faint and Mara looked at him with concern. 'Come on, boys, we'd better be going,' she said, 'we have a climb ahead of us.'

'Keep your eyes on the village, Newtown, as Sorley used to call it,' said Toin as he walked to the gate with them. 'You have to go right through that. Then you have another short climb. You see up there, the top terrace is just above the village, if you can call it a village – it's just a collection of hovels – no farmer would house his cows in a place like that. Anyway, you'll see it for yourself. Go about halfway up to that and you will be at the mine entrance. Bring the boys in for something to eat on your way back. I'd enjoy their company.'

'I don't think I will,' said Mara gently. 'Brigid will have their meal ready and would be annoyed if they didn't turn up.' A message could be sent to Brigid, she knew, but Toin would probably find six sweaty, tired boys a bit too much for him.

'Well, you would have been very welcome, but, in the meantime, here is something to keep them going.' Toin beckoned to Tomás who came up with two large linen bags. 'Just a few oatcakes for the lads,' he said, and Enda stuffed one bag into his satchel with a beaming smile and an elegant bow while Fachtnan took the other with murmured words of thanks.

❈

The lower slopes of the small mountain were full of beauty. The limestone glittered in the slanting rays of the sun as it moved over towards the bulk of Slieve Elva. Silver-blue harebells tossed their silky heads among clumps of grass deep in the fissures and small stunted holly trees, with the gnarled trunks of fifty-year-old veterans, showed their gleaming berries, different on every tree, some orange, some scarlet and some a deep crimson.

When they were about halfway to the summit, though, Mara could see how the bare smooth sides of Cappanabhaile were scarred with the ugly workings of the silver mine. Great rocks, showing the dark blue of newly cut limestone, had been hacked out of the hillside, leaving ugly gaps; small wheeled wooden carts were piled high with crushed stone and the grykes were filled with dead and dying heaps of blackened vegetation.

'Let's stop here to catch our breath,' she said, whistling to Bran to recall him to his mistress's side.

'You can see the men,' said Hugh pointing. 'Look, Brehon.'

Mara's eyes followed the direction of his pointing finger. Silhouetted in front of the deep blue of the sea, and the pale hazy outlines of the Aran Islands, she could see a long line of men toiling down its stony slopes carrying leather buckets.

'The village is just over the brow of this next bit, Brehon,' called Enda who had gone ahead after depositing his satchel at her feet.

'Let's look at it, then,' said Mara. 'You can eat the oat-cakes afterwards.' She was curious to see the little village of houses that Sorley had built for his workers and she followed the boys up the last bit of hill and then stopped.

As Toin had described, it was indeed an ugly, sordid place, the single-roomed hovels built from loosely stacked stones, even one that seemed to be made entirely from sods of turf. All of the roofs, made from decayed rushes, had large gaping holes. Here and there, the doors were rotten and hanging crookedly from their hinges of leather. There were very few people around, just a couple of heavily pregnant women with some very small children. Everyone else seemed to have gone to work in the mines above. The children upset her. They were dressed in rags and were all very thin and lethargic-looking. Mara sent a friendly smile in their direction, but no one moved or smiled back. One mother clutched at two small boys and firmly marched them into the house behind and slammed the door. Mara turned to go back. This place disturbed and distressed her. No human beings should live in conditions like these. However, live they did and it was their homes. She should not invade their village with her troop of well-fed and well-dressed boys. She snapped her fingers at Bran, who was trying to make friendly overtures to a few of the ragged children, and she had turned to go when she heard a hoarse chuckle from behind her.

'No sense in staying too long here,' said a voice almost from under her feet. 'There's nothing here for anyone.'

Mara started in surprise and almost fell over the body at her feet. It was the man whom she had seen at the graveyard, twisted and gnarled with a missing arm, a hunched-up body and a disfigured face. He had been sitting on the ground beside the little cabin made from the sods of turf and the rags which half covered his mutilated body were so mouldy and stained that it was hard to distinguish him against the greens and browns of the vegetation around. Indeed, he hardly looked like a man, crouched there, peering up at her, but Bran had no hesitation. Like his mother before him, Bran was a dog that loved all mankind and with a bark of pleasure he bounded forward. The man screamed, a horrible sound, a scream which seemed to be dragged from the depths of a body which had known so much suffering that it could take no more.

'Get back, Bran!' shouted Mara desperately; but for once the dog did not obey her. Bran was already on top of the man, overjoyed to find one of his beloved humans at his own level and was enthusiastically licking the man's face. She grabbed Bran's collar and tried to drag him back. She had no fear that Bran would hurt the man, but that scream had been unnerving. However, the man was now smiling, at least Mara thought he was smiling – it was hard to be sure – and his remaining arm had gone around the dog's neck. Mara could now see that one of his legs was useless, withered and twisted beneath him. He was an appalling sight, a repulsive sight and, with shame, Mara knew that if the dog had not run over, her own instinct might have been to avert her gaze and move away as quickly as possible. Something of the loneliness and the desire for comfort within the unfortunate man seemed to have been communicated to Bran. Always friendly, he was now showing the degree of love that he normally kept for a few favoured special friends.

The boys huddled together in an aghast group and Mara knelt down in the wet soil and looked into the man's face. 'You have been badly hurt, my friend,' she said gently.

The man grimaced. 'It's not new,' he said. 'This happened a while ago, about eight months ago. A mine shaft collapsed, the lucky ones died, but I was dragged out from under the rocks and I lived, but I could never work again.'

Mara glanced at the wretched cabin behind. 'You live in there, Anluan?' she asked, appalled.

'Yes,' said the man indifferently. His speech was hard to understand, he spoke a mixture of the Welsh dialect with the Irish Gaelic language; she could follow that well enough, but his mouth had been mangled and very few teeth remained. 'I live there, if you can call it living. The neighbours are good to me, poor things; they don't have much themselves, none of Sorley's riches comes to this place, but they give me a crust from time to time.'

Silently Fachtnan opened his satchel and took from it a few oatcakes. Hesitantly he handed them to the man who instantly crammed them into his mouth, like a starving animal. But then Anluan stopped, looked at Bran's pleading eyes, broke one cake in half and handed the larger bit to the dog. Mara felt tears come to her eyes.

Fachtnan took the linen bag off his shoulder and placed it beside the crippled man. 'You eat these, yourself,' he said, gesturing to show the meaning of his words. 'We've all had our dinner and so has Bran.' He took Bran firmly by the collar. Bran gave the man's face a last lick and then allowed himself to be hauled away.

❋

'I had to give them to him,' asserted Fachtnan when they had left the village. He gave a challenging look at Moylan who was the big eater of the law school. But Moylan's eyes fell beneath his gaze. Even Moylan had been shocked by the poverty and air of starvation in the little village.

'This is disgraceful,' muttered Mara between her teeth. 'I shall speak to the king about this. How could Sorley have allowed it? Well, it's not going to go on. I shall see to that.'

'There's thirteen cakes left in my bag,' announced Enda

after a careful count. 'If you have one, Brehon, then it's two each for the rest of us.'

Mara took the cake to avoid arguments. She bit into it and was surprised by the sudden rush of flavour from the fresh blackberries with which it was stuffed.

'Last day for blackberries – shouldn't have blackberries after *Samhain*,' said Aidan. 'The devil spits on them on the eve of *Samhain*.'

'Don't talk nonsense,' said Mara irritably, getting to her feet. 'Why blame the devil for everything; man has enough of the devil in him to account for most evils. Come on all of you, if you're going to see the silver mine and get back home in time for supper then you can't delay any longer.'

'I'll eat yours if you like,' offered Moylan, picking the last crumbs of his oatcakes from his *léine* before jumping to his feet. Aidan did not reply. He crammed the rest of the oatcake into his mouth, though he looked aggrieved. Mara did not often snap at them for no reason. She felt a twinge of remorse; she was still upset after what she had seen at the mining village, but that was not Aidan's fault.

'How did you know that poor fellow's name, Brehon?' asked Shane.

'I saw him at Father David's burial,' said Mara. 'I heard one of the other workers call him that.'

'I'm amazed that he managed to get all the way down and then back up again,' said Shane, with a glance over his shoulder at the steep climb.

'He had a stick when I saw him.' She spoke mechanically because her mind was still occupied with thinking about the mining village. She felt ashamed that she had never taken the trouble to come up here before. They were Welsh, the occupants, and the Welsh had exchanged Brehon law for English law over three centuries ago, but that was no excuse. As the king's representative, she should have made it her duty to know what was going on in all parts of the kingdom. With an effort she dismissed the thought from her mind. When she first became Brehon she had resolved never to think about the past unless it held any relevance to the future and, usually, her strong will had enabled her to keep that resolution. She gave herself a mental shake. The important thing now was not to allow this situation to go on: the family at Newtown Castle was going to be forced into rebuilding this wretched place and feeding these workers properly. And it was then that she suddenly realized what she had said to Shane. Yes, of course, Anluan did have a stick.

'He couldn't have given the straw skep a poke with the stick, could he?' asked Shane, reading her preoccupied face with his usual sharp intelligence.

'I was just thinking about that stick,' admitted Mara.

'He'd never have the strength for that,' said Moylan.

'How much strength does it take to push over a straw skep, birdbrain?' asked Enda scornfully.

'And he did come in late,' said Fachtnan. 'I remember you saying that.'

'So would you if you were as lame as that, clodhead,' persisted Moylan.

'And he would hate Sorley,' persisted Fachtnan, ignoring the insult. 'After all, Sorley was responsible for his injuries.'

'He wouldn't know about Sorley always swelling up after a bee sting, though, would he?' argued Moylan who seemed to have constituted himself the defender of Anluan.

For a boy with a huge appetite, the sight of Anluan's obvious hunger seemed to have come as a shock.

'Only his family and the beekeeper and a few others would have known about that.' Aidan came to Moylan's aid.

'Do you think this crime was planned, or was it a spur-of-the-moment thing, Brehon?' asked Enda.

'I'm not sure how it could have been planned,' said Mara. 'Of course, on the one hand, you could argue that the murderer might have heard about Sorley's problem with bee stings, and perhaps was waiting for an opportunity, but on the other hand, it is such an unusual crime that I feel it was an impulse that was immediately acted upon. It may not have worked. The bees might have gone in a different direction; they might have concentrated on saving the honey from their damaged hive. No, the more I think of it the more I feel that this crime was not planned. Someone hated Sorley and seized the opportunity to either injure him or kill him.'

'But it could have been Anluan.' Enda was determined to prove his point.

Mara nodded her head. 'Yes,' she said. 'I suppose it could have been Anluan. He is a man who has not much to live for, a man who would feel he had nothing to lose.'

❋

As they approached the gaping hole in the side of the mountain, there was a buzz of conversation. One small dark man, who was speaking loudly to another with the shafts of a barrow held in his hands, stopped talking abruptly, turned his back on the party from the law school and rushed into the mine entrance.

'Gone to get the manager, probably,' said Enda, his face alight with interest as he looked around.

There was a small stone cabin built into the shelter of the mountain about fifty yards away. In front of the cabin a dead heifer calf, its stomach swollen, lay spread-eagled on the ground. There were two people inside the cabin, but one was doing most of the talking. The door stood open and it was easy to hear the words. The boys looked at each other and grinned. The stream of swear words was embarrassing even to the older scholars and Shane and Hugh were wide-eyed with amazement. The small dark man hesitated before the doorway as if reluctant to enter, and then compromised by gingerly stepping over the body of the calf, reaching out and knocking on the frame of the doorway.

'Someone is losing his temper,' murmured Enda as the stream of words went on unabated.

Then there was a final scream of obscenities and a small narrow-framed man burst out through the door. His face was dripping with sweat and was a strange shade of white, patched with red. He kicked the body of the heifer and plunged on. Mara stepped forward instantly; she recognized the man, the young face and the almost bald head were instantly memorable. She thought she had seen him climb the hill after the burial of Father David and he had been standing near the gate to the church while she had been talking with Toin this morning. She had noticed how no one seemed to speak to him, or even to greet him.

'You are Sheedy,' she stated, standing in his path.

He gave her an uncertain look, and then suddenly turned and bolted back over the lumps of scattered rock and heaps of crushed stone. Enda gave a long low whistle.

'Shall we go after him?' asked Aidan eagerly.

'Never catch him,' said Moylan. 'Look at him. He can jump like a goat.'

'He was probably brought up on the mountainside,' said Fachtnan wisely. 'Moylan's right – it would be impossible for us to overtake him now.'

'I could have a go,' said Aidan optimistically.

'No, leave him,' said Mara firmly. She had no intention of allowing the reckless Aidan to chase this man over rocks and chasms. It was interesting, though, she thought, how Sheedy had fled at the sight of her. He would undoubtedly know who she was and normally there was huge respect and deference paid to the Brehon within the kingdom of the Burren.

'Sorry, Brehon.' The mine manager looked apologetic. 'He's a madman,' he added, taking out a square of linen and mopping his brow. He gave the body of the heifer a distasteful look before continuing with heartfelt emphasis, 'Back in our own country someone like this would be locked up.'

'What's his problem?' asked Mara mildly.

The mine manager hesitated. 'Well, it's not for me to talk about it, Brehon,' he said. 'The master . . .' then he stopped and gulped. A look of horror came over his face.

'Oh my God,' he said slowly, his Welsh accent suddenly becoming more apparent. 'He was there, too, at the church, I mean. I know he was there . . . I saw him coming back up the mountain. Do you think . . .' again he stopped.

'And you are the manager of this mine.'

'Yes, my name is Ifor.'

'So is this all common land, Ifor?' Mara looked around

her with interest. She was not going to discuss the possibility of Sheedy being involved in the murder, she decided, though she would have welcomed some incidental information.

'It's shared between four farms, and my master owns – well, owned – three of these four farms.' His tone was guarded as he gave the explanation and he looked at her warily.

'And Sheedy owns the fourth.' Mara nodded her head. Everything was beginning to become clear.

'He has had plenty of opportunity to sell the farm, he and his father before him.' Ifor's voice was defensive. Obviously he identified with Sorley and his interests. He looked well fed and well dressed, unlike the poor unfortunate poverty-stricken miners.

'Was it to talk about Sheedy and his threats that you came to see me, Brehon?' His tone was assured and, though perfectly polite, had an undertone of belligerence.

'At the moment I am just interested in the mine and how it works; these scholars of mine have never seen one.' Mara kept her voice casual; she decided not to question him further about Sheedy. Toin could probably tell her the whole story and she would have to see the farmer himself. When he had calmed down she could question him about his presence at the church this morning and decide whether he was involved in the murder of Sorley.

'I am just on my way down to the castle to see Mistress Una.' He looked at Mara with a trace of impatience. Obviously he wanted to get rid of her.

'Perhaps you would have a moment to answer a few of my scholars' questions before you go.' She was not going to stand for any nonsense from this young Welshman, she

76

decided. If he lived in the Burren, then he had to live under the laws of the kingdom.

'Are they trying to get the silver out of the rock over there?' asked Shane pointing to some men hammering a large boulder of limestone.

'That's right,' said Ifor shortly.

'Perhaps we could look when they stop for a break,' suggested Mara.

'Very well.' He made a quick signal to the men and they stopped instantly, leaning on their sledgehammers. They were out of breath and dripping with sweat, their eyes dull, their faces white with exhaustion.

Ifor led the way in silence, obviously hoping that the interruption would be as quick as possible, but the eager curiosity of six boys made that unlikely, thought Mara. The questions began to fly as soon as they neared the crushed rock.

'How do you get out the silver?'

'That looks like lead, is it lead?'

'How much silver would you get from a rock that size?'

'Do you find big lumps of it, or is it all little tiny bits?'

'That's the silver, that gleaming stuff there, isn't that right?' asked Hugh, whose own father was a silver merchant.

'No, that's calcite,' Ifor answered sourly.

'Calcite is crushed and used on the land as a fertilizer,' put in Mara with a smile at Hugh. Certainly the gleaming heap of powder did look like silver in the sunlight.

'So how do you extract the silver?' Enda fixed the man with a stern look. He wasn't going to be fobbed off by silence.

'We burn it,' said Ifor reluctantly.

'Over there.' One of the men pointed, his accent was strong but he spoke in Irish Gaelic.

Near to the summit of the mountain it looked as if some giant hand had hollowed out a huge basin. A beautiful place originally, surmised Mara, as they walked over to look. It should have been filled with those lovely plants that grew in profusion in the shallow, scooped-out basins on Mullaghmore Mountain. This hollow, though, was stained with yellow and from the hazelwood fire in the centre of it a pungent smell was rising up.

'Disgusting,' said Shane wrinkling up his nose.

'Smells like rotten eggs,' said Aidan, fanning the air in front of him vigorously.

'Makes me feel sick,' observed Hugh, putting his hand across his mouth dramatically.

'Sulphur,' said Enda with a superior air.

Mara moved across to the western edge of the hollow and looked down towards Lios Mac Sioda. Sheedy certainly had a reason for his grievance, she thought. A small spring rose nearby and trickled down the slope. In the past it would have been a valuable resource for thirsty cattle on this common land during the rare dry spells. However, now the water foamed a pale primrose yellow and the smell was, indeed, sickening. A broad band of dead foliage outlined the stream's progress and for quite a distance around, the grass, normally so green on this limestone land, had a sickly tint. Mara knew little about cattle, but she was sure that poisoned land would result in poisoned cattle.

Ifor had said that Sheedy was mad: perhaps that was not true. Perhaps he had a true grievance which she wished that he had brought to her. Nevertheless, she now had to consider the fact that this young farmer was certainly filled with an almost insane rage and hatred of the mine and of its owner. She turned back towards the mine. The dead body of the young heifer still lay on the ground and flies hovered over it.

Mara's eyes went from the dead animal down to the valley where Newtown Castle stood, its conical, stone-slated roof gleaming in the sunshine. Within its walls, there was another dead body, the body of Sorley the mine owner, which would, by now, have been laid out, surrounded by all the splendour of the silver that had been gouged out of this ruined land.

SIX

MELLBRETHA (SPORT JUDGEMENTS)

There is no right to a fine or sick-maintenance if a boy is injured in most games such as swimming, hurling, jumping, hide-and-seek, or juggling, but the kin of the culprit must provide sick-maintenance if a boy has been injured by javelin-hurling or rock-throwing. All contests must be even in numbers.

The foster parents of a boy must take responsibility if they do not forbid dangerous pursuits.

❦

BY DUSK EVERYTHING WAS ready for the party at Cahermacnaghten law school. The turnips had all been carved and illuminated by candle ends placed in their hollow centres and every window within the enclosure had a ghostly skull glaring from it. *Samhain* was a time where the barriers between the real and the supernatural world are dissolved and where humans and spirits can penetrate each other's world for a few short hours. However, it was also a time of feasting on the last fruits of the season and Mara always tried to emphasize this aspect for the younger children in her care.

The benches and tables within the schoolhouse had been pushed together and spread with a linen cloth. Baskets of cakes and pies had been laid out on it. Brigid always made a great effort to ensure that nothing but the fruits of autumn would be served for this *Samhain* supper. There were little clusters of sticky cakes made from honey and hazelnut flour, bowls of walnuts, sweet cider made from windfall apples, dark purple elderberry paste and pale pink crab apple jelly stood in clay dishes beside the usual oatcakes. Everywhere there were heaped-up pottles, woven from the willow stems, filled with the apples from the *Samhain* tree, golden apples with yellow flesh and skins where the russet blended with the amber.

Daire, the silversmith's apprentice, was there. Taller than any of the others, he was leaping high in the air to catch, with his splendid white teeth, one of the apples tied to strings from the beams that supported the thatched roof of the schoolhouse when Aoife came in. She didn't look well, thought Mara. The girl's cheeks had lost their previous rosy glow and her blue eyes were deeply shadowed. Her brother had almost to push her into the room, though she had known the law school scholars since they were all children together.

'Come in, Aoife.' Mara seized the cold hand and drew her over towards the fire, calling over her shoulder, 'Careful, Daire! Don't break your teeth.' This had the desired double effect of leading Aoife's eyes towards Daire and of calling the young silversmith's attention to the girl.

He was over in a second, holding the apple he had secured, in his hand. It was the largest and the most beautiful apple in the room. Quickly he took out his knife and sliced off the place where his strong white teeth had marked the skin and held it out. 'Would you like it?' he asked gently. 'Please do have it.'

'You're like the fellow we were reading about in our Latin, Daire,' remarked Shane with the unselfconsciousness of a ten-year-old to whom girls were still just inferior boys. 'He offered an apple to the most beautiful woman in the room.'

'Come and let me see if I can duck for apples; I used to be very good at that,' said Mara, hastily ushering Shane away. As she pushed her way through a boisterous crowd of O'Lochlainn lads, trying to urge Brigid to jump for an apple, she heard Daire say: 'He's right, you know. When I saw you come through the door, I thought you were the most beautiful girl that I had ever seen.'

So it was love at first sight. He had rejected the silversmith's daughter; he was fancy-free and had now given his heart to a farmer's child. Well, they would make a lovely pair, thought Mara, as heroically she dipped her face into a bowl of water and tried to capture one of the small apples that moved tantalizingly away as her teeth neared them.

'Thanks, Brigid.' She accepted a piece of linen and wiped her face. 'You have a go, Shane. You'll be better than me at this.'

'He's in a great mood tonight.' Brigid's eyes were directed towards the young couple by the fire. Mara nodded. There was no doubt that Daire had the look of a man who has had a huge weight removed from his shoulders. He was chatting easily to Aoife, though she appeared to be making little response. Still, her eyes were on the blond, broad-shouldered young man and the night was only beginning. Mara felt cheered. However, Rory would probably be at the *Samhain* bonfire with his new zither and his sentimental songs, so she hoped that Daire would make the best of his opportunities before they got there. She kept an interested eye on the couple as she moved around the room, hospitably inviting everyone to eat and drink and turning a tolerant eye away from Enda and Mairéad O'Lochlainn, who, mouth close to mouth, contested for a small apple in a dark corner of the room.

❀

The weather was still fine as they all set out to walk across the stone pavements of the High Burren on their way to Eantymore, the traditional fair site for the people of the kingdom. However, the west wind was strong to their backs and the silver moon sailed in and out of rapidly expanding purple clouds.

The crowds had gathered by the time that they arrived. This was one of the two great fire festivals of the Celtic year; for weeks before, farmers, during the annual clearing lands of hazel scrub, had deposited bundles of sticks on the rocky field. The bonfire was lit just at the entrance to a large cave that went for miles under the limestone of the Burren. This cave was of great symbolic importance. In ancient times it was considered that on the night of *Samhain* the spirits of the dead could float between this world and the next. The legends spoke of a cave leading from the world of the living down to the otherworld: the world of the dead, and the shrieks of the daring youngsters who dashed in and out of the cave holding up their pitchpine torches held a note of real panic underneath the fun.

'There's Roderic,' said Fachtnan as the deep mellow notes of a horn reached them. 'It's good that he's here. Aoife, Roderic is here; Emer is surely with him.'

By the light of Fachtnan's torch, Mara could see Aoife's face. Last summer, Roderic and Emer, Rory and Aoife were a pair of inseparable couples. Now Roderic had married Emer, and gone to live in the kingdom of Thomond to become one of the king's musicians there. And Rory had rejected Aoife and taken up residence in the silversmith's magnificent tower house. Mara could see all those memories coming to Aoife, but, to her pleasure, she saw the girl stiffen slightly and take Daire's arm for the first time. Well done, thought Mara, wishing Brigid were here so that they could exchange satisfied glances. However, Muiris, Aoife's father, was there and this reminded her of something.

'Fachtnan,' she said, 'I just want to have a word with Muiris.' She would call his attention to Daire and emphasize the young silversmith's eligibility as a suitor. 'Could you keep an eye on Shane and Hugh for me? I don't want any of this running in and out of the cave. Hugh is a bit inclined to nightmares and I don't think it would be a good idea for him.' Hugh's mother had died earlier this year, on the boy's twelfth birthday and he had been nervous and tense ever since. 'You can pretend not to see Aidan and Moylan, if you like,' she added light-heartedly. The terrors of the cave would be all part of the fun for a pair of tough adolescents like those two.

'Muiris,' she greeted the farmer as she came up behind him and he swung around quickly, looking slightly shocked.

'Sorry,' she said immediately, 'did I startle you?' By the light of the torch that he was carrying, she thought that he looked ill at ease.

'No, no, Brehon, I was just thinking of something.'

It was easy to know what he was thinking. Right in front of them was Rory waiting his turn to sing a ballad to the crowd.

'Aoife's looking well tonight,' Mara said in the easygoing, gossiping tone which was second-nature to her in her dealings with the people of the Burren. 'What do you think of young Daire? They seemed to be getting on well together earlier on.'

He gave Daire an indifferent glance. His eyes were fixed on Rory and his bushy eyebrows were knitted into a frown of concentration. Mara looked also. She had always thought that Rory was an extraordinarily beautiful young man, his hair was a pale blond with a shade of red in it, his eyes were intensely blue and he had an elegant figure with broad shoulders and slim hips. She glanced appraisingly from him to Daire. If she were sixteen, whom would she prefer? Daire was more strongly made. Whoever christened him had named him well for the sturdiest tree in the forest, *dair*, the oak tree, but Rory had a showy glamour about him. Reluctantly, honesty compelled her to acknowledge that if she were Aoife's age, Rory might appear the more attractive. Perhaps this was why young people had parents; parental indulgence was all very well, but possibly her own father, Sémus O'Davoren would have been a better father if he had forbidden the marriage between herself and Dualta, the son of the stonemason, who had not had the industry to make the most of his opportunity to achieve the status of a Brehon. Her lips tightened as she thought of Dualta. He had hoped that his marriage to Mara, when she was fourteen and he was sixteen would guarantee him an easy and luxurious life, especially after the death of her father. Only by taking matters into her own hands and conducting her own divorce case had she been able to get rid of him. She turned away from those memories and turned back to Muiris.

'I would use all your influence with Aoife to help her forget about Rory,' she said decisively. 'Someone like Daire would be a much better match.'

Muiris nodded and a look of resolution came over his strong face. He thought for a moment and then nodded his head as with approval for a resolution to speak out.

'Brehon,' said Muiris abruptly. 'That was a terrible thing that happened this morning.'

'It was indeed, Muiris.'

'A terrible accident.' Muiris had a note of enquiry in his voice.

There were times that Mara wished people would come to the point more quickly, but she curbed her impatience. Words did not come quickly or easily to Muiris. He would have to be given his time. 'Terrible,' she echoed gravely.

That disconcerted him; she watched him sifting through the already-prepared words in his mind, just as a wool merchant hunts for his best sample of fleece.

'You see I keep bees,' he said eventually.

Mara nodded. Most farmers, especially those with large families like Muiris, did keep bees. The honey was the only means to sweeten the oatcakes and to brew mead and also had a valuable use in preventing infection in wounds for both animals and people. She said nothing, though. Muiris would have to tell his story in his own way.

'So I know the way that they behave,' he ploughed on. 'You see, if you disturb a hive they will fly at you if you are very close, but if you keep out of the way, they will just get back to guarding their honey. That's their nature – you leave them alone and they'll leave you alone,' he added, now gaining in fluency.

'But they went after Sorley.' Mara looked at him with interest.

Muiris nodded. 'I reckon that they must have been disturbed when he was very near to them.'

'Do you think that he overturned the hive himself?'

'No, no, no man that has his wits does a thing like that.' He hesitated. 'Of course, though, it might be that another man pushed over the hive when he saw that the silversmith was exactly opposite the bees.'

'That makes sense,' said Mara thoughtfully. It was interesting that this man, experienced in bees, was also thinking of Sorley's death as murder.

'And it could be that a man who did that might still have a few bees lurking when he rushed into the church, quite late.'

'You saw someone?'

Muiris nodded. 'I saw Rory come in late and he had his hood pulled well over his head and almost covering his face, as if he were shielding himself. I was watching him, keeping an eye on Aoife to make sure that she didn't turn around and give him the satisfaction of seeing her yearning for him. I saw him stand there at the back of the church and brush his hood before he took it off.'

How much of this was significant and how much was it a question of Muiris wanting to wreak vengeance on the young bard? And what use would the death of Sorley be to Rory? From what Mara had seen yesterday and this morning, Sorley seemed more friendly to him than did Una. She couldn't really picture the solid, middle-aged Una indulging in fun and games with Rory behind her father's back, whatever Brigid said.

'And that's not all, Brehon. I went looking for Rory afterwards, once I knew that the bees had stung Sorley to death and I saw him rub his arm. I got as close to him as I could and I'd swear there was a big lump, like a bee sting, on his wrist.'

'Well, thank you for telling me this, Muiris,' said Mara gravely. She looked at him carefully. There was an uncomfortable look in his eyes before he looked away. He turned away from her and looked intently across the grass at Rory standing chatting to Roderic. She could not see his eyes, but she saw his fists clench in frustration before he swung around and strode away.

Well, thought Mara, what is to be made of this? She looked all around. The reels and jigs were beginning. Fachtnan, with Nuala, Shane and Hugh and some of the younger members of the O'Lochlainn clan, had made up a set for a reel. Diarmuid O'Connor, Mara's near neighbour at Cahermacnaghten, was playing his fiddle and they were all dancing on the damp grass. Aidan and Moylan were dashing in and out of the cave leading to the underworld, Moylan giving vent to a ghostly shriek that sounded more like a cow in labour than any self-respecting denizen of the under-world. That only left Enda, who seemed to be on the point of dragging Mairéad O'Lochlainn into the darkness of the undergrowth between Eantymore and Eantybeg.

Mara thought for a moment, but then raised a beckoning finger. Enda hesitated, but the habit of obedience was too strong so he whispered a word in Mairéad's ear and came reluctantly across.

'Yes, Brehon,' he said.

'I just want you to do a little task for me, Enda,' said Mara mildly.

His high-cheeked, tanned face was flushed and his very blue eyes seemed to be burning like a piece of lapis lazuli that she had once seen in the abbey's scriptorium. He swal-lowed hastily, trying to regain his composure and she was filled with affection and sympathy. There was no point in ignoring the situation. She was not just an instructor to these young scholars of hers: she had to take the place of mother and father to them.

'Enda,' she said gently, 'you have done very well with your studies this term. If you work like this through Hilary and Trinity, I think that there will be no doubt in my mind that you will pass your examinations in June and that you will then be an *aigne*, able to earn money that will help your family in Mayo. What you must not do, now, though, is to allow anything to get between you and your books for the next few months.'

Then she stopped and watched the hectic flush fade

from his face. He was a good-looking boy with all the normal instincts of someone of his age. If he got involved with Mairéad O'Lochlainn at this stage, he was bound to be distracted from his studies. He had confided in her that his father in Mayo was almost ruined by a plague of the murrain which had spread amongst his cattle; he was very young, he would be barely seventeen by the end of the year, but it was essential for his own pride and his belief in himself that he qualify as a lawyer this summer. Mara watched while the memory of his father's distress came back to Enda, and she saw the flush fade from his cheeks and his eyes look at her steadily.

'Thank you, Brehon.' That was all that he said, but she gave a satisfied nod. Mairéad would have to look elsewhere for a lover. Enda would keep his mind on his work until the examination was passed and he had established himself as a lawyer.

'I just wondered, Enda, if you could find some opportunity to look at Rory's wrist. You see, Muiris implies that he has a possible bee sting there and that might just, though not necessarily, have some relevance to the death of Sorley. It's not an investigation yet; I haven't completely made up my mind, but bee stings fade, so if you could think of something, Enda . . .'

He was gone with a quick nod and without a sideways glance at Mairéad, who watched him from the shadow of the hawthorn hedge.

Enda took a long time over chatting with Rory. Obviously he took his mission seriously. His eyes never strayed towards Mairéad who was tossing her red curls impatiently. Mara watched him with some compassion, but also with some compunction. She was right, she knew, but that did not stop her feeling guilty and rather sorry for him. Most farm lads of his age would be getting betrothed by now; their fathers would be looking out for a suitable small farm so that they could set up in their own right. Enda, with his brains, his looks and his charm, would probably end up as a wealthy man, but for now he had to concentrate on his studies and avoid any unwise entanglements. Let him pass his examinations, get a position as an *aigne* in the service of some *taoiseach* or with some Brehon and then he could think about marriage.

Enda and Rory were now wrestling playfully: Rory pretending to cuff Enda. And then the two heads were bent together looking at something. After a few minutes Enda left with some joke shouted back. Rory lifted his hand in a parting salutation and the light from the bonfire showed as a red flash on his wrist.

'He is wearing a silver bracelet, Brehon,' said Enda in a low voice as he returned. 'I think the silversmith, Sorley, probably gave it to him. I admired it and eventually he allowed me to slip it on. I pretended that I didn't want to give it back so I had time to have a good look at his wrist.'

'And?'

'Muiris is probably right,' said Enda. 'There is still a slight lump just on the back of his right wrist.'

'I see,' said Mara thoughtfully. Of course it was natural that Sorley should give Rory a present of a silver bracelet and equally natural that he should wear it at *Samhain*. He was a showy young man and jewellery like that would have been part of the price that Sorley was willing to pay in order to secure a husband for his plain daughter. On the other hand, it was not natural to slip the bracelet over a sore wrist; why not wear it on the left wrist?

Unless, of course, thought Mara, Rory's was the hand that pushed over the hive of bees and caused the death of the silversmith.

SEVEN

CÁIN LÁNAMNA (THE LAW OF COUPLES)

In the case of a divorce, desired by husband and wife, the property is divided between them.

When a divorce between a man and woman of equal status occurs, the woman gets one-sixth of the fleeces, but if the wool has been combed she gets one-third of it and if the cloth has been already woven she gets a half.

In the same way, the husband gets five-sixths of the flax standing in the field, but only a half if the flax has been turned into linen.

☙❧

'I think,' SAID MARA to her scholars, as they lined up in the schoolhouse after breakfast on Friday morning, looking clean and neat in snowy white linen *léine* and well-combed hair, 'I think that we will go to the All Saints' Mass at Rathborney today instead of to Noughaval as usual. I would like to have a look around the graveyard and you can all be of help to me.'

'Does that mean that you are definitely considering the death of Sorley to be murder?' enquired Fachtnan after a moment's silence while the boys looked at each other and then at Fachtnan as the eldest scholar.

'I'm not sure, Fachtnan,' said Mara honestly. 'You see there seems to be a quite a few people who hated Sorley and then this sudden death – well, it just worries me a little. I feel that it is a murder.'

'Are you thinking about Cathal the sea captain, Brehon?' asked Shane.

'What about Daire?' asked Enda.

'Why do you say that, Enda?' Mara was interested. Had Daire told of his unfair treatment last night? As far as she knew her lads had not seen him for a long time before. 'Did Daire say anything to you?'

Enda shook his head. 'No, it was Rory who told me,' he said and added thoughtfully, 'in fact, he told me at great length how much Daire had hated Sorley and how unfair the silversmith had been to Daire and how he had refused to warrant him as a silversmith and had cheated him.'

'At great length?' Mara raised an eyebrow and Enda nodded.

'I got the feeling that I was supposed to take that information to you, Brehon,' he said astutely.

'Sorley was a moneylender; Brigid told us that,' said Aidan eagerly. 'Could you find out anything about that, Brehon?'

'Has anyone borrowed money from him? We could go around the Burren asking about that,' proposed Moylan.

'Is there anyone else that you suspect, Brehon?' asked Fachtnan.

'I saw Sorley's son, on Wednesday night,' said Mara quietly. 'His name is Cuan and Sorley has rejected him as an unsatisfactory son quite recently. He gave him a farm of twenty acres, but the lad is not used to farming and I don't think that things have worked out for him. I think that if we are making a list of those who had reason to dislike this man Sorley, we might have to put Cuan's name on it.'

'It couldn't have been legal, though, could it, Brehon?' asked Enda. 'I mean Sorley's repudiation of his son. After all, he would have had to come to you and I don't remember any such case.'

'Unless he went to the Brehon at Kinvarra,' said Mara. 'I don't think that could be the position, though. I'm sure that, out of courtesy, I would have been notified. Though, I can't remember being notified about the divorce granted against Sorley's wife, either, but then that was about seven or eight years ago; perhaps I've forgotten, or perhaps Sorley was not living at the Burren at all at that time. He had a house in Galway as well as a castle in Kinvarra. I know that he bought Newtown Castle from the O'Lochlainn about twenty years ago, but he didn't live there much, I think.'

'Exactly how old was Cuan when he was rejected, Brehon?' asked Enda alertly.

Mara looked at him with respect. 'Why do you ask that, Enda?'

'Well, if he were under seventeen, even by a day, then it

is illegal, and, come to think of it,' he added, his blue eyes thoughtful, 'even if he were over seventeen a mountain farm of twenty acres would not, in the eyes of the law, be suitable provision for the son of such a rich man.'

'Well done, Enda,' Mara eyed him jubilantly. 'That is my feeling exactly.'

❋

The church was still half-empty when they entered. The six scholars sat in the back row while Mara went further up the church looking keenly at the row of people in the top right-hand seat; Una was there with her faithful maidservant on one side and Rory on the other side. Daire was in the same row and also a middle-aged man – probably Sorley's steward, surmised Mara. She glanced around from time to time as the church began to fill. Toin came in, leaning heavily on his stick and on the arm of a body-servant. She saw that he too glanced around the church after he had seated himself beside her. He was obviously looking for someone and expected to see them at the back of the church. Mara's eyes followed his and she saw Cuan, Sorley's rejected son, slip in through the door; with him was a plain-faced, middle-aged woman in a threadbare cloak.

Just as the door to the vestry opened to admit the altar servers with their tapers extended carefully in front of them, there was a slight stir and Ulick Burke came hurrying up the aisle. He hesitated for a minute, his eyes on the party from Newtown Castle, but then he turned into Mara's pew, squeezing past Toin with a beaming smile.

'Well, my dear Brehon, this is a terrible affair, isn't it?'

whispered Ulick as he squeezed past Mara and insinuated himself into the space between her and the wall.

Mara turned resigned eyes on him. The altar boys were lighting the candles and carrying the sacred vessels out to the table and there was a murmur of conversation in the church; if Ulick kept his voice down there was a good chance that no one would overhear.

'You're upset by Sorley's death?' Her question wasn't too seriously meant. She had seen the look of fury that Ulick gave his sneering host that night she had dined at Newtown Castle and guessed that there was little genuine regret in his protestations.

'Uncanny, though,' he said with a quick look over his shoulder. 'It almost seemed as if he foresaw his death.'

Mara frowned. 'Why?'

'Oh, of course, I haven't told you what happened after you left on Wednesday night. All the excitement yesterday morning put it out of my head ...' he paused dramatically.

'Tell me now.' Mara gave him her full attention. There were times when a gossip like Ulick was indispensable. He was obviously bursting with news.

'Well,' he said dramatically, 'as soon as you and the king had departed, well, that hatchet-faced lawyer from Galway said that he was going to bed and Sorley said there was just a little business for him to do before he retired for the night.'

'Business?' queried Mara. Had Sorley decided to reopen the affair of Cathal and the boatload of silver, she wondered. Cathal, and what was probably his son, were there in the church today. She had a quick look at Toin, but he was lost in his own thoughts and seemed to be ignoring Ulick.

Ulick nodded. 'Yes, business. You see before you, my dear Brehon, a broken man. I have been disappointed in love.' He waited for a tantalizing moment, his eyes dancing with amusement, before adding dramatically, 'She is not for me, alas!'

'What are you talking about?' Mara sat back in her seat to enjoy the story. She cast another glance at Toin and saw that now he was listening. He had a faint smile on his purple lips. He knew Ulick of old, of course. She remembered Turlough and Ulick staying with Toin last summer when they were on their way to the Aran Islands.

'Yes, the fair Una, she is for another. She has been betrothed!'

'What!' Mara realized that the word was louder than she intended. She looked hastily over her shoulder, but no heads had turned. The church was full and the air was full of murmurings of prayers and creakings of seats and of people sitting down, or kneeling or pushing past others with whispered apologies. Several women were walking around the church, reciting the Stations of the Cross in pious voices. Nevertheless, she lowered her voice to whisper, 'Betrothed to whom?'

'To Rory the bard! It was all signed and sealed the night you had supper there. As I said, do you think perhaps our dear friend, Sorley, had a premonition of his demise? The Bodkin lawyer took out, not a bodkin, but a quill and covered the vellum, not as beautifully as you would have done it, my dear Brehon, but I am sure that it was adequate. The bridegroom was very drunk and tried to kiss his future bride who was obviously pining for me because she slapped his face and told him not to be a fool.'

'Well . . .' Mara's breath was taken away for a second. She had not realized things would progress as quickly as that. She felt furious for the sake of Aoife, the lovely girl that Rory had courted for the last year, but she was glad that she had not been asked to draw up the betrothal contract. Aoife was in the church, she noticed, and her father and mother were with her. How would she take this news, or was her new-found interest in Daire enough to carry her through? Mara hoped so.

'And that's not all, my dear Brehon!' Ulick paused dramatically and then rose to his feet as Mauritius, Bishop of Kilfenora, came out on the altar steps. Everyone else rose also and as the bishop's sonorous voice sang out the Latin words: '*In nomine Patris, Filii, et Spiritus Sancti,*' Ulick's voice hissed out: 'He drew up a will as well. His last will and testament.' Reverentially he crossed himself and then added in Mara's ear: 'And, I must say, my dear Brehon, that the lovely, innocent bride-to-be, Una, showed much more interest in this than she did in the betrothal contract.'

'And why was she so interested?' Despite her resolution not to indulge in gossip, Mara could not help putting the question. Hastily she looked back at the altar and crossed herself piously.

'Because, my dear Brehon,' Ulick paused while the bishop intoned: '*Introibo ad altare Dei,*' and crossed himself profoundly again, making sure to touch forehead, breast and each shoulder, 'because everything is left to her. You can understand, Brehon,' he said, while the altar boys shrilled out the response of '*ad Deum qui laetificat juventutem meam*', 'why you see me now as a broken man. You couldn't believe it, my dear Brehon, the amount that man owned. I had a quick look when we placed the vellum scrolls in the chest up in the gallery. Such a shame about his death, though, my dear Brehon,' he said as everyone rose for the recitation of the gospel.

This time there was a genuine note of regret in Ulick's voice and Mara gave a few curious glances at him as she listened to Christ's discourse on the resurrection.

'You think he would have favoured your suit?' she whispered under the cover of everyone sitting down in preparation for the sermon.

'Of course, my dear Brehon.' Ulick's face was complacent. 'Wait until you hear . . .' but he said no more as a hush came over the church as the bishop delivered his sermon.

Mara kept an attentive face turned towards the altar but did not hear a single one of the bishop's well-chosen words. Her mind was running over the accusation made against Rory by Muiris. Ridiculous, she had thought at the time, but now she was not too sure.

As the Mass progressed Mara puzzled over Ulick's story. It seemed very odd that everything had been left to Una. What about the son? Did Lawyer Bodkin know that there was a son alive when he drew up the will? Certainly under Brehon law a son, unless publicly disowned for a good reason, could not be excluded. She did not want to betray Ulick, who should never have repeated all this, even if he were a witness, but she felt that, some way or other, she would have to interfere in this matter and get the boy his rights. Probably Ulick had got it all wrong and Sorley had left a substantial amount of his moveable property such as the treasury of silver, to his daughter, while his son inherited the castle, land and farm.

As soon as the service was over the church emptied quickly. Mara turned an expectant look towards Ulick. 'So you think Sorley would have favoured your suit, even though he had just betrothed his daughter to Rory the bard.' She injected a note of scepticism into her voice.

Ulick responded instantly. 'Well, I had a word with him afterwards. "Sorley, my dear fellow," I said to him, "the story goes that this new king, Henry VIII, is happy to hand out earldoms. You would like your daughter to be a countess, wouldn't you?" Of course, Brehon, he was very interested in this idea and I put it to him that, with a little help from him, I could afford to divorce the Earl of Kildare's daughter. Kildare would not have a leg to stand on if I were negotiating an earldom and a "surrender and regrant" with the King of England, himself. We had quite a little chat about it on Wednesday night, myself and Sorley. However,' he heaved a sigh, 'I don't think that Una the Plain will see it like this. I confess that I am beginning to have a strange feeling that she doesn't like me much.'

'Were Rory and Una present when you had this interesting conversation?' asked Mara.

'Certainly not.' Ulick looked affronted. 'These matters were very delicate. No, they had both gone out. Although', here his voice grew thoughtful, 'I wouldn't be surprised if Rory hadn't been lurking outside the door. He seemed very surly with me the following day. Now, my dear friends, I must leave you; I must go and greet the bishop. I have a fancy to go and stay with him in Kilfenora for a few days. Oddly enough, I don't feel very welcome at Newtown Castle at the moment.'

When Ulick had gone, Mara turned to Toin. 'I suppose you heard all of that?'

The old man smiled. 'Gossip is my weakness,' he said lightly. 'Ulick told me all about that business when he dropped in to see me before Father David's burial Mass yesterday morning. I told him that I didn't think it would work out. Sorley was too shrewd to fall for something like this. A divorce could be granted under Brehon law, but the English hate these Brehon laws and refuse to recognize them. Henry VIII is supposed to be very strictly religious. He would not be likely to grant Ulick an earldom with his scandalous past. In any case, the Earl of Kildare is far too important to the English. They would never risk offending him just to gain over someone as fickle and unreliable as Ulick. It isn't as if he had any great lands or influence. No, that was all a piece of Ulick's nonsense. He was a bit upset, though. I noticed that he did not come into the church until after the service started.'

It may not have seemed like nonsense to Rory, thought Mara as she made her way to the back of the church. Rory was not too intelligent a young man and would have little knowledge of affairs outside his daily life. Did he perhaps think that the glittering prospects before him were about to vanish? After all, he had the betrothal document signed by Una as well as by her father. Without her father's backing or influence it would seem an easy matter to a young man like Rory, accustomed to getting his own way with women, to persuade Una into a speedy marriage and then he would be able to enjoy an easy living amidst all of the luxury of the silversmith's home. Mara decided that if Rory had overheard the conversation between the silversmith and Ulick, he might well have decided that the death of the silversmith would be essential to allow his plans to go forward. Thoughtfully, Mara beckoned to her scholars waiting by the door of the church.

'Go and see if you can find Giolla the beekeeper, Fachtnan,' she said when they joined her.

Giolla must have been waiting just outside the door as Fachtnan returned with him almost immediately.

'I wonder, Giolla, could you come with us when we go and look at the ruined church; I want to see the place where the hive was pushed over.'

Giolla did not reply, but bowed his head gravely. His face looked apprehensive, but Mara said no more until they reached the graveyard and she carefully examined the hole in the wall. Giolla was eager to talk now. He had been worrying about things, in fact, he had lain awake most of last night, he said, wondering whether Sorley's family would be able to demand a blood price from him if it were certain that his bees were the cause of Sorley's death.

'I was thinking about what that woman, the mother of the lad Marcan, said. Do you remember, she said that I shouldn't have them in a public place? Could I be in trouble over that, Brehon? The priest, Father David, gave me permission. You see, you have to put these straw hives under some sort of shelter, you can't leave them open to the sky or the rain would damage them, but you have to have them somewhere where the bees can fly in and out without hindrance and these little alcoves in the ruin were ideal. What do you think? Could I be held to be responsible?'

Mara shook her head, 'I don't think that the question will arise,' she said, 'it is not as if the hive was blown over or something like that. If that were the case, then it could be said that you should not have left them where that could happen, but they are well tucked into the stone alcoves and a good distance from the path. From what we saw the last time it looked as if someone had pushed the hive, at least I thought so at the time. I'd like to have another look now, though, if you don't mind.'

Followed closely by six scholars, they went through into the ruined church where, once again, the bees hummed placidly as they pursued their normal orderly and industrious life. Mara carefully examined the hole at the back of the still empty alcove.

'What do you think, boys?' she enquired, turning around.

'Not been there for long, that hole,' said Aidan sagely.

'You can see how there is no moss here and the stones look paler here on the inside,' Enda nodded agreement.

'These stones haven't been exposed to the weather for many a long day, I'd say,' said Fachtnan.

'So what do you think happened?'

'I'd say that someone took out a stone,' began Fachtnan.

'There it is,' said Shane excitedly. He leaned over and picked a stone from the grass at the base of the empty alcove. 'That looks like it, doesn't it, Brehon? Look, you can see the way the back of the stone has been weathered and the front, a little bit, but the sides are clean.'

Mara looked at the stone carefully. There was a strand of pale green lichen on the back of the stone and a clump of bright green moss on the front of it – but the sides were a pale untouched grey.

'Wait,' said Shane. 'Come on, Hugh, you come and be a witness.'

Both darted off and ran around the wall of the ruined church. After a minute a black head and a red head appeared over the uneven remains of the wall.

'We're on the other side, now, Brehon,' said Hugh.

'And I can see the stones at both sides of the little gap have lichen dangling from them.'

'It matches exactly.' Shane's high clear voice was triumphant.

'Have a look around and see whether you can find a stick lying in the grass,' called Mara and then turned back to Giolla.

'Have you got the overturned hive here?' she asked.

Giolla shook his head. 'I can't show it to you just now,' he said, 'I am draining all the honey out of it and if I take it out of the cabin all the bees will come over to it. But there is definitely a hole in the straw. I'll show it to you later this night if you like, if you come back when it is dark. The bees don't come out after nightfall.'

'I'll take your word for it for the moment,' said Mara, 'but make sure you keep it. It could be used in evidence. Could you clean it out when you take the honey?'

'The bees will do that for me,' said Giolla happily.

'When I finish with it, I'll just leave it out here a few paces from this new skep that I've got over there and they will have it as clean as a new pin by the end of the day. They will take back every drop of honey from it.'

'Strange that no one heard him shout,' remarked Shane. 'You would think that he would – at least one shout.'

'I was thinking about that, too,' said Enda.

Mara cast her mind back to yesterday morning. 'Of course,' she exclaimed. 'The bell was tolling for five or ten minutes before the service began. Father David was seventy-six years old – the bell tolled seventy-six times. That sound would have drowned any other sounds – and, of course, we don't know how soon he was stung on the back of the throat. He would not have been able to call out after that.'

So now it was of the utmost importance to discover who was late into the church.

'Thank you, Giolla, for showing us everything,' she said, 'Will you make sure to keep that hive safe and not to show it to anyone else? My scholars and I will go through the law texts to see if you face any problems, but I must tell you now that I am inclined to regard the death of Sorley, not as an accident, but as *duinetháide*, an unlawful, secret killing.'

Her scholars were looking at her with bright-eyed interest and Giolla seemed startled, but Mara said no more so after a minute he asked courteously: 'Would you like to come back to my house and have some mead with me? I make it from my own honey.'

'Thank you, but no, I must find Toin, bid him farewell and then we must go back to Cahermacnaghten.' Mara was conscious that her voice sounded absent-minded, but her mind was busily scrolling through the names of all those people who might have come in late for the burial service of Father David. Which one of them had stood there, behind this ruined wall, perhaps crouched down – it was less than the height of her two youngest scholars – and which one had gently tipped over the hive as soon as Sorley had seated himself on the top of the ancient tomb?

Mara gave a last look around and then saw Toin who was walking slowly and feebly. He stopped in the middle of the path and stood waiting. He was not looking towards the Brehon and the boys, but back down the path. The woman whom Mara had seen earlier in the church, Cuan's mother, she guessed, came and joined him. There was no sign of Cuan himself.

'You stay here,' said Mara to her scholars. 'Spread out and search the long grass carefully. See if you can find the stick that was used to poke the stone through. I'll just go and have a word with Toin.'

'Are you all right? Should you sit on the bench and wait for your servant?' Mara asked as she approached the old man, standing deliberately in the middle of the path as she realized that the woman was about to slip past her.

'I'm all right.' Toin's reply was given in a dismissive tone and Mara did not pursue the subject. No doubt he was sick of questions about his health. She looked enquiringly at the woman by his side.

'This is Deirdre,' said Toin after a minute. 'She was Sorley's wife.'

'Divorced wife.' The woman's voice was harsh. Though

her shoulders were wide, she did not have the bulk of her daughter, probably she did not have a surplus of food, Mara guessed, but otherwise there was a great resemblance.

'I've been telling Deirdre about the death of her husband, Brehon.' Toin seemed to lay emphasis on the word 'husband' and this time Deirdre did not contradict him. She made no further effort to move away but stood looking from Mara to Toin.

'You are the Brehon of the Burren,' she said after a minute.

'Yes,' said Mara. 'I'm sorry that we have not met before.'

'I live on the side of the mountain,' said Deirdre with a short laugh. 'Not many come calling where I live! I'd better be getting back there, now.'

'Stay a while.' Toin placed his hand on the woman's torn cloak. 'You can talk to the Brehon. Your position may be changed now. You must think of your son.'

She stood very still then, watching the old man intently.

'Could we go and talk somewhere?' Mara was determined not to let this chance go. Toin seemed to be on familiar terms with Deirdre; it would be a help to have him present while she talked to the woman.

'Come back to my house.' Toin tried to smile. 'I can offer you both a cup of wine and for myself I can have something stronger that Malachy left for me.'

'I'll just tell Fachtnan where I am going.' Mara hastened along the path but as she went she heard Deirdre's voice say gently: 'Take my arm; you're not fit to walk.'

❄

Toin's face was grey by the time that they reached the house. He poured a cup of wine for Mara and for Deirdre, then went to a small chest, unlocked it, took out a flask and swallowed some of the contents. After a minute he sat down and a faint shade of colour seemed to come into his corpse-like face.

'My best brandy,' he said with a smile. 'Malachy's poppy syrup is all very well, but it makes me fall asleep.' He glanced at Mara and then looked compassionately at the woman sitting bolt upright and awkwardly on one of the velvet-cushioned chairs. 'Deirdre, my dear,' he said gently. 'I have told the Brehon some of your sad history. I have also told her that few who knew you believed in your husband's accusations.'

'That's all a long time ago,' said Deirdre. She had a deep voice for a woman. There was almost a rusty sound from it as if the voice itself was seldom used.

Toin took another swallow from his brandy flask. Mara drank some of her wine, but Deirdre, she noticed, touched nothing. She made as if to stand up, but Toin stopped her with a quick gesture.

'Don't return to that dreadful place up on the mountain, Deirdre,' he said urgently. 'Go back down there to the castle. Your putting aside was unlawful, now you must take your rightful position. Your son will need you. Cuan will not be able to manage all the affairs of that great castle and the silver mine – you know that. You and Una have strength, but he has none. You must be his strength.'

Deirdre sat down again. Her face showed little, but the eyes were sharp and intelligent.

'What makes you think that the boy will get anything?' she said after a minute.

'Talk to the Brehon,' said Toin. His voice was faint and he took a gulp from his flask like a man who is desperate to keep life in his body for another few hours.

'You were legally divorced?' Mara put the question as gently as she could but there was no trace of embarrassment or shame on Deirdre's face as she gave another one of her short, gruff laughs.

'Legally,' she echoed. 'Though the church says no, the man, that lawyer in Kinvarra, he said yes.'

'What was the evidence?' asked Mara.

'My husband . . . Sorley gave evidence.'

'And what did that consist of?'

She shrugged. 'Lies.' She said the word impassively.

'And did you deny the accusations?'

'I wasn't called to give evidence.' Her tone was as flat as if she were talking of someone else.

'You weren't even called to answer the accusation?' Mara was startled. Her voice rose and she saw Toin look across at her keenly.

'No,' said Deirdre. 'I wasn't asked, so I said nothing.'

'And who else spoke?'

'No one, Sorley spoke, the Brehon gave judgement and that was it.'

'But surely the Brehon asked you to speak!' And then when Deirdre shook her head silently, 'Didn't he ask if anyone else had something to say?'

Deirdre shook her head again, emphatically this time. 'No, he didn't. It was all over in the time that it would take a swallow to fly past. Then he went on to the next case.

Sheep stealing, I think it was. That one took a long time, I know.'

'And how have you lived since?'

'Sorley sent his steward over to me. He had everything arranged. He knew beforehand what the verdict was going to be. The steward took me in a cart. There were clothes already packed on it. He took me back to Rathborney, up the valley and then up to Lios Mac Taidhg. There was a house there, not much of a place, there were a couple of goats, and a bit of a garden. The steward told me that it was mine now, but that I was never to show my face at the castle again. If I did I would have nothing.'

'And you didn't?'

'I used to wait around in the bushes to try to see the children whenever they visited here. After a while Una didn't want to see me anymore. She was her father's daughter. It was different with Cuan.' Suddenly the woman's face seemed to soften. There was even a hint of tears in her eyes. 'He needed someone and he didn't get much from his father.'

'I see,' said Mara. Was there any means of corroborating the woman's story, she wondered? Toin was right, of course. If Cuan were the inheritor he would need his mother.

'Tell me about Cuan,' she said. 'What happened there?'

Deirdre shrugged. 'His father rejected him.'

'Legally?'

'I don't know.' Deirdre's voice was bitter. 'What is legal? I only know that it was not right.'

'There was no law involved as far as I know, Brehon,' said Toin. His hand was clenched into a fist and was driven into the wasted depths of his stomach. 'I made enquiries about this. It only happened less than a year ago. My steward told me that the boy was just ordered to leave. He was given a farm, a twenty-acre farm, worthless land, just up there beyond the place where Deirdre was sent. It's called Lios na gCat.'

'What did your son say to you?' Mara turned to Deirdre, but the woman presented a blank face to her.

'I understood from him that he was disinherited,' she said carefully. 'He told me that he was to get nothing and his sister, Una, was to get everything. He said that his father had made provision for him and that was all that he could hope to get.'

'A twenty-acre mountain farm for a boy who once had everything.' Toin's rich, full voice could not disguise the bitter tone.

'It probably would count as provision if the boy had been convicted of being an unsatisfactory son,' said Mara thoughtfully. 'Do you know if there was any misdeed on the part of young Cuan. Had he stolen anything? Injured his father in any way?'

Deirdre shook her head and said quietly: 'I don't know, Brehon.' Toin laughed scornfully. He took another sip of brandy.

'You don't know Cuan, Brehon,' he said. 'If you knew him you would know that he is not capable of anything like that. The lad was terrified of his father from an early age. He would never have done anything deliberate to incur his father's wrath.'

'I think,' said Mara looking from one to the other, 'that

Deirdre should fetch her son and they should both return to Newtown Castle and stay there until I can have a chance to sift through the documents. I shall send Fachtnan, my assistant, to ride over to Kinvarra, or I may go myself. Mahon O'Brien may not have appointed a new Brehon, but he will know where the papers are kept. In the case of Cuan, I should certainly have been informed and I have heard nothing. Deirdre's case is nearly eight years old so I would have to look back into my records, but again, I do think that I was not informed. However, tonight is the wake for Sorley and Sunday is his burial; his wife and his son should be present for both these occasions.'

'Will you do it?' Toin eyed Deirdre eagerly and when she didn't reply, he added, 'It's for the boy's sake. You must give him his chance.'

She considered the matter for a moment and then bowed her head and slowly got to her feet. 'I will go,' she said.

'Wait.' Toin rang a small bell by his hand and in a minute his servant was in the room. Toin spoke to him in a low voice and then when he had gone out, turned back to Deirdre.

'They'll have a cart ready for you in a few minutes. You should take what you want to take from your house and then go on and fetch Cuan. The driver will take the two of you back to the tower house.'

She nodded in an indifferent way as one who cared little about what became of her. There seemed to be no strong feelings about her husband, thought Mara watching her carefully. No hatred, no distress, just indifference. On the other hand, she might be a woman of strong character who was used to hiding her emotions. And there was no doubt about her devotion to her son; the plain face had lit up with passion when his name was first mentioned.

✸

'Tell me a bit more about Cuan.' Mara waited until the woman had been gone for a few minutes before speaking. She was conscious that she herself should leave. Brandy would only keep Toin going for a while; already his face was grey with pain and his lips were livid. However, he had shown himself interested and concerned about this unfortunate mother and son and he was probably her only source of information for the moment.

'Tell me about Cuan,' she said again, and was careful to say it lightly. 'He seems quite different to his sister.'

'You probably think that he is an idiot,' said Toin eyeing her carefully.

Mara smiled invitingly and drained her cup of wine. She would not ask the question, but she was interested to know what Toin thought. From the point of view of the inheritance of Sorley's property it would be important to know whether Cuan was, in fact, lacking in normal wits. Toin reached for the flagon and refilled both their wine cups. He put away the brandy with a decided gesture and Mara leaned back and prepared to listen.

'I don't know,' said Toin taking a long swallow of his wine and cautiously easing himself against his cushions, 'I don't know if you have ever seen a dog, who from the time he was a young pup, has been continually shouted at and beaten when he thought he was doing the right thing and beaten when he did not know what he should do.

Well, that poor dog grows up useless and terrified. In a way, that is what happened to Cuan. He was a nice little fellow when he was young, before his mother was divorced, nothing special, you know, but a friendly little fellow and anxious to please. The boy had a deformity, of course, nothing too bad, his right hand was crippled, but Sorley kept trying to force him to do things which he had no possibility of doing and jeering at him when he failed and beating him for things that he had not done so the result is that he grew up the way he is now. No one ever taught him or trained him. And then Daire was taken into the house as an apprentice and Sorley thought the world of Daire, then anyway. He was always praising him and telling everyone how good Daire was and showing his work to visitors when they came. Cuan, in the meantime just hung about the house, or did a bit of shovelling in the mine. He seemed to get worse and worse and have less and less to say for himself until people did begin to think of him as some sort of idiot and then about a year ago, Sorley grew sick of having him around the house and so he gave him a farm. Well, it was the sort of farm that not even the best of farmers could make much of and this boy was not a farmer. No one had ever shown him anything about farming and, of course, he had no one to turn to for help. Sheedy was his nearest neighbour and Sheedy hated anything and anybody to do with Sorley.'

'Why did Sheedy hate Sorley?' interjected Mara.

'Sheedy.' Toin pronounced the name thoughtfully, but added no more for a few minutes. 'I'm not sure what to say about Sheedy,' he said thoughtfully. 'He owns the farm just below where Sorley's mine is situated. He's had very bad luck with the farm – lots of cows dying and the grass turning yellow. He blamed Sorley for it, but I wouldn't like to say for certain that it wasn't Sheedy's own fault. He's a strange fellow. I'd keep away from him, Brehon, if I were you.'

'And Daire stayed on in the castle?' Toin looked distressed and worried so Mara turned the conversation with her customary ease, but she resolved to go to see this Sheedy.

'Yes, as you say, Daire stayed on, almost like a son of the house, you could say and, for ages, he could do no wrong in Sorley's eyes and I do think that the lad is an exceptionally skilful silversmith. As time went on, we did not hear quite so much of what he had done and I suspect that Sorley began to get a little jealous of him; also there was some talk that Sorley wanted him to marry Una, but Daire didn't want to.'

Toin stopped, took a long swallow from a cup of some sticky, red liquid which stood on a press. For a minute he stayed very still and then continued.

'So then recently Rory the bard came along – but you probably know more than I do about this. He comes from your own part of the Burren. Of course, it was obvious that he was kept there as a possible husband for Una. I didn't need Ulick to tell me this. Everyone knew that Sorley hadn't a note of music in him. He hated music, called it noise! Anyway, Rory was there, living in the lap of luxury and Sorley's only son was out there on the hillside, trying to do something that he had no training for.'

A sad story, thought Mara, listening attentively. But would the story have a happy ending? Deirdre had been very careful to discount the possibility of Cuan inheriting. Surely, though, she was intelligent enough to know that he would be his father's heir in absence of any formal legal proceedings? Was she, perhaps, trying to blind the Brehon as to her possible part in the death of Sorley?

Could this deeply wronged woman have been instrumental in opening the way for this docile, childlike son to inherit the castle and the vast wealth of the husband who had so wronged her?

EiGhT

CÁIN LÁNAMNA (THE LAW OF COUPLES)

There are seven kinds of union between a man and a woman:

1. Marriage of First Degree: the union of joint property

2. Marriage of Second Degree: the union of a woman on man's property

3. Marriage of Third Degree: the union of a man on woman's property

4. Marriage of Fourth Degree: the union of a man visiting a woman with her kin's consent

5. Marriage of Fifth Degree: the union where a woman goes away openly with a man, but without her kin's consent

6. Marriage of Sixth Degree: the union where the woman allows herself to be abducted without her kin's consent

7. Marriage of Seventh Degree: the union where a woman is secretly visited without her kin's consent

In a union of joint property neither partner can make an agreement detrimental to the other partner's interests.

☙❧

It was soon after the bell for vespers. The scholars had done a good afternoon's work so when Turlough unexpectedly turned up, Mara was in a mood to indulge him. Together they rode over to look at the progress of Ballinalacken, a home that would be theirs for the few weeks that they could snatch from their busy lives. A wonderful place to live in, Mara thought. The scholars would all go home to their own families during the months of July, August and September and also for the month of January. This would be her home then, perched up here on the top of the hill overlooking the turbulent Atlantic.

'Wait,' she said, reaching her hand out towards Turlough. 'Wait for a minute, I want to look at the sea.'

It stretched out in front of them, blue as woad, the waves streaked across its ruffled surface like cream whipped to rough peaks. The colour was so intense that the sky itself paled before it and the limestone rocks were black and formless against the continuously moving water. A single-sailed carrack moved swiftly towards the coast and the gulls cried and screamed overhead. An energetic breeze was blowing strongly from the west, but the air was like wine, full of life-giving vigour. The slopes of the steep hill that led up to Ballinalacken Castle were bright with the tiny purses of pink and mauve heather, almost every flower busily probed by an industrious bee and the bracken glowed golden brown in the bright sunlight. Mara breathed in deeply and looked all around her. This is a moment that I will remember, she thought.

The castle itself was full of workmen, measuring spaces, building walls, carving stone and sawing wood. It would be a splendid mansion when it was finished. The new extension was more than double the size of the original tower. Some of the windows were already in place and the mullions were beautifully carved from smooth columns of blue limestone.

'You see,' said Turlough, eyeing her with the excitement of a four-year-old with a new toy, 'these old tower houses are all very well, but they are cold and dark. This new wing that they're building here will have good big windows facing south, see, look across there; that's the hall.'

'Could it have a window to the west, also?' asked Mara. 'I'd love to be able to sit and look over the sea and across to the Aran Islands.'

'You see,' said Turlough triumphantly. 'Aren't you glad that you came? Now, if you hadn't come then I would just be saying yes, yes to my builders. A big window to the west will be fine. We'll sit there on the window seat when the day's work is done and we'll watch the sunsets over the islands. I'll tell them to make it triple mullioned and then it will have plenty of space for the two of us. Now I want to show you everything. This is to be your house and I want everything to be just right for you.'

❊

'So this is your new home,' said Turlough when she had seen every inch of the new castle. 'This will be yours, yours only. You will invite me to visit you here and I will come humbly, cap in hand. You remember that I said this is to be a marriage of first degree. Now what would you like to see next?'

'I'll have to go soon,' Mara told him regretfully. 'I want to go to Sorley's wake at Rathborney; I didn't like the man much, and I hardly know his kin, but I am beginning to think that this is a case of murder, not just an accident and a wake is a good opportunity to see the family and friends together.'

'I'll go with you.' Turlough did not protest at her departure, she was glad to hear, but she did not want him at the wake. Somehow she felt it was lowering his dignity. It would be unusual for a king to attend the wake of anyone lower in status than a *taoiseach*. In any case, she had a job to do and she could do it more easily without the distraction of his presence.

'Why don't you ride on to Cahermacnaghten and we'll have supper together when I come back and then you can stay the night,' she said softly. And then before he could worry about her riding alone, she said quickly: 'Young Donie from my farm will be waiting for me at Toin's place and he will escort me home.'

He looked relieved at that. 'Toin will make sure that Donie has a good torch if there is no moon,' he said. 'Toin is the best of hosts, poor fellow.'

'Did you tell me once that you knew Toin when you were young?' she asked.

He shook his head. 'No, not then, he would be about eighteen years older than I am. I knew his father though, at my father's court. Toin's father was a harpist. He served my father, Teige of Coad, God have mercy on him, and when he died, the old man went on playing for my two uncles, Conor na Sróna and the Gilladuff.'

'So Toin himself did not become a harpist?' Mara was surprised. These skills and positions were usually passed from father to son. Her own father, grandfather, great-grandfather and his father before him, had all been lawyers.

'No, he didn't,' said Turlough indifferently. 'He became a physician, first one in his family to do that. I think I heard some story of a physician curing him of something when he was young and he set his heart on learning the skills himself. He must have done well to accumulate enough silver to set himself up as a *briuga*. He's a nice man, very like his old father who was always kind to us all when we were children. I can remember him trying to teach me to play the harp and he was the soul of patience with me.' Turlough laughed heartily. 'I was all fingers and thumbs, all right with a sword in my hand but no good with the strings. The old man would sing a note and I would try to play it. Toin has a beautiful singing voice, too, he's probably not able now, poor fellow but I can remember a few years ago, when Teige and I stayed with him on his way to the Aran Islands; I'd never heard such wonderful singing!'

'I'm afraid his singing days are over now,' said Mara softly. 'I think, from the way Malachy looked at him, that he has only a few weeks to go. He looked very ill today, but determined to keep himself going and to help others to the end.'

'I know, Ulick told me when I met him earlier today.' Turlough looked uncomfortable. He was as brave as a lion when facing danger in the battlefield, but he hated illness.

His own eldest son, Conor, was very ill, and Turlough could seldom bear to talk of him. She could see him casting around to change the conversation.

'There's something I want to discuss with you, something that I was talking about to Ulick,' he said hurriedly.

'What was that?' asked Mara gently. It had taken a long time to wander around the half-finished building. She cast a quick glance to the west at the spectacular sky of primrose-yellow streaked with orange and darkest blue. The sun would soon set. She should be on her way, but she had to give Turlough another few minutes. He had a thoughtful, worried look about him, almost as if he were looking for an opportunity to broach a difficult subject.

'Well, you know Ulick. He's a very clever fellow. He's been to Rome and then back through France and England. He has even stayed a few nights in London with Sir John Morton, the king's counsellor.'

'King Henry VIII?'

'No, before that, this was last year. It was Henry VII, his father, the king that died last April.'

Mara waited. Normally Turlough took no more interest in England or English affairs than she did herself. He had something of importance to say.

'He was talking about Henry VII and saying that this Sir John thought the king was a great legislator and that he had reformed the currency – that's their money – they never use barter as we do – anyway Henry VII brought out a set of new coins with his own picture stamped on them. There's three gold coins called "sovereign", "royal" and "angel" and then some silver coins: a "shilling", a "testoon" and a "groat" as well as pence and halfpence and farthings –

I'd heard of them, of course, but not of the more valuable ones.'

Mara looked at him in a puzzled way. 'Why is all this so interesting to you?' she asked.

He avoided her gaze and fixed his eyes on the distant islands. 'Ulick thought I should have my own currency, put my picture on it, make all the clans buy it from me and use it instead of milch cows and ounces of silver.' He swung around to look at her and when she still said nothing, he added defensively: 'Well, it would stop English money creeping in over here. You can't do much in Limerick or Galway without English money, these days.'

'And how would you make this money? What would you use to manufacture it?'

His eyes fell before hers. 'I was thinking about this silver mine here on the Burren,' he said. 'If Sorley has disowned his son as Ulick told you, if Sorley has made a will that excluded the boy, then the daughter should not inherit anything as valuable as that mine; surely that's the law, isn't it? I met Ulick at the bishop's house in Kilfenora and he was talking to me about this.'

'The law,' said Mara cautiously, 'is concerned to preserve clan land within the clan. If there is no son, then the daughter is the heir. However, if a daughter inherits a large amount of land from her father, then this land would be lost if she married into another clan. The law, therefore, just grants her the house in which she dwells and enough land for seven cows and the rest of the possession goes back into clan land and is available for the *taoiseach* to allocate to someone else.'

'Exactly,' said Turlough eagerly. 'Now Sorley was not a

member of a clan, he was a Skerrett from Galway, wasn't he? And that land on the mountain, that's common land to everyone who lives around it; I was asking about that. There's only one man, an *ócaire* called Sheedy, who farms around there and I could compensate him – more than Sorley ever did. He just bought the tower house from the O'Lochlainn and then, because he owned the farm around it and bought up a couple more farms, he just took what he wanted from the mountain. He just marched in and grabbed it.'

'Yes,' said Mara dismissively. 'I suppose that was the way that Sorley conducted his affairs. Not a very admirable character.'

There was a silence for a few moments. She could see the king turning matters over in his mind. He had flushed quickly at her last words, and then gnawed a finger for a minute.

Mara watched him carefully. 'Once when Enda was at his most rebellious he said to me that he thought there were far too many Brehon laws. He said that people should make up their own minds about what to do and not always be thinking of what the law says and what the law allows.'

He said nothing in reply so she said quietly, 'Do you want to know what I replied?'

'Something wise no doubt.' He tried to smile but his eyes did not meet hers.

'I said that men could not always be clear-minded about decision when their own personal affairs were involved. I told him that I found the wisdom of the past to be a great help to me in deciding what is the right course of action to take.'

'And what would the law say about this silver mine, then?' Turlough asked the question with resignation.

'I think that the law would say that the mine was built with the wealth of the owner and that this was personal wealth and therefore he had a right to will it where he pleased, whether to a daughter or to the church.'

Turlough smiled. 'I should have known that you would have an answer.' And then with a quick change of mood, he said hastily, 'In any case, I don't suppose really I wanted to do all this. It's just that Ulick thought . . .'

'I don't think that it would be worthy of you,' said Mara decisively. She decided not to talk about Sorley's son, though she had been about to. Let Turlough forget this idea. He would never be a man to make personal wealth and possessions his god. He was happiest as he was, following the way of life of his noble ancestors. Ulick was a poor model for him to take.

❋

The courtyard in front of Newtown Castle was full of people when Mara arrived. It was a pretty castle, she thought, as she dismounted and gave her mare into the hands of the porter at the gate and then looked around her. It had been built in the latest style, not rectangular and forbidding like most of the tower houses in the Burren, but rounded with a neat turret of well-cut stone slates capping it. The buildings around the courtyard, workshops, kitchen, stables, were well built also.

A long line of the Welsh workers at the mine was filing out of the main entrance; no doubt they had already been to see the body and were now sent out to leave room for others. A fire had been lit in the courtyard, and the appetizing smell of stewed meats rose in the air as the workers gathered around and accepted wooden trenchers piled high with food and horns brimming with ale.

It was all very well organized, thought Mara as she entered through the huge, heavily studded main door. Sorley's body had been laid out on an elaborately draped trestle in the exact centre of the guardroom on the ground floor. Those who came to view it were efficiently organized to move in a sunwise direction around the corpse and then, as they came to the doorway again, were, according to their status, either sent upstairs to the great hall or outside to the courtyard.

Mara viewed the corpse: it had been competently cared for, richly dressed, and the terrible congestion partially smoothed out from the face and the neck, the staring eyes closed, the hands folded on the breast. She murmured a prayer and then passed on. Her business now was with the living, not the dead. Outside the dividing of the sheep from the goats continued; Mara did not wait for an invitation, but mounted the steeply circling stairway right up to the third floor. The door to the great hall stood wide open, a fire was burning in the chimney and glowing braziers of charcoal stood at the other end of the room and along the passageway of the gallery overhead. The table was spread with wooden platters loaded with food and flagons of mead, wine and ale stood dotted around the central table and on small tables at the side of the room. Everything had been organized with a lavish hand.

The two women of the castle stood, side by side, at the top of the room, near the glowing fireplace. They looked so alike, thought Mara, both heavily built, the same sallow skin and hooked nose, the same lank dark hair. They might have been sisters. In fact, Deirdre, according to Toin, had been only sixteen years old when Una was born. With those features she would have been a plain girl even then, so why had Sorley married her? Perhaps he had made her pregnant and, like all ambitious men, he wanted a son.

'Let me get you something to eat and drink, Brehon,' said a quiet voice at her elbow and she turned and looked up into Daire's light blue eyes. He was looking better, she thought instantly. There was a hint of colour in his cheek and a softness around the mouth that had looked so grim before.

'I won't, Daire,' she said. 'I eat too much and I will get fat if I'm not careful.'

He laughed then, quite at ease with himself and with her.

'Did you enjoy last night at the *Samhain* celebrations?' she asked and was pleased to see his eyes gleam. 'And you got on well with Aoife, I noticed,' she said teasingly.

He turned abruptly so that his back was to the room. 'Is it true about her and that Rory? One of your boys was telling me . . .'

'You'll suit her better,' said Mara with a determined nod and was pleased to see the white teeth flash in a delighted grin. 'So Deirdre came back,' she added in a low voice.

'Yes, she turned up a few hours ago,' he murmured, with a cautious glance over his shoulder.

'Tell me what happened.' Mara moved a little back and sat on the window seat, patting an invitation to Daire to sit beside her. Now they were partially screened by a velvet curtain.

'Well, she arrived and Una just looked at her. The two of them, they just looked at each other. And then Una asked her whether she would be staying and Deirdre said that she would.'

I wish I had been there, thought Mara, and aloud she said: 'And what happened next?'

'She sent for the sewing maid and I think she borrowed a gown from Una, anyway she was soon all dressed up and enjoying herself, even giving a few orders. All this,' he glanced around at the luxurious arrangements, 'all this, of course, was organized by Una, but Deirdre is the one who ordered the food for the miners – first thing they've ever got from here that they didn't pay for in sweat and blood.'

'That was kind.' Mara gave a nod of approval.

'She is kind. She has certainly been kind to me. I think the fact that I tried to stand up for Cuan has made her friendly towards me.' Daire hesitated for a moment and then he said, the smile pricking at the corners of his mouth again, 'she even made time to have a talk with me about my prospects. Did you know that she is the sister of a silversmith?'

'No, I didn't. I know very little about her,' confessed Mara. That was surprising, she thought. Surely this man should have stood up for his sister when she was pushed aside by her husband.

'Yes, she was the daughter of a silversmith, but her father died just about the time that she was divorced. This brother was apprenticed to a silversmith in London, but he has recently come back to Galway. She told me all this, just a couple of hours ago. She said that she was going to get her brother to be my guarantor if he was happy with my work and then I could be a master smith and my indentures be cancelled.'

'That's wonderful news, Daire,' said Mara warmly. He would make a very good match for Aoife, she thought jubilantly, congratulating herself on having asked him to the *Samhain* party.

'And Cuan?' Mara looked around the room but there was no sign of the young man. 'Where is Cuan? I expected to see him here as well.'

'He's up in my room. Deirdre asked me to find him something to wear, but he didn't want any of my clothes; they are all much too big, anyway, so he refused to come down. I left him up there. He seems terribly changed. He's quite half-witted at the moment.'

'Rory's clothes would have been a better fit,' said Mara with a glance across the room at the slightly built young bard. He was standing at a distance from his bride-to-be, scowling heavily.

'He didn't offer,' said Daire curtly.

'How did Rory react to the arrival of Una's mother and her brother?'

'Not happy,' said Daire with a slight grin. 'In fact, he is not happy at all at the moment. Una is pretty rude to him. I wonder why he stands for it, unless there is some reason. What do you think?'

He looked at her enquiringly, but she did not respond. It was time to offer her condolences to the newly bereaved wife and daughter. They were sitting now, still side by side, near to the fireplace – an outward sign of unity, but there did not seem to be any warmth or closeness in the glances that they exchanged with each other. Rather, thought Mara, studying them with interest, there seemed to be a wariness, a suspicion, rather like the furtive looks between two hooded crows each watching the dying agonies of a wounded fox.

However, they had a dignity about them, both of them. They accepted her murmured words of sympathy and made suitable comments. It was as if they were speaking of a well-loved husband and father. As so often at these affairs, the conventions were what mattered, not the truth.

'Could you spare me a moment of your time?' Mara was conscious of a tremor of surprise that seemed to pass from mother to daughter. Both sets of grey-blue eyes were suddenly fixed intently upon her. 'I would like, also, if Sorley's son could be present.'

They glanced at each other. There was almost a wordless communication between them.

'I'm sorry,' said Deirdre, 'my son is not well at the moment. But of course, anything you say to us will be communicated to him.'

Una nodded solemnly as if they were talking about the head of the family rather than a distraught, handicapped boy. Mother and daughter, though probably for very different reasons, were as one about handling this affair without reference to Cuan.

'Perhaps there is somewhere that we can go?' suggested Mara.

Una was the one to lead the way to a small chamber just off the stairway below the great hall. She brought forward the chair and did the honours of the small room as the mistress of the house. Deirdre seated herself on a comfortable chair, but said nothing. There was a wary, watchful look on her face.

'You see,' said Mara, 'I'm not happy about Sorley's death.' Both women were looking at her with expressionless eyes. 'It looks like an accident,' she went on firmly, 'however, from the evidence given to me by the beekeeper, Giolla, I don't think it was an accident. He has shown me the place where a stone was dislodged, obviously recently, and how the straw hive was poked by a stick and thrust forward so as to end on the ground to the tomb where Sorley was sitting.'

She waited for a moment, but no glance passed between the two women this time. Now they had themselves strictly under control.

'I think,' went on Mara, 'that this was a deliberate attempt to kill Sorley. Any man might die if a whole hive full of bees stung him, but it seems that this man was unusually susceptible to bee stings so the chances of his dying were higher than normal.'

They did not question this, she noticed with interest. Obviously Sorley's problem with bee stings was known to both.

'So I am going to announce this as a *duinetháide*, a secret and unlawful murder, at Poulnabrone tomorrow,' she concluded firmly. 'I shall, of course, ask if anyone wishes to admit to this crime, and whether anyone knows any of any evidence as to the culprit.'

'Is this necessary?' A look had passed between mother and daughter, but it was Una who spoke. Her grey eyes, sharp and intelligent, were fixed intently on Mara.

'The murderer must be given the chance to confess to the crime, to express penitence and to pay restitution.' Mara's voice was matter-of-fact, almost as if she were explaining the law to a young scholar at her school.

'And if no one confesses?' This was Una again – almost a note of aggression in her voice now.

'In that case,' Mara met the challenge in her eyes with a firm look, 'in that case,' she repeated, 'I continue my investigations until I have solved the crime and brought the murderer to justice.'

'We understand, Brehon,' said Deirdre. Una did not speak further but led the way with dignity, back into the great hall.

❈

It suited Deirdre to be back in this affluence, Mara thought a while later as she made conversation with a farmer's wife from Rathborney. The woman almost seemed to have put on some weight since the morning. Her cheeks were faintly flushed and she nibbled continuously on the sweetmeats from the silver dishes. From time to time she surveyed the rich hangings, the velvet cushions, the gleaming silver and the rich food with the air of one who had been starving and is now offered a banquet.

Mara moved among the crowd greeting the people from the Burren and looking with interest on the prosperous-looking men and women, speaking English and dressed in the English style, the men wearing short jackets, tight hose and thigh-high cloaks, the women in elaborate full-skirted dresses and steepled headdresses heavily encrusted with embroidery. They were undoubtedly silversmiths and their

wives who had come out from Galway to attend the obse-
quies of one of their brotherhood. Una must have sent a
messenger to Galway yesterday morning. An efficient pair,
mother and daughter, she mused, watching Ulick in ani-
mated conversation with a well-dressed, grey-haired silversmith. She paused for a moment, her eyes on the little man.
Normally she avoided him, if possible, but now there was a
piece of information that she needed and he would be one
to give it to her.

'You know these people well, Ulick,' she said with a
smile as he joined her.

'Rich, my dear Brehon, rich,' he said with satisfaction.
'We always have to pay homage to the rich.'

'Why?' asked Mara with raised eyebrows, but Ulick was
not disconcerted.

'Take advice from an old man,' he said paternally, 'I
always take people at their own valuation; it saves a lot of
trouble. Go where the riches are, that's my motto.'

'So you've met most of these people before?' Best to go
directly to the point. It was never difficult to get Ulick to
talk.

'Yes, indeed.' He gave a satisfied glance around.

'Were you at his big hunting party three weeks ago?'

'At the party, my dear Brehon, not at the hunt.' Ulick
laughed merrily. 'I came for the food, not the exercise.'

'Good party?' Mara kept her tone light and did not
allow her satisfaction to show. This must have been the
occasion when Giolla arrived with his swarm of bees.

'Exciting, we nearly had roasted bees for supper!'

'Oh, I've heard of that. Why did he do it?'

'I've no idea.' Ulick's tone was dismissive. Strange,

thought Mara. If the porter had told Giolla about Sorley's susceptibility to bee stings, she would have expected Ulick to mention this. However, basically he was interested only in himself.

'So was Rory there?' she asked with a quick glance over at the young bard.

'He was indeed, and very sympathetic, too. Everyone else was too busy laughing. I didn't know what he was up to then, of course. I hadn't known that the daughter was up for grabs at that stage. Ah well, we live and learn!'

'I'm sure I do,' she said with a smile and moved away quickly before he thought of an answer.

'You haven't seen Cuan, Rory, have you?' she paused in front of the young bard.

'No, Brehon, I haven't,' he was making an effort to be polite, but his eyes were dark with anger. Una was completely ignoring him and so was Deirdre. He had not been introduced to any of these affluent people; even the servants with platters of food and flagons of drink were starting to pass him by while they were doing their rounds. This is interesting, thought Mara. If Una does inherit vast wealth, then perhaps she will change her mind. Ulick had spoken of the contract of betrothal. It had been signed and sealed. If Una now did not want the marriage to go ahead it might be expensive for her to extricate herself from it since Rory would have a right to compensation, but she might consider that worthwhile. There were obviously no feelings of affection or even of friendship on her part. However, she might wish for a husband at all costs and could make up her own mind now as to whether this reluctant lover, ten years younger than herself, was worth it.

'I'm afraid that I have no idea where he is, Brehon.' Rory's voice was emphatic, the tone slightly over-loud and slightly slurred. Mara turned her attention back to him.

'So you are getting married, Rory,' she said chattily. 'Has a date been set for the wedding?'

He didn't seem surprised that she knew, just shook his head, eyeing Una gloomily. Mara wondered whether he was comparing in his mind this plain, heavily built, indifferent woman with the beautiful, affectionate Aoife. Aoife would only have brought him a couple of cows, perhaps, but she was young, pretty, full of high spirits and she adored him. Was this bargain ever worth it?

'I suppose it will be a union of man upon a woman's property,' she said sweetly. That would be Brehon law and would give Rory very few rights. The ownership of the wealth would still be Una's. He would not be able to incur a debt or to sign a contract without the permission of his wife.

Rory flushed angrily. 'No, indeed,' he said stiffly. 'I've insisted that the marriage will be according to English law. I will be master in my own house and I will make provision for my wife.'

'I see.' Mara tightened her lips. He had told her what she had wanted to know. If this were true, and if Sorley had legally disinherited young Cuan, Rory would move from being a penniless bard, literally singing for his supper on many occasions, to being one of the richest men on the Burren. What had he felt like, she wondered, if he had overheard Ulick's offer to make Una a countess?

NINE

AN SEANCHAS MÓR

(THE GREAT ANCIENT TRADITION)

The éraic, or blood price, for killing a person is fixed at forty-two séts, twenty-one ounces of silver or twenty-one milch cows.

To this is added the honour price of the victim.

An unacknowledged killing is classified as duinethάide and this doubles the fine to eighty-four séts.

☙

'I HAVE SENT SEÁN with a message to all the churches to sound the bell at two o'clock this afternoon,' said Mara to her scholars on Saturday morning. Her voice was grave and they looked at her with quick attention.

'You're summoning everyone to Poulnabrone?' questioned Moylan. Poulnabrone was the name of the ancient dolmen in the centre of the High Burren. It had been the place of judgement and of law courts since time immemorial.

'Because of Sorley's death?' Fachtnan's voice was quiet and matter-of-fact.

'You think it wasn't an accident, then, Brehon?' asked Shane.

'Murder,' said Aidan with relish. '*Duinethâide*, secret and unlawful killing!'

'Can it be *duinethâide*? Is it forty-eight hours yet?' questioned Hugh. 'This is Saturday morning at nine o'clock. What time did you find the body on Thursday, Brehon?'

'It must have been just after noon,' said Mara.

'So you have to wait until noon today before it can be declared to be *duinethâide*.' Twelve-year-old Hugh said the words with satisfaction and a sidelong glance of triumph at Moylan who was two years older.

'That means that if someone admits to the crime this morning then he saves himself half of the *éraic*,' said Fachtnan lightly. Fachtnan was very good with the younger boys; he always tried to avert arguments between them if possible.

'The fine for *duinethâide* is eighty-four *séts*, forty-two cows, or forty-two ounces of silver, twice the fine for an acknowledged murder,' chanted Shane.

'So if a few thousand bees come in the door now, waving little white flags, then they will only have to pay twenty-one cows,' said Aidan with a smirk.

❀

By the time Mara and her scholars had reached Poulnabrone at three o'clock that afternoon, most of the people of the Burren had gathered in the field that surrounded the ancient dolmen. Traditionally, they had come here to listen to the judgement of cases by their Brehon: the guilty to receive fines, the injured to gain compensation. There were no prisons, no savage punishments. The Brehon delivered judgement; the fine was paid. The clan tradition of responsibility for the family ensured this obedience from its members.

This ancient system of Celtic laws was already over at least a thousand years old, perhaps two thousand years, thought Mara, looking around at the assembled crowd who had come here from the four quarters of the hundred-square-mile territory of the kingdom of the Burren. The laws of property – theft, damage, inheritance – the laws pertaining to children, the laws of livestock, the laws of marriage and of divorce, the laws of injury to persons – killing, wounding, disabling – all these laws were in place when St Patrick came to Ireland over a thousand years ago. The oldest manuscripts had been written at the time of St Patrick, but the laws had existed probably for a thousand years before he arrived in Ireland to try to convert the people from their worship of the sun, the fire, the water in spring wells and the earth that they tilled, to a belief in one God.

It was a dramatic spot, this ancient judgement place at Poulnabrone. The dolmen itself was constructed from four huge upright slabs, each of them the height of a man, supporting the soaring capstone of rough lichen-spotted limestone. The field around it was paved with limestone clints, the grykes between the clints filled with ferns and curling strands of purple vetch, and the dolmen stood high above their heads, silhouetted against the sky. In the background, behind a large hollow, was a towering cliff, now bright with clumps of pink and purple heather, that rose a good hundred feet above the level of the field. When Mara began to speak she automatically half turned towards this cliff. She, and perhaps hundreds of Brehons before her, had learned that this rocky cliff face enhanced the human voice and bounced the sound back so that it could reach the farthest person in that crowd.

It was the custom that each household send at least one person to these summonings at Poulnabrone. Mara's eyes searched the crowd. Neither Una nor her mother Deirdre was here, but Daire and Rory were, and so was the steward from Newtown Castle. Cathal, the sea captain was here and by his side, Giolla the beekeeper. Toin, understandably, had not made the journey but he, also, had sent his steward.

Mara greeted the people and the murmured blessings came back to her. There was curiosity on each face. This was a specially convened court so no other cases were waiting to be heard. The news of Sorley's death was probably not yet widespread; he had been a man from Galway, not a member of one of the four dominant clans: the O'Briens, the O'Lochlainns, the MacNamaras and the O'Connors. Few, except for the small community at Rathborney, would have met him.

Mara took the scroll from Fachtnan, unrolled it, glanced at the details mechanically and then rolled it up again, holding it in her hand like a rod of office.

'On Thursday morning, shortly after noon, Sorley Skerrett, silversmith, silver merchant and mine owner, of Newtown Castle on the Burren, and of Galway city, was killed.' Mara automatically paused after each few words and allowed the sonorous rocks to echo her words. There was an air of interest in the faces before her, but no sorrow, no appearance of worry. This was a close-knit community here. An unlaw-ful death normally involved the members of one clan or more; a relation, a friend or a neighbour would be implicated and the repercussions considered. The killing of a silversmith from Galway would be different; it was unlikely to involve many of them.

'I have considered this matter very carefully,' went on Mara, waiting until the last syllable of the word *cúramach* had ceased to ring. 'These are the facts as they occurred. The man, Sorley, was in the ruins of the old church at Rath-borney, when a hive of bees was knocked over, just behind where he sat. There is no doubt in my mind that the action was deliberate. Grievous bodily harm was intended, at the very least, and the law tells us that if this results in death, the crime is murder.'

Mara paused while the swell of words rose and fell; this would give everyone something of interest to discuss. Most kept bees so their habits would be well known. She could see the tall figure of Ardal, chieftain of the O'Lochlainn clan, bending down to discuss the matter with his steward, Liam. Ardal was always interested in legal matters. Several heads turned in the direction of Giolla whom many would have recognized from his honey stall at the Noughaval and Kilfenora markets.

'I now call on the person responsible for this crime to accept responsibility and pay the fine,' continued Mara after a minute. She waited calmly looking from face to face. There would be no answer, of course. If anything were to be confessed, it would be in private and after much thought. She was prepared to wait, but the formalities had to be gone through with. *I give them sixty seconds,* her father used to say, and she counted the numbers carefully through in her mind before lifting her hand to silence the murmur of conversation.

'Forty-eight hours have passed since this crime and no one has acknowledged it,' she said. 'I now declare the killing of Sorley Skerrett to be a case of *duinetháide*, an unlawful and secret murder. The *éraic*, or blood price for this is eighty-four *séts*, forty-two ounces of silver, or forty-two milch cows. Added to that is the honour price of the victim. Sorley, as a silversmith, had an honour price of seven *séts* so the total fine for the murder is ninety-one *séts* or forty-five-and-a-half ounces of silver or forty-six cows.' Again she paused and then added, almost perfunctorily, 'Has anyone anything to say?'

'I have.' Muiris stepped out of the crowd and stood sturdily in front of her. All heads turned towards him with interest.

'Yes, Muiris?' Mara kept her voice and expression neutral.

'I understand, Brehon, that the murder of Sorley the mine owner, took place just before the burial Mass for Father David.'

'That is correct.' Already several eyes were turned towards Rory the bard. Muiris had obviously been sharing his suspicions.

'So it might be of interest to you to know the names of any who came late into church?'

'Any information about that time and day is of interest to me,' said Mara warily.

'Well, I was standing at the back. I'm not from the parish myself, but like a lot of other people on the Burren I had reason to be grateful to Father David. He baptized and buried my first child, and my wife and myself will always remember his kindness, then.'

There were nods from all around. Father David had been a popular priest, always ready to give credit where there was doubt as to whether a child had been alive for a hasty baptism and whether a suicide might just possibly have been an accidental death.

'So, not being of the parish, I didn't want to push myself forward,' continued Muiris, gaining in confidence. 'I came in early, but I stood at the back. I watched the people coming in and ...' Here he stopped and when he spoke again his voice was hard. 'I saw Rory the bard come in late. He wasn't the only one who came late, but I watched him rub his wrist during the service and I saw a big red swelling on it.' Muiris waited for a moment and then added, 'it looked like a bee sting to me.'

'I see.' Mara increased the power of her well-trained voice to drown out the surge of comments and exclamations. She looked enquiringly towards Rory, but he shook his head firmly. It was his decision to answer the accusation, here in public or in private to her afterwards. On the whole, she thought he had made the right decision. 'Thank you, Muiris,' she continued rapidly. 'I was just about to ask if anyone who was present at the church that day would come forward. My scholars will take your evidence,' she quickly improvised, 'I won't need to delay anyone else, so if no one else has something to say in public, I will bid you now to go in peace with God and your neighbours.'

They didn't, of course, she thought with a suppressed

grin. This was far too interesting; there would be plenty to discuss and the day was crisp and sunny. They all stood around in groups chatting and eyeing those who were coming forward. Some perched themselves on several of the huge boulders that seemed to have been deposited in the field by some giant hand of the past, others sat on the clints or leaned against the gnarled trunks of the few wind-deformed hawthorn trees that grew in a large hollow while some of youngsters started a quick game of handball with *slíothar* from someone's pouch.

Many, however, left their friends and relations and started to line up near to the dolmen itself, whispering to each other with a lot of looking over shoulders and nodding wisely. Rory the bard stood irresolutely at some distance, and then, as if suddenly conscious of his isolated position, hastily joined the queue. Mara turned to her assistant.

'Have you got a horn of ink and some pens, Fachtnan?' she whispered, delving into her own satchel. 'Oh, good, at least I have three quills as well as my ink horn.'

'I've got a set of two large and two small quills as well as an ink horn, Brehon,' said Enda. He handed them and some small pieces of vellum to Fachtnan and then said in a low murmur, 'You don't think that I should have come forward about the swelling on Rory's wrist, do you, Brehon?'

'No, Enda,' said Mara. 'You did the right thing. That is not really evidence. I suppose it's past the season for midges, but that swelling could have been a flea bite or something like that. I think I'll keep that bit of evidence safely shut up in my mind.'

'Oh good.' He looked relieved. I wouldn't have called

him, anyway, thought Mara. Rory had been a near neighbour to the boys at Cahermacnaghten law school. They had
hunted together, gone fishing, danced at *céilís*, had picnics,
played hurley, celebrated festivals and been companionable
together. She would not have asked him to give evidence
against a friend, unless the matter had been of vital consequence.

'Shane and Hugh, you are responsible for lining up the
people who want to give evidence,' she said, as her four
older scholars seated themselves on the flat clint at the foot
of the dolmen. 'Make sure that no one comes near enough
to overhear the one that has gone before,' she added. It
didn't matter really as everyone would probably tell everyone else what had been said, but the boys enjoyed a bit of
secrecy and she was always careful to give Hugh and Shane
their fair share of the law school work.

She stood and watched for a while. To her surprise it
seemed as if about thirty people were there in the queue.
There must have been a very large crowd at Father David's
burial Mass. The two young boys had efficiently divided
them into four lines, though Mara noticed with interest that,
when their backs were turned, Rory moved himself from
Fachtnan's line to Aidan's.

Mara felt proud of her scholars. Each was showing
himself to be sensible and adult in front of the huge crowd.
Enda was demonstrating to Moylan and Aidan how to tab-
ulate the answers and Fachtnan, with his beaming smile and
his gentle voice, was extracting a lot of information from the
mother of the boy Marcan, who had been accused of overturning the bees. Marcan, himself, was saying very little, she
noticed. He looked overawed, which was probably not his

145

natural state. Mara made a mental note to check on his evidence afterwards. Boys like that were often quick at noticing things and had good memories. These lists would be invaluable. She would study them later that night and plan the work for next week.

'Brehon, could I have a quick word with you?' Daire was there, looming over her, his shadow huge on the grass.

'Certainly,' she turned to face him. She had been aware of his presence and was glad he had not attempted to talk to Aoife. Muiris's public announcement had probably made his daughter feel sorry for the young bard. Daire would be best to bide his time until another rebuff from Rory convinced Aoife that she had no hope of him. The young silversmith would suit her better, but it would take time to get over an infatuation that had lasted over a year.

'How is everything going at Newtown Castle?' she asked and he seized on her words with an air of relief.

'Well, that's just it, Brehon. Things are not going too well. There seems to be quite a bit of trouble brewing.'

'Between Una and her mother?'

Daire smiled. 'They're a match for each other and as far as I am concerned they can fight it out between them,' he said tolerantly. 'The problem is that Una has said that neither Deirdre nor Cuan have any right to be in the castle; that it is her house and she did not invite them. Deirdre took no notice of that, but Cuan got straight up from the table and walked out. I heard him going down the stairs and I followed him, but he had taken his horse and he was out the gate before I could say anything.'

'Oh, dear,' said Mara. 'Well, I'm sorry to hear that.' He's not much more than a child, she thought indignantly, picturing the woebegone figure. What a hard-hearted woman that sister of his was. After all, she must have been about ten years old when Cuan was born. Normally you would expect, with that age difference, the girl to be maternal towards a much younger brother. And what about the mother of the boy? Why didn't she interfere? There was no doubt of Deirdre's affection for Cuan. However, she had been exiled, herself, for almost ten years and perhaps she felt for Cuan's sake, as well as her own, she should stick grimly to her rights to live in Newtown Castle.

'So what's your understanding of the position, Daire?' she asked eyeing him cautiously. 'Was it generally considered that Una was going to be her father's heir? Had he mentioned anything to you about this?' She was curious to know whether this betrothal was just a spur of the moment decision evoked by the presence of Lawyer Bodkin on the night of 30 October.

'I'm not sure,' said Daire cautiously, 'but I do know that a week ago Rory got very drunk and he hinted at it. He had just come out of a conversation with Sorley,' he added with a quick glance to where Rory was giving his evidence to Aidan.

'Well, thank you for telling me about the unkind treatment of Cuan, Daire,' said Mara, resolving that she would not let another day go by without solving this problem at least. She gave him a quick nod and then moved slightly apart. She would stand there and wait. Somebody else might wish to talk to her; this would be their opportunity. Cathal, the sea captain, was standing in the queue ready to give his evidence to Enda. She was glad of that; Enda was quick and clever; she would not be able to rely so well on Moylan and Aidan. Cathal was at the back of her mind; undoubtedly he would have been aware of the silversmith's malevolent intentions. That cask of silver belonging to Sorley would have been worth more than the value of his boat itself.

Hugh and Shane were beginning to look bored; their duties were over as the queues were now diminishing to small manageable lines. They were watching enviously Marcan who, while waiting for his mother, chatting animatedly to some other women, was occupying his time in hurling some small pieces of limestone at a disdainful hooded crow that perched on top of the cliff. Mara approached her two young scholars.

'Go and have a chat with Marcan,' she said in a low voice. 'Ask him about the morning when Sorley was found dead. See if he saw anything of interest. He'd be more likely to tell you than me, especially now that he's away from his mother.'

'Shall we tell him that you said to ask?' Hugh was always timid and unsure once the support of the older boys was withdrawn, but Shane was made of a tougher material.

'We'll just ask him to tell us what Sorley looked like when he was found dead,' he said with relish. 'I was wondering about that myself and whether he was really blue, like they said.'

Mara stifled a laugh. Shane was a bright boy; that approach would immediately focus Marcan's interest, where an adult's questions would probably cause him to clam up. She watched as Shane picked up a few stones himself and began joining in on the onslaught of the hooded crow. After a few minutes of this the crow departed with languid sweeps of his large dark wings and the three boys began to chat animatedly. From what she could see, Hugh hung back while Shane was asking all the questions. He was like Enda, she thought, the one was dark-haired with an olive complexion, the other golden-haired and fair-skinned, but they were both quick and clever. She hoped that Shane would not be as awkward to deal with as Enda had been during his early adolescence.

After a few minutes, Marcan's mother retrieved her son and the two young scholars returned to Mara.

'He doesn't know much,' said Shane disgustedly. 'He went to have a good look around when he heard that Sorley had been stung to death and he found the place where the stone had been taken out, but he didn't find anything else.'

'That's useful, though,' said Mara thoughtfully. 'It probably means that there was nothing to be found. Now, do you two want to start walking back to Cahermacnaghten? You'll probably catch up with Brigid if you hurry. I want to wait for a while longer until the older ones finish taking evidence. Someone else might want to talk to me.'

No one came to speak to her, however, and the day began to turn colder. There would be a grass frost tonight. The crowds began to disperse and soon no one was left at Poulnabrone, except Cumhal, the farm manager, Mara and her scholars.

'Anything significant?' she asked, gathering up the lists from them.

'There is just this on my list,' said Fachtnan leaning over her shoulder and pointing with his quill.

'So Toin's servant saw Rory coming through the grave-yard after the service had begun,' said Mara thoughtfully.

'Well that seems to fit with what Muiris said about him coming in late.'

'Toin must have seen him then,' said Aidan, 'because Cathal the sea captain told me that Toin was on the bench in the churchyard.'

'Toin mightn't have noticed. Apparently he collapsed just near to the door of the church. He was in terrible pain. He went to sit on that little wooden seat around the other side, the one near the sundial. He sent his servant to run and fetch some poppy syrup from his house. The steward told me that Tomás took him home before the service began,' explained Fachtnan, his face solemn.

'Poor man,' said Mara. 'He should never have come.' She spoke the words automatically because her mind was on Rory. 'Who took the evidence from Rory?'

'I did.' Aidan handed his sheet with a slightly dubious look at the number of blots on it.

Mara scanned it rapidly. 'You've put that he left Sorley talking to the bishop, did he volunteer that explanation?' She was interested; most of the evidence from others seemed to be concentrated on position in church and remarks on the arrival of others.

Aidan nodded. 'Yes, he told me to write that down.'

'He probably heard Cathal the sea captain telling Muiris that he saw Rory coming late into the church,' said Enda. 'He was in the queue for Fachtnan, but he has a very loud voice – he's probably used to shouting at sea. Rory perhaps thought it was better to explain before he was questioned.'

'Enda,' said Mara thoughtfully, 'you and Rory went around to a lot of fairs together. I seem to remember you saying that he sometimes had plenty of money to spend. Is that right?'

'Yes, I think that I said that,' said Enda cautiously.

'Where do you think that he got that money?'

Enda's face cleared. 'Oh, that's easy. He got it from betting on horses. He was always lucky with that. I . . .' He stopped abruptly. Mara did not question him further. She had always forbidden her scholars to place wagers; the law school fees were a heavy enough burden without the additional problem of gambling debts. However, Enda seemed to be a much more sensible character for the last few weeks and was certainly better from being away from the influence of the fun-loving young bard, so she decided to ignore that slip of the tongue.

So Rory was a gambler, well, that crime, that murder of the man Sorley, within sight and sound of about hundred people, that was a crime of a gambler, a crime of an opportunist – probably not even planned, just a spur-of-the-moment decision.

'And he said that he walked down from the castle with Sorley and then left him,' said Mara thoughtfully, looking again at Aidan's untidy script.

'That's right, Brehon.' Aidan was eager; no doubt he was glad that the interest of the information had distracted the Brehon from the blots and crossings-out on his piece of vellum.

Mara smiled. Aidan was easy to read, a nice boy with an exuberant, puppy-like nature. 'You've done very well,' she said warmly to her scholars as she gathered in the vellum leaves and stored them carefully in her satchel. 'Now, you three should go straight back to Cahermacnaghten with Cumhal; Brigid will have your dinner ready. Fachtnan, will you come with me? I think that I will ride around by Rathborney. There are a few questions that I wish to ask.'

'It was interesting, wasn't it,' she added, as they cantered across the clints, 'that neither son nor daughter, nor wife turned up here today?'

Ten

There are seven people who should never be given a loan:

1. A person who has been proclaimed an outlaw

2. A person who is without legal responsibility

3. A person who does not recognize the law of the kingdom

4. A person who has no land

5. A person who will use the loan for dangerous purposes

6. A person near to death because his heirs may not have to repay it

7. A king, because of the weight of his honour

It WAS still DAYLIGHT, though the sun was low in the sky, when Mara and Fachtnan arrived at Rathborney, talking earnestly, as Mara explained to Fachtnan the family situation of Sorley Skerrett, his wife, son and daughter. They were just about to turn to go in through the gates, when Mara felt her mare hesitate and looking around she glimpsed a miserable figure, sitting on a stone, gazing moodily across the prosperous green fields in this fertile valley.

'That's Cuan, Sorley's son,' she said quietly to Fachtnan. 'Let's not allow him to get away. His place is in his father's house.'

'Cuan,' she called. 'We're just going to see your mother. Come with us and you can show us the way.' She had pulled her mare to a halt just in front of him and Fachtnan sat impassively in the path behind him. Cuan gave a hasty glance around and then bowed his head. He would be a biddable boy, she thought, and addressed him as she would one of her own young scholars.

'That's right,' she said encouragingly. 'You just walk ahead of us. This lane is too narrow for three. What lovely weather it is, I can't believe that it is November, can you? Pull the bell, will you?' she chatted freely until they reached the gates and she heard the sound of the lodge door being opened. 'Please take our horses,' she added to the porter immediately when he came to the gate. She gave Cuan no chance to escape, tucking her arm inside his, once her feet had touched the ground.

He smelled, she noticed compassionately. He looked as if he had not washed, nor shaved, nor even combed his hair for days. There was a sore on one hand that would turn bad soon if not attended to and she made a mental note to ask Malachy or Nuala to look at it.

The scene around the castle was full of activity when they arrived at the gate. There was no sense of chaos after the death of its owner; men and women moved busily in and out of the cottages, cabins and stables that lined the sides of the large *bawn* in front of the castle. The porter was at the gate before they arrived there and stablemen came forward immediately to take their horses. At the sound of the porter's bell, the steward quickly opened the front door and came down the steps to greet them and escort them up to the hall.

The room was as perfect as always, the floor was luminous with beeswax polish, the wooden tables and chests shone and the silver candelabra held new candles. Una was sitting at a window examining what seemed to be a book of accounts while Deirdre was scrutinizing some velvet hangings, by the fireplace. Unlike her daughter who was plainly dressed, Deirdre's gown was made from dark-red damask, heavily encrusted with small gems. An elaborate headdress, made from the same material and laced with silver wires, covered her lank, coarse hair.

'The Brehon to see you,' the steward hesitated there, gazing from one woman to the other, but then added an impartial, 'my lady'. Both women turned their eyes attentively towards Mara. Una gave Cuan a contemptuous glance and then turned her eyes away from him, but Deirdre stepped forward towards her son and then stepped back again with a hesitant look at Una. Rory was lounging on the window seat, idly strumming the strings of his zither. He stopped and sat bolt upright when he saw Mara.

'I just thought that I would come and see you this evening,' said Mara comfortably ensconcing herself in one of the velvet armchairs. 'There were so many people here last night, and of course, tomorrow you have the burial Mass so it seemed best to come now and to talk to you about your father's death and to give you the latest news.'

'News?' It was Deirdre who spoke. Una said nothing, but her expression was wary.

'Yes, from Poulnabrone,' said Mara, making a sign to Fachtnan to take his seat at a small low table. She handed him her satchel and watched with pleasure while he smiled at Cuan and unselfconsciously pulled out another seat for the boy. Fachtnan was such a nice boy; he was not very clever, but he was gifted with people. If he could only pass his final examinations she would always be proud that he had attended her law school. She could imagine him as Brehon of a small kingdom, showing all the people courtesy and warmth, being sensitive to all, never lacking common sense or humanity. Book learning was of little consequence to that. He could always look things up in law texts, she thought.

'Well,' she continued, 'I have declared the killing of Sorley to be *duinetháide*, a secret and unlawful murder and the fine of ninety-one *séts*, forty-five-and-a-half ounces of silver or forty-six cows to be paid to Sorley's heir, but no one admitted to the murder.'

There was a flicker of avarice in Una's rather dead eyes as the enormous sum of compensation was mentioned, but Deirdre's face was impassive. Cuan was fidgeting uncomfortably, but still sat beside Fachtnan.

Mara sat back and stretched her legs. 'Which, of course,'

she added carelessly, 'brings us to the question of who is Sorley's heir.' She looked around. There they were: the wife, that was no wife, the son that had been disowned, and the daughter, well, thought Mara – who knows about the daughter? Had she loved her father, or hated him? 'I thought it was best to see the whole family here in private,' she continued and then glanced across at Rory. 'It's for you to say whether anyone outside the family should be present while we speak of this matter.'

'I am here at Una's invitation, Brehon,' said Rory smoothly. He smiled at Una; she did not smile back, but looked directly at Mara.

'My mother and my brother are here at no invitation of mine,' said Una in a low harsh voice. 'They have no right to be here. I have told my mother this, but she still refuses to leave. My father divorced my mother ten years ago for the crime of unfaithfulness, and last year he disowned my brother as an unsatisfactory son and a ne'er-do-well. The castle and all the goods within it, the shop in Galway and the mine, they all belong to me and to me only.'

There was a dead silence, broken only by a sudden spurt of flame from the fire. Fachtnan made a note on the vellum and then looked up, his quill in his hand. Mara allowed the silence to continue. 'Ten years ago,' she said evenly, 'I was Brehon of this kingdom. I remember no petition come before me at Poulnabrone concerning your mother. I searched through my records last night and there was nothing. However, Deirdre, you were not born in this kingdom and you only lived part of your life here, so it is possible that your divorce should have been quite legal without notification to me – though it is unusual since you did have a residence in this kingdom. I want to have a little more time to check through the records at Kinvarra before I say any more on this matter.'

Deirdre bowed her head. Her face remained indifferent.

'But, in the case of Cuan, your brother, Una, the matter is different.' She looked towards the boy, but Cuan had nothing to say. He just sat there, beside his mother, his mouth slightly open, his eyes blank. Mara wondered whether he could be an idiot. Somehow she did not think so. However, if he were, it would have given Sorley a reason to get rid of him. But, in that case, why not bring him before the court at Poulnabrone? Cuan was looking at his mother now, but Deirdre grimly held her silence and waited for the Brehon to finish speaking.

'Cuan was born in Rathborney; he lived most of his early life here and large portions of his adolescence. If Sorley wished to disown him, he should have brought him to Poulnabrone – after his seventeenth birthday. That was not done, therefore any measure that Sorley took was not a legal one, and Cuan, as the only son, has the right to inherit his father's goods.'

'He was not brought before the court at Poulnabrone,' Una told Mara confidently, 'but everyone knows that Cuan had been banished. My father did not find him satisfactory as a son. Cuan argued with him and wanted his own way.' There was a sour note of satisfaction in the harsh voice, it was almost as if she said, *I did not, I bided my time and now I will have my reward.*

'Be that as it may,' Mara replied patiently. 'Your father, Sorley, is now dead. You have no other brothers so Cuan is the heir.' Was this true, she wondered as she said it? Ulick seemed to think that it had all been left to the daughter, but he was the sort of man that often got things wrong.

Cuan did not look as delighted at this news as one would have expected of a young man who last Thursday had declared that he was starving. He turned his big vacant eyes towards his mother again and waited. Still Deirdre said nothing. In her turn, she looked towards her daughter and Una gave a short laugh.

'What you say may be true, Brehon,' she said, 'but there is something else to tell. Last Wednesday, the day you dined here, my father made a will, it was drawn up for him by Lawyer Bodkin from Galway, and in that will he left all his property to me, his daughter Una.'

'It was made at the time that our contract of betrothal was signed,' said Rory eagerly.

'That's a different matter,' said Una sourly. 'I'm talking about the will.'

She leaned back and looked at Mara triumphantly. Mara tried to keep her face neutral and not betray the fact that Ulick had already told her about this. Out of the corner of her eye, she could see Fachtnan's astonished face and had to suppress a smile. It certainly was unusual to leave all of the property to a daughter when there was also a son left alive, but it was not illegal. Sorley was a man who had made his own wealth and he would have been able to dispose of it as he willed. It was hard luck on the boy and on the unfortunate wife, especially as it did not look as if Una would do much for either. Mara determined that she would have to try to do her best for the dispossessed pair and to achieve this she would have to guard against antagonizing Una.

'Could I see the will?' she asked mildly, addressing Una and ignoring Rory.

'Certainly,' said Una. 'It is in the small chest on the gallery. My father kept all his documents there.'

Ponderously she got to her feet and pulled out from the pouch, which she wore around her waist, a small brass key. Mara stood up too and followed her and from behind she could hear the other footsteps, the soft noiseless tread of Rory, the heavy footsteps of the wronged wife, the uneven shambling of the boy and behind them all the springing step of Fachtnan who had obviously decided that he too might as well see the opening of the chest.

The gallery was beautifully made of handsomely carved oak, its wooden walls hung with fine tapestries, its polished floors softened with rich rugs. Around the circular walls, candles were held in silver sconces and the soft light was reflected on the many polished surfaces. Even so Mara was glad that Fachtnan had the foresight to bring with him a candle from the room below because the chest, though small, was deep and full of documents, all tied with the pink linen legal tape which Mara herself knew so well. It looked as if Sorley had left everything in good order. One by one Mara took the documents from the chest, murmuring to herself as she did so:

Deed of Ownership of the townland of Croagh North on the mountain of Cappanabhaile.

Deed of Ownership of the townland of Bally-conry on the mountain of Cappanabhaile.

Deed of Ownership of the townland of Lios Mac Taidhg on the mountain of Cappanabhaile.

Deed of Ownership of the townland of Lios na gCat on the mountain of Cappanabhaile.

Leases for sundry messuages in the city of Galway.

Deeds of Ownership for houses at Rathborney.

Valuation of silver objects in the Great Hall at Newtown Castle.

Valuation of silver objects on stairway, gallery and in bedchambers.

Bills of Sale of thoroughbred horses.

Profits pertaining to the sale of silver in the country of France.

One by one she took the carefully rolled-up scrolls out and laid them neatly on a side table continuing until the chest was empty.

There was no will.

It was Rory who broke the strained silence. 'I know he made a will,' he stammered. 'I watched the lawyer draw it up, I saw him sign it; the steward and Ulick Burke witnessed it. The lawyer tied it up himself and then Sorley put it in the chest and locked the chest and put the key back in his pouch.'

Mara looked at Una, but she was not looking at Rory. She had made no move, no sound, but her eyes were fixed accusingly on the face of her mother. Mara looked at Deirdre in her turn, but there was nothing to be read in that face. Long years of suffering had taught the woman to keep her face blank and her eyes void of feeling. Cuan, also, showed no understanding of the way the fleeting minutes were turning him from pauper to rich man, back to pauper and now to rich man again, in giddy succession. There was only one person in the group behaving normally, thought Mara, and that was Rory.

'He must have put it elsewhere,' he said desperately searching through the documents on the table and then looking up with his face glistening with sweat. 'It will be in the chest in his bedchamber.'

Mara looked curiously at Una who turned and led the way in silence, down the steep winding staircase and wordlessly the others followed. Sorley's chamber was almost as ornate as the great hall above it. The bed was huge, roofed with a tester of the finest silk and at the foot of it was another chest. Once more, Una produced a key. She must have taken them from the body, thought Mara. I cannot imagine Sorley allowing her to have a key to all his chests. She watched Una's face with interest. She looked to be going through the motions perfunctorily, it was obvious that she did not expect to find the will.

This chest was less orderly than the one in the gallery and seemed to be mostly bills of sale. Mara went through them rapidly, noting with interest as she did so the high prices that Sorley's silver seemed to fetch. He must be enormously rich, thought Mara, passing the deeds to Fachtnan to retie; Sorley was definitely even richer than anyone had imagined. Like many silversmiths, he was a moneylender, mostly to denizens of Galway. One bill, though, made her pause, tighten her lips and then replace it with the others. No wonder that Ulick Burke had been willing to put up with the sneers and jibes of the silversmith. He could never have repaid this huge loan; and what on earth was Turlough doing getting himself involved as a guarantor?

It was not surprising, of course, that Sorley had that much silver to lend. He was immensely rich. There was a huge fortune at stake here. As she took each piece of vellum out, scanned it, then Una took it from her, read it, put it down, and then Rory picked it up and re-examined it. Mara felt amused. The young bard acted as if his own fortune was at sake. The fact that Una was eight or nine years older than he and certainly not attractive would not have deterred him. He now seemed almost beside himself with anguish and when the last document had been removed from the chest, he could contain himself no longer:

'I know there is a will,' he repeated again and again, and then with rising hope, 'if you speak to the steward, Brehon, he will tell you. He witnessed the will. And Ulick, he'll tell you when he returns from Galway.'

Mara surveyed him with a half smile. She was not a malicious woman, but the memory of Aoife's agony and the distress of her parents made her feel little sympathy for him.

'You must know that would be no use without the will itself,' she said quietly. 'I certainly take your word and that of Una for the fact that a will was made, but Sorley may have changed his mind. People do. He may have burned the will. That is possible.'

'No,' said Rory emphatically. 'He would not have done that. He promised me that...' His voice tailed off and his colour rose slightly. Fachtnan, Mara noticed, was looking at his former friend with amusement so he had obviously grasped the situation. Mara picked up the documents and carefully and tidily replaced them in the chest. Now what comes next, she asked herself and to her surprise, Deirdre was the one who broke that silence.

'He must have burned the will,' she said flatly, the harsh, hoarse voice sounding alien amidst the scented luxuries of her former husband's bedchamber.

'Is there anywhere else he could have put it?' appealed Rory to Una. He did not sound like a lover, more like a man who has been cheated of a prize.

She did not answer but shook her head.

'Among his garments?' he pressed.

'No,' she said and then added almost indifferently, 'It was there yesterday, in the chest in the gallery. I looked yesterday morning. It was on top of all the other documents.'

Rory turned to Mara in triumph. 'Well, there you are, then,' he said, 'it has been stolen.' He stopped and looked at Deirdre and then at Cuan. 'One of you stole it. It must be one of you. It could be no one else. Nothing else is missing. All the silver is there. No one could get into this castle. It is guarded like a king's palace.'

Mara looked politely at Deirdre, her eyebrows slightly raised.

'No,' said Deirdre firmly. Her eyes were expressionless.

Mara had not expected her to say otherwise. She looked at Cuan who said nothing.

'I think that I should ask you, Cuan,' she kept her voice gentle, 'did you open the chest belonging to your father, in the gallery, and take out anything?'

Cuan stared at her for a minute and then shook his head. There was a flash of fear in his eyes, but that might not mean anything. He might just be confused and worried by all the undercurrents. Mara stood up and closed the chest. Silently, Una locked it. She seemed to be deep in thought. This time it was Deirdre who led the way back to the great hall and now the position between the two women seemed to have changed. Now Deirdre assumed the manners of mistress of the house and rang the bell for the servant to replenish the logs on the fire.

'Will you have something to drink or to eat?' she asked Mara.

'No, I thank you,' said Mara. 'We must be getting back to Cahermacnaghten.'

'And you?' Deirdre said, addressing Fachtnan. 'What about you? At your age boys get hungry quickly. Would you like some honey cakes, some sweetmeats?'

The change in her was amazing. Even the harsh voice sounded softer and more relaxed. Whatever she was bracing herself for had not happened and now she suddenly seemed to have shed some years. Mara looked at Una and wished she knew what the woman was thinking, what she was going to do. She was obviously intelligent and had grasped the point, even more quickly than Rory, that without a will, there would be no fortune for her. Una met her eyes openly for the first time.

'What is the position now, then?' she asked gravely, her voice neutral and dispassionate.

Mara's respect for her grew. Sorley had obviously passed on his clear-thinking business sense to one of his children.

'The normal position would be that the wife would get one-third of a man's personal wealth and belongings,' she said carefully, 'and then the remaining two-thirds would go to your brother. In this case, there was a divorce so possibly the whole fortune goes to Cuan, but I think that there were some slightly unusual features about this divorce, a certain lack of evidence, and I feel that the case could be reopened. Could I ask you, Deirdre, was your dowry returned to you after the divorce?'

Deirdre gave a short laugh. 'No,' she said.

'Well, in that case, if it were to be proved that the divorce was illegal, then you would have your dowry or its value returned to you as well as one-third of your husband's wealth.'

'But there would be nothing for me?' Una's gaze was clear and her voice was steady.

Mara nodded reluctantly, but then added: 'No, but no doubt your brother will make ample provision of a *spre*, a dowry for you. This would be customary for a brother who is the sole heir of his father to do for his sister. You certainly should have your share of your father's goods. I think both your mother and your brother would agree to this.'

Una looked at her thoughtfully and then turned her eyes on her mother who met the gaze unflinchingly. Neither spoke; Cuan just looked miserably into the fire. He wore the expression of one who had no interest and no understanding of the subject under discussion.

There was another long silence. I have never met people who said so little, thought Mara. She glanced at Fachtnan. Carefully he made some more notes on the vellum and in that quiet room the slight sound of the pen against the horn of the inkbottle almost sounded intrusive. He finished the last note, put the pen carefully on its stand, and turned to Mara who rose to her feet. It was time to go.

'It is your decision,' she said to Deirdre, 'but would you

like me to look into the divorce case and if I consider that justice was not done, then to reopen it?'

Deirdre thought carefully for a while, glancing at her son, but not, Mara noticed, at her daughter. 'Yes,' she said eventually.

'Would you wish a lawyer to act for you?' he asked.

She shook her head. 'No,' she said. 'I'll trust it to you.'

'In that case,' said Mara, 'I think it might be best to leave the sorting of Sorley's affairs until that question is settled. I will do it as quickly as possible and it can be done in private. The inquiry does not need to be held at Poulnabrone, unless, of course, either your son or your daughter feels that the divorce should stand.'

Mara looked at Una and she looked back, a long considering look directed first at the Brehon and then at her mother.

'No,' she said eventually. 'If the divorce was rescinded, I would not contest it.'

Again she looked at her mother, and this time it seemed to Mara as if the two women made some unspoken agreement.

'Could I have a word with you before you go?' Deirdre's voice was abrupt, full of tension.

'Certainly,' said Mara.

'Stay here,' said Una. Again there was that curious exchange of glances between the two women. 'We'll go and you can talk here.'

One by one they got to their feet and went out, leaving Mara and Fachtnan with Deirdre.

'Let's sit by the fire,' said Mara. She smiled at Deirdre

and, to her surprise the woman smiled back and then went to sit in one of the luxurious over-stuffed chairs by the fireside. Almost as a cat does, she settled herself into it, her square hand, with its broken nails and rough discoloured skin, stroking the silken nap of the velvet. With a sudden flash of insight Mara imagined what it must mean for her to have suddenly changed her existence from a poverty-stricken cabin on the side of the mountain to the position of mistress once again of all this luxury.

Fachtnan with his usual tact had moved and modestly seated himself at a small table behind Deirdre but in full view of Mara in case she needed to communicate with him. Noiselessly he dipped his quill in the ink horn and sat waiting quietly.

'Do you think that you can manage to overturn the divorce?' Deirdre's voice sounded curious.

'I am not sure,' Mara replied cautiously.

'It doesn't matter too much, anyway,' Deirdre said almost as much to herself as to Mara. Her eyes softened. 'Cuan will not turn me out. If he has the money and the castle I will have my share, law or no law. He is a good lad and has always been a good lad. I'll make sure that everything goes well for him now.'

Mara nodded. That was obvious. Deirdre would be the one who would manage the estate and mine and the silver merchant business. She could not imagine Cuan being able to cope. No matter what came of her investigations, Deirdre was firmly back in her position as mistress of Newtown Castle. The question that was now troubling Mara's mind was: could Deirdre have killed to get this position back for herself and her son? The woman was strong, independent and had reason enough to hate Sorley, but would she have taken that risk? This was a murder that could so easily have gone wrong. Sorley could have seen her, could have escaped the bees and Deirdre was dependent on the small income that he gave her. Also, Mara felt this was a crime of chance – a crime of an opportunist and it did not fit with Deirdre's character, as far as she could judge.

'So you're a Brehon,' Deirdre mused. Her tone was friendly. 'It's good to see that women can have situations like that. Mostly it seems to me that women don't have much of a life.'

'You were young when you married Sorley?' Mara was sympathetic to any woman forced into a too early marriage.

'Too young.' The rejoinder was flat. 'But I never thought he would divorce me, though I knew that he had no interest in me.'

'And now he's dead.'

'And now he's dead.' The echo was thoughtful, and then with a quick change of mood Deirdre looked across at Mara and her eyes were sharp with intelligence. 'You probably want to ask me some questions about the death. I'd prefer to answer them here, alone, rather than outside with everyone listening.'

Mara nodded briskly. 'Let's make a start then. When was the last time that you saw Sorley alive?' she asked, signalling to Fachtnan to begin writing.

'Last Sunday,' said Deirdre confidently, 'I see him every Sunday at church. We never speak, of course, but I see him.'

'Did you see him on the morning of Father David's funeral?'

Deirdre shook her head. 'No,' she said firmly.

'What time did you arrive, then?'

She shrugged, 'A while before the service, not long.'

'Which gate did you use?'

'The Rathborney gate.' Deirdre's voice was brisk and assured.

'And afterwards? Did you go to the graveyard?'

She shook her head again. 'No,' she said, 'I went home straight after the service in the church. I was busy that day, but I wanted to come. Father David had been very good to me. He had tried to talk to Sorley about me many times, had done his best for Cuan, too."

It was probably true that she did go home straight after Mass, thought Mara. Her mind went to the figure of a boy and middle-aged woman that she had seen on the pathway to the mountain. It seemed strange, though. After all, if she had spared the time to come to the service, surely she would have waited to see the old priest buried. It might be possible to press her a little on this.

'Why did you not go to the graveside?' she asked eyeing Deirdre carefully.

There was a pause. She could hear Fachtnan finish writing and then dip his pen into the ink horn before the woman spoke again.

'I was busy,' she said briefly. 'I had to get back. I had a long walk ahead of me.'

Mara let it go at that, in any case Sorley was dead by then.

'Let's go back to the time you arrived, did you speak to anyone, did anyone see you come?'

'You forget,' she said the words with some bitterness, 'I

was the wife who was put aside for adultery. Not many people spoke to me, ever. Toin, and one or two others, but no one who was connected with Sorley in any way.'

'So when you arrived,' pressed Mara, 'did you go straight into the church, or did you go around near the ruins?'

Again there was a pause, not as long as before, but Mara could have sworn that she was going through her mind to see if anyone could bear testimony against her.

'I went straight to the church,' she said.

Mara nodded. There were no reports of Deirdre coming late into church. In fact, no one had mentioned her name. She waited until Fachtnan had finished writing and then said, almost perfunctorily, 'And there is no other help you can give us? You heard or saw nothing to do with this matter?'

Deirdre gave a half smile. 'I am afraid not,' she said and then rose to her feet. 'I will send one of the others to you. Will you stay the night?'

Mara glanced out of the window. The lines of the stone mullions were dark against the faded pink of the sky. This business of the missing will had taken up a lot of her time and she was reluctant to leave the journey home much later. She considered the invitation to stay the night. It would be the sensible thing to do and it might give her some insight into the relationships in this warring family, but she felt that she could not really bear it. She would prefer to get away and consider the facts in the open air, and not be smothered by the heat and perfumes of Sorley's tower house and the tensions within. She rose to her feet.

'Thank you for your invitation,' she said, 'but I am afraid that I cannot stay. I will be back soon; I will see Una and, of course, Cuan, then.'

And it was of Deirdre's face, softened, but apprehensive, when the name of her son was mentioned that Mara was thinking as they rode out of the great iron gates and it was of Cuan that Fachtnan spoke as soon as they were out of earshot of the guards around the gates.

'Deirdre is worried about Cuan, isn't she?' he said sagaciously. 'Do you think that she suspects him of having a hand in his father's death?'

'Hard to know,' said Mara thoughtfully. 'I suppose that it would have been tempting for anyone in Cuan's position to take a quick poke at the beehive when he saw his father pass by.'

'Can you imagine Cuan doing anything quickly?' said Fachtnan with a grin.

Mara laughed, but then the picture of Deirdre's grim face came before her and her own face grew solemn at the thought. The rejected wife was certainly someone who would have had the quickness of mind to push over the beehive and then to disappear rapidly into the church. It was almost positive that she had gone to the gallery yesterday, possibly at the time when Una was occupied with the preparations for the wake, and had taken the will out and burned it. No doubt she had retained her bunch of keys from her time as mistress of Newtown Castle. Toin had said that Deirdre spent a lot of time there at Rathborney when her husband was in Kinvarra or in Galway. There was no other explanation of what had happened today. Sorley had taken everything from her including her good name, and when the opportunity had arisen she had taken back what she could. Mara was sure in her own mind of that, but had Deirdre also taken the life of her erstwhile husband? And if she had, was it a justified act in her eyes, an act of vengeance for the long years of suffering and for the sufferings of her son? Mara had a momentary sympathy for her but then the words of St Paul came to mind and as the last shafts of sun struck glints of silver from the rock ahead of them, she seemed to see them written in shining letters: *Vengeance is mine; I will repay, saith the Lord.*

Vengeance was the province of the Almighty God: but it was for the Brehon of the Burren to establish the truth and to see that justice was done.

ELEVEN

URCUILTE BRETHEMAN

(A JUDGE'S FORBIDDEN THINGS)

If a judge does not swear on the gospel to utter only the truth, then he must leave the kingdom.

If a judge makes a mistaken judgement he has to bear responsibility by paying a fine to the injured person, but if he hears only one side of the case or takes bribes then he is deprived of the office of Brehon and loses his honour price.

TRIAD 96

Three things will cause ruin in a kingdom:
1. A judge who takes bribes
2. An unlearned judge
3. An unjust judge

'I think that i will go to Sunday Mass at Rathborney and attend the burial of Sorley Skerrett,' said Mara the following morning to her scholars. 'You can all go to nine o'clock Mass at Noughaval and then you can have the rest of the day to yourselves. Make sure that you tell Brigid what time you will be home and where you are going.'

'Mass again!' grumbled Aidan. 'We seem to have done nothing but go to Mass this week!'

'You could always try praying to the Almighty to help you in your studies, especially with your handwriting,' said Mara sweetly. 'Stop grumbling; you know that Mass at Noughaval is the quickest service in the Burren. You can enjoy yourselves for the rest of the day.'

'You don't need any help, Brehon?' asked Fachtnan respectfully.

'No,' said Mara, 'but, if by any chance you see Nuala today, Fachtnan, you might ask her to ride over to Rathborney with you. Young Cuan's hand looked very bad to me. If Nuala could bring something with her she could dress it for him.'

Fachtnan's face lit up. 'We'll do that,' he said enthusiastically, while behind his back Aidan made some kissing motions with his lips much to the amusement of Moylan, Hugh and Shane.

❋

The burial Mass for Sorley was to be the usual nine o'clock Sunday Mass at Rathborney. Mara rode over on her mare Brig, followed by Bran, his long legs loping effortless over the stony road that led downhill from Cahermacnaghten to the valley. At the gate of Toin's house, Mara hesitated, the church bell had not yet sounded; they had made good time and the old man was already up and moving around in the pear orchard next to his house.

'Good morning, Toin,' she called.

'Come in, come and look,' he called out. 'I must show you my pears, it's been a great year for them. I was a bit concerned by a few early morning frosts in May but I needn't have been worried. Just look at them. Have you ever seen anything like the crop that I have this year? I must get someone to fill up a few barrels and send them over to Cahermacnaghten. Your boys will enjoy them, I know.'

Mara dismounted from her mare and handed the horse to a servant who came rushing forward.

'Gently now, Bran,' she murmured, as they went forward. Bran was a great lover of people and inclined to place his paws firmly on the chest of anyone who showed any interest in him. Toin looked like a wraith this morning, so unsubstantial that a breath of air could almost knock him over. He was in good spirits, though, and greeted Bran with a pat on the wolfhound's narrow head.

'This pear orchard is my pride and joy,' he said. 'I planted it when I came to the Burren first, before you were born. I was a young man then, a physician. They say you plant pears for your heirs, and it's only in the last ten years that the trees have borne such fruit.'

'You've made it inside an old enclosure, haven't you,' said Mara glancing around. 'That should be just right to protect the trees against the frosts and wind damage.'

'There are fifty trees here,' boasted Toin. 'You've seen it in the spring, haven't you?'

'Yes,' said Mara softly. 'I've never seen anything so

beautiful.' She spoke with sincerity. Toin's pear trees, in the spring, were like a fairyland of lime-white blossom, shining intensely in the shelter of their ancient grey stone walls. She promised herself that she would visit it next spring in memory of the old man who had created such beauty.

Some of Toin's servants were picking the pears, taking each one carefully from the branch and laying it in the flat baskets which they all carried. Toin reached up and plucked a pear from a magnificent tree near to the gate and handed it to Mara without a word. It was a perfect pear, its pale yellow skin just flushed with rose. It smelt faintly of aniseed and when Mara bit into it the juice ran down her chin; she was speechless in her appreciation.

'Is it all right?' asked Toin anxiously.

Mara took another bite and nodded. She swallowed it carefully and smelt the pear again. The king of fruits, she thought, and took a piece of linen from her pouch and wiped her face and hands. 'Perfect,' she said, 'I have never tasted such a beautiful one.'

'You're on your way to the burial service,' said Toin.

Mara nodded. 'You're not thinking of going there, yourself, are you?'

'No, I'm not. The man wasn't worth it. Anyway, Tomás won't allow me; will you, Tomás?'

The servant smiled, leaning down to pat Bran whose long muscular tail was wagging so energetically that it threatened to knock the pears from the basket he was carrying. 'No, my lord, Father David's service was far too much for you. You weren't well all that day afterwards. I'm going to ban visits to the church for you, you do far too many of them,' he said with a mock severity which showed Mara the good relationship between man and servant. 'Anyway,' he added, 'the young bard is coming to play for you.'

'Rory?' questioned Mara with surprise. 'Isn't he going to Sorley's burial, then?'

'I'm not sure,' said Toin. 'Perhaps it is after the service that he is coming. It doesn't make any difference to me. The days are long and the nights even longer when you are in my condition. Anyway,' his voice became more cheerful, 'it's nice for the young fellow to have a chance to play that zither of his. There's not much music asked for up there at the castle.'

'Could I leave my horse, and Bran, here with you?' asked Mara watching Bran walking around Tomás in circles, his tail wagging and his eyes adoring. 'I could leave him outside the church; he's well trained, but I think he would prefer to stay here with you. He seems to be making great friends with Tomás. I won't disturb you when I come back.'

'You won't disturb me; I'll love the company, what's more I'll have a glass of muscadet ready for you when you return,' promised Toin. 'It's perfect with the pears.'

'Only if you have a good rest though while I am at Mass.' Mara looked anxiously at the old man.

'It looks as if I am going to have another visitor; there's Ulick at the gate,' said Toin. His voice sounded weary.

'I'll take him off with me,' promised Mara. 'Mass will be good for his soul.'

❉

When Mara emerged from the gate Ulick Burke was standing by the wall examining a bee exploring the dusty golden antlers on a piece of flowering ivy. He had a thoughtful look on his face.

'Toin wondered whether you were coming in to see him, Ulick, but I think he is a little tired for a visit at the moment. You weren't thinking of going in, were you?'

'No, no,' he said with a slight start. 'I'm on my way to church. I was just looking to this little furry fellow here and thinking of how extraordinary it is that he and his little brothers and sisters were able to cause the death of that huge man, our valued friend, the master of Newtown Castle.'

'So you mourn Sorley then?' Mara looked at the man appraisingly. He was one of Turlough's dearest friends and yet no two men could be more unalike. Still the bonds of early childhood friendships were very strong.

'Who wouldn't?' Ulick summoned up a pious expression. 'Such a generous, big-hearted man. Always willing to share his wealth.'

'At a price.' Mara's tone was blunt as she thought about the document that she had seen in the chest.

'As you say, my dear Brehon,' murmured Ulick. 'At a price . . . There are some consolations attached to his demise, I suppose.'

'You'll still have to pay the debt,' warned Mara as they arrived at the church gate.

'What!' Ulick looked genuinely startled. 'I thought death cleared all debts.'

'Certainly not under English law. And your agreement and the subsequent guaranteeing of the debt was enacted under English law. You will still have to pay that sum of money to Sorley's son and heir.' Or, rather, since Turlough had guaranteed it, he will probably have to pay it, she thought with some irritation.

'Daughter, my dear Brehon, daughter!' said Ulick as he politely held the gate open for her.

'Son,' repeated Mara firmly as she passed through and waited for him on the path.

'But he made a will; he left all that silver and property to his daughter; I told you about it. I witnessed it myself.'

'The will cannot be found.'

'Really?' Ulick looked at her enquiringly and she nodded.

'So it all goes to the son, now.' Ulick began to move forward, his face thoughtful.

'Do you know, my dear Brehon,' he said as they passed the wooden bench, 'this is quite a relief to me, it was getting to be very hard work paying court to that plain-faced girl. The brother is a sweeter character. Dear boy, I will be a father to him. I will guide his infant footsteps through society. I will teach him the joys of high living. I will instruct him on how to spend his money. I will even find a nice little wife for him.'

The church was full of the people who lived around in the parish of Rathborney, attending their usual Sunday Mass, but there was no sign of any additional people for the burial of Sorley. None of the silversmiths from Galway was in the church. They had paid their respects at the wake; obviously they felt that to be enough; they probably had little liking for the man in any case. The mineworkers were there; no doubt the overseer was under orders; they were huddled in the back of the church, while the family of Sorley sat in the traditional mourning place on the left-hand side of the altar.

On the right-hand side, at the top of the church, was a burly figure, leaning back, legs sprawling, head turning from side to side. Mara went up the middle aisle, conscious of the stir of interest that her appearance caused and slipped in beside him.

'What brings you here, my lord?' she whispered as she knelt demurely by his side.

'You, of course.' Turlough's smile beamed and his green eyes twinkled. 'I've been visiting Conor and his wife at the abbey – the monk there, Father Peter, has a great reputation for cures for the wasting sickness. He's looking better, Conor. He's put on a bit of weight and got a little colour in his cheeks.'

It was early days yet, thought Mara. Conor was Turlough's eldest son and the *tánaiste*, or heir, to his father's position of king of the kingdoms of Thomond, Burren and Corcomroe. In the normal way of things he would be king when Turlough died, but he was sinking rapidly under the onslaught of the deadly wasting sickness that seemed to affect many of the young and strong.

'That's wonderful news,' she whispered back, unwilling to disappoint him by expressing any doubts. She hoped that he was right: Turlough, of course, had an incurably optimistic temperament. Conor could only have been about a fortnight at the abbey; the last time that she had seen him he had looked like a man close to death.

However, Father Peter of the Cistercian abbey in the north-east of the kingdom was famed for his cures of seriously ill people and it might be possible for him to work a miracle and to cure the wasting sickness that racked poor Conor with constant fevers and seemed to strip the flesh from his bones.

'Will you come back there with me, to the abbey, I mean?' Turlough's voice took on a pleading note which she was coming to know well these days. 'The abbot, Father Donogh, would like you to come for a Sunday dinner. He wants to discuss the wedding arrangements with you.'

'So that's the new parish priest.' Mara stood up with the rest of the congregation as the Bishop of Kilfenora came out from the vestry followed by a very young priest. She wanted to think about this invitation. She needed to collect her mare and Bran from Toin's hospitable care and she had planned to walk around Rathborney, perhaps to climb the mountains and see Sheedy.

'Straight from Rome.' Turlough was diverted as she expected. 'Or from the cradle,' he added in a loud whisper.

Mara felt sorry for the young priest. It was an ordeal facing his first parish, and to do it under the eyes of the bishop and the king made it doubly difficult. The people of the Burren were intensely clannish and they would take a long time to get used to a stranger in their midst, especially one taking the place of such a deeply loved priest as Father David had been.

'I have a surprise for you,' mumbled Turlough, devoutly beating his breast as the congregation recited the act of contrition. 'Do you remember young Cormac, that nice lad that you had at the law school a year or two ago? Well, I met him last night with my cousin Mahon. Cormac is now Mahon's lawyer and he has been appointed as Brehon of

Kinvarra now. He's coming to the abbey today to meet you. I told him you would be bound to come.'

Mara smiled. That was an incentive. Cormac had been a bright, clever scholar with plenty of common sense and initiative. She would enjoy meeting him again and, of course, he might be able to give her information about Deirdre's divorce case.

'Did you tell him about the murder of Sorley?' she whispered as they stood for the recital of the gospel.

Turlough nodded and then, as he saw his cousin, the bishop, Mauritius of Kilfenora, turn a cold eye on him, he clutched his rosary beads, and signed himself devoutly with the small silver cross on the top of them.

That will be almost worth putting up with the pompous abbot for an hour or so, thought Mara, sinking down to her knees again at the end of the recitation of the creed.

Cuan had been smartened up, she thought, glancing across at the family group. He was now richly dressed and his hair was clean and well combed. He was kneeling beside his mother who glanced at him proudly from time to time. To her amusement, Ulick had placed himself on the other side of the boy. Deirdre, herself, was also richly dressed and looked indistinguishable now from the wives of the prosperous silversmiths whom Mara had seen at the wake. Una was looking the same as usual, but there was no sign of Rory. Had he already decided that it was not worth his while marrying this plain woman with no fortune? Had he just walked off, or perhaps engineered a quarrel, or possibly just taken too much to drink last night and not bothered to get up in time for the burial?

Daire was there, and Mara was pleased to see how, from

time to time, Deirdre bent down and whispered something in his ear. Obviously they were on good terms with each other and this might mean that the young man might be able to finish his term at Newtown Castle with honour, be spoken for by Deirdre's brother, or transfer his apprenticeship elsewhere and become a master smith before the year finished.

The service passed in an almost perfunctory manner. The bishop could find little to praise about Sorley, and wisely decided to confine his eulogy to a few facts. Surprisingly, for one of his wealth, Sorley had no personal bard attached to his household, and obviously, Rory had not been deputed to recite his lineage, so quite quickly they were all standing over the newly dug grave watching the body being lowered down into it.

There was a deep silence as the workmen began to fill the grave. This was usually the moment when the bereaved broke into loud sobs and had to be led away by solicitous friends. However, Sorley's wife and daughter showed no emotion, but stood looking quietly on, obviously waiting for the moment when they could walk away with dignity. Cuan passed his sleeve over his eyes in a childlike manner, but Deirdre gave him a quick glance and a pat on the arm so he controlled the emotion and stood with his eyes fixed on the bare branches of the ash tree above their heads. Anluan, the severely mutilated mineworker, made some inarticulate sound – it almost sounded like a cackle of laughter – and another mineworker took him by the arm and half-helped and half-dragged him away from the graveside.

'Go and greet the bishop,' said Mara in Turlough's ear when all was finished and the procession wound its way back towards the church. She waited until he had obediently departed and then slipped around to the rough grass behind the ruined wall. The boys had reported that no stick was to be found there and she knew, that under Fachtnan's super-vision they would have searched it thoroughly. They were young and keen and their eyesight was at its strongest. There was no chance that they would have missed anything of significance, and yet she didn't feel satisfied until she had checked it through thoroughly for herself. The grass was long and interlaced with nettles but she persevered, going over every inch of the ground.

The bishop's voice was still booming in the distance when she straightened her back. No, there was certainly no stick to be found in the grass, nor was it, as far as she could see, to be found it the sparse hedgerow behind. Mara went around the ruined wall and once again viewed the spot where the hive of bees had been placed in the empty alcove of the ruined church. This was where the stone had been removed and the hole that it had left still showed bright and clean-looking in the lichen and moss-besmirched wall.

There was something else there, though. Mara went closer. It was quite small; perhaps that was why it had not been seen before. It was small, and round and it lay in the shadow on the stone surface. She picked it up and held it to the light and then it flashed silver. It was a small round, hollow object, just the right size to fit over a thumb. She might not have recognized it, she thought, if she had not seen Rory, tuning and plucking his musical instrument, sitting in the gallery in Newtown Castle. It was the silver plectrum for a zither.

'Brehon.' It was Giolla's voice. Hastily she picked up the

small object, put it into her pouch and went out onto the path to greet him. He was carrying something in his hand.

'This is that skep you wanted to look at,' he said, holding it out. 'You can see that the bees have picked it completely clean. You can handle it without fear. There is nothing left.'

Mara stretched out her hand and murmured her thanks. The skep was made from soft rope, spun from the straw of oats after they had been harvested. The sides of the skep were made from coiled rope and so was the base and the roof. She examined it carefully, fascinated by the workmanship. The roof, she saw was detachable, presumably so that the honey could be taken from it with ease, but it was the hole, not much bigger than the girth of her thumb, in the back which held her attention. The soft straws were bent inwards and forced apart, not torn nor cut.

'What do you think made the hole?' she asked holding it out to Giolla.

'A stick poking into it,' he said without hesitation.

'Not a knife?'

'No, not a knife: that would leave a different hole; a knife would cut and would leave a sharp narrow opening. You can see here how the stick has pushed in the straw.'

'But you haven't seen any stick?'

'No, I haven't.' His tone was dissatisfied. 'I've searched everywhere trying to find something that would have made that size of hole. I'll keep my eyes open, though, Brehon, and I'll let you know if I do find anything.'

Mara nodded. 'Yes, Giolla, thank you; please keep the skep safe and don't use it again until I give you the word.'

Where was the stick, she wondered. What had happened to it after the deed had been accomplished?

❀

Rory and Toin were sitting in the pear orchard when Mara and Turlough came in after Mass. Bran came across to greet them and then returned to the wooden bench where Rory was strumming his zither, taking up his position at his feet. The boys always said that Bran loved music, but Mara suspected that he just liked to be in the centre of any group. Mara crossed over and sat beside Rory, looking closely at the zither. It was quite a new instrument, obviously bought for him by Sorley – there had been nothing but a simple lute in evidence when Rory had played in the garden of Cahermacnaghten during the summer months. He held the instrument flat on his lap, the fingers of his left hand plucked at the strings on the narrow top while his right thumb, gloved with a gold plectrum, softly stroked the notes from the body of the zither.

'Leave the lad to play and come and have your glass of muscadet,' ordered Toin. He was looking better than earlier: never better than when he was attending to the wants of his guests, surmised Mara as she came across to him and accepted a pear while Tomás filled the delicate fine glass with the golden wine. Mara bit into the pear, holding the juice in her mouth and then swallowing it with a sip of the sweet perfumed muscadet. Toin was right; they did go well together. She leaned back on the grassy seat and closed her eyes. The November sun was as warm as if it were still September and the bees were searching the flowers at the side of the orchard. For a while their busy noise was soothing but then it brought her mind back to the graveyard and the man who died there.

'Toin,' she said tentatively, 'I know you were feeling very ill on the day that Sorley was killed, but do you remember seeing Deirdre going into the church?'

Toin nodded vigorously. 'I do indeed. I remember that she passed me just as Tómas was giving me my poppy syrup. She went down the path and followed Cathal the sea captain into the church.' He added with a quick smile, 'and, before you ask it, Sorley was still by the gate at that stage.'

Well, that's two people off my list, thought Mara. Una, I saw myself. She had her maidservant with her, but Cuan? What about Cuan? From the reports at Poulnabrone, he, as well as Rory, came quite late into the church.

'No more,' she said with a smile, shaking her head as Toin held out the flagon invitingly. 'The king and I have a long ride ahead of us. We are having dinner at the abbey.'

'Leave Bran and collect him on your way back,' said Toin. 'Tomás has taken a fancy to him and he seems fond of young Rory also. Come and look at the rest of my garden before you go. You should see my flowers,' he boasted. 'It's like the height of summer.'

Mara got to her feet willingly. I'm going to miss Toin when he goes, she thought sadly. No one else quite shared her passionate love of flowers.

'It's wonderful, this year, isn't it?' she said, surveying the ranked masses of peonies, pinks and loosestrife. 'It almost seems as if winter has forgotten to come, and yet we're past *Samhain*.'

'The dying of the year.' Toin's voice was reflective with no trace of melancholy in it.

Mara stood for a moment looking around. Toin's garden was packed to the last inch with flowers and the late autumn colours of purple and gold, all blowing slightly in the gentle breeze, seemed like a banner. At the edge of the garden, the tiny Rathborney river curved its way through the flowers, towards the mountain gap. Tall velvet-brown bulrushes lined its sides. Mara bent down and stroked one. Its surface was as soft as fur to her fingers.

'I wish I had a river in my garden.' Mara looked admiringly at a few last creamy flowers of meadowsweet, the pale pink bistort and the solitary purple loosestrife that lined the banks. 'Look at those reeds – still such a vivid green. Don't they make a gorgeous background to the lovely colours of your flowers!'

'You should see it in the spring,' said Toin boastfully. 'I've got primroses and violets and kingcups and marsh orchids all along here.' He stopped for a moment and then said quietly: 'You will come and see it in the spring, won't you? I'd like to think of you doing that.'

'I will,' said Mara. She knew; and knew that Toin himself knew; that he would never see the springtime glory of his garden again, but she understood his feeling. The pleasure in a garden was doubled when it was shared with an admirer.

'You go on, now,' he said, with a change of tone. 'King Turlough will be waiting for you. Enjoy your day.'

❖

There were bees everywhere. Never had Mara been so conscious of them. The slopes of Cappanabhaile Mountain were clothed in brightly coloured pink and purple plants of stiff-stemmed heather. Many beekeepers had moved their hives up here, she noticed as she and Turlough cantered along the path beside the steep slopes of Cappanabhaile. Some were wooden hives, with pointed wooden roofs; others were the old-fashioned straw skeps used by Giolla.

'Great honey,' said Turlough following the direction of her eyes.

'Why? Not that I know much about honey. I don't really like the stuff. It's too sweet for me.'

'Heather makes a lovely honey,' explained Turlough. 'Not like ivy; that makes a dark, bitter honey. I think most of the beekeepers just leave ivy honey to be used by the bees themselves. It keeps them alive during the winter months. Now, heather honey, well you can make a great mead with that – but then, you don't like mead much either, do you?'

Mara shook her head with a smile. 'Again it's too sweet for me; I prefer wine. I'd imagine most people do. Otherwise why would so many thousands of tuns of wine be imported into Galway every year? I think that Oisín, you know, my son-in-law, told me that about 120,000 gallons of wine came into the docks in Galway last August, while I was staying with them.'

'There's Galway Bay for you,' said Turlough pointing. 'I always love the first sign of the sea. I suppose it was because I was born and brought up in an inland place and, you won't believe this, but I never actually saw the sea until I was fourteen years old. I had finished school at Emly –

the monks had decided that they couldn't leather anything else into my thick head – so my uncle, Conor na Sróna, big-nosed Conor, he thought I should do some work for my living and so he sent me with his steward to collect tribute from the O'Lochlainn at the Burren. That was Ardal O'Lochlainn's father and he was a very nice man. He invited us to stay with him, he was living in Gleninagh Tower, over there, just near the sea and I thought it was all wonderful.'

'Imagine not seeing the sea until you were fourteen years old,' said Mara. She looked all around and took in a deep breath of the salty air. The mountains of Cappanabhaile on their left and of Moveen on their right gleamed silver in the sun and the sea was a deep blue, as blue as the sapphire in Turlough's ring. A sturdily built ship, with sails of bleached linen, moored by the pier, rocked gently and a fishing boat steered for the harbour followed by a cloud of hungrily squawking seagulls. She narrowed her eyes. There was a man walking down the small narrow street that led to the harbour. His back was turned but there was something about the rolling gait and the squat figure that was familiar.

'Cathal,' she called and he turned instantly, a squarely built man, with weather-stained clothes and a very brown face.

'How are you, Brehon?' he said, crossing the road and standing by her horse. 'My lord.' He made a deep bow in the king's direction.

'How is everything going, Cathal?' asked Mara.

'Very well.' He hesitated for a moment and then said, 'I was going to come to see you tomorrow. I wanted your advice.'

'Well, you can have it now if it won't take too long,' she

said good-humouredly. In her hard-working, overcrowded life she had early learned the value of never postponing anything that could be dealt with instantly. 'Do you want to see me privately?' she asked with a quick glance at the king.

'No, no, nothing private about it at all.' Cathal was relaxed and affable, a man who was sure of himself and of his place in his world.

'Is that your ship down there?' asked Turlough. 'I'll just ride down and have a look at it. Looks a fine vessel.'

'The king will enjoy looking at your boat,' said Mara reassuringly, seeing that Cathal looked rather concerned. Like most men of the kingdom he was a courteous man with a high regard for the king. He would not have liked to inconvenience him in any way. 'What was it that you wanted to ask me about?'

'Well, it's to do with the man who died, Sorley the silversmith.' He hesitated and Mara nodded.

'You were there at the church, of course, weren't you?'

'That's right,' Cathal eyed her a slightly apprehensive way. 'I had nothing to do with the bees going after him, though,' he said bluntly.

'No, no, you were seen going into the church while Sorley was still alive. You were just in front of a woman called Deirdre.' She waited for a moment, but he said nothing. That meant little, though. He would probably not have known her so would have taken no notice of a middle-aged woman behind him. 'I just wanted to ask you whether you could remember anyone coming in late. You were at the back of the church, weren't you?'

'I remember the young bard, Rory, isn't it? I remember him coming in late.'

'Do you remember whether he had his hood up or down?' asked Mara.

'Up,' said Cathal confidently. Mara nodded. This was a useful confirmation.

'I wonder why he had the hood up coming into the church – especially as it was so fine.' Her tone was conversational, but Cathal gave her a keen look.

'Well, you know these young lads, Brehon,' he said tolerantly. 'He pulled the hood down and then that gave him a chance to comb through his hair and show all the young maidens his golden curls.'

Mara laughed. 'But you wanted to see me – is it about the silver that was lost? I know about this troublesome affair, Cathal,' she added quickly as she could see him trying to marshal his thoughts to explain the whole matter to her.

'It's just that I wondered, now that Sorley is dead, should I approach the son and ask for more time, or is it the daughter who is the heir?'

'I think,' said Mara thoughtfully, deciding to ignore the last question, 'it might be best if you left the matter to me. Would that be all right, Cathal? Would you be happy for me to handle it?'

'More than happy,' said Cathal gratefully. 'I was talking to Toin the *briuga* – I'm going to bring some goods over for him when I return from my next voyage so I went to tell him that I would be leaving in about ten days' time – and he suggested that I have a word with you about it. I'll leave it to you then, Brehon, and I'm sorry that I interrupted your Sunday ride with the king.' His eyes went to Turlough who had handed his horse to one of the bodyguards and was now walking up the gangplank closely shadowed by the other bodyguard.

'I'll ride down and look at your vessel, too,' said Mara, 'though we mustn't be long as we've promised to have dinner with the abbot and the sun is going around; it will soon be noon. So you'll be staying around here for a while, will you?'

'Yes,' said Cathal. 'I'm picking up some flagstones from Doolin in about ten days' time and taking them over to the north of France. That will be my outgoing cargo.'

❄

The king's cousin, the abbot, was pacing the fine green grass of the garth outside the guesthouse of the abbey when they arrived. He was not alone, but was deep in conversation with his brother, Mahon O'Brien. Mara was struck by the resemblance between the three cousins as Turlough dismounted from his horse and greeted them. This resemblance was particularly strong between Mahon and Turlough who shared the same heavy build and height as well as the high-bridged O'Brien nose and lofty forehead.

However, it was not the royal cousins that engaged Mara's interest as she handed her reins to the porter, but a young, fresh-faced man who leaned against the stone wall of the cloisters, smothering a yawn. His eyes brightened when they saw her and he took a few eager strides forward.

'Brehon,' he said enthusiastically, 'it's good to see you again.'

'Cormac, how are you? I don't need to ask – you're looking wonderful. How was Cork?'

'Good,' said Cormac. 'I got a lot of experience there, then I had a few months as an *aigne* in Oriel and now here I am.' He turned to smile politely at the stately figure of the abbot.

'Well, Brehon, it's good to see you. You are well?' Father Donogh O'Brien, abbot of St Mary of the Fertile Rock, the Cistercian abbey in the north of the Burren was the king's cousin. Like him, and yet quite unlike him Mara always thought. She made suitable replies to the queries and listened respectfully to his plans for the wedding on Christmas Day while all the time she was wondering how to get Cormac to herself.

'And now you will wish to see Conor,' the abbot was saying to Turlough. 'I'll escort you to the guesthouse.'

'I'll wait here with Cormac,' said Mara quickly seizing the opportunity. 'We don't want to be all crowding in on an invalid at the same moment. I'll join you in a little while, my lord.'

Without waiting for an answer, she seized Cormac by the arm and led him into the enclosed cloisters' garth.

'I've got something to show you,' said Cormac when they were alone. He opened his satchel and she could see inside it rows of scrolls all tied neatly with the legal pink linen tape. 'I heard that you were investigating the murder of the silversmith. Well, believe it or not, all of these are to do with cases that Sorley the silversmith brought to the court at Kinvarra. He seems to have been a great man for the law,' Cormac lowered his voice and added, 'and by some strange coincidence things always seemed to go his way.' He gave a quick look at her face: 'That doesn't surprise you, Brehon, does it?'

'No, it doesn't, Cormac,' said Mara shaking her head wryly. 'I understand that there was some very fine silver at the Brehon's house in Kinvarra, also.' She spoke lightly, but there was a deep distaste within her for a Brehon who could be bribed and would betray his oath for some silver.

'Hmm,' said Cormac with a grin, 'well, an innocent young lad like myself would know nothing about that sort of thing. Anyway, this may be the scroll that you are interested in.' He had it out before she replied and had begun unwrapping it.

'This is the divorce of Sorley from his wife Deirdre; I just made a few notes here to save you time.' He gave a quick glance around. Mara nodded. She understood. Cormac was newly appointed; he would not want to offend Mahon O'Brien in any way by appearing to question the judgements of his successor.

'Just keep an eye on the gate to cloisters like a good boy,' she said as she quickly scanned down through the pompous legal phrases and then looked at Cormac's note. She nodded with satisfaction as she read that. 'Neat, succinct and to the point,' she commented. 'Remind me again: who taught you?' He grinned at that and she handed him back the scroll. 'Just tie that up again and put it away,' she said. 'Your notes are all that I need.'

The notes were clear, concise and informative. The husband had made the accusation; no witnesses were called. Deirdre's testimony was not asked for and the judgement had been delivered without any defence or denial being entered.

'*You are a simple man,*' one Brehon had remarked, perhaps rather impatiently, to a victim, '*but fear not; the law is greater than any of us and it will protect you.*'

The law had manifestly not protected Deirdre on that occasion, but Mara was determined that justice would ultimately be done.

TWELVE

GÚBRETHA CARATNIAD

(THE FALSE JUDGEMENTS OF CARATNIA)

There are seven things which a husband may cite if he wishes
to divorce his wife:

1. *Unfaithfulness*
2. *Persistent thieving*
3. *Inducing an abortion*
4. *Smothering her child*
5. *Bringing shame on his honour*
6. *Starving her child*
7. *Absconding from the marriage home*

ග❧

'THERE ARE MANY DIFFERENCES between English
law and Brehon law,' Mara informed her scholars. The
boys were finding it hard to concentrate. It had rained

heavily all day on Monday so they had no fresh air and exercise yesterday. It had still been raining this morning so even their midmorning break had to be spent indoors. An hour of Latin, followed by an hour of Greek and then an hour spent memorizing pages of the thousands of judgement texts meant that they were all now tired and looking sleepy. 'I was thinking about this on Sunday,' she went on, 'when I was riding home from my visit to the abbey with the king. I met Cormac there – you all remember Cormac – and he was telling me the details of Deirdre and Sorley's divorce. Sorley divorced Deirdre for infidelity. It appeared that she made no defence and no witnesses were called. I found that strange, don't you?'

'You mean he gave no proper evidence?' asked Moylan, abandoning his attempt to carve something on his desk and looking at her alertly.

'None.' Mara nodded.

'So she was convicted on his word.' Enda looked thoughtful.

'Perhaps she had a baby and he wasn't around to . . . well, you know . . .' said Aidan.

'I wish you'd learn to put matters into words, Aidan,' said Mara crisply. 'Words are the tools of a lawyer, just as a chisel is the tool of a stonemason.'

'He was absent at the time of conception,' said Enda primly and Mara nodded gravely in acknowledgement.

'I don't know whether he was absent, or not,' she said, 'but there was no baby. Deirdre had two children, only two. One, Una, was born, I think, shortly after the marriage. The other, Cuan, that lad we met on Saturday, Fachtnan; well he was born about nine years before the divorce. There were no more children and according to Toin, Deirdre has lived alone, ever since.'

'So why were you saying about English law and Brehon law being so different?' asked Shane.

'Well, I was thinking that Brehon law allows for a wife to divorce her husband and to retain her bride-price and a share of his property. It will not allow a husband to put aside his wife for no reason.'

'But it did in this case, is that right?' queried Shane.

Mara shook her head. 'The law didn't; the man who administered the law was at fault. The law is quite clear. Deirdre should have had a chance to bring her own evidence, to make a protest.'

'So it's better for a woman to live under Brehon law than under English law,' said Hugh thoughtfully.

'And of course, Brehon law also allows for women to have a profession such as being a lawyer or a physician,' Mara agreed. 'Can anyone remember what Fithail says on this subject?'

'*A woman physician is a glory to the kingdom*,' Fachtnan recited with a quiet smile.

'Nuala keeps telling him that,' Aidan smirked.

'But English law allows a girl to inherit if she has no brothers, and Brehon law doesn't,' said Fachtnan hurriedly, propping his chin in his hands to hide his burning cheeks.

'Well, yes, and no,' said Mara. 'You see it's a question of clan territory.'

'So if Mairéad O'Lochlainn didn't have any brothers and Donogh, her father died, then she would only get land fit for seven cows,' said Aidan with a quick glance at Enda.

'And her house,' replied Enda, calmly ignoring the jibe.

'But,' said Mara, 'if it's not a question of clan territory, and the wealth has been earned by the individual, then he or she can make a will leaving it to anyone. Sorley, the silversmith, mine owner and merchant, made, according to his daughter Una, a will leaving all his possessions to her and excluding his divorced wife, Deirdre, and his repudiated son, Cuan.'

'Well, lucky old Rory,' said Moylan enthusiastically. 'I was wondering why he gave Aoife the push for the sake of Una who's got a face like a mountain goat.'

Mara raised her eyebrows admonishingly, but stifled a laugh. Moylan, it was to be hoped, would learn some diplomacy before he was released to the world as a Brehon.

'Ah, but the will can't be found,' said Fachtnan. 'When the Brehon and I were there on Saturday, Una searched everywhere and so did Rory. There was no will, so now the wealth goes to the son.'

'So Una will have nothing and Rory will have nothing, either . . .' Moylan broke off with a glance at Bran who had stood up, his long thin tail wagging.

'There's Rory now,' said Aidan, standing up and peering out of the window. 'He probably wants to talk to you privately, Brehon, about the will. I think I smell dinner, would it be all right if we went to eat now and that would leave you in peace?' he finished helpfully.

'Well, don't get in Brigid's way if she's still preparing the meal,' Mara warned them tolerantly.

'We can play hurley if the field has dried a little,' said Moylan joyfully.

'If I may, I'll just borrow *Cáin Lánamna* about the laws of marriage, Brehon. This is an interesting case about Sorley and his wife, Deirdre,' Enda said. He returned Aidan's stare of amazement with a superior look as they strolled outside.

'Shall I tell Rory to come in, Brehon?' asked Fachtnan.

'Yes, please, Fachtnan.' What did the young bard want? she thought. Her mind went to the discovery she had made in the graveyard yesterday.

Rory looked troubled and hesitant when he came in. He made a few uneasy remarks about the weather and enquiries about her journey yesterday and fidgeted with his fingers until Mara, worried that he would never get to the point, asked him bluntly: 'Well, what brings you over here, Rory?'

'I wanted to talk to you, Brehon,' his voice was hesitant, but his eyes were assessing her.

'Yes, Rory.' He was a handsome boy with some musical ability, she thought. It was a pity that he had not stayed longer at bard school and qualified as a *file* (poet). As it was, he had left once he had attained the lowest qualification and had spent a couple of years idling, living in an old house in Dooneyvardan, the fort or *dún* of the bard, selling songs or his services as musician at fairs and festivals, dining with whosoever would give him a meal, and perhaps a bed for the night. He had little prospects ahead of him; it was no wonder that he had succumbed to Sorley's offer. The sight of all that ostentatious wealth would have seduced a stronger character than his.

'You see I am a bit worried about something that I saw on Thursday, the day of Father David's burial.' His tone had a rehearsed sound; the words, even the slight hesitation after the word 'worried' flowed like the words of a well-practised tale.

Her interest sharpened. She had thought he was about to talk of Aoife.

'Go on,' she said.

'Well, I walked across from Newtown Castle with Sorley on that morning,' he said. 'He wanted to go early, wanted to see the bishop. He tried to hurry Una but she wouldn't be rushed so I said I would go with him. I was fond of him, really. I liked to please him.'

Making sure to ingratiate himself, Mara thought cynically. Or had he some other idea in his head? In any case, he was trying to convince her that an affection existed between himself and his future father-in-law, looking at her appraisingly, trying to see how his words impressed her. She said nothing, looked back at him with a blank, though interested, face, so he continued.

'We walked across and then he delayed a bit so that he was waiting at the gate when the bishop arrived on his horse. Sorley made a big thing of helping the bishop off his horse. He handed the reins to me as if I were a servant.' Now there was a genuine sound of indignation in his voice. She believed that; he had probably been made to suffer many humiliations during his stay at Newtown Castle. Sorley would take the view that he had bought Rory and he would extract due payment from him.

'So what happened then?'

'Oh, Sorley was just chatting to the bishop, introducing himself, telling the bishop about the communion cup that King Turlough Donn had purchased for him as a gift to the abbey. Described what it looked like and the jewels in it: he did that sort of thing very well,' said Rory, a certain note of admiration creeping into his voice. 'I could see the bishop wondering whether to order an even more splendid one for the cathedral at Kilfenora.'

'And then he left the bishop?' queried Mara. It occurred to her that no one yet had given a detailed account of the movements of the murdered man on that Thursday morning so she sat down on her chair and prepared to listen patiently.

Rory perched on Enda's desk and shook his head. 'No. Well, I don't know, really. The horse was getting restless, tossing his head and sweating, Bishop Mauritius told me to take him over to the stable at Father David's house. He even told me to rub the horse down and give him a good drink. He just waved his hand at me.'

'And did you do that?'

'No,' said Rory indignantly. 'I'm not a groom. I met Toin's servant and he pointed out Father David's man to me so I handed the horse over to him.'

'And when you returned, did you go back to Sorley and the bishop?'

'I'd had enough of that,' said Rory resentfully. 'I just waited at a distance until they finished talking. The bishop went to the vestry to robe for the service so I joined Sorley.'

'And stayed with him.' Mara allowed a note of puzzlement to enter her voice.

'I talked with him for a while, but then he seemed restless. He got out his wax tablets and started sketching a communion cup – I suppose he thought that if he had a design ready for the bishop when he met him after the service, then he might get an order there and then. Anyway, he said that Una would be coming and that I should escort her into the church. Sorley was always very anxious that I did everything for Una, not that she ever seemed to notice or bother doing anything to please me.' A note of resentment had crept back into Rory's voice and Mara suppressed a smile. As she thought, this proposed marriage was more Sorley's idea than Una's.

'Well, this is what I wanted to tell you about, Brehon,' said Rory. His eyes were a very dark blue, now, very focused as if they followed some inward script. 'When I turned to go I thought I saw a head over the ruined wall of the old church. Do you know the one that I mean?'

'I do,' said Mara. 'It's not very high, is it?' She pictured the two heads, one black and one red, of ten-year-old Shane and twelve-year-old Hugh, appearing over the top of it.

'That's right,' said Rory eagerly. 'That's what caught my attention. It wasn't someone just strolling along the pathway in the way that the people were doing, going into the church for the service. It looked like someone was ducking down behind the wall, trying not to be seen.'

'So you were curious.' Mara always found it best to keep these confidences flowing by interjecting little remarks.

'Well, I just went to the end of the wall and had a look,' said Rory. He sounded more confident now. His voice was fluent and assured. 'I must say that I wasn't surprised when I saw who it was; poor fellow he's always hanging around trying to have a word with his father.'

'Was it Cuan, then?'

Rory nodded, 'Yes, it was.'

'Did you speak to him?'

Rory shook his head. 'No, I didn't,' he said. He made his voice sound low and miserable – a fine performance, thought Mara. 'I keep thinking that I wished I had. I could just have gone over to Cuan and shook his hand, chatted with him, taken him into the church, but you know it's stupid, but I got the feeling that he resented me. There I was, a stranger, living in his father's house while he was stuck out on that terrible little farm on the mountainside. I suppose it wasn't very fair on him, though Sorley was always full of complaints of him, and I think that, to give the old man due credit, he did try to teach Cuan something of the silversmith's trade and then when he couldn't master that, he tried him in the mine, but nothing worked.'

'So you didn't say anything to him?' Rory was building a case rather cleverly and certainly artistically against Cuan. He had obviously decided to give up casting suspicion on Daire. But why try to cast suspicion on anyone? After the accusation that Muiris made at Poulnabrone, it was understandable that Rory would feel threatened but could there be a more sinister reason?

'No, I didn't. I was pretty sure that he hadn't noticed me as he was concentrating on peeping at his father, so I just crept away.'

'And went straight into the church.' Mara watched Rory carefully as she said this. Muiris, after all, had given public testimony to the late arrival of Rory in the church.

'No, I didn't.' The answer came quickly. Obviously Rory expected this question. 'You see,' he said with a charming smile, 'I just got a bit worried about the bishop's horse. The manservant, that I handed him over to, seemed in a bit of a state, what with it being the burial of his master and everything, so I thought I'd just quickly nip around and check on the horse.'

'And he was all right?'

'Yes, he was, I even checked that the water in front of him was fresh and that there was hay in the net before him.' Rory's eyes went to the elaborate silver bracelet on his wrist and he added, 'and got bitten by a horsefly for my pains.'

'I see,' said Mara rising to her feet. 'Well, thank you, Rory, that was very interesting and valuable evidence for me. The more I know about everyone's movements on that morning, the quicker I will be able to solve this crime. Have you mentioned this to anyone else?'

'I did speak of it to Toin the *briuga*,' said Rory. A slight flush came over his face. 'He advised me to forget about it. He seemed to think it was not of any interest to say any more. However, I felt that you should know, Brehon. You should be the one to decide whether it is of any importance.' His tone was filled with the self-importance of one who will always do the right thing.

Mara imagined that Toin had probably felt that Rory was motivated by a desire to save his own skin. His steward would have carried the news of Muiris's dramatic accusation of Rory at Poulnabrone to the old man.

She led the way to the door and he followed meekly, politely reaching around her to lift the heavy wooden latch.

'There's just one other thing, Brehon,' he said holding the latch in his hand, but not pulling the door open.

Mara turned to look at him curiously and he met her eyes with that frank open look, which he could assume at will.

'Cuan was carrying a stick,' he said.

Once Rory left, Mara went around to the kitchen house
to find the boys sitting around the big table, eating their
substantial midday meal of salted beef and leeks. She herself
seldom ate dinner, preferring to have a tasty supper and a
cup of wine when the day's work was finished.

'Just give me a couple of oatcakes, Brigid,' she said,
swallowing some ice-cold buttermilk which Brigid normally
kept stored in a cool damp cabin next to the kitchen house.
'I think I'll take Bran and go for a walk. We can't expect to
have this weather for long. Back to work at two o'clock,
boys,' she said indicating the candle clock which Brigid kept
meticulously synchronized with the church bells.

Bran was sitting on the wall above the piggery, absorbed
in watching the long line of fat piglets feeding from the
mother sow. For some reason pigs endlessly fascinated
the dog and he was always to be found at the pigsty when
nothing else was happening. He jumped down as soon as he
saw her, his tail wagging.

'Let's go across the fields, boy,' she said, sharing an
oatcake with him. He was a meat eater, but any food from
his beloved mistress tasted wonderful to him.

The fields that stretched east across to Baur North from
Cahermacnaghten were named the High Burren, a flat table
land, high above the valleys and reaching over to the spiralling heights of Mullaghmore Mountain, that lay in the centre
of the kingdom. Today, though it was already the sixth of
November, the midday sun was warm enough to heat the
rounded lichen-spotted stones of the wall beneath her hand.
It was strange, thought Mara, as she threw a stick for Bran,
how autumn and summer seemed to mix in this landscape.
The small, stunted, twisted hawthorn trees, that grew in gry-

kes, between the clints, were already bare of leaves, their clusters of crimson berries glowing in the sunlight. But the limestone still held the heat of summer preserved in its crystals, so the grykes were also filled with pale yellow foam of lady's bedstraw, tiny blue and white eyebright flowers, and here and there that special flower, called *virgin of the grasses* by the country people, reared up on its tall stem high above the arrow-shaped leaves. Its five white petals, faintly veined with green, and arranged around a centre of tiny cream and green antlers, were as cool and smooth to the touch as satin. Mara bent down to touch the flower and then straightened. Bran had stopped, stiff-legged, pointing in the classic pose of a hunting dog. This would be no prey, though; Bran was not a killer by nature. This meant that someone Bran loved was nearby. Quickly Mara slipped a leash over his head. Bran loved everyone, but farmers, kneeling down mending walls or tending an animal, were often not very appreciative when a huge dog, the size of a man, hurled himself on their backs and licked their ears.

'Wait.' Mara had spoken the word when she caught a flash of red-gold hair from behind one of the upright stones of an ancient circle. She relaxed: it was only Rory. She could let Bran go; Rory and Bran were great friends. She was just about to take the leash off when she heard the sound of voices, a man's voice and a girl's. Rory was not alone, a flaxen plait tossed suddenly and she heard a voice. Yes, it was Aoife with Rory. Well, he had not wasted much time. Was it he, or was it Una who had decided to end the betrothal, wondered Mara. She hoped it was Una, though it was a fine point of law as to whether she had the right to do this if a betrothal contract had been drawn up. Una was a strong-minded girl, though, and who knows whether, having heard of the accusation that Muiris had made, she had used this to get rid of an unwanted suitor.

'You weren't saying that last week,' Aoife's voice rose suddenly. No tears now, Mara noted with pleasure. Reluctantly she turned to go back. Really she had no business listening in to a private conversation; she could not even tell herself that it might have something to do with the killing of Sorley. This was just an everyday story of an ambitious, fairly callous young man doing the best possible for himself all the time and caring little for the hurt that he caused to an unsophisticated girl who had fallen for a handsome face and a melodious voice.

But when Mara turned around, she saw that Aoife's father, Muiris, was driving a large herd of cows up from the small valley of Poulnabrucky onto the High Burren. No doubt more rain was on its way. Traditionally the farmers of the Burren kept their cattle on the dry uplands and mountain slopes during the winter months. There would be great movements of herds from now on.

Mara stayed very still. At the front of this herd was a large, brown bull, walking with confident step, leading his cows and their calves. Mara was wary of bulls and it would be folly to proceed, especially with a dog that might arouse the animal's protective instincts.

'Quiet. Lie down,' she whispered to Bran and seated herself on a low stone by his side. Here she would be well out of the way of the path being taken by the herd, and while she was there she might as well listen – so she told herself, anyway.

'You see, I always wanted to marry you,' pleaded Rory.

'It was just that I had nothing to support you. I couldn't do that to you.'

'My father promised us some cows; I told you that.' Aoife's voice was stony with no hint of yielding.

'Yes, but . . .' he wouldn't have been much of a hand with cows, thought Mara with a grin, picturing the elegant Rory up to his knees in muck or out in a freezing field at midnight trying to pull a calf from a cow in labour. She whispered another 'quiet!' to Bran whose tail started to wag again at the sound of Rory's voice.

'You can marry this Una for all I care. I hope you're both very happy.' Aoife did not sound as if she hoped anything of the sort, but there was plenty of spirit in her voice and Mara willed her to remain firm. 'There are better men than you around. Twice as good, twenty times as good.' Was Aoife perhaps thinking of Daire, the silversmith, with his broad shoulders and tall strong frame? He would certainly make two of the slender young bard, though perhaps not twenty.

'No, Aoife, listen.' Rory was good at pleading. His musical voice now broke artistically. 'Things are different now. 'You see I think I have a patron now. The *briuga* Toin is very rich. He's almost as rich as Sorley.'

There was an inarticulate sound of disgust from Aoife. The mention of Sorley had been a mistake. Perhaps Rory was not too bright, after all.

'He loves my playing. I'm staying with him now. I think I can get a permanent place there.' No mention of the fact that Toin was an obviously dying man. Perhaps Rory hoped that he would leave him something in his will. It was possible, of course; stranger things had happened. Mara had never heard of any relation of Toin's; he belonged to no clan on the Burren. As a professional man, his wealth would be his own, to dispose of as he saw fit.

'I suppose you could always kill *him* if you thought you were coming into some silver.' Mara was surprised at the girl's sneer. However, Aoife's mind was obviously moving along the same lines as her father's. A tough girl, far too good for this idle young bard!

'Aoife, how can you say that?' Now there was a genuine break in Rory's voice. It obviously shocked him that the girl who had loved him so much had turned against him. 'In this very place...' He broke off and Mara saw his head droop as he walked away from the girl.

There was a silence for a few minutes. Perhaps Aoife, too, was recalling memories of soft murmurings and love-making during the summer months at this spot. Obviously Rory thought so because Mara saw him return.

'Aoife...' the rest of the words were drowned by the bellowing of a cow after a straying calf, but then the cattle fell silent and Mara heard the end of the sentence. '...so if only you'll agree to marry me now, I'll be the happiest man on earth.'

'You'd better go now,' Aoife's voice was loud, and as hard as the stone beneath her feet. 'I'm going to go and help my father with the cattle. You'd better clear off. If he sees you he will turn the bull on you.'

And then she was gone, running fearlessly across the stone clints towards her father. There was an affectionate teasing greeting from Muiris and a laugh from Aoife. Muiris shouted after a straying cow and Aoife called back merrily. After a few minutes the voices and the slow thudding of hoofs on the hard surface were just a distant echo and then Rory emerged and walked in the direction of Rathborney. He was not near enough for Mara to see the expression on his face, but she could imagine it.

He was an idle, mendacious, exploitative young man and she was glad that Aoife had not given way to him. But was he also a murderer?

Thirteen

Bretha Déin Chécht

(Judgements of Dían Cécht)

A physician must cultivate healing herbs in his garden.

He must remember also the great service given by the garden plants such as cainnean *(leeks), and* imus *(celery) because feeding is as important as medicine to a sick person.*

A physician's bag must contain many compartments so that there is no mingling of the herbs in it.

∂G;

'Brigid, I'm just going down to Rathborney. Could you get Seán to saddle Brig? I should be back in plenty of time for supper. I just want to see someone.'

Mara had considered the matter for the whole of the day; by the time school had finished, she had made up her mind. She would have to question Cuan; even if it were just self-defence, or possibly spite, that had led Rory to make that accusation, she could not ignore it. Certainly Rory had found a plausible explanation for his late arrival at church on that fateful Thursday. What would Cuan say, she wondered.

Mara's mind recalled all the details taken down by her scholars at Poulnabrone, as she waited patiently for Seán to emerge with Brig. Most of the statements had been checked and a certain pattern had evolved. The time of Sorley's death was almost certainly in the few minutes before Mass began. The silversmith probably just delayed to make sure that he had a finished sketch of the communion cup to show the bishop after Mass and the burial of Father David was over.

Rory, Cuan, Daire had all arrived late. All three could have benefited from the death of Sorley. And there were, doubtless, others who might be relieved at that death. Ulick was unlikely to be the only man to owe money to the greedy silversmith. She frowned slightly; did Ulick really think that his debt would cease when the life of the money-lender ceased?

Sheedy was another name that came up. He was one of the last to come into the church.

'Enda,' called Mara. 'Just one moment, Seán, I want to have a quick word with Enda.'

Enda was still in the schoolhouse, though the others were energetically whacking a leather ball around the field with their hurleys.

'I'm just reading through that book on English law, Brehon,' he said sauntering out. 'I know it won't be in the final examination, but I'm interested in the differences. It's amazing that someone can actually be thrown in prison before their case is heard in court. So if they are innocent, they will already have been punished!'

'I must confess I haven't read all of that myself, Enda,' said Mara. 'You shame me. And of course, you are right. We need to know about this English law. What we also need to do is to make good records of our own laws. It's one of those things that I must discuss with other Brehons when we meet in the summer. The king seems to feel that we, even over here in the west, may be in danger of being swamped by England eventually. It's a very rich and power-ful country. Anyway,' she said with a hasty glance back to where Seán was walking Brig up and down, 'I just wanted to ask you something, Enda. I noticed that quite a few peo-ple in your list mentioned Sheedy coming in late to church on the day of Father David's burial, but Sheedy, himself, was not actually at Poulnabrone, was he? He's on no one's list.'

'No he wasn't there,' said Enda, closing his book and coming to look down on the lists. 'I think he might be a strange sort of fellow. Most people seemed to hesitate a bit and look over their shoulder before mentioning his name – almost as if they were a bit afraid of him.'

'I see,' said Mara thoughtfully. 'Well, don't work too hard, Enda. It's important to take a bit of fresh air and exercise as well.'

❈

Toin was in his garden when she arrived at Rathborney. He was leaning heavily on his crutch and looking very ill. He was alone, but as she dismounted at the gate his manservant came out from the house carefully carrying a small flagon. Toin smiled a welcome to Mara, but drained the flagon before speaking. Mara watched him compassionately.

'That's better,' he said after a minute. 'What we owe the east! These poppy seeds that Malachy grinds up for me – bless him, he even flavours it up with honey and rosehips – they have the most marvellous effect. First a warm feeling creeps over you and then you find yourself relaxing and then the pain becomes bearable. Talking about Malachy, he's left me his assistant. She's here to take care of me while Malachy goes to treat a man gored by a bull.' Toin lowered his voice. 'I sent her to pick some pears for me; it's not good for the young to have to watch too much pain.' Then he raised his voice, now full and rich, 'Physician, where are you?'

Nuala came running from the orchard, her black plaits swinging, her *léine*, as usual, hitched up to calf level by her belt. Her tanned face was flushed slightly pink and her brown eyes were full of concern.

'You're looking a little better,' she said, tucking her arm into his. She sniffed the air and then looked at him accusingly. 'You've been having poppy syrup again; just as soon as my back is turned,' she scolded. 'So that was why you sent me to the orchard. You know, it's not good to have too much of that poppy syrup. The more you have: the more you crave. My great-grandfather wrote that down over a hundred years ago when poppy seeds were first brought to the Burren by the monks at the abbey. You should have some of my chamomile tea. I gave some to your cook, Mael, for his stomach pain and he said that it did him a power of good.'

'You see how she orders me about,' said the old man affectionately.

'She's probably right,' said Mara with a smile. 'Nuala knows a lot about medicine. She is always studying her grandfather's notes and experimenting with herbs.'

'She does know a lot.' Toin's voice was full of admiration. 'I keep putting questions to her and she never gets one wrong. At her age I knew very little, though I had the best of physicians for a master. I even watched him take out gallstones from a living man's stomach and the man was still alive twenty years later.'

'I wish I could do something like that,' said Nuala seriously. She thought about it for a moment and then said resolutely: 'I wouldn't mind the blood; I would just concentrate on how much good I was going to do. I suppose you couldn't show me, could you? Perhaps that is what is wrong with you,' she added hopefully.

Toin shook his head smiling. 'No, my dear child,' he said gently, 'that's not what's wrong with me. I know what is wrong with me and I don't think the greatest physician in the country could cure me; I have a growth here in the stomach. I must endure it. In any case,' his voice lightened, 'I'm not the person to show you how to use a knife; I never did any cutting of people myself. My hand was not steady enough. I was a herbalist more than a surgeon.'

'Father says the same thing,' said Nuala. 'I wish I could find someone to teach me. Mara, why aren't there schools for physicians as well as for lawyers?'

'I don't know,' said Mara. 'That's something to ask your father, but I've never heard of them. Mainly physicians learn from their fathers and then the knowledge is passed down like that. The O'Hickeys have been physicians to the O'Briens of Thomond for generations.'

'I think a school would be best,' said Nuala seriously. 'Fachtnan and Enda spend lots of time arguing about the law; I'd like to have someone to talk about things like that; Father is usually too busy.'

A lonely child, thought Mara compassionately – no, not a child, she contradicted herself, a woman with a gift for medicine who was being frustrated by a lack of training and instruction.

'Well, I promise you, Nuala, that I will make enquiries about a school for medicine. Perhaps there might be one in the north of Ireland. I'll ask Shane's father when he comes to collect him at Christmas time.'

'Perhaps Nuala will have the first one,' said Toin lightly, 'and where are you off to, Brehon, or are you paying me a visit?'

'I was looking for directions, actually,' Mara explained. 'I want to pay a visit to Sheedy.'

'Sheedy, the *ócaire*,' said Toin musingly. 'You've never met him, have you?'

'No,' said Mara and waited. Perhaps Toin would know why people spoke warily of the farmer. 'Is he a young man?' she asked. A farm of twenty acres or so was usually given to an *ócaire*, a young man, though some who were inefficient farmers remained an *ócaire* for the rest of their lives.

'Yes, he's a young man,' confirmed Toin, yielding to the gentle pressure from Nuala's arm and allowing her to guide him across the grass towards a wooden bench by the stream. 'Well, not too young,' he amended. 'He inherited the land from his father a few years ago. It's not much of an inheritance . . .' And then he fell silent for a couple of minutes before adding hastily, 'I wouldn't go there on your own, Brehon. I don't know what I would say to the king if I had to tell him that you went up there alone. I'd feel happier if you were to send a couple of men up and fetch him down here for questioning.'

'Why, what's the problem with Sheedy?' Mara gave him a puzzled look.

Toin frowned a little. 'He's had his problems,' he said after a minute and Mara did not press him.

'Well, I'll just have a look at the land around there,' she said vaguely. A hasty glance at the sun which now stood over Slieve Elva showed her that she had only another hour or so of good daylight left.

'You won't take long to get there,' said Toin following the direction of her thoughts. 'Just take that path, there, outside the gate and follow it up the hill for about a quarter of an hour; it stays beside the bank of the Rathborney river, if you can call it a river,' he said with a disparaging glance at the tiny stream trickling through his garden. The name of the place is Lios Mac Sioda, but you can't miss it; the cabin is just at the spot where another little stream joins this one.'

'I'll go then, take care of your patient, Nuala, won't you?'

'Come and have supper with us on the way back,' called Toin as Mara swung herself up onto the mounting block by the gate. 'King Turlough is coming, staying the night, also, as we have some business together. Malachy and Nuala will be here, of course, so you will have their company on your way back to Cahermacnaghten, unless, you too would like to stay the night.'

'I won't do that,' said Mara, 'I have to be back for the scholars, but I'd love to have supper with you.'

※

What was Turlough doing visiting Toin, she wondered as she rode up the path. He hadn't mentioned anything about it to her on Sunday. And what was his business with the old man?

The path to the mountain was well paved with stone for about half a mile but then it turned into a deeply rutted track, full of ancient potholes and water-worn channels. The ditches on either side were choked with weeds and it was obvious that the track would become impassable in the depths of winter, but on that fine autumn afternoon it was a pleasant place to be. The sun was surprisingly warm in the deeply sunken lane, framed on both sides with hedge-rows of blackthorns still laden with purple-blue sloes. Mara pulled her mare to a halt and took off her cloak, slipped it into her saddlebag and looked around her. Ahead of her to her right there was a small cabin set in a filthy farmyard. It looked derelict but there was a figure of a man there leaning against the doorpost. Mara came over to the wall meaning to check on the directions to Sheedy's place and then to her surprise she saw that it was Cuan, Sorley's son.

'God be with you,' she said courteously, wondering all the while what had brought Cuan away from all the luxuries of his father's house back to the miserable place where he had almost starved.

Cuan made no reply, or at least none except an inarticulate grunt and Mara was about to call him to her when she saw the traces of tears on the smeared cheeks of the young man. She hesitated and then dismounted and walked into the farmyard, carefully hitching up her *léine* and her gown so that they would not be smeared by the liquid dung.

'Could I sit down for a few minutes?' she asked and then as the young man did not reply, she added meekly, 'I'd like a little rest.'

Cuan said nothing for a moment and then he turned and went into the cabin and came back with a three-legged stool.

'You can rest on that,' he said. 'It's better out here than in the house. It's very dirty and dark in there.'

'Won't you sit down yourself?' asked Mara lowering herself cautiously onto the unstable seat.

'I've only got one stool,' said the young man. 'I made that myself,' he added contemplating with pride the ungainly piece of furniture.

'Not an easy thing to do, unless you have been brought up to it,' commented Mara gently.

'I wasn't brought up to do anything,' said Cuan miserably, 'that's the trouble – I can't do anything.'

'How old are you, Cuan?' asked Mara.

'Seventeen, I'll be eighteen next month,' he said looking puzzled.

'I see.' Mara thought for a moment. 'And you were sent to live on this farm a year ago. Was that before your birthday or after it?'

'I can't remember,' said Cuan miserably.

'Can you remember *Samhain* last year?' asked Mara

shrewdly. 'Surely you can remember the bonfires. Were you up here then, or down at the castle?'

Cuan shook his head. 'I can only remember that it was cold and wet and I didn't know what to do with the cows. I'm no good at doing anything like that.'

'You're a rich man now; you don't really need to do anything. You can just enjoy yourself.' Mara made her voice sound encouraging though inwardly she was annoyed that he couldn't remember the date of his banishment. A child of five would remember his birthday, she thought with a mild irritation.

And then Cuan burst into a torrent of weeping. He cried like a child, with great noisy gulps and sniffs, smearing his face with his grubby hands. Mara watched him in silence. She wanted to comfort him, but she also wanted to know what was troubling the lad so much so she sat quietly waiting and eventually the storm of weeping ceased. Still Mara said nothing but handed over a square of linen for the boy to wipe his face. The simple gesture of friendliness seemed to upset the boy even more and he broke down again, but this time he regained control more quickly and attempted an explanation.

'I didn't want him to die,' he said, his voice still thick and choked up with the violence of the sobbing. 'I just wanted to come home again and to please him. I didn't want my father to die. I don't know which of them killed him, but I didn't want it to happen, not like that, not stung all over his face and neck. It was horrible. I can't forget it.'

So someone does mourn Sorley after all, thought Mara, and by all the wonders, it is his neglected and abused son.

'Which of them did do it, do you think?' she asked, in an easy, conversational tone.'

'I don't know, do I,' said the boy petulantly. 'They were both always talking about it. Una said that she would get all the money, when father died, but she hasn't so that has gone wrong. My mother was just the same, muttering that she would like to kill him. I don't know what to think, but I don't want to be blamed for anything, because I never told them to do it. I don't want all that silver, only a little bit. I don't want to be in charge of the mines. My mother keeps talking and talking to me and telling me what to do and trying to change me and I just came up here for a bit of peace and quiet.'

'That's the right thing to do,' said Mara gently. 'I always do that myself. When I want to get away from people and do some thinking, I just take my dog and go for a walk until my thoughts clear.'

Cuan looked at her with gratitude. I suppose people don't often agree with him, or tell him he has done the right thing, thought Mara. She went on sitting there quietly, though conscious that time was passing and that the sun was getting lower in the sky all the time. She would give the lad all the time he needed, she decided. Already the few broken words had given her a very different picture of Deirdre to the one which Toin had painted for her. When everything was added up, the most likely murderer is the one who had the most to gain. But in this case, the one with the most to gain was, in mind at least, a broken-spirited child. She reached over and patted Cuan on the shoulder.

'So what did you like best when you were at home with your father, when you were young?' she asked softly.

Cuan looked surprised and then thought for a while. 'Listening to music,' he said eventually.

'So, you are musical,' said Mara thoughtfully. She glanced at the boy's deformed right hand. No point in asking him whether he played a musical instrument.

'Can you sing?' she asked with a sudden inspiration.

The boy's face lit up. 'Yes,' he said, 'would you like to hear me?'

As unselfconsciously as a bird he lifted his voice and sang, a melodic little ditty, popular at the time with the bards. His voice was not very strong, but it was true and very sweet. Mara listened appreciatively and prayed for the right words to come to her when the song had finished. When the last note had died away, she spoke with all the authority with which she delivered her judgements at Poulnabrone.

'It would be a shame for a man with your musical talent to waste your time with mines and the silversmith business. Put your mother in charge of the mine. She is a clever woman; a competent woman and she will manage the business well. Put Daire in charge of the silversmith business. Let him recruit other young smiths. He will do that well for you. Pay him what he is worth; he will not let you down. When you have fixed all that up then go to the bard school at Finvarra and engage some musicians. Spend your days making music, perhaps writing songs. Be happy and enjoy your life. Don't let others run your life for you.'

Cuan stood up. He looked bewildered, but already he held himself straighter. He could be quite a good-looking lad if he dressed himself and groomed himself the way other boys of her age did. His features were not as harsh or as heavy as his sister's. In fact, he did not resemble either his mother or his father in looks, or in character, thought Mara. She patted him on the shoulder again, made her way towards the gate. Sheedy would have to wait, she thought. Turlough might well have arrived; he and Toin would be wondering what had kept her. When she reached the pathway she turned back and called out, 'Cuan,' she said.

'Yes,' said Cuan.

'Get yourself a comb. Musicians always look well dressed and well groomed.'

'I will,' said Cuan fervently. 'I think I'll ask Toin. I was thinking of talking to him about the bard school at Finvarra. I know he goes there sometimes. Toin is very fond of music. He will advise me. He is always very kind to me.'

Mara paused. Would it be fair to burden Toin with this lad? On the other hand the boy was quiet and unassuming and it might prove a distraction.

'Why don't you come down with me, now,' she said. 'I'm going to see Toin just now.'

'May I?' he asked the question in such a childlike way that she was touched. 'You can ride, I'll trot,' he said. 'I am a very good runner,' he boasted.

He was light and lissom, thought Mara, as she watched him run along the path beside her mare. He seemed to be enjoying the exercise so she did not rein in the mare until they came to the flat path outside the church of Rathborney. She stopped there and allowed him to catch his breath.

'Oh, by the way, Cuan,' she said casually. 'I was going to ask you about Father David's burial service. You came in a bit late, didn't you? I wondered if someone delayed you.'

'I was just talking to the son of Cathal the sea captain,' he said earnestly, looking at her with the touching faith only shown by the very young, or the very naive. 'I was asking him if he had managed to find the silverware. He had been diving for it; I heard that. He said he hadn't managed to find it yet, and then he started telling me about sea voyages that he had taken to places like Spain. We stayed there talking until he realized that the bell had stopped tolling.'

✽

They were all at the window when Mara handed her horse to a waiting servant at the gate. Toin came to the door himself.

'Cuan,' he said with surprise.

Mara opened the little wicket gate to the inner garden and pushed the lad inside. 'Cuan would like some advice from you, Toin,' she said, as she walked up the garden path, making sure that the embarrassed boy was ahead of her. 'He would like to be a singer, not go into the silversmith or the mining business. He sings well. He just needs to employ a good musician for a bard, some lute player perhaps and he could have a fine life there in Newtown Castle. I think that he needs the sort of clothes and grooming that a musician would have so I brought him for you to advise him.'

Toin did not hesitate. 'I would be honoured,' he said. 'Come indoors and we will talk it over. My manservant would like to have a handsome young man instead of a decrepit old one to work with.' With a quick glance that was as effective as any barked order, Toin made eye contact with Tomás who came forward, bowed before Cuan and swept him out of the small hallway.

'Come inside,' said Toin to Mara. 'The king has been waiting eagerly for you.'

Mara followed him into the warm room richly furnished with polished oak furniture and hung with tapestries sewn in rich colours. Malachy was sitting over by the fire, Nuala was at the window and Turlough had just jumped up from his chair.

'Just in time for supper,' said Turlough greeting her with a hearty kiss. 'Tell her what we've planned, Toin.'

'We've sent over to Cahermacnaghten to say that you'll be staying the night, Brehon.' Toin's voice was amused.

'Oh, am I?' said Mara, raising her eyebrows.

'Don't look at me,' said Turlough innocently. 'Nothing to do with me; it's Toin's stableman that has gone galloping off.'

'If you stay, we'll stay,' said Nuala eagerly. 'Would you like to see your room? I've just been up there making sure that everything is all right. Would you like me to take you up there?'

'I'll do that, Nuala. You have a patient to look after, remember, isn't that right, Malachy?' Turlough took Mara's arm and steered her towards the stairs. 'Herself and Toin have been talking about physician schools and herbal remedies of the last hour. It's time she did a bit of nursing now.'

'She's doing me out of a job,' said Malachy with an indulgent smile. 'Toin tells me that he feels much better with her than with me.'

'So what's your business with Toin?' asked Mara as soon as the door closed behind the two of them.

He didn't answer immediately, just crossed over and sat on the bed and she went to join him, slipping her hand into his. He looked a little embarrassed, she thought, and it was a minute before he spoke.

'Well, you see the last time that I was here I was telling Toin what a fool I was to have fallen into Sorley's hands, by guaranteeing Ulick's loan. I was a fool, I know that.' His voice was rueful.

'I know,' said Mara. 'I saw your signature on that document among the scrolls in Sorley's chest. And witnessed by that Galway lawyer! Didn't you have the sense to ask Seán Mac Flannchadha to have a look at it for you? Or me, why didn't you ask me?'

'I just wanted to get it over and done with and put Ulick's mind at rest. I was so sorry for the poor fellow,' he said uncomfortably.

'But didn't you understand what interest was?' queried Mara with an exasperated look. 'He was charging very high interest: twenty marks for every hundred that Ulick borrowed from him. You do understand, don't you, that if, as I imagine, Ulick could not pay the interest, you were making yourself responsible for it?'

'He did mention something about interest,' confessed Turlough, 'but I didn't understand; I thought it was a bit like our system of making a man a client by giving him a gift. I thought that he might want my protection, something like that . . .' His voice trailed away.

'It's a good job that I'm marrying you,' said Mara fondly. 'You need looking after.'

'Yes, but listen.' Turlough's face was beaming now. 'Toin has promised that I need not worry about it any longer. He's going to look after everything for me. All my troubles are over now!'

'I think in future we can manage without this. If you want silver, ask me. Half the time I don't know what to do with the fees I get for the scholars. I go to Galway in summer and buy gowns for Sorcha and for the children, or give her money for goods that she wants for the house, but I could always lend you some. Still,' she relented, seeing his disappointed face, 'I suppose if you have to owe silver to someone, Toin would be a nicer person to be in debt to than Sorley. Now let me just comb my hair and wash my hands and face and then let's go down to supper. I like that smell.'

And then, touched by his downhearted expression, she combed his moustaches and the thatch of brown hair which had earned him the nickname of 'Donn', the brown-haired, and by the time that they arrived back into Toin's hall he was looking his usual self, all borrowings from silversmiths forgotten.

After all, she thought, with Sorley dead and the debt transferred to Toin, perhaps there would be no further problem. Once they were married she would keep an eye on his dealings with Ulick.

FOURTEEN

An Seanchas Mór

(THE GREAT ANCIENT TRADITION)

The king is bound by law to do justice to his meanest subject.

A king carrying building material to his castle has only the same claim for right of way as the miller carrying material to build his mill.

The poorest man in the land can compel payment of a debt from the king himself.

The man who steals the needle of a poor embroidery woman must pay a far higher fine than the man who steals the queen's needle.

☙❧

WHEN THEY GOT DOWNSTAIRS, the whole house was filled with savoury scents, the table was spread with snowy linen, glittering goblets and shining silver.

Seated by the fire was an elegant young man, freshly bathed and combed and richly dressed. The manservant had obviously found clothes for him, also. The snowy white *léine* and rich crimson gown, tailored to suit an emaciated old man, fitted the slim young figure perfectly and the rich colour enhanced a pair of beautiful brown eyes.

Toin led him up to present him and visibly enjoyed the start of surprise from Turlough when he said, 'My lord, this is Cuan, the son of Sorley the silversmith.'

Toin had already told Nuala all about Cuan, Mara guessed from the gentle way that Nuala greeted him and from her rapturous pleasure at the little song, which with childlike obedience he had sung for her at Toin's request. Nuala was fourteen and Cuan was seventeen, but she seemed the elder of the two. She had always been very grown-up. The long illness and the tragic death of her mother over a year ago had forced her into an early maturity. She sat and chatted with the boy when he had finished the song, and although he did not say much, what little he did say was sensible and, in his new clothes and with the wine bringing colour to his cheeks, he almost looked like the son of the household. Nuala was good with him. She treated him just as if he were one of the boys at the law school and he was soon at ease with her, and also with Toin whom he had obviously known for a long time, though he stammered over his words when Turlough or Malachy addressed a kindly remark to him. He was certainly not to be classified as a *druth*, thought Mara listening carefully. She was inclined to think that Toin's account of the boy, in his childhood, was probably correct. He was a pleasant boy, not overburdened with brains, but friendly by nature and certainly not suffering from any mental handicap. His murmured replies to Nuala's questions were all quite rational.

Rory came in a few minutes later and then there seemed to be a change in the atmosphere. Rory gave Cuan a long, thoughtful look and Cuan blushed like a child. Had Rory already accused him of being close at hand when Sorley met his death, wondered Mara. There was certainly an unease between them, though perhaps that could have been the fruit of past resentments.

'What glorious weather we've been having,' said Malachy and Mara, usually bored by discussions of the weather, seized on the subject with relief. While Turlough, Toin, Malachy and she shared memories of past autumns the silence between the two young men passed unnoticed. In any case, the door was open to the banqueting hall and that was full of bustle as servants came and went carrying in, first of all, long cloths of linen, followed by trays of costly silver and precious Venetian glasses, flagons of wine and of ale, then platters and baskets heaped high with food. When all was ready, Tomás approached Toin with a low bow.

'Will it please you to be seated, my lord,' he said. The words were formal, but the care with which he stretched out an arm to escort Toin through into the hall and gently helped him to his seat at the head of the table showed the depth of feeling that existed between servant and master. Though wifeless and childless, Toin, because of the essential sweetness of his nature, was being carefully cared for by his servants in these last months of his life.

The banqueting hall was a magnificent room, a long high room with a ceiling of great arched beams of oak wood, a floor of gleaming green and white Connemara marble, the walls, in the Italian fashion, boarded in chestnut wood, with candle sconces carefully placed so that each illuminated the beautifully carved panels. The table was a long one, left over from the days when Toin held his great banquets. Places had been laid for each guest at a rather unfriendly distance of a couple of yards from each other. Mara cast a quick glance around when the servants retired to fetch the hot dishes of food.

'Shall I sit here, Toin?' Mara quickly moved a place setting and inserted it into a gap, 'Cuan can sit next to me, and then Nuala on his other side. Is that all right, Toin? My lord, you sit here, next to Toin and opposite me. And Rory down there on Malachy's other side.'

Turlough was surveying her with an amused look, but she didn't care; it wouldn't matter to Toin who sat where, but Cuan might as well have a good dinner, cocooned between herself and Nuala. The boy was nervous and ill at ease with Rory; that was obvious. He took up a knife, then looked at his deformed right hand, flushed, transferred the knife and tucked the other hand under the table.

'Could you always sing, Cuan?' asked Nuala. He turned to her with surprise, dropping the knife onto the table. He was poor with his left hand, thought Mara, watching him carefully from the corner of her eye. Obviously he had tried to use it in preference to the right hand, but it didn't work for him. She herself was the same. Once when she had injured her right wrist, she had tried very hard to write with her left hand, but she just could not do it.

'I mean,' continued Nuala, 'Fachtnan says he could sing like an angel before his voice broke, but now he makes a noise like a bull calf.'

'Whereas,' said Rory, helping himself to some more wine, 'Cuan has always sung like a nanny goat.'

It wasn't so much the words – the law scholars bandied much worse insults between them in a carefree way every day of the week – it was more the concentrated malevolence in Rory's voice, thought Mara, eyeing him across the table with a steady, cold look as she noticed Cuan flush and clench his hands, his eyes full of misery.

'I wouldn't drink too much wine, Rory,' she said evenly. 'I notice that it can often lead young men into saying silly things.' And then she filled her glass and sipped it appreciatively. 'Wasted on young people, Toin,' she added lightly. 'Just give them ale.'

Turlough roared appreciatively at that and Malachy's dark face lit up with a smile.

'I'm drinking ale, but then I have the patient to look after since my father has already had two glasses of wine,' said Nuala primly.

Malachy protested, though with an indulgent smile. Turlough teased Malachy and in the ensuing merriment, the angry flush died down from Cuan's face.

'I was talking to Cuan about a bard school,' said Mara to Nuala. 'And now I find you want to go to a medical school. I suppose a day will come when there is a school for everything.'

'Well, I went to the monks at Emly,' said Turlough 'and I just can't imagine what Nuala wants to go to school for. Hell has no terrors for me now.'

'You were probably not concentrating on your studies, my lord,' said Nuala severely.

She was looking very well this evening, thought Mara,

wishing that Fachtnan were present. A confident girl, one who could speak sociably to a king and yet was gentle and deferential to poor Cuan. Toin's admiration for her skills had brought a flush to Nuala's cheek and a gleam to her eye. She was a pretty child, with her dark eyes and hair and her brown skin, still bronzed by the summer sun. Her whole face and bearing shone with intelligence and sensitivity, also. Cuan was trying desperately to separate the pink succulent flesh of the salmon from its bone, swapping his knife from his deformed right hand to his unhelpful left and, quietly, with no fuss, she took the plate from him.

'Let me do it,' she said. 'Boys are no good at this sort of thing. I'm always having to open shellfish for Fachtnan.'

Cuan was best left to Nuala, thought Mara. She sat back and relaxed and devoted herself to the dinner and to the wine. The rich taste of the pinot noir grape filled her palate. Perfect with the slightly gamey taste of the woodcock, she thought, making a note to tell Brigid about the sauce. Malachy, from his pleased face, was still enjoying the salmon and the flinty coldness of the bottle of Montrachet which accompanied it. She leaned against the cushioned comfort of her chair and looked around her, holding her glass to the light of the beeswax candle in its candlestick of silver. Not as beautiful a candlestick as those she had seen in Sorley's house, she thought, and at that moment Turlough, following the direction of her eyes, and forgetting Cuan's presence for a moment, said to Toin: 'Did you buy your silver from Sorley?'

'No,' said Toin, shortly. 'No, I didn't.'

With a glance at the boy sitting silently beside her, Mara

intervened hastily, 'I don't think I have ever eaten a meal quite like this before. What is that wonderful sweet, but slightly sour, taste in the sauce, Toin?'

'That's probably the oranges,' said Toin. 'Cathal the sea captain brought me some from Spain the last time he came. I sent a messenger to him this morning to bring me some more back from his next voyage. I'll ask him to bring some for you, too, Brehon, if you would like some. What about you, Malachy?'

'Why yes,' said Malachy with a start. He and Turlough had been deep in a discussion about coinage and its advantages and disadvantages over barter. 'Yes, I'm sure that Nuala would love to taste an orange. I don't think I've ever seen one myself.'

He turned back to his conversation with Turlough, saying, 'The thing is, my lord, if I have bred a fine saddle horse and you have a prize bull then we can get together and if the value seems equal then it's a straight exchange that benefits both. If you use coinage, someone else is making money out of both of you.'

'We dry the oranges and store them for the winter,' said Toin turning to Mara. 'But Cathal tells me that they never taste the same as they do when they are picked straight from the trees in Spain.' He was speaking with an effort now. Mara eyed him with concern and noticed that Malachy was doing the same thing. The wine and the company drove Toin's pain and weakness into the background for a short time, but his twin enemies had obviously reasserted themselves.

'I wish I could eat some more,' said Nuala sadly, putting

down her silver fork reverentially. 'This is gorgeous food, your cook is almost as good as Mara's Brigid,' she added with the tactlessness of youth.

'I went on a voyage once with Cathal,' said Turlough. 'It was in the carefree days before I became king. We were both young men then; we went to France. I don't remember anything about oranges.'

Sheedy, thought Mara. I must go up there tomorrow afternoon. If Sheedy were guilty it was important to find out as soon as possible, or, if he wasn't then he needed to be eliminated. She took another sip of the burgundy and rolled it carefully around in her mouth and then took a bite of the woodcock. That sauce was just perfect. She would put off thinking about the murder and just concentrate on enjoying every mouthful of the wine.

'Let's have some music,' said Toin when they were all sitting around the fire. The long linen cloths had been cleared from the table and the servants had all retired to the kitchen house to have their own supper. 'Rory, play your zither, Cuan, you'll sing for us.'

The song would not be a success; Mara knew that before Cuan stumbled to his feet. She was not very musical, but even she could hear that Rory was playing the zither very fast and very loudly – too fast and too loud for Cuan's high sweet voice – the words and the tune did not blend together but seemed at odds with each other and there were times when the notes of the zither seemed to drown out Cuan's voice. He faltered and then turned red and suddenly stopped. He sat down, shaking his head, as Rory cocked a quizzical eyebrow at him.

And then Rory, himself, started to sing. Unlike Cuan he had a powerful voice and was well used to singing at open-air festivals and assemblies. Now the zither took its rightful place as a backing to the song. For a few minutes, Mara did not realize what was happening. It was a clever mimicry of a typical rural song – but this was about Nanny the goat that went courting. The continual use of the word *ciotógach* was neatly slipped in. The word, of course, just meant 'left-handed' but in the rural idiom it had all sorts of other meanings attached to it: *clumsy, awkward, stupid,* even *deformed.*

With a howl of rage, Cuan was upon him, Rory holding the precious zither well out of reach, but otherwise taking little notice of the blows that were rained ineffectually upon him, while keeping an infuriating smile on his face.

'All right, all right, it was just a joke, calm down,' he was saying. There was a note of triumph in his voice.

'Malachy,' said Mara quietly, as Turlough got to his feet and Malachy obediently came across and took Cuan by the arm in his powerful grip.

'Take it easy, boy, take it easy,' he was saying, but Cuan was now sobbing hysterically, tears of rage and of humiliation pouring down his cheeks.

'Come on, lad, take no notice of him,' Malachy now had Cuan by the shoulders and was gently shaking him to and fro, his face distressed.

'Let's take him outside in the garden for a minute, Father.' Nuala seized the boy's other hand, his deformed hand. Mara suppressed a smile as she noticed that Nuala, despite all the genuine pity that showed in her voice, was, as she led the boy through the room, stroking the hand with the expertise of a physician undertaking a diagnosis. She's wanted to do that all night, thought Mara, the girl is born to be a great physician. I must do what I can to help her, but first this young man must be dealt with, and she turned a stern face towards Rory.

He had a half-smile on his face as he surveyed Toin and Mara. Neither spoke so he took his eyes from them and carefully scrutinized the zither. He turned it over and over in his hands, examining it minutely to see whether any damage had come to it. Mara waited. She was interested to see what he had to say for himself. Toin moved across the room, opened the flask that he kept on a small side table and swallowed some liquid. Mara smelled the sweet-scent of honey mixed with rosehips. So Toin needed some more of his poppy syrup. She wished she could spare him, but this matter had to be sorted out immediately. It was lucky, she thought, that none of the servants was within earshot. The kitchen house was on the other side, connected to the main house by a long stone passageway.

'So why did you do that?' Her question whipped out and Rory flinched slightly. His eyes went to the window where the sound of Nuala's voice chattering lightly about the moon could be heard from the garden.

'I suppose I feel a bit annoyed about seeing someone get away with murder,' he said lightly, strumming a single note from his zither.

'What do you mean?' Mara reached out and took the zither from him, placing it on top of a nearby cupboard.

'You know what I mean,' he said sulkily. 'I told you that I saw Cuan hiding behind the wall just before Sorley was murdered. I told you that it looked like someone was ducking down behind the wall, trying not to be seen. I told you that Cuan had a stick in his hand.' He looked around. Turlough was looking at him with startled attention so, encouraged, he repeated in a belligerent tone: 'I told you and you did nothing. Now I come here and find that he is an honoured guest – him a murderer!'

'Are you taking it upon yourself to act as Brehon for my kingdom?' snapped Turlough.

Mara gave the king a quick signal. It was for her to handle this matter herself.

'My lord,' she said formally. 'It may be that I will need to refer this matter to you if it goes any further, but in the meantime I think that I should question this young bard myself. I need to remind him about the law on several points.'

'And why are you not questioning Cuan? He's the one that killed his own father. I liked Sorley; he was good to me. I don't like to see his own son, a man guilty of *fingal* – and your youngest scholar will tell you that the killing of a near relative is the worst crime of all – I don't like to see a man guilty of *fingal* just getting away with this crime.'

Rory's voice rang out – too late Mara realized that the window had been left open in the mild autumn air and from outside there was an answering howl from Cuan. Obviously he had torn himself free from Malachy: in a moment he was back in the room, crashing through the door, his face white, his eyes half-mad with terror, followed closely by Malachy and Nuala.

'I d . . . didn't, I didn't, I didn't.' He screamed the words and then fell on his knees before an embarrassed Turlough. 'Don't let them do it, my lord, don't let them declare me an outlaw, don't let them cast me out to sea in a boat with no oars. I didn't kill my father; I swear it to you, my lord. I didn't kill him.'

Turlough patted his shoulder awkwardly and looked an appeal at Mara.

'Cuan, stand up immediately,' she said, her tone crisp and authoritative. 'Yes, that's right, now go and sit on that chair over there and control yourself.' She waited until he had done her bidding, and then she moved to the centre of the room. Malachy sat down heavily on a large carved chair, his face full of sympathy, and Nuala perched next to him. Turlough stretched his bulk across a bench by the fire and Toin sank into a cushioned chair and leaned his head against the back of it, watching her with his dark intelligent eyes. Tomás came to the door, hesitated, then withdrew, closing the door quietly behind him.

'Sit down, Rory,' said Mara in a tone that brooked no argument. 'I want to explain a little law to you and I want no one to interrupt me. Cuan and Rory, neither of you is to speak without my permission.' She eyed them both carefully. Cuan was sunk in apathy, mopping his face with a square of linen which Nuala had pressed into his hand. Rory stared ahead with a slight mocking twist to his lips, but neither spoke so she continued.

'In the first place,' she said carefully, 'there is a recognized procedure for accusations in this kingdom. Any accusation may be made, in public, when the matter is under consideration at Poulnabrone, the judgement place. This is called "bearing witness". Any other accusation has to be made to me, personally, in private.' She looked around; no one moved nor spoke. Nuala watched her with interest, but the two boys looked at the floor.

'So,' she continued, 'what happens if an accusation is made, unasked for, in public, and it cannot be verified? Well, the person making that accusation is deemed to have caused an injury under the laws of satire, and recompense has to be paid. The recompense is the victim's honour price.' What was Cuan's honour price, she wondered. His father, as a silversmith would have had an honour price of seven *séts*, but the son? An *ócaire*, she decided; it didn't matter anyway. Rory had nothing: no land, no cows, no silver, no family: he could pay no fine.

'There is another matter that occurred here tonight. Brehon law is always concerned to prevent trouble between neighbours. That is why such a trivial matter as bee trespass is so carefully provided for. And that is why the laws of satire forbid, not just false accusations, but also public ridicule. You would do well to remember that, Rory, in whatever part of the country you next visit.'

Rory gave her a startled look and then looked away. And now what happens next, she thought. Was Rory staying here? If so, would it be better for Cuan to go back to his mother and unwelcoming sister at Newtown Castle this very night, or even to his sordid mountain farm? Perhaps Newtown Castle would be best, but she wanted to be able to accompany him. There was no doubt in her mind that he was now the owner of the castle and she intended to establish that with Una, herself. She glanced across at the candle clock on the marble shelf over the huge fireplace.

Nine o'clock – rather too late for a visit from the Brehon on formal business. This would have to be left to the next day. She looked across at Toin and he bravely rose to his feet.

'If you have finished speaking to Rory, Brehon,' he said, 'I just want to . . .'

And then there was a knock on the door. A sharp double knock and for the first time since Cuan's ill-fated song, Toin smiled.

'Ah, that must be Daire,' he said with pleasure. 'Could you open the door, my dear?' he said to Nuala. 'You asked me earlier, my lord,' he turned to Turlough as Nuala left the room, 'if I had ever bought any silver from Newtown Castle, well I haven't until now, but I got a fancy to see this chess set that you talked of a few days ago so Daire agreed to bring it over so that I could see it. If I like it, then Cuan and I can agree a price, I'm sure.'

So now it was said: Cuan was the owner of Newtown Castle and of all its fabulous riches. Mara saw Rory's head shoot up. He eyed Cuan with malicious dislike and Cuan stared back at him with a murderous hatred clouding his dark eyes. These two would have to be separated; they were like two dogs which would not give over a fight until one was beaten to the ground.

When Daire entered he immediately noticed the atmosphere. His eyes went from Cuan to Rory and then politely back to Toin. He was a mature and sensible young man; the more Mara saw of him, the more she approved of him. She felt sure he and Aoife, the farmer's daughter, would have a future together if the mutual attraction blossomed into love.

All the time that Daire was showing the magnificent

chess set Mara pondered over the problem of Cuan and Rory. Of course, Rory had given evidence to her and she was at fault for not asking for witnesses to corroborate his statement. This should be done, she decided; and it should be done as soon as possible. The fact that she was sure in her innermost mind that there was nothing in it should not have any influence with her. She could not afford to show herself to be more on the side of the wealthy young man than of the indigent young bard who had nothing.

'This is beautiful,' enthused Nuala examining the chess pieces. 'Look at the pawns, just like Bran; and the castle, that's Newtown Castle, isn't it? Did you make it, Daire?'

'Yes, I did.' His voice rang out with a firm and determined note. He saw Mara look at him and then fished in his pouch and produced a piece of vellum which he handed to her.

'Una, the daughter of Sorley, has certified that I was the sole maker of the chess set,' he said proudly.

'So she has,' said Mara, skimming through the few lines of writing. Una wrote a clear, good hand, she thought. The writing was fluent, the work of someone to whom the pen was an accustomed instrument. An educated woman of intelligence, she thought.

'I see she says that she watched all stages of the work,' she commented, handing back the vellum to him.

He stored it away carefully before replying in a low voice, with a quick glance at Cuan, who, sunk in misery, was sitting, slumped in a chair, with his head in his hands. 'Una's a good silversmith, herself, Brehon. She made quite a number of the vases that you've seen at Newtown Castle. She often spends most of her days in the workshop.' He paused, glanced across with a malicious smile at Rory and then incautiously his voice rose slightly. 'There's no reason why a woman shouldn't be a good silversmith,' he asserted. 'I took Aoife there this morning and Una showed her how to make a pretty little ring. It was lovely. She gave it to me.' Proudly he displayed the crudely made ring on his finger and Rory winced.

His voice was still quite low, but the room was silent. Cuan's head swivelled around, then jerked up when he heard his sister's name. His face was torn by different emotions, but the foremost one was shame. It must be galling for him to hear of his sister's competence as a silversmith, thought Mara watching him carefully and wishing she could comfort him.

'I think I will be going now, Toin,' he said rising to his feet with a valiant attempt at dignity. 'Thank you for a lovely meal.'

He was gone from the room before anyone could stop him. Toin gazed after him compassionately and then looked back at Rory. His expression hardened. 'Just a quick word before you go, Rory,' he said rising to his feet and firmly leading the way to the door.

There was silence in the room after the door closed behind the two men and no sound of voices from outside either. Toin must have taken Rory into one of the small side rooms. No doubt, as a *briuga*, Toin would have had to deal in the past with many quarrelsome young men. Despite the man's feebleness, Mara felt it would not be right to interfere. There was no doubt in her mind that Toin could manage this situation properly. She herself would have another word with Rory, she promised herself. He was not too clever and if his accusation of Cuan was manufactured then it should be easy to trip him up. If not, it was very serious, but it still proved nothing unless it could be corroborated in some way. No Brehon would convict a man on the bare word of another, especially involving such a serious crime as *fingal*. She joined Nuala who was inspecting each chess piece and questioning Daire.

'What about the knight?' Nuala was fingering the little piece. 'Who's that. Oh, I know, it's you, isn't it?'

Daire laughed, looking embarrassed, but Nuala was right. There was something about the athletic, squared shoulders that did make it look like Daire.

'The trouble is that the silver and copper pieces look different,' continued Nuala. 'I could see that the copper queen was Mara, but the silver queen didn't remind me so much of her and the silver knight looks like you, but not the copper knight. He is the dark knight. Perhaps you could have made the pieces look different? Still, I suppose you couldn't do that for a chess set.'

'It's wonderful to have the skill to make this,' said Malachy, joining them and examining the bishop. 'So this is my lord bishop of Kilfenora,' he mused with a smile, balancing the little figure in his palm.

'Poor Cuan,' said Nuala changing the subject suddenly. 'Father, what do you think is wrong with his hand? I felt it, and I could feel the tendons all bunched up inside the palm.'

'He was probably born with it,' said Malachy thoughtfully. 'I've seen such things.'

'Could it be cut open?'

'Nuala's mind is still dwelling on surgery,' said Mara looking at her with an affectionate smile.

'Not something I'd like to undertake,' said Malachy firmly. 'However, I suppose it would be possible. It might work, though I don't suppose that the hand would be too strong afterwards. Still I have seen a tendon sliced open after an accident with a flail and it healed up eventually. However, I would think – not that I know much about it – that the surgery might have had to be performed when he was a child.'

'Well, the lad is rich enough to get the best surgeons in Ireland, now,' said Turlough. 'That's true, isn't it, Mara? He's immensely rich, isn't he?'

'If there is no will, and it begins to look as if there is no will, then Cuan will get at least two-thirds of his father's wealth,' said Mara reluctantly, after a minute. She disliked talking about legal matters in public, but there was no harm in it, she supposed. The whole kingdom of the Burren was probably discussing Cuan and his mother and sister by now, especially after Muiris's evidence against Rory at Poulnabrone. She was still considering the matter when the door reopened.

'Well, that's two young men departed,' said Toin as he came back in.

'Where has Rory gone?' asked Nuala.

'I advised him to go back to his own house at Dooneyvardan,' said Toin firmly. 'I don't think that Newtown Castle is the place for him at the moment. I put a bit of pressure on him. He'll be back tomorrow and in a more reasonable mood and then I can talk properly to him and get him to apologize to Cuan.' He cast a glance up at the top of the cupboard where Mara had placed the zither, before adding lightly, 'What is the old story about the poet who sang a satirical verse about the river that refused to yield a salmon and the river rose up and threatened to drown the poet? He quickly sang a song of praise and then the river returned to its normal bed. If Rory praises Cuan and asks his pardon all this will blow over.'

'Has Cuan gone back to Newtown Castle?' asked Daire. 'If he has then I might rush and try to catch up with him. It would be easier for him if we came in together.'

Toin shook his head. 'No, I don't think that he has. I had a word with Tomás and he told me that the stableman saw Cuan going up the path to the mountain. No, Cuan has probably gone back to his farm.'

'He'll cool down better there,' said Nuala wisely. 'He was mad with rage. I could feel him shake all over.'

'Shame for this to happen,' said Daire thoughtfully. 'It's not right to say it perhaps, but now with Sorley dead, all his troubles should be over. In fact . . .'

He stopped and said no more and soon afterwards made his farewells and left without finishing his sentence.

Mara knew what he was about to say and she finished it for him in her mind. *With Sorley dead, most people's troubles are over.*

Fifteen

BRETHA NEMED DÉIDENACH (LAST LAWS ON
THE PRIVILEGES OF PROFESSIONAL PEOPLE)

Heptad 33

There are seven kinds of satire:

1. Wrongfully accusing someone of a crime

2. Making public an untrue story

3. Making sport of a man's appearance

4. Ridiculing a defect or deformity

5. Devising an insulting nickname

6. Teasing or taunting beyond the norm

7. Being the author of a song that satirizes

The penalty for unjust satire or mockery is a sum equivalent to a person's honour price.

&

'**H**AS EVERYONE COPIED DOWN the laws of satire now?' asked Mara, as, damp sponge in hand, she prepared to wipe the lime-washed board on the wall clear of the charcoal words.

'Just doing the last one,' said Hugh.

'This means that when Enda calls me a birdbrain then he has to pay me a fine,' said Moylan triumphantly.

'What *is* your honour price?' queried Enda with a superior air.

Moylan hesitated and looked at Mara for help.

'You don't know,' said Enda triumphantly. 'That's because you don't have one – you're under seventeen.'

'What would Cuan's honour price be, Brehon?' asked Fachtnan, ever the peacemaker.

'I'm not sure myself, Fachtnan,' confessed Mara. She glanced around at the eager, lively faces and said gently, 'there is no necessity to remind you all of the oath you swore at Michaelmas to preserve silence about any matter discussed here at the law school, is there?'

Emphatic nods greeted these words; she tried not to remind them too often of this point, as she liked them to feel that she trusted them. However, in this case when they were discussing Rory, who had been a close companion of the older boys, she felt the reminder was necessary.

'You see,' she went on, 'last night, when Rory sang that offensive song and when he shouted out these public accusations that Cuan murdered his father, I was considering this matter. First I thought that Cuan might be classified as an *ócaire*, since he has twenty acres of land, but now I think that cannot be right. After all, if he is his father's heir, he is one of the richest men in the kingdom.'

'Surely he will have the same honour price as Sorley?' Fachtnan sounded puzzled. 'And you said at Poulnabrone that Sorley's honour price was seven *séts*.'

'Yes, but you see,' said Mara rapidly, 'Sorley was a qualified silversmith – that determined his honour price; Cuan, poor lad, is qualified for nothing.'

'Strange, isn't it, Brehon?' Enda's active brain was working on the problem. 'Why do you think that there is no provision in the law for a man who is rich just because of inheritance?'

'I think it is because these laws are so old, Enda. They probably mostly date from over a thousand years; we know that they were in place when Saint Patrick came from Ireland. One of the first things that he did, apparently, was to review them and to reject those that he disliked, like the law of a fine, instead of a death, for murder.' It didn't do much good, she thought triumphantly. Here we are, more than a thousand years later and the Brehon law still rules in most of Ireland.

And then, because she was always careful never to criticize the Church in front of the boys, she hastened to divert their minds.

'I think that there is much work to do to update these laws; for instance, my own son-in-law, Oisín, in Galway, is a trader; he buys goods such as skins, Irish mantles, even silver; takes them to other countries, sells them, buys other goods in those countries, brings these goods back to Ireland and sells them in Galway, or even in Thomond. He makes a good living out of this, but there is nothing in Brehon law about a trader so he has no honour price.'

'He'd better stay in Galway, then,' said Shane looking aghast.

'But isn't Cuan now the owner of the silver mine?' asked Aidan. 'What's the honour price for a mine owner?'

'The nearest that I can find is the honour price for a mill owner,' said Mara. 'I suppose that if I were to have to judge a case where Cuan was involved then I would take that as my example and give him an honour price of seven *séts*. I would then tell as many other Brehons as I could of my decision and see what they think. Last summer King Turlough organized a meeting of the Brehons of the three kingdoms of Thomond, Corcomroe and Burren, to discuss these matters and we are hoping that next summer we will be able to include Brehons from other parts of Ireland – Cormac from Kinvarra will come, I'm sure, and his father from Cork. Perhaps your father will also come, Shane, although it is a long journey from Dungannon in the north.'

'About the murder,' said Aidan getting bored with the theoretical discussion, 'can we make a list of possibilities, Brehon? May I write them on the wall?'

'If you do it in your very best handwriting.' Mara tried to inject a note of severity into her voice, but Aidan was like an over-enthusiastic young puppy; it was hard to make him take any of his shortcomings seriously. He jumped up with a quick glance of triumph at Moylan, seized the long charred stick and wrote SUSPECTS in large letters on the whitewashed board on the wall. It was so beautifully written with a sweeping tail to the letter S that Mara, though she was worried about having a list of names under that heading, did not have the heart to tell him to rub it out. She cast a quick glance at the doorway. It was raining heavily so it was fairly unlikely that anyone would visit; in any case, Bran was now lying up against the door so no one could get in without a few minutes' delay and she could quickly wash the words off with the damp sponge lying in its bowl of water on the windowsill.

'Let's do them in alphabetical order,' suggested Enda. 'Otherwise people might be prejudiced by the name at the top of the list.'

'Good idea,' said Mara.

'I think,' said Fachtnan, hesitating a little, 'that we might have to put Anluan at the top of the list.'

'No,' said Moylan indignantly. 'He couldn't. He hasn't got the strength of a fly.'

'He's strong enough to poke a stick through the hole,' said Shane. 'But I agree that he is not very likely.'

'Let's give them points.' Enda, as usual, was bursting with ideas. 'Each reason to murder Sorley will be worth a point. Now who can name a reason for Anluan to murder?'

'Revenge for the lack of safety at the mine and no compensation for his terrible injuries,' said Shane.

'One point,' said Aidan, slashing down a stroke on the wall.

'Had a stick handy.' Hugh looked pleased with himself.

'Two points,' said Aidan, adding another stroke.

'Let's have minus points,' said Fachtnan. 'And I think I have one for Anluan; I think he is so afraid of pain that he would not risk being stung by a bee. Do you remember how he screamed when he thought Bran might hurt him? That's one minus point; the other is that he didn't know

Sorley would swell up and perhaps die from a bee sting, so that's two. And that leaves Anluan in the clear.'

'Shall I wipe his name?' Aidan looked around, all heads were nodding.

'And Cathal the sea captain was cleared by Toin.' Mara thought back to her interview. Yes, Toin had been quite certain.

'Then the next must be Cuan,' said Moylan, 'I can't think of anyone beginning with the letter B.'

Aidan wrote the word *Cuan* carefully and then looked around.

'Point one: he inherits his father's goods,' said Moylan rapidly.

'Point two: he probably hates his father,' added Hugh.

'Point three: he would know that Sorley swelled up after a bee sting,' said Shane.

'Point four: we know, from Rory, that he was there near to his father just before the murder.' Enda was triumphant. The line of strokes was looking impressive.

'Any minus points?' Mara looked around at her scholars.

'This isn't any point of law, or factual point,' said Fachtnan hesitating a little, 'but I just think, from what I've seen of him and from what you've told us, Brehon, that Cuan is just too gutless to do a thing like that. After all, whoever murdered Sorley that day, he or she had to act very fast and not care about the consequences. If Sorley had not been killed, had not even been stung, he would have seen what had happened and would have been very angry. I don't think that Cuan would have risked that.'

'What does everyone else think?' Mara turned to look at her scholars. The younger ones were looking unsure, but Enda nodded vigorously.

'That's worth a minus four mark,' he said. 'Especially when you think that the crime would have been *fingal* since it was his own father who was murdered; Cuan would not want to have been put out to sea in a boat without oars, to die or live out his life in banishment from the kingdom.'

'Possibly.' Mara looked dubious. 'It's a very good point, Fachtnan, and you made it very well. However, sometimes a boy like Cuan, who has always been abused and denied affection, can be pushed beyond the bounds of reason. Let's give him minus two and that leaves him on the list.'

'Deirdre is next,' said Moylan. 'I vote we give her a point as she has now got back to the castle and the life as a rich lady.'

'I agree,' said Aidan writing the name quickly and then putting a stroke beside it.

'I disagree,' said Shane calmly. 'She couldn't have known that the Brehon would have taken her part. I vote we give a minus for lack of knowledge of the future.'

No one argued with that and Mara said nothing. Of course, Toin had cleared Deirdre as well as Cathal, but Cathal had not noticed Deirdre. It would be difficult to say who was right. Personally she thought that a clever, self-contained woman like Deirdre was unlikely to have taken a chance like that. This murder was a quick-thinking, but very reckless act.

'Rory must be next,' said Hugh who had been counting the alphabet on his fingers and muttering under his breath.

'Well, one big fat point for all the silver and goods that he was going to get his hands on when he married Una,' said Enda with emphasis.

'And another for the fact that the betrothal document stated, according to him, that it was not a union of man upon woman's property, according to Brehon law, but a union according to English law where the man has complete control of the woman's property.' Mara looked around. Every head was nodding solemnly; they all saw her point.

'And he was last into the church,' she continued. 'All the evidence points to that. Of course, according to himself he came from a different direction, but I only have his word for that.'

'Four points for Rory; so he's our front-runner,' said Aidan.

'But couldn't he have had everything without murdering Sorley?' Morley asked.

'He might have had to wait a long time for it, and Sorley might have given him very little for himself once they were married. Sorley sounds like the sort of man who would have enjoyed keeping Rory at his beck and call.' Enda, as usual, passed judgement shrewdly.

'And there was another suitor.' Briefly Mara told them about Ulick and the dazzling prospect that he had held out to Sorley.

'So Sorley might have been the father of a countess.' Enda gave a long low whistle, while the other boys tried to look impressed, though Mara suspected that none of them actually knew what a countess was.

'And the grandfather of an earl if Ulick died,' added Enda. 'Well, that certainly is worth another point. Rory might have seen Sorley's riches vanishing out of his sight unless he moved quickly.'

'Any minus points?' Mara looked around at the eager faces.

They all thought about this very carefully, she was glad to notice. This was an important part of their training: the ability to weigh the facts and to decide without reference to claims of either friendship or affection was essential for any qualified Brehon.

'None,' said Fachtnan solemnly and they all echoed the word.

'What about Una?' asked Hugh after a minute.

'She believed that she was going to inherit. That must be worth one point,' said Aidan, looking at his friends enquiringly and then putting a stroke beside the name when he received a few nods.

'Yes, but if she had to marry Rory then she would not have had control over her possessions, if it were a union of equality,' said Hugh. 'I vote a minus point for that.'

'But she didn't have to marry him, once Sorley was safely dead; she could always have said no.' Enda was emphatic and as usual everyone nodded agreement.

'Or burned the agreement.' Mara smiled. Una might not be very likeable, but she had plenty of guts, as the boys would say.

'But she would have risked *fingal* as well as Cuan. I vote a minus for that. Everyone agree?' Aidan added the minus after a cursory glance around.

'Also, I'm sure she was there in church with her maid quite early on.' Mara nodded as Aidan went along the names, crossing out most.

'So now we are really left with Cuan or Rory as possible murderers,' remarked Enda.

'Points are all very well, but they don't tell you everything.' Fachtnan looked thoughtfully at the list and tugged his curly brown hair.

'There's one name that we haven't put down,' said Shane, his black eyes sparkling with fun. 'I'll spell it for you, Aidan. It's U N K N O W N.'

'Someone who hates Sorley,' said Moylan in a rush. He, as well as the others, had been looking at the names with an air of disappointment and dissatisfaction.

'Someone who was in his debt.'

'Someone from his past.'

'Someone whom he had cheated.'

'Someone who was mad with rage.'

'The hunt is on, lads,' said Enda grimly. 'No one can get away with a secret and unlawful killing in our kingdom of the Burren.'

sixteen

BRETHA COMAITHCHESA

(JUDGEMENTS OF NEIGHBOURHOODS)

Every neighbourhood has a duty to its members. In the case of a disaster:

    1. By fire

    2. By flood

    3. By going astray

neighbour must come to the assistance of neighbour.

☘

'CUMHAL, IF YOU ARE sending a man to Drumcreehy Bay for the fish could he carry a message to Cathal the sea captain to come and see me?' asked Mara.

'Fish,' exclaimed Aidan with disgust.

'It will do you good,' said Mara bracingly. She was not too keen on fish herself, but the priest at Noughaval, after a recent visit from the bishop of Kilfenora, had become very emphatic on the observation of the Friday fast and Mara felt that the law school should set a good example.

However, when she released the scholars from the schoolhouse at dinnertime Brigid was waiting for her with a message from Cumhal.

'You won't be seeing Cathal for a month of Sundays, Brehon,' she announced. 'Cumhal was told at Drumcreehy that the sea captain set off in his ship last Wednesday, going to France, he was; so Cumhal was told.'

'Strange! I thought he said that he wouldn't be going for another week. We met him, King Turlough and I, when we were going to the abbey on Sunday.' Mara looked around for Cumhal, wanting to question him further. Normally he took his dinner at the same time as the lads. Perhaps he had heard the reason for the sea captain's sudden change of plan.

'He's gone over to the bard's house at Dooneyvardan, Brehon,' said Brigid, following the direction of her eyes. 'There's some men come over from Rathborney, from New-town Castle. That young bard, Rory, is missing and the silversmith's wife is trying to find him.'

Wife, not daughter, noted Mara, listening with interest. Perhaps Deirdre wanted to get rid of this strong-minded, surly daughter of hers. She would probably be able to get Cuan to agree to give his sister a substantial dowry – perhaps almost as much as the father had intended.

'The story is that Rory was seen going up Cappanab-haile Mountain yesterday morning and there hasn't been sight or sound of him ever since, and you know what a heavy rain and mist there was the last few nights,' continued Brigid with relish. Though the kindest of women, she did enjoy a disaster.

'What! Do they think that he's still on the mountain?'
Mara was startled.

'That's exactly what they do think, Brehon,' said Brigid
with heavy emphasis. 'There was plenty saw him go, but
there's none to say that they saw him return. Muiris is getting
up a *slógad* to hunt for him. And there's Cumhal now, coming across the Moher Field.' She rushed to the wall, closely
followed by all the scholars, who had forgotten their hunger
in the excitement.

'Muiris,' said Mara thoughtfully. Of course Muiris was
usually the one who organized the mountain rescue parties.
Despite his low stature, he was immensely strong, had huge
endurance and always seemed to be very competent at directing a large crowd of well-meaning helpers.

'Any news,' shrilled Brigid, as Cumhal crossed the last
wall. He said something, but his words were lost in the
distance. However the shake of his head was ominous.

'Would it be all right if I took young Donie and a few
ropes, to join in the *slógad*, Brehon?' he said when he came
near.

'Could we go, too, Brehon?' pleaded Enda.

Mara looked at the noontime sun, illuminating the pale
yellow hazel leaves and warming the nut clusters to a rich
fawn, and then turned to gaze at Cappanabhaile Mountain.
The sky was a clear blue with no clouds in it and the folded
terraces of the mountain shone silver. This day would probably be bright and sunny until dusk and then would come a
mist, filling up the valleys and spreading gradually up to the
High Burren and on up to the mountains above. Cumhal
said nothing; the decision would have to be hers, but it he

had any fears for the safety of the boys he would have voiced them instantly.

'Yes, we'll all go, for a couple of hours only, though. And we'll take Bran.'

'That's a great idea, Brehon,' enthused Shane. 'Bran knows Rory very well. He's bound to find him.'

Cumhal said nothing still; he was a man of few words, but he took from his pouch a purple fillet and handed it to her. Mara had often seen Rory wearing this around his head. Undoubtedly Cumhal had found it at Rory's house in Dooneyvardan. She hid a smile. She often thought that Brigid and Cumhal knew her mind before she had fully made it up, herself. Cumhal had obviously expected her to join in the hunt for the missing young man and had brought something for Bran to track.

'Feels sweaty,' said Moylan taking it from her. 'Bran will definitely be able to find him if you show him this.'

'Don't put too many other scents on it,' warned Mara taking it back and storing it carefully in her pouch. It probably didn't matter too much; Bran was quite familiar with the name 'Rory' and would look for him once she gave the order.

'Rory's probably broken his leg,' said Aidan with relish.

'Or arm,' said Hugh, not to be outdone.

'A broken arm wouldn't stop him coming back down the mountain, birdbrain,' said Aidan scathingly.

'Now then, Aidan, you mind your tongue, or else there'll be no dinner; take no notice of him, Hugh,' said Brigid, ushering the boys into the kitchen house. Brigid had a very soft spot for Hugh; his red-gold curls and his small freckled face seemed to bring out her maternal instinct. 'They'd better put on their heavy boots once they've had their dinner, Brehon,' she called back. 'And put their mantles in their satchels, too.'

'Thanks, Brigid,' said Mara. She could leave everything to Brigid and have a quiet half an hour to think carefully about this disappearance. In all probability this disappearance had nothing to do with the murder of Sorley, but perhaps it had. Something told her that it fitted the pattern which was beginning to form in her mind.

❧

Muiris had gathered a large crowd by the time the group from the law school had arrived at the foot of the mountain. There were many people there from Rathborney, but also a big group from the High Burren and its valleys. Some of these had walked, but the majority had ridden. Toin's field had been pressed into service for the horses and his stableman was there revelling in the excitement. He had been the last to see Rory and so his story was greatly in demand.

'I said to the master, *that's Rory all right, my lord*,' he was saying as Mara handed over her mare into his charge. Toin, himself, was there, his face grey and anxious. Mara crossed over to him.

'Don't worry,' she said reassuringly. 'With a crowd like this, they'd uncover a fieldmouse up on that mountain.'

He smiled at that, but his eyes were dull, sunken deep into the sockets on his emaciated face. Mara looked at him sharply and then looked all around. There were a few of the servants there from Newtown Castle. Daire was there, she discovered, chatting to Aoife and to her brothers, but Cuan was nowhere in the crowd.

'Have you seen Cuan since Wednesday night?' she asked.

Toin looked uncertain, shook his head, and then nodded it. 'I think so,' he said hesitantly, and then immediately contradicted himself, saying, 'or perhaps that was Sunday.' He looked confused and Mara did not press him. There was a pungent smell of poppy syrup from him; his pain was getting to an almost unbearable stage, she thought compassionately and the dose that he needed now was robbing him of his wits. She saw Malachy chatting to her neighbour Diarmuid and signalled to him with a lift of her eyebrows. He came across instantly.

'Toin, I think you should be in bed,' he said, feeling for the old man's pulse. 'Shall I leave Nuala with you? I'd like to go up the mountain, myself. If the lad has broken a leg or an ankle, it will be better if I bind it up on the spot and stop any further damage while they are carrying him down, but Nuala would wish to stay with you. She enjoys your company. She told me yesterday that she has learnt so much from you that she is writing it all down.'

Toin managed a smile. 'No, take the child,' he said. 'It's not right for a young girl to be cooped up with an old man. Let her enjoy herself with the boys and girls of her own age. I'm beginning to feel a little better now. I'll go back to the house.'

Tomás was on hand and they set off, Toin leaning heavily on his servant. Mara looked a question at Malachy.

'A matter of weeks,' he said briefly. 'The heart's slowing

right down now. When I put my hand on his chest this morning, I could feel it stop, and then start again, very slowly. He's an old man. That's probably the way that he will go – that would be the merciful way.'

'We have to get into groups.' Fachtnan came running across, followed by Nuala, her black plaits bouncing against her thin back as she strove to keep up with his long legs.

'Four or five to a group, Muiris says,' she gasped. 'Who will come with us?'

'Well, perhaps if I lend you Fachtnan, Enda and Moylan,' said Mara to Malachy, 'I'll keep Aidan, Hugh and Shane and with Bran that will make five in our group.' She had been going to ask Cumhal to take some of the boys, but he had already planted himself next to Muiris and some other habitual climbers. Cumhal would be of more use if he did not have to be burdened with the care of the scholars. It would be better for them to go with Malachy. Moylan would be well behaved without Aidan, and Nuala would enjoy their company. She looked around. Everyone was moving quickly and efficiently into groups and waiting quietly for Muiris to give the orders.

It was wonderful the force of neighbourly solidarity, thought Mara; a few days ago, this man Muiris was looking for the blood of the young bard, and now he, and all of the others, few of whom could have liked Rory much, none of whom was related to him; all of these people had given up a day's work at a busy time for them and had turned out to search for him.

'Keep together until we reach the foot of the mountain and then spread out,' shouted Muiris. He had Daire and his two sons and Aoife by his side. 'If anyone finds him then give a good loud bellow, not a shout or a screech – these sounds don't carry on the mountainside, just a good old *béic* on two notes, that's what will be heard by us all.'

A few of the younger ones, his own sons and daughter amongst them, giggled as he gave a demonstration yodelling sound, slapping his horny hand against his mouth, but he hushed them with a glance.

'I've got a hunting horn,' he continued, and blew one short blast on it. 'One means I've found the man. But if I blow two long blasts, it means that the mist is coming up and you'd better all get down the mountain as best you can. I'll keep blowing until everyone is safe down. With the help of God,' he added in a perfunctory fashion. It was obvious that Muiris was going to rely on himself rather than on God.

'We've got a horn, too, Muiris,' shouted the O'Lochlainn boys. They had Mairéad with them, noticed Mara, feeling thankful that she had allocated Enda to Malachy's group, as she watched how the girl tossed her red curls, eyeing the young men around her.

'I've got a tin whistle,' called Nuala in her clear voice and Muiris gave her one of his rare smiles. Nuala was very popular among the people of the Burren, more so than Malachy, who tended to be rather distant in his relationships with them.

'The physician's group better stay fairly near my group,' he said. 'If the man is injured, then we can get Malachy to him by the quickest route. And now, in the name of God, let's get to work.'

Never once, thought Mara, as she and her little group followed the long procession trailing up the path beside the little Rathborney river, did Muiris mention the name of Rory. It was probably best that way. Now Rory was a man lost on the mountain for twenty-four hours – not Rory the bard who had deceived and humiliated the beloved daughter of Muiris.

❀

It was easy walking for some time as the pathway led along a valley between the Cappanabhaile and Gleninagh mountains. The river ran beside the path; once it must have been a large river to have carved its way between the two great peaks, but now it was just a trickling stream that dived into an underground cave as soon as the hill began to get steep. Many ancient enclosures, their walls still massive and towering over the humans, lined the way. In a place where water was scarce and before man lacked the iron tools to dig for wells through the rock, this was the place to live.

The crowd, mostly the young and the fit, made rapid progress and when they reached Drumbrickaun, most turned and began to climb the lower slopes of the mountain.

'Spread out,' shouted Muiris. 'No point in everyone going up the same way, bunched together like that: spread out and check behind every rock.'

'Aren't we going up Cappanabhaile?' complained Aidan, watching his friend Moylan scrambling over the rocks like a mountain goat.

'Not yet,' said Mara serenely. 'There's no point in releasing Bran here; he would just be dashing around and licking everyone. Let's go up as far as Lios na gCat.' She hadn't taken the purple fillet from her pouch yet, though the reason she had given Aidan was not entirely valid. She was puzzled by the absence of Cuan; he was probably the only male from Rathborney who was not present; she was anxious to see whether he was still at his mountain farm.

A few other groups followed them, obviously thinking of going around by the west-facing slopes at Feenagh. There was no hurry, though. Judging by the sun it was only about an hour after noon; the light would last another four hours or so and, with luck, the mist should not fall until dusk. The air was still balmy; as they rounded a bend on the narrow stony lane they surprised a mountain hare, sleeping peacefully against a warm rock. He bounded away merrily, his white tail waving an impudent salute to the indignant Bran, who strained at the leash until Mara admonished him.

'It shows how warm the weather is still; that hare will be almost white all over when another month goes by. The king told me that our hares are different to the hares in England; they have much smaller hares which remain brown in winter and summer,' Mara told her scholars. None of them was listening; they were all looking over their shoulders at the crowd that was now fanning out across the mountain slopes.

'There's Lios na gCat,' said Shane thankfully. 'Are we going to turn off here, Brehon?'

'Let Bran smell that sweaty hair fillet,' said Aidan eagerly. 'It really pongs . . .' He stopped abruptly because a slight figure had emerged from the filthy, derelict house. 'I didn't know anyone lived there,' he muttered, looking around at the filthy farmyard and the moss-covered cabins.

Mara waited for a moment. The two groups behind them overtook and then turned right to go up the mountain slopes. She could hear them call to each other as they separated, one going to the left and the other keeping straight ahead.

'Ah, Cuan,' called Mara, her tone bland and friendly. 'Have you heard the news? Rory the bard has been missing since early on Thursday morning.'

He came towards them slowly. He had heard her; she was sure of that. It seemed more as if he were giving himself time to think before he replied.

'No,' he said eventually, 'no, I hadn't heard that.'

He was still dressed in the fine clothes that Toin had lent him, she noticed. They were no longer so fine, though. The red tunic was torn in one place and splashes of mud marred its smooth wool. The *léine*, which he wore beneath it, was grubby and soiled with yellow sweat stains. The hem was filthy and so were his sandals.

'Have you seen him since Wednesday night?' demanded Mara.

His eyes went from her to the listening boys and he flushed. His dull eyes suddenly became full of fury. She could see how the memory of humiliation was still fresh in his mind. She wondered whether Rory had come to apologize. And if he had done so, what had been his reception? If the apology had been accepted, there would have been no point in Cuan staying up here in his mountain farm. Where was the young bard, then?

'No, I haven't seen him,' he said eventually.

'We're searching for him,' persisted Mara, 'would you like to join us? He's been missing since Thursday morning, now.'

'No, I wouldn't!' he shouted, thrusting his face almost into hers and causing Hugh to step back in alarm. 'Why should I? Why should I look for that fellow? He's done nothing but insult me and mock me from the day that my father brought him to Newtown Castle. What do you come bothering me like that for?'

It was like a small child having a temper tantrum, thought Mara, eyeing him severely. Her grandson, Domhnall, used to have fits of screaming like that, before he learned to talk properly and to argue with his mother, instead.

'Don't you dare speak to me like that, Cuan,' she said sternly, once the sound of his hysterical outburst died down. 'Now, I would advise you to clean yourself up and to go down and take your rightful place in your father's house. It's for you to uncover his hearth, as the law says, and to take possession of his goods.'

'I'm sorry, Brehon,' he muttered. His eyes sought hers, like an apologetic dog. She felt sorry for him and sorry for his humiliation. Perhaps she should have sent the boys away before speaking to him. She made them a quick signal and obediently they moved down the path towards the rusty gate. Mara waited for a moment then, but he said no more. It was time to leave; she would get no more out of him. The boys moved restlessly. They wanted to be off finding Rory.

'I will meet you there tomorrow, Saturday afternoon,' she said firmly giving him a quick pat on the arm. 'We will settle everything, then. Don't forget. I will be expecting you at Newtown Castle on Saturday afternoon.' She repeated the words with emphasis. There were times when she began to doubt again whether he had all of his wits. There was something very unstable about him today.

Cuan stared up the mountain, almost as if he were looking at a distant figure. He kicked a stone violently, clenched his fists as if about to hit someone and then turned on his heel and went back up the path and into the house. He slammed the door with such violence that the leather hinge, holding it in place, split and the door gaped open.

'Whew!' whistled Aidan. 'Temper!'

'Brehon, when are you going to release Bran?' asked Shane impatiently.

'Now, I think,' said Mara. She took the purple fillet from her pouch and held it for a moment. It was woven from bright threads of purple with a few of red in the weft between. Was it Aoife that made it for the young bard? She held it out towards the dog's eager nose. 'Seek, Bran, seek,' she urged and then bent down and released the leash from his neck.

The dog understood her; she was sure of that. He sniffed at the fillet, looked along the path to the house, took a few steps back and then started to smell the path behind, the way that they had come up. His nose travelled along the grass-covered middle of it and once again he started to move back down the mountain.

'Rory didn't come up as far as this,' said Aidan impatiently. 'I knew we had come up too far.'

'Hush,' said Mara. 'Don't distract the dog.' She would slip on the leash when he had found the scent properly, she planned.

Bran was obviously confused, going back down the lane and then drifting up it again, his nose glued to the ground. Then he came to the gate and stood for a long time there, glancing up at Mara and then down at the ground again.

Mara's heart sank. What was the dog trying to tell her? That Rory had come here, to the gate of this farm? That he had stood there for some time. Stood in the shelter of the large hawthorn bush that grew by the gate. That was what Bran was trying to say.

And if the dog was indicating a true and faithful account of Rory's movements yesterday morning, what happened next? Had Cuan come out? He would undoubtedly have done so. Very few people passed on this track. Surely Cuan must have come out. And if he did, what happened after that? Was there a fight between the two boys? They would have been evenly matched, both slightly built, neither used to hard labour. But there would have been a difference. Rory would have been unconcerned, slightly mocking, perhaps, but Cuan would have been filled with a murderous rage. She glanced around. The place was untidy, littered with farmyard utensils and tools – most of them covered with dung or even moss – but on top of a large boulder an iron rod was lying, and that had no moss on it.

And then Bran finally made up his mind. With a quick bark, he left the gatepost and began to zigzag up the hill. Mara followed as quickly as she could; the three boys were running but none could not keep up with the fast pace of the dog.

A huge enclosure stood to the left of the path on the brow of the hill, built into the face of the cliff. This was Lios Mac Sioda, the home of Sheedy. Mara had planned to call in there and have a word with him, but Bran was going too fast, scurrying along with his nose to the ground. She would not break his concentration now, she decided. In any case, it looked like a steep climb to get to the house within those ancient walls.

'Bran's turning, Brehon,' shouted Shane.

'He's going the wrong way,' wailed Hugh.

The path they were following would have still led along the old river valley between the two mountains, but Bran had turned left. The boys scrambled after him and Mara followed as quickly as she could. She had just rounded the corner in time to see Bran, no longer on the gentle slope, but now scaling the rocky surface of Gleninagh South.

'Bran, come back,' she called, breaking her own resolution. It would be impossible for them to keep up with Bran here; he had four legs, they had two. He was two years old, at the height of his strength and fitness. He was bred for chasing wolves and could outrun any one of them.

'Bran,' she shouted again, but he ignored her. It was useless, she knew that, but she toiled on, scrambling up the clints, which, like endless steps of stairs, scaled the heights of Gleninagh.

'I can see him, Brehon,' shrieked Shane who had got ahead of the others. Wirily built, like Bran he was supremely fit and could outrun others taller than himself. 'He's heading down to Formoyle.'

'Formoyle!' Mara stopped for a moment to draw breath. Formoyle was another one of these ancient settlements in the dry valley of the Caher river. What possible reason could Rory have for going to Formoyle? There was nothing there but ancient ruins. She sat down beside a small stunted juniper bush which was sheltering a clump of burnet roses. Amazingly one pure white flower bloomed among the black hips. She waited fingering the petals until Shane had climbed back down again.

'I've lost sight of him,' he said disconsolately. Shane was especially fond of Bran so Mara assumed a nonchalant air.

'We'll follow on across the saddle,' she said. 'He'll slow down soon.'

The saddle was the high plateau of rock that lay between the two river valleys. The ground seemed as if some ancient plough worked by giants had chopped the stones into hundreds of small rocks. The flat slabs were heavily scored with lines as if a coulter had been dragged along their surface. Here and there, where goat droppings had fertilized the small hollows, there were exquisite little rock gardens of ferns and even, in one of them, three tiny white flowers of wild strawberries, warmed by the stored heat of the limestone, blossomed among them as if it were May again. But mainly it was just unrelieved boulders and crushed stone. The slanting sun made it a dazzling sight.

Mara did not rush. There was no possibility of anyone catching up with Bran; he would return once he lost the trail. In any case, the ground was treacherous and she had no wish for anyone to sprain an ankle.

'I haven't been up here for ages,' she said looking around. 'I remember that there was an old fort here, a huge one with a door high enough to let a giant walk through, that's why it's called Caher Ard Dorais. Can you see it yet, any of you?'

Shane, who was still ahead of the others, shook his head. Mara began to get a little worried. As she remembered it Caher Ard Dorais was about halfway on this rocky ground between the two river valleys. The sun was now directly in their faces. It was moving rapidly into the west. They would go as far as the ancient enclosure, she planned, but then they should turn back.

It took quite some time to reach the fort. They climbed

on the high banks and could see for a long distance from there. The green valley of the Caher river was quite visible, but there was no sign of Bran. A herd of cattle walked slowly along, pausing to take a bite here and there from the succulent clumps of grass beside the river. Bran had been trained to ignore sheep and cows, but it was unlikely that the cows would be so at ease if he were anywhere in the vicinity. They would have been glancing nervously over their shoulders at the slightest smell or sound of a dog.

'We'll have to turn back now,' she said decisively as they scrambled down. 'We came out to find Rory and there is no sign of him anywhere. We'll find the others and join in the search around Cappanabhaile. That's the place where he'll be found.'

'But what about Bran?' asked Shane anxiously.

'Don't worry about him, he'll be back soon,' she said reassuringly and then raised her voice to summon Aidan and Hugh who had gone to explore inside the giant's door. 'Come back, boys, we'll go back to Cappanabhaile,' she called. 'We'll just see if Sheedy is at his place on our way back. He might have some more sensible news of Rory than Cuan had. In any case, he was at Father David's burial so I do need to ask him a few questions. Bran will join us when he's caught whatever he's chasing, or when he gets tired of it.'

It was true, she told herself. There was no point in trying to follow the dog; he would come back when he had found his quarry. There was little doubt in her mind now; Bran had lost Rory's scent when he had been hesitating around the gate of Lios na gCat. He had lost that faint twenty-eight-hour-old scent of the young bard and then picked up a newer stronger scent – of a fox, perhaps, or even of a wolf. Either would have accounted for his sudden excitement. She wasn't worried about the dog; like all of his breed he had a strong homing instinct; he would come home by nightfall. She dismissed the matter from her mind.

But had Rory come to Cuan's gate? And if he had, where had he gone then? Was he really lying injured somewhere on Cappanabhaile Mountain? Or was there a more sinister explanation for his absence?

seventeen

Bechbretha (bee judgements)

Dírann, unshared land, is land available for all to use. It is mainly mountainous land, deep forest land or marsh land.

A man is entitled to hunt freely upon such places.

If he finds a swarm of bees there, he may make it his own if he pays one-third of its value to the Church or to his taoiseach.

❦

Lios Mac Síoda had been built for defence. Its western face stood directly over a hundred-feet-high cliff of sheer rock, the small house dwarfed by the huge double walls that curved in a semicircle behind it. At first it seemed as if only an eagle could broach this impenetrable stronghold, but on the southern side there was a small gap in the wall and a well-worn track leading up showed this was the way that Sheedy himself entered the stronghold.

'No one around, I'd say,' said Hugh as Mara and her scholars dragged themselves up the steep path.

It was true that there was a deserted feel about the place. No cows lowing, no dogs barking, no geese cackling; everything was very quiet. Even though the path they followed was obviously used, the grass beaten down, yet it seemed to be the width of one man only with long thorny briars of dog roses reaching across their heads, and the tiny ivory heads of pointed ink-cap mushrooms remained unbroken in the cool depths of the mosses on either side of the path.

And yet there was someone living there. A pungent, bitter smell of peat filled the air and a plume of purple-grey rose from a hole in the roof of the cabin-like house. Beside the gap leading into the small haggard in front of the house was a pickaxe. It was thick in fresh mud and had a strange smell from it. Mara sniffed at it. The pickaxe had a smell of sulphur, just the same smell as they had all noticed when they had visited the silver mine.

'Do you think that there is anyone there?' Hugh spoke in a low voice. Mara wasn't surprised to hear a slight tremor in it. There was something strange about this place. However, she had to see Sheedy again at some stage and it would be ridiculous to pass his door without making an effort. She raised a hand to tap on the door, but it suddenly opened and the man was on the doorstep staring at them as if he had never seen humans in this place before.

He was such a strange-looking little man – a small, neat man, with a bald head and watery blue eyes. He was not much above thirty, guessed Mara, but the loss of hair made him look older. He said nothing and made no gesture to invite them inside. This was strange in the Burren where the words, 'come in, come in,' always seemed to be inseparable from the action of opening the door. This man just stood and looked and expressed no surprise at seeing a woman and three boys on his doorstep.

'You are Sheedy?' asked Mara in a friendly way. He still stared at her; it was obvious that he had not remembered her from the day at the silver mines so she added, 'I am Mara, Brehon of the Burren, and these boys are my scholars.'

Was he going to ask her in, she wondered. And while she was wondering, he took one step forward, pulled the door behind him so vigorously that it slammed loudly and then began to walk down the path towards the gap.

'I must be getting on with my work,' he muttered, as if they had just finished a half-hour talk.

'You've heard that Sorley the silversmith was murdered in the graveyard on the day of Father David's burial?' asked Mara quickly, raising her voice. She felt she needed to pierce through a fog in this man's brain.

'What?' he stopped for a moment and then went on. Mara hastened after him.

'You were there, on that Thursday morning, over a week ago. Many people testified that you were there. You came in late, didn't you?'

'That's right.' He gazed at her with annoyance, rather as one might look at a bee impeding progress.

'When you were outside, did you see anyone? Did you see anyone near the graveyard, after the bell had gone for the service.'

He stopped then and considered the matter for a

moment. Then he spoke. His voice had the rusty air of one who did not use the organ too frequently.

'I hold this land from the king,' he said, a note of fanaticism entering his voice. 'I, and my father before me, we held this land. We pay tribute for it, we pay tribute to the O'Lochlainn and he pays tribute to the king. What more can we do?'

'No more, surely,' said Mara soothingly.

'I must get on with my work,' he said again. It seemed as though he clung to the one sentence as his way out of this unexpected encounter.

'Have you any milch cows?' asked Shane, gazing around at the overgrown haggard. The question was understandable. It did not look as if there was any work in progress for Sheedy to do. There was no trace of any farmyard, no haystacks, no cow muck; the stone-girt haggard was filled with frothing masses of the small pink Herb-Robert flowers, each small blossom set daintily amongst its lacy foliage. No cow had tramped through here for months, or even a year thought Mara, as she waited to hear what the man would say; there was nothing here but a strange silence and emptiness.

'Cows! How can I have milch cows?' Sheedy stared at Shane with a bemused expression. 'How can I have any cows, little gentleman, when all my land is poisoned by that man, Sorley? No grass can grow with that filthy stuff flowing down the hill. Cows need grass, you know, and they need clean water, too, you know that, don't you?' He spoke in the voice that would be used to a very young child, bending down slightly to look into the boy's eyes.

Shane ignored that; he was a boy who was always confident with adults. 'What's wrong with your water, then?' he asked with a puzzled frown.

'The hill is poisoned, that's what's wrong, little gentleman. He's poisoned the hill, the king's own hill has been poisoned.' He said the last words in a sing-song tone of voice. 'My spring has been poisoned. Will you tell the king that, little gentleman? Even the bees will be poisoned soon and what will we all do, then?'

'Bees?' queried Shane. 'How can the bees get poisoned?'

Sheedy said nothing. He did not appear to hear Shane's question. He walked briskly down the feet-worn path, bent down and slung the pickaxe over his back.

'I must be getting on with my work,' he said again.

'Wait a minute. You haven't answered my question.' Mara made her voice authoritative but it had little effect on this strange man. As if directed by an inner voice, he marched down the lane, calling over his shoulder, 'I must get on with my work'.

'You should answer the Brehon when she asks you a question,' reproved Aidan, taking his responsibilities as a senior member of the law school seriously and dodging in front of Sheedy to block his progress.

'It's for the king to answer all questions,' said Sheedy in a high-pitched, strange voice. He pushed Aidan aside with great ease and then went on down the hillside singing lustily in a strange, high-pitched voice: 'The king is the king of all of the bees . . .'

'Is he mad?' Hugh asked the question in an awed voice.

'He does seem strange,' said Mara thoughtfully, 'but

that could be because he lives alone. When you are Brehons you may have to decide if someone is a *dásachtach* and to do that you must hear all the available evidence and detach external mannerisms from real insanity.'

They received this in silence and she thought with some compunction that at times they must feel that there were too many laws for their brains to absorb.

'What do you think Sheedy is doing with that pickaxe?' she asked. That was a simpler and more down-to-earth question.

'Perhaps he's hoping to find silver on his land,' said Hugh eagerly. 'I've been wondering whether there might be silver on the land around my father's place at Carron. My father says that it is very expensive to buy the ore from the merchant ships that come into Galway from Spain. If he could find silver he could have a mine.'

'I reckon that Sheedy is going towards Sorley's mine,' said Aidan, stopping to listen. 'He's going down the Rathborney path, now. Listen, you can hear him singing his strange song about the king of the bees.'

'Surely it should be the queen of the bees.' Shane had a logical mind.

'He's definitely crazy, Brehon.' Aidan sounded scared. Suddenly he had realized that he was the eldest scholar present. All of his years at the law school he had relied on the older boys and now a note of deep worry sounded in his voice. Mara decided to allow Sheedy to go. Her first responsibility was to her young scholars.

'Perhaps you're right,' she said gazing after Sheedy. He had a lethal weapon there, slung carelessly across his back;

she had no right to expose these young boys to any danger. 'Let him get ahead,' she said in a low voice, 'and then we'll join the others on Cappanabhaile.'

'Shall we go down the Rathborney path after him?' asked Hugh in a slightly uncertain voice.

'No, we'll just climb up here at the back and go across Feenagh and then down the other side.' It would be simpler to go by the Rathborney path, but Mara was determined to let Sheedy get well ahead and, if possible, have people like Cumhal and Muiris nearby when she encountered him again.

'Yes, let's,' said Shane enthusiastically and, followed by the others, began the steep climb at the back of Lios Mac Sioda. They were all soaked in sweat and panting hard by the time they reached the top of the cliff face, but there was a disappointment ahead of them; there was no possibility of turning to go back towards Cappanabhaile and Rathborney as the cliff on the eastern side dropped down, sheer as the wall of a house.

'What'll we do, Brehon?' asked Hugh.

'I think we'd better go on up to the next terrace,' said Mara, looking back down the way that they came. 'I don't think that I fancy going back down that way again. It was hard enough to climb up it, but I think it could be quite dangerous to try to climb back down.'

She was annoyed with herself. She wished that she had never bothered with Sheedy, or with Bran, either. Both of these had delayed her little group and now the sky had turned a pale shade of gold and the air was suddenly cooler and damper. When they reached the top of the next terrace the pale blue sea was visible with a streak of amber across its smooth surface. The misty outlines of the Aran Islands were beginning to dissolve and merge with the sky beyond. The sun was near to setting.

'If we go on up here a little this way, Brehon,' said Shane returning from a quick reconnoitre, 'we can actually get back down again – it's quite an easy path, this way.'

'We'll follow you then, Shane,' said Mara, trying to impress on her mind never to do this sort of thing again. Her great fault was her impulsiveness. It worked much of the time: a quick decision, and then a task was done, or a problem solved, but there were times when it got her into trouble and this looked like being one of those times. If she did get those boys back safely, she promised herself, she would send Cumhal and Seán to fetch, in a dignified way, any future suspects for questioning to Cahermacnaghten, and never go scrambling around a mountainside again after them.

Shane's way down was a good one. It was steep, but the rocks were broken into slabs and they could go down, step by step, in perfect safety. However, the mist was now rising in erratic leaps and bounds. One minute they were gazing around an ocean of grey stone, the next they could barely see a few feet in front of them. Mara began to worry that her sense of direction, never her strongest point, might lead her astray. The trouble was that they could not steer a straight path; there was always a boulder to go around, or a small chasm to avoid. She prayed that they would reach the Rathborney path before the mist completely engulfed the mountain.

'If we keep our face to the sun until we reach the path, we should be all right, Brehon,' said Aidan voicing her thoughts. She was touched by the reassuring air of hearty courage which he had assumed. At times he could be a nuisance, but today he seemed to be showing another side. The steepness was levelling off now and she wondered whether they had reached the path; however, the silent bank of fog was now completely wrapped around them.

'Wait a minute,' she said. 'Are you all here? Aidan, Hugh, Shane, are you all there?'

'Yes, Brehon.' Three voices answered at almost the same moment.

'I was wondering whether we have reached the path?' Mara tried to keep her voice from betraying her anxiety. 'Have any of you been as far up this path before? I think it leads right up to a gap in the mountain and you can look down and see the sea by Black Head. I've been along it once, but it's twenty years ago.'

'It doesn't feel like a path,' said Shane doubtfully, scuffing his feet on the stone.

'We'll go another bit,' said Mara, 'but make sure that you can see each other, there's just enough light to do that.'

The ground began to rise a bit so that must have been the right decision. They could not have reached the path yet. She prayed that they would do soon, because the mist was disorientating.

'Surely by now, we should have reached the path, Brehon, shouldn't we?' said Aidan.

Before Mara could reply, she heard Shane stumble.

'Are you all right, Shane?' Her voice was sharp with anxiety, but he answered readily.

'I'm all right, Brehon, there's just a bit of a hollow here, I stumbled, but I didn't fall.'

'Look, the mist is clearing a little,' said Aidan thankfully. 'We're still facing the sun, look you can see it behind the mist right there in front of us.'

Mara took her eyes from Shane and looked. Yes, the sun was in front of them but the ground seemed to be rising rather than falling. She looked around and got a shock.

'We've been here before,' she said. There was the hollow which had caused Shane to stumble. The mist had lifted for a few minutes, just enough to allow her to see the exquisite little rock garden of ferns dotted with the three tiny white flowers of wild strawberries. She had seen this earlier; she knew instantly. The mountains were full of these fertile hollows, but it was unlikely that another had the same arrangement of May blossoms growing among the November ferns.

'We've gone too far,' she said blankly. 'We're on the way over to Formoyle. We must have crossed the path without realizing it. We have to turn back.'

None of the boys said anything, but she could imagine their thoughts. If they had gone wrong before, perhaps they would go wrong again.

'Let's turn around now,' she said briskly. 'Perhaps it will stay clear long enough to allow us to get back on the path. Keep your eye on the sun from time to time. We must keep it to our backs.'

Even the watery streak of pale gold did not stay for long, though. When Mara turned around after a few minutes of stumbling along the rocky ground of the 'saddle' she saw that the mist had closed down again and now there was nothing but endless banks of vapour enclosing them. She was desperately worried now; as they were coming down from Lios Mac Sioda she had been confident of recognizing the path once her feet met it, but now that confidence had been shown to be unjustified. The path, no longer grassy at this height, probably would feel, to the feet, very much like a small flat piece of the stony ground of the mountain.

'I think that I heard the two notes of the horn,' said Shane. His voice sounded more optimistic than certain, but Mara seized on the slender hope eagerly.

'How stupid of me,' she exclaimed. 'We should try calling. Can any of you make the noise that Muiris demonstrated? Do you remember? A two-note *béic*. Try it one at a time, and leave a few minutes' space in between. We'll keep walking, though. I'm pretty sure that we are going in the right direction now and remember that Lios Mac Sioda is built on a cliff face so there is no danger of us wandering ahead this time. When we meet anything steep then we'll turn right.'

Easily said, she thought as she listened to the boys yodelling enthusiastically. Shane's would carry the best, she thought. He had a high clear voice. After one of his yells she thought she heard something and she quickly hushed Aidan.

'Listen,' she said.

Yes, there it was again. She was quite sure of it. But it wasn't a two-note blast from the horn. This was a bark, very distant ... Probably just a farm dog roused by the noise from the mountain ... Nevertheless ...

'Do it again, Shane,' she said urgently.

This time there was no mistake. The bark came from the Formoyle direction. It was coming nearer and she had no doubts. This was no sheep dog. This bark was a deep note, the bark of a huge dog.

'Bran!' yelled Shane and the others joined in instantly.

'Thank God,' breathed Mara. 'Bran,' she called, 'here, boy.' She could hear the sound of tumbling stones and feet running on the uneven ground. 'Steady, now, Bran,' she called. Dogs had been injured running on ground like this and Bran would be anxious to get back to her as soon as possible.

The next minute his hard, narrow head was under her hand and she was stroking the harsh wiry coat. And then he was licking the boys frantically, and his whipcord-like tail was flailing them all.

'I've got hold of his collar, Brehon,' said Shane. 'Better put the leash on him before he goes off again.'

'I don't think that he'll do that,' said Mara. All of her worries had now vanished. She took the leash from her pouch and passed it to Shane.

'He's got something stuck in his collar,' said Shane. 'Wait a minute; it's a piece of heather, I think. No, it isn't. It's sort of crackly. I think it's a bit of seaweed, a dried-up bit. Yes, that's what it is – it smells of that. Here it is, Brehon.'

'You shouldn't have run away like that, Bran,' reproved Aidan, 'we were all worried about you.'

'He was just following his mistress's orders, weren't you, Bran?' Mara took the dried-up crumpled strip from Shane's fingers and sniffed it carefully. 'Yes, you're right, that smells of the sea,' she said thoughtfully as she placed it in her pouch.

'Come on, Bran, home, boy, home,' she commanded taking the leash into her own hand and she signalled to him to go ahead of her.

Bran did not hesitate, nor did he put his nose to the ground. He just strode out confidently. The mist was still blanket-thick, but Mara had no fears now. After about five minutes of trotting steadily, Bran turned to the right and began to lead the way downhill.

'He's going the right way now, I just felt some grass brush my leg, and the ground feels softer, too.' Hugh hadn't spoken for quite some time and now his voice was full of relief.

Mara shared his feeling. Now there was nothing else to worry about. Bran would lead them straight down to Rathborney.

'You might try calling again,' she suggested. 'I thought I heard the horn just now.'

'All together, now,' said Aidan, reasserting his mastery of the younger boys. 'On the count of three, lads . . .'

The two-note yell that burst from them was enough to raise the dead and it was immediately answered by the horn.

'And once more for luck,' shrieked Aidan.

This time there was a triumphal, celebratory note from the horn and a cacophony of exuberant yodels in return.

'They know we're on our way down,' said Aidan with satisfaction.

'Do you think that Sheedy might have anything to do with Sorley's murder, Brehon?' asked Shane chattily as they made their way down the hill, Mara holding Bran's leash and the little party following the big dog confidently. Through the mist she could see that there were a string of torches coming up the hill and the heavy air smelled strongly of burning pitch.

'He's got a thing about bees,' said Hugh. 'He might be

290

brooding over the time that he pushed a hive over and killed a man.'

'And he certainly hated Sorley,' put in Shane eagerly.

'He'd be high on my list if I was Brehon,' said Aidan wisely.

'And he wouldn't have to pay a fine if he were a *dásachtach*,' said Shane knowledgeably.

'Everything all right, Brehon?' Muiris's powerful voice reached them a minute before they could see his outline.

'We're all fine, Muiris, thank you. I'm sorry that you've had such trouble.' Mara said no more; none would question her further.

They walked on until the two parties met. There was Muiris, and Cumhal, his face impassive, but his eyes full of relief. He would make a good story of this to Brigid, tonight, guessed Mara.

'Glad you're all safe, Brehon.' Muiris's voice was relieved, but held something else, also. 'I'm afraid that we have some bad news for you,' he continued. His voice was grave and for a moment her heart stopped. Had an accident happened to one of her boys? Her eyes scanned the crowd of the young and active who had accompanied Muiris up the Rathborney lane and then she let out a breath of relief. There was Fachtnan with Nuala and beside him Enda and Moylan.

'Bad news?' she echoed, turning back to Muiris.

'I'm afraid so, Brehon,' he said. 'We haven't found the man. I had to call everyone off the mountain,' he explained. 'I daren't let them up there any longer with mist coming down so early.'

Mara considered for a moment. She had almost forgotten about Rory, as her mind was busy with another person.

She sought for the right sentences to utter. She knew well that her lightest words were repeated and spread all over the kingdom.

'Well, you've all done your best, Muiris,' said Mara consolingly. 'I should leave the matter now,' she said, picking her words carefully. 'I will make some enquiries tomorrow and I'll let you know if anything further needs to be done.'

'Bran ran away.' Aidan's loud, adolescent, uncontrolled voice could be heard by all.

'No, he didn't!' Shane's was just as loud and more vehement. 'No, he didn't run away. The Brehon asked him to track Rory and he tracked him right as far as Fanore. I found the seaweed in his collar.'

Muiris swung around to listen and then turned back to Mara. 'I see,' he said evenly and there was a look of comprehension and also of triumph in his grey eyes. He had done his best for Rory. He had hunted all day and used every ounce of his skill and his expertise, but it had come to nothing and now he was interested in the latest news. She could see surmises, suspicions and finally enlightenment flash through his mind.

'I see,' he repeated. 'Well, we'll call it a day and go back to our homes, Brehon.'

'That's right, Muiris,' said Mara meeting his eyes frankly. 'You've done all you can now and everyone can go home with the feeling of a good day's work being done. I shall send Cumhal to make further enquiries tomorrow.'

EIGHTEEN

DIN TECHTUGAD (ON LEGAL ENTRY)

This is the legal procedure to be used by the lawful owner for taking possession of land, unjustly occupied by another person.

The claimant must enter the land accompanied by one witness and two horses. If possession is not yielded, then ten days later the claimant comes back with two witnesses and four horses. If still not allowed possession, he returns after twenty days with three witnesses and eight horses.

The claimant then spends a night on the property, kindles a fire and allows his horses to graze freely.

The following day the case must be heard by the Brehon of the kingdom and judgement given as to the rightful owner of the property.

∞

'Oh, BREHON, BRIGID SAID to remind you that the king is coming to have supper with you tonight,' said Cumhal at the end of Saturday morning schooling. He had waited for the boys to go off for their dinner before giving his account of the mission she had sent him on.

'No, I won't forget about the king,' Mara said, still pondering on the news that he had brought her. 'And the man was sure that Cathal said that?'

Cumhal nodded silently, scanning her face, but he asked no questions.

'I must ride over to Newtown Castle now,' said Mara decisively. 'Tell Brigid that I will be back in plenty of time for supper. I've given permission to all of the boys to spend the night with the O'Lochlainns so you and she will have a quiet afternoon and evening. They won't be back until nightfall on Sunday.'

He nodded. 'Yes, Fachtnan told me that they'll be off after their dinner – going hunting on Aillwee tomorrow at dawn apparently.' He lingered for a minute and then said, 'You might be interested to know, Brehon, that the lad Cuan, the silversmith's son, is back staying with Toin the *briuga*. I met Tomás from Rathborney and he told me the news.'

'Oh, is he, indeed?' Mara saw a grin on Cumhal's face and waited. There would be more to come, she knew that.

'Apparently young Cuan was up in that mountainy farm of his when the rain came bucketing down last night and the thatch of that old cabin he lives in started to leak and the place flooded out, so down came your man, with his pride tucked into his pouch, and the *briuga*, decent man that he is, welcomed him back,' finished Cumhal who had obviously heard the full story of Cuan's outburst on Wednesday night from Tomás.

So Cuan had been taken back under Toin's wing, well that didn't surprise her, but she hoped that the young man would have the courtesy to be there to meet her at Newtown Castle as she had ordered him.

❈

The road that wound steeply downhill from Cahermacnaghten to Rathborney was running with rainwater when Mara rode her mare towards Newtown Castle. The air was cold and the skies overcast with a hint of more rain to come. One of the green meadows deep in the valley of Gragans was flooded; already a flock of white swans had discovered it and they rocked peacefully on its grey surface.

'We're getting our winter at last, Brehon,' said Eoin MacNamara, as she reined in her mare to allow him to cross the road after an endless herd of sheep. 'Just helping Lorcan take these ladies of his up to Gleninagh South,' he added, closing the field gate as a frantic sheepdog, circling around the heels of four lagging sheep, finally drove them across the road.

'It's a bit wet for them down there now, I suppose,' said Mara, looking down at the flooded valley. Many of the valleys in the Burren had underground lakes which spilled above ground when they overflowed.

'That's right,' he said cheerfully, 'they'd get foot rot before you could turn around if they were left down there any longer. I'll be bringing my own cattle up to the mountains soon, too, and then it will be Lorcan's turn to give me a hand.'

And with that he followed the sheep through a narrow gap in a wall on the side of the road, just pausing to replace a few large boulders before striding up the lower slopes of Gleninagh South.

This way of life on the Burren was a custom that had probably gone on for thousands of years, thought Mara as she rode on; soon all of the animals from the valleys would be brought up onto the common land in the hills. It was a way of life that depended on neighbours sharing mountain space, helping each other with the movement of herds, keeping a friendly eye on each other's animals.

The thought set her to thinking about yesterday and how the whole neighbourhood had turned out to hunt for the missing bard. Where was Rory now, she wondered, and, more importantly, who had been instrumental in his disappearance?

✻

Three men on horseback rode out from Toin's gate as Mara came down into Rathborney. They greeted her with great respect, hesitated, but when she made no effort to overtake, they bowed again and rode on ahead of her towards Newtown Castle.

Who were they, she wondered. Their faces were familiar, but it was only when one glanced over his shoulder at her that she realized she knew them; all three were members of the king's household back in Thomond.

Ulick was in the courtyard chatting to Daire when they all rode in through the instantly opened gate and he came forward immediately.

'My dear Brehon, how wonderful to see you,' he said enthusiastically, but his eyes were on the riders and the leather satchel that the foremost bore at his saddle. These messengers from the king were obviously expected.

'I won't keep you, Ulick, I've just come to see Deirdre. I'll wait until she's free.' She made no attempt to dismount but waited while the king's men came forward hesitantly towards Ulick. All five looked at Mara, but she lingered, engaging the porter in conversation about the night's rain.

The first of the king's men dismounted, took what seemed to be a heavy box from a satchel, and handed it to Ulick, who carried it across the courtyard to the workshop where Deirdre was waiting. The once-rejected wife seemed to have taken complete charge of everything: castle and silversmith's business. Mara watched with interest how Deirdre took the box into the workshop, probably carefully checked its contents and then re-emerged a few minutes later with two small leaves of vellum in her hand. She gave one to Ulick and stood waiting while he tucked it into his pouch, then handed the second to the dismounted man and then, with more low bows to Mara, all three galloped back out through the gate. Mara watched them go and then eyed Ulick sharply. The king's messengers, coming from Toin, obviously on business that also concerned Ulick; there could only be one answer to that. Mara set her lips in a gesture of annoyance. Ulick gave her a hasty glance – no doubt, even he was embarrassed about having involved the king in his money affairs – and then smiled with all the charm at his disposal.

'Well, my dear Brehon,' he said smiling amiably, 'I must

congratulate you; I hear you have solved the case of the silversmith's death.'

'Really!' Mara raised a reproving eyebrow at him, but Ulick was incorrigible.

'So it was Rory all along.' His light, slightly high-pitched voice seemed to carry around the yard. Several men stopped what they were doing and turned to look at him. 'I must say that I suspected him from the start and now he's fled to France. What a shame! Still he would not have been able to pay the fine, would he? Perhaps Cuan could have had him as a slave. What do you think about that, Brehon?'

'I suspect that you are calling my attention to Rory because you wish to distract my attention from another person.' Mara stopped and looked at him keenly. Suddenly the easy-going, slightly effete, man-of-the-world mask had slipped and it was a warrior's eyes that confronted her own.

'*Ulick's the best companion in the world until you cross him, and then, God help you,*' Turlough had said once, but Mara didn't care. Her eyes met his steadily and Ulick was the first to look away.

He leaped lithely onto his horse and, without any farewells, followed the king's servants through the gate as Daire came towards Mara.

'You're looking very fine today.' Mara gave Daire a friendly smile, as he helped her to dismount from her horse. She wondered whether Deirdre was going to come over to greet her, but then turned her full attention to Daire. He was indeed looking very well dressed, and in Gaelic rather than English-style garments. He was wearing a pale blue *léine* and a mantle chequered in squares of blue and purple.

An elaborate silver torc was around his muscular neck and the mantle was fastened with a large silver brooch.

'Where are you off to, then? Not to Poulnabrucky, by any chance?' she asked teasingly.

He flushed, but then smiled in return. 'Muiris invited me over there to spend the night. Apparently there is going to be a big hunting expedition on Aillwee Mountain tomorrow morning at dawn.'

'I hope the weather is kind and that you have a wonderful time,' said Mara heartily. It looked as if there would be full approval from the father of the girl, and the girl herself had seemed to be hanging on Daire's arm when Mara had seen her last at the hunt for Rory yesterday evening. So much had changed for this handsome young man since the death of Sorley. But did that mean that he had a hand in it? No, she thought, it's fairly unlikely. After all, he couldn't know that things were going to turn out so well for him. If Una had been left mistress of Newtown Castle and of the mine and the silversmith business, then his position would probably have remained unchanged. Una would have been as likely as her father to exploit the young man's talent. Cuan would have had no spirit, no will-power to change anything. Deirdre had been kinder but it could never have been predicted that Deirdre would just walk back into the castle as if she had never left it. No, Mara decided with a sense of relief: this young man, at least, can be put from my mind. With a last smile and wave, she turned to walk across to the mistress of the house.

Deirdre now came forward with a few murmured words of welcome. She was even more richly dressed than on the last occasion when Mara had seen her. She flashed in the watery sunlight with silver brooches pinned on every possible spot of her gown and mantle and her work-worn fingers were laden with silver rings.

'I was hoping to meet Cuan here, Deirdre,' said Mara. 'I went up to see him at his farm and told him that I thought he should take up his rightful place at Newtown Castle. I don't think it's a good idea for him to live up there on the side of the mountain, do you?' Her voice was easy, chatty, a one-mother-to-another-mother tone. The last thing she wanted was for Deirdre to feel that the Brehon was interfering in private family matters.

'He's not here.' Deirdre seemed taken aback and uncertain.

'Perhaps he's still with Toin, then,' said Mara. 'My farm manager, Cumhal, told me that he heard, when he passed through Rathborney this morning, that Cuan was with the *briuga.*'

'I think he might be there,' said Deirdre cautiously.

'Would it be possible to send a servant to fetch him?'

Deirdre thought about that for a moment. Her heavy face betrayed no emotion, but her eyes were intelligent and when she spoke her voice was resolute. 'I'll go myself; it will be best that way.' She called an order to a servant who came running with a heavy fur-lined mantle held carefully in her hands, and then Deirdre turned to Mara. 'Ciara will take you up to Una; she will entertain you until we get back.' She shrugged on the mantle and then turned to speak in a low tone to the girl. Orders were given for refreshments in a decisive clear way. There was no doubt that

Deirdre could manage this house, and probably the business, with no problems.

But what about Una? Where did that leave her?

❈

Una was sitting by the western window of the hall. Her embroidery frame was beside her and she continued to stitch even after the girl had announced Mara.

'Shall I sit here beside you?' Mara took a chair and bent to look at the work and then gave a gasp of surprise. The picture was of a beautiful girl, sitting on a grass seat in a garden and beside her was a young man strumming a zither. And the man was the living image of Rory. Everything was right. The blue eyes, the red-gold hair, the slim figure, even the clothes that the youth in the picture was wearing were identical to those that Rory wore when Mara had visited Newtown Castle on the day before Sorley's death.

Una followed her eyes with a malicious grin, but said nothing until Mara blurted out, 'But that's Rory! How marvellously you have captured the likeness. How did you do it? It seems amazing to be able to paint an exact portrait just with some pieces of embroidery silks.'

Una gave a harsh laugh, and short, explosive bark of amusement. 'I'm afraid that you credit me with too many powers, Brehon,' she said. 'Embroidery takes longer than you might think. I first saw Rory the bard about three or four weeks ago. He came here to sing at a banquet held for some noble lords and silversmiths from Galway. I had been working on this tapestry since last year and it was almost completed then.'

'I see,' said Mara, but she was puzzled not so much at the resemblance now – she herself had often thought that Rory looked like a picture from an ancient tale – but more because of the intense bitterness with which the woman spoke.

'Yes,' said Una, carefully outlining a daisy on the grassy sward at the lover's feet. 'You are not the only one to see the resemblance. My father's guests that evening made much sport about the likeness between the bard and my tapestry picture.'

She filled in a daisy petal with tiny precise stitches before adding thoughtfully, 'It was a very successful banquet: my father sold many valuable pieces of silver that night. He poured the wine unsparingly and high prices were paid, but,' she paused to pick out a pair of tiny silver shears from the basket at her feet, before continuing, 'despite all of his efforts he had not managed to sell me too by the end of the night. That's probably when he first began to think of bribing Rory the bard to marry me.' And then she set her lips and snipped the thread decisively.

'Why?' Mara put the question bluntly.

Una looked up at her with surprise. 'Why?' she echoed.

'Yes, I would have thought you were useful to him, here at Newtown Castle. He could leave everything in your care when he was in Galway, you looked after the house, the mine, you even did some of the smith's work, I understand. I would have thought that he would want to keep you.'

'That was in the bargain,' said Una, carefully threading some yellow silk through the tiny eye of her needle. 'We were both to live here, Rory was to father a child on me – I think, though I was not told this, that the bargain was that, if the child were a healthy boy, there would be no obstacle to Rory obtaining a divorce if he wished, and no doubt he would leave with a substantial sum of silver in his satchel. 'You see,' she said, stitching the tiny centre of the daisy with a knot of the yellow silk, 'my father was desperate for an acceptable male heir; his own son was not worthy.'

'And yet you say that your father made a will leaving everything to you.'

'That was my price,' said Una calmly. 'I made that very clear to my father. He knew me better than to try to trick me. And the will was made, Brehon, I can assure you of that. It was made in this very room, in my presence and when it had been signed and sealed I took it and locked it into a chest. I refused to sign the betrothal contract until I had checked through the will. My mistake was', she spoke calmly and dispassionately, 'not to realize that my mother had kept her bunch of keys after all those years.'

'And what about the betrothal contract between you and Rory?' And then as, for the first time, Una hesitated, Mara said sharply, 'Don't deny that there was one.'

Una carefully snipped the end of the yellow silk, put shears and needle back in their places and closed the lid of the basket. It was as if she were getting ready for battle.

'I had no interest in the betrothal contract – my father probably put it straight into his own chest that night.'

'But it wasn't there when we looked after his death?'

'No,' said Una. 'Like the will, it had disappeared.' Her eyes moved over towards the fire of pinewood burning noisily in the chimney hearth. Like mother, like daughter, thought Mara, both quick-witted and ruthless. There was little doubt in her mind that the betrothal contract had been burned by Una just as soon as Sorley's dead body had been carried back to Newtown Castle.

'Did Rory have a copy of that contract?' she asked and then quickly added before a denial could be uttered, 'It would be customary.'

'Perhaps.' Una shrugged her heavy shoulders. 'I don't remember anything about that.'

'And if so, then he would be within his rights to demand that the contract be fulfilled.' Did Rory know his rights, wondered Mara. He was not a particularly clever young man. From the smug expression on Una's face it didn't look as if he had demanded a copy of the betrothal contract.

Una shrugged her shoulders again.

'Well, he appears to have disappeared, now,' she said indifferently.

'As you say,' said Mara clearly and distinctly, 'Rory has now disappeared.' For a long moment she held the eyes of Rory's betrothed.

Una got to her feet and went towards the door. 'I think they are bringing you some refreshments now,' she said with the air of one who wishes to finish the conversation, as she flung the door open.

It was the maidservant with a well-furnished silver tray, but behind her was Deirdre, followed by her son, Cuan. Quick and efficient, thought Mara, noting that Cuan was once again washed and well dressed. Toin's kindness and patience with this awkward young man seemed endless.

'I'll take that.' Una took the tray, brought it in, placed it on the table, but made no effort to invite anyone to partake of the cakes and small glasses of wine. She stood and glared at her brother, but waited until the door was closed before saying anything.

'What are you doing here?' she snapped then, looking him up and down.

He flinched and, though still irritated by his bad manners and surly behaviour, Mara felt herself, once again, sorry for the boy. She remembered Toin's thoughtful estimate of him; Cuan did indeed look like a dog that had been savagely mistreated from his early days.

'Sit down, Cuan,' she said, ignoring Una. She took him by the hand and led him over to a cushioned bench by the fire. 'Deirdre, could you sit beside him, and Una,' quickly she dragged over a chair to place beside another, already in position in the favoured place beside the fire, and completed the semicircle, 'you sit here.' She waited until everyone had obeyed her instructions, but then began to talk quickly, anxious that no irredeemable insult should be offered.

'I've just been chatting to Una while we were waiting for you to arrive, Cuan,' said Mara in an easy conversational tone. Carelessly she leaned across, picked out a small round pine log from the basket by the hearth and threw it on the crackling fire. Not one person relaxed, however, nor moved a muscle. Mara, after the one quick glance, kept her eyes on the fire.

'The position is,' she continued, 'though Sorley may have made a will, none can be found so the disposal of his goods goes according to the law.'

She put on another log and then looked around. Deirdre, one beringed hand folded within the other, gazed thoughtfully at the burning firewood, Cuan's chin was sunken upon his chest and Una watched Mara as a man watches another across the length of two crossed swords.

'These are the facts,' said Mara, speaking slowly and carefully with her eyes now on Cuan's downcast face, 'Sorley Skerrett was a silversmith from Galway, with, at the time of his death, his principal place of residence here in the kingdom of the Burren. He left no will.' Una snorted contemptuously, but didn't interrupt and Mara continued smoothly. 'Sorley was not a member of any clan: his wealth was the result of personal exertions; he could, if he had wished, will his property where he pleased, but as there is no will available, therefore the land, houses and property owned by Sorley, including the mine on that land, go to his only son, Cuan.'

Deirdre looked at Una with a gleam of triumph in her pale eyes, but Cuan himself showed no interest.

Mara waited a moment, and then continued. 'His daughter, Una, has been left with no provision although if I were advising Sorley Skerrett and helping him to draw up a just and equitable will, I would have recommended that she should receive one-quarter of what is termed moveable property, furniture, household fittings, and,' Mara's eyes went to the glittering array of silverware on every table and window seat in the room, 'of course, this would include the objects made from silver in the house and in the workshop.' There was a silence when she finished. Neither Cuan nor Una showed any emotion. Mara turned her eyes towards the mother.

'I have not dealt with the position of Deirdre, who was divorced by Sorley. There were certain irregularities about the procedure that lead me to say that this case should be heard at Poulnabrone and since it involves the work of the now deceased Brehon of Kinvarra, then I feel that three Brehons should hear this matter so I shall ask the Brehon from Corcomroe and the Brehon from Thomond to sit with me on this case. Would that be acceptable to you, Deirdre?'

Deirdre considered the matter for a moment, staring steadily into the fire.

'Leave things as they are,' she said eventually. 'There's no sense in raking over old stories.'

'If that's what you feel,' said Mara briskly, 'then I won't proceed against your wishes. You may wish to think about this matter and come back to me at a later date. Now is there anything else that I can explain to you? Please ask me any question that occurs to you.'

Una broke the silence. 'You have explained the law very clearly to us, Brehon, and I'm sure that we all understand the position. But perhaps you can explain this to me now.' She paused and looked at her brother. There was no trace of affection or pity in her glance. 'What happens,' she said with heavy emphasis, 'when the son who inherits has ensured his inheritance by murdering his father?'

Mara glanced at Cuan. He reddened, but said nothing.

'I think, Cuan,' she said kindly, 'you should reply to that accusation. Take your time and reply slowly and carefully. A simple yes or no will suffice.'

Cuan clenched his fists, but Deirdre put a hand on his arm and he relaxed. They would get on all right, mother and son, if Una were removed from the scene, thought Mara.

'No,' said Cuan. 'I did not kill my father. I had nothing to do with it.'

'Thank you,' said Mara with an approving nod. 'Now

Una, you've made an accusation; what are your grounds for saying this?'

'He was seen by the bard, Rory,' said Una vehemently. 'He was seen dodging . . .' she broke off and then continued in an exasperated manner, 'but you know all of this. You were present last Wednesday at Toin's supper when Rory told what he had seen.'

'Tell me again,' encouraged Mara. 'I hear many things and my mind is not as young as it used to be.'

'He told you that he saw Cuan hiding behind the wall just before Sorley was murdered. He told you that it looked like someone was ducking down behind the wall, trying not to be seen. And he told you that Cuan had a stick in his hand.'

'Ah,' said Mara. She looked at Una with a half-smile. 'Now I remember. But how do you know what happened at Toin's supper? Have you seen Rory since?'

'No.' Una hesitated for a moment and then rallied. 'I heard what happened,' she said briefly.

'From whom?'

Una shrugged. 'Servants' gossip.'

I doubt it, thought Mara. Toin would not have said anything. The servants were all in the separate kitchen house when the row broke out. They would have known that Cuan had stormed out and not waited to stay the night as expected, but they would not have heard the exact words of the quarrel.

'So, did you and Rory discuss this matter, arrange it beforehand?' she suggested. 'It was perhaps agreed between you that he should make the accusation.' She looked keenly at Una and Una stared defiantly back.

Mara was not deceived, though. Of course; if Cuan were convicted then the punishment would be permanent exile, or perhaps even death by being placed in a boat with no oars and launched out to sea in an offshore wind. The killing of a parent or close relation was the only crime that merited a savage punishment under Brehon law. If Cuan were guilty then there would be no possibility of him inheriting his father's wealth and possessions. Even if not convicted, the young man could be blackmailed. He would be easily frightened.

Una hesitated. Then her eyes left Mara's and went, not to Cuan's distressed young face, but to the face of the woman so like herself. The two pairs of grey eyes met, Deirdre's looked worried, distressed even, but Una's eyes were full of calculation. Was this an attempt at blackmail, an effort to make Deirdre uneasy about Cuan, perhaps even to elicit a confession? After all the murder of a divorced husband would not be as serious a matter as the murder of a father. Mara felt that she could almost see how various possibilities were being shifted and arranged in Una's acute mind, but in the end she shook her head and said simply, 'I haven't seen Rory for some days.'

That's probably a lie, thought Mara, but aloud she said, 'In that case, I suggest you make no accusations that cannot be backed by solid evidence. By solid evidence I mean the sworn testimony of at least two people, preferably without any interest in the outcome of the case.' She rose to her feet. 'Now I must go,' she said. 'Una, will you accompany me to the door? Cuan,' her voice softened slightly as she saw his miserable face, 'I hope that soon you will get to enjoy your possessions and the freedom that wealth will bring you. I'm sure that in your mother you will find a useful friend and counsellor. Think of what we discussed and live your life to the full. *Slán leat,*' she added, thinking that it was not health so much as happiness, that she wanted to wish him – a more difficult matter altogether for a boy with his upbringing and sensitivity of spirit.

Una, to Mara's surprise, looked quite willing to accompany her to the door. She said nothing on the way down the stairs, but her expression was thoughtful and receptive when the light of the opened door shone on it.

'Walk to the gate with me,' said Mara quietly, seeing that an efficient stableman was already leading her mare from the stable.

'You have some advice for me,' said Una and there was a glint of humour in her grey-blue eyes. 'You'd suggest that I should enter a nunnery, I suppose.'

'No, certainly not!' Mara's voice was vehement. 'If you had nothing to do with this murder, then I would advise that you come to terms with your brother; you will find it surprisingly easy to do, I would say. Suggest to him that you take over the Galway side of the business. There's a house in the middle of the city, I understand. You can have a shop there; you can market the goods, you can engage a silversmith; do your own work also. You are clever, efficient and artistic. I'd say you could manage a business well – make beautiful silverware also. Who's to stop you if you are the owner of the business? Make that bargain with Cuan, Una. Deirdre, your mother, will back you up. She is a sensible woman.'

'And she would prefer to have me out of the house.' Now a smile twitched at Una's lips.

'Of course she would,' said Mara robustly. 'No grown mother and daughter should share a house. It doesn't work. You have your own establishment and if you fancy getting married, then just choose your own bridegroom. Manage your own affairs.' There'll be suitors and plenty once word gets around of the wealth involved, she thought, cynically watching Una's eyes considering the matter.

'I'll do what you say,' she said briefly. She hesitated slightly and then added, 'What about Rory?'

'Rory,' said Mara thoughtfully. 'I don't think Rory will be seen again in these parts.'

NINETEEN

A man may open a mine if he has ownership of all the land around it. He may only dig one shaft and may not dig side shafts leading towards the lands of other men.

He must cause no harm to other property.

If harm is caused, then a fine must be paid. This will be decided by the court and will take into account the damage caused.

The fine for removing stones from another man's land is five séts or two-and-a-half ounces of silver or three cows.

***

JUST AS MARA REACHED the gate of Newtown Castle on her way back home, the most extraordinary roar suddenly filled the air. Ignoring the groom, she ran through the gate, closely followed by Una. They both crossed the road and turned around towards the mountain. Before their horrified eyes a great torrent of water was sweeping down the hillside. It was foaming and bubbling as it came and the force of it was so great that it carried along great boulders, turning and tossing them like pebbles in its pathway. There were trees in it, too. Not big stately trees like those around the castle, but those twisted, gnarled, bent bushes which came from the top of the mountain. This river was coming straight down from the steepest part of Cappanabhaile, not twisting and flowing sinuously inside its valley down the gentle slopes to Rathborney, but plunging precipitously from the summit of the mountain down to the castle yard. There were living things in it, too. A sheep with a sickening, twisted leg, and then a man, alive but only just, his black sodden head rising above the flow and sinking beneath it.

At that, the sense of unreality which seemed to have numbed them was suddenly broken and without a word the porter flew to the bell and began to clang it wildly. Men appeared from the fields.

Mara rushed towards the man noticing that Una seemed to have left her and returned inside the castle gates.

'Quick,' she shouted to the nearest worker.

Instantly he was by her side. The ground was flat here and the torrent was beginning to spread out. He plunged into it and pulled out the drowning man efficiently grasping him by the hair and pulling him free of the water and onto a slight hump in the uneven ground. There was a sickening smell in the air, sulphur, thought Mara; it smelled just like those sulphur sticks that Turlough had given her to replace her faithful old tinderbox.

'Turn him upside down,' she said urgently. 'He'll have water in his chest and perhaps worse than water.' The smell was poisonous and she was relieved when vomiting began. One of the Welsh mineworkers, she guessed, and wondered, looking up at the torrent still pouring down, how many others might still be trapped within the mine.

'I'm going up there, Brehon.' Daire's horse leaped the stone wall of the field in one agile bound. He shed his fine new mantle on the ground as he galloped past. 'I saw it when I was halfway across Gragans,' he shouted over his shoulder. Within a few moments he and his strong horse had began to climb the lower slopes of Cappanabhaile.

A group of miners were straggling down the hillside. They looked as if they were dragging someone between them. Mara put up her hand to shield her eyes from the slanting rays of sunlight. Daire had reached them now. He had stopped, had dismounted from his horse and was listening to them.

'Bring that man inside. There's a fire in the guards' room and they have a pallet ready for him to lie on. Carry him in. Aodh, you bring the other men in when they come down. I've told them to light a fire in the courtyard and there will be hot drinks, and beds for any that are injured.' Deirdre was by Mara's side, efficiently organizing.

'The courtyard is flooding,' the girl Ciara, no doubt left in charge of the hot drinks, shrieked hysterically.

'Get the sandbags from the gatehouse.' Deirdre's voice was loud and authoritative. 'I'll take these men back in with me to the yard to help to protect the buildings,' she said to Mara. 'Will you tell the others to come in as soon as they are down?'

There was something familiar about the man who was being dragged down the hill. Mara narrowed her eyes. A small man. The late afternoon rays of the sun shone directly on the figures now and she saw the gleam of a bald head. It was Sheedy; she had no doubt about it. The picture of him, yesterday, with his pickaxe in his hand, flashed into her mind. '*I must be getting on with my work*,' that was what he kept repeating.

Daire was now leading his horse down accompanying the small group. Mara decided to wait until they arrived down in the meadow; there was little point in going to meet them. The flood was decreasing every minute. Probably some water had been pent up for some time and the rain of yesterday had caused it to burst forth. She walked across to the courtyard gate and looked in.

The tower itself was in little danger as it was built on a small mound, but the *bawn* or yard was already filling up with water and the cabins built around its outside walls were in danger of being flooded. Deirdre was there, her cloak wrapped around her and her harsh voice directing the men. Bags of sand were being placed in front of the kitchen, the workrooms and the stables and in front of the gate. Several women with large brooms were sweeping the water towards some drains set into the back wall of the courtyard. Mara stood by the gate watching, her eyes fixed on the mountain, now a fast-flowing sheet of turbulent water. It was strange, she thought, how she had felt Cappanabhaile to be evil and menacing the last time that she had looked at it and now it had taken its revenge on those who had despoiled it.

More men had now arrived and were battling with the flood. Regardless of the wet, Deirdre was now outside the gate and was directing them. Mara could see what she was doing. A drain was being dug which would turn the water harmlessly into a low-lying meadow beside the road-way into Newtown. It was a good solution and she admired the woman for being able to think of it so quickly. Where was her son, who should be safeguarding his property, she wondered, and come to that, where was her daughter? Just as she thought that, from behind the door opened and Una came out; she was not wearing her cloak and obviously had no intention of joining in with the work to save the castle. Her eyes, like Mara's, went to the mountain and she drew the same conclusion as Mara had done.

'The mine must be flooded,' she said in the low steady voice which never seemed to express much emotion. And then she said, almost as an explanation, 'I've been looking after the man who was saved from drowning. Would you like to come to see him, Brehon? He has an interesting tale to tell.'

❈

The man who had been dragged from the flood was look-ing a little better. He was in the guards' room, a dark room with only gunslits to admit the light, situated just beside the front door on the ground floor. Ciara was holding a hot drink to his lips and someone had brought some blankets and put them around him and a brazier filled with newly lighted turf smoked at his feet.

'How are you, my friend?' asked Mara gently.

The man shuddered. 'I thought I would never keep my head up,' he said hoarsely. 'I was mending a wall up there and then I heard the sound of it. It burst out of the mine and came thundering down at me. I climbed on top of the wall but it was no good. The water swept me off and I couldn't get to my feet. I kept trying to grab at things but the water was too fast for me.'

'Don't be thinking of it now,' said Ciara comfortingly. 'Take a drink of this. It will do you good. It's carrageen and honey. It will keep the cold out of you.'

The man took another gulp while Mara waited.

'You don't know what caused the flood, then do you?'

The man nodded. 'It must have been that madman, Sheedy,' he said. 'People say that he killed the master and now he's probably killed the mine, too.'

'Did the water came out of the mine?'

'Yes, it spurted out of the mine all yellow and foamy. That was the first I saw of it.'

Una got up and left the room. Mara patted the still bewildered man on the shoulder and joined her on the doorstep.

'So the mine is destroyed,' Una said briefly.

'It may not be,' Mara answered cautiously, 'it all depends on how much harm the flood has done.'

She did not answer, so Mara asked curiously: 'Where is your brother?'

'Cuan is in his bedchamber,' she answered contemptuously. 'He came down at the first alarm and then he turned and went back. He is afraid. He is afraid of water, he is afraid of fire, he is afraid of his own shadow and because I am a woman and he is a man, you say that he is more fitting to inherit my father's wealth and property than I am.'

'It is not I that say it,' said Mara mildly. 'The law says it and I just interpret the law.'

'You should change the law, then, shouldn't you?' said

Una harshly. 'After all, we are both the children of Sorley. I am the elder, but because I am a girl I get nothing and my brother gets everything. And I have to go down on my knees to a coward like that in order to get my share.'

She gave a short laugh and left with a scornful glance, and in her heart Mara found it hard to blame her. Perhaps, it would not have been too great a crime, after all, if Una had given a quick push to that hive of bees and reaped some rewards for all of her years of servitude to that unpleasant man, her father. Mara walked thoughtfully back to the field to meet Daire and the men dragging the captive, Sheedy.

❉

'He's been working at this for weeks,' said Daire. His voice was loud and clear and he continually looked back at Sheedy and each time Sheedy nodded happily, his watery eyes full of the pleasure of a child who has achieved a skilful piece of work.

'He wanted to stop the water that washed the silver and the lead from poisoning his land so he dug a hole and diverted it back into the galleries that drain the mine. Ifor,' here Daire indicated the dark-haired Welshman whom Mara had seen at the mine on Monday, 'Ifor says that he was puzzled how full of water they seemed to be since we had been having such a dry spell.'

'Is this true, Sheedy?' asked Mara mildly.

'I am the king, the king of the bees,' he assured her, singing the words in a strange high voice.

'He's completely out of his wits, I'd say,' said Daire in a low voice.

'What is your name?' asked Mara, looking at Sheedy intently, but he just continued to sing: 'I am the king, the king of the bees.' Was he a witness to the death of Sorley, she wondered? Was that the reason why he continued to harp on about the bees? In his deranged mind, the bees had obeyed the command of their king and had brought about the death of the despoiler of the mountain, Sorley Skerrett.

'What shall we do with him?' asked Daire.

Mara thought for a moment. Brehon law decreed that an insane man should be held by his nearest relative until he could be questioned at the law court on judgement day. If he were found to be permanently insane then the kin group, that was all of the descendants of the same great-grand-father, would have to care for him, either by drawing lots or by some other arrangement. The usual thing was to pass the insane person around from household to household on a monthly rotation, unless some charitable person could be found to take permanent care of him.

'Could you send someone for Diarmuid O'Connor?' she said after a minute's thought. 'I'm sure he would care for him until the next judgement day. In the meantime, have you somewhere here where you can keep him in safety?'

'I'll have a word with Deirdre,' said Daire and took the man coaxingly by the arm. 'Come on, Sheedy, let's go over there.' Mara followed him, watched him cross the courtyard and saw Deirdre nod her head and point to a small stone cabin beside the gatehouse. Why was Sheedy obsessed with the words 'king' and 'bees' she wondered? What had he seen, or what had he done that Thursday at Father David's burial?

Mara climbed up to the top of the steps by the front door to the castle. The danger was now averted and the water was running steadily into the meadow. It would flood the meadow, but that was of little consequence. The castle and all its treasures were safe. The mist had cleared and the sun was beginning to edge the clouds. Daire was now directing men to go up the mountain and Ciara was busily handing out drinks to the drenched miners. There is little more that I can do here, today, thought Mara. There were a few hours to spare before suppertime, but she would leave now. There was just one more piece of information that she needed. The porter had emerged from one of the cottages, wearing dry clothes and had gone back to his place of duty in the lodge. Everyone was busy so Mara crossed the court-yard and followed him in.

'A terrible business, this,' she said chattily, smiling at him as he gulped from a steaming cup. By the fragrant smell she guessed that it was liberally laced with mead. Deirdre would soon have the loyalty as well as respect from all the workers at Newtown Castle. It didn't take much, she reflected; just a bit of fellow feeling, an understanding that people like to be valued, like to have their efforts appreciated.

'It is, indeed, Brehon,' he replied, wiping his mouth and then draining the last few drops from his cup before setting it down on the table.

'And coming the day after the disappearance of the young bard, Rory,' she continued. 'Of course, that would have been shocking for you here at Newtown Castle. He was here a lot during the last few weeks, wasn't he?' She watched him carefully and saw his expression change.

'Quite a lot,' he muttered with a lack of enthusiasm. Rory had obviously spent most of his efforts on charming the master of the house and had not bothered with the underlings.

'When was the last time that he was here?' Mara made the enquiry in a careless manner, walking over to look out of the window where there was a sudden shout of laughter.

'I suppose it must have been early on Thursday morning.' The porter came over to join her. Ciara was crossing the courtyard and she had a flagon of the mead-laced hot drink in her hand; he made a quick signal to her before turning back to Mara. 'I'd say I was one of the last to see him, Brehon; he came to see Mistress Una at dawn and it must have been after he left here that he went up the mountain.' He accompanied Mara to the door with a show of great courtesy, picking up his cup as he passed the table. 'There's the mistress over there, probably looking for you.' He sounded relieved as he pointed out Deirdre so Mara left him to replenish his drink and walked over to where Deirdre was emerging from a cabin.

So Deirdre is the mistress now, thought Mara. She went over and joined the woman. 'I'll go now, Deirdre,' she said aloud to Sorley's despised former wife who was sitting wearily on the steps, her long cloak, her elaborate gown and even the linen *léine* soaked wet and making a trail of water behind her. 'You have enough to be thinking of for the moment without me bothering you. There's nothing I can do. You have plenty of people here to help you.'

Deirdre smiled. She looked tired but there was a glow of happiness and fulfilment in her eyes. A woman of ability, thought Mara. Why did Sorley ever let her go? She would have managed his affairs so competently. 'Everyone has helped,' she said happily. 'Even poor Toin has sent to offer assistance.' She pointed and Mara recognized one of the *briuga*'s men and raised a hand to beckon him over.

'How is your master?' asked Mara. The man hesitated. All of Toin's household must have grown used to those queries during the last few months, but that did not make them easier to answer; Mara knew that and felt sorry that she had asked the question.

'Not well,' replied the man after a minute. 'He gets a bit depressed, and he's in pain most of the time. The physician came in the middle of the morning and gave him something else and the girl, Nuala, the young physician, she's wonderful with him; she's in and out of the kitchen making him soothing drinks, and poultices, too; that's the latest, Tomás was telling me.'

'Do you think I could drop in on my way home?'

'He'd like to see you, Brehon,' said the man enthusiastically. 'Tomás was saying the other day that you do him a power of good. Not many come to see him these days; more's the pity, because company takes his mind off the pain.'

❊

'So have you solved your murder case yet?' Toin's voice was cheerful. He was stretched out before the fire on a cushioned bench, well propped up on pillows, a small linen bag placed over his stomach.

'That's my invention,' said Nuala beaming with satisfaction as she saw Mara's eyes go to the bag. 'Toin finds that heat helps the pain, but he cannot bear anything like a hot brick, so I stitched that bag last night and Tomás and I keep it filled with hot bran.'

'That was clever.' Una would not have thought much of the workmanship – the stitches were large and uneven – but Toin looked rested and clear-eyed. Perhaps the bran poultice worked as well as the poppy syrup, thought Mara.

'I have so many problems to solve connected to this case,' she said aloud, sitting down beside the sick man. She told him the story of Sheedy and the flooding of the mines and he listened with keen interest.

'Go down there and see how they are all doing,' he said to Nuala. 'You know what an old gossip I am, I love to have news of my neighbours.'

'Will you be all right while I'm gone, though?' Nuala looked at him with a worried glance.

'Of course, I will.' He was still able to force a note of energy into his voice. 'The Brehon will look after me. We'll have a game of chess together, she and I. Let's use Daire's fine set.'

❋

'So you do believe that Daire, not Sorley, made the chess set,' said Mara as she set out the silver pieces after Nuala had left.

'Of course,' said Toin. 'Give me the black pieces; I enjoy defending. Yes, of course Daire is to be believed. Even without Una's testimony I would still know that it was Daire. Sorley never told the truth whenever a lie suited his purposes better. How are they all getting on over there, now?'

'I think they might settle down now,' said Mara, pushing out her little wolfhound pawn to the king-four position.

'If Una were out of the way, the boy might have a chance,' commented Toin slipping out his knight to cover the centre of the board.

'So which of them did you bargain with to buy the set?' asked Mara sliding out her bishop in return. 'This piece is so like Mauritius of Kilfenora I almost feel that I should kiss his ring,' she added in a light tone of voice. She shouldn't really burden him with the cares of the self-centred people at Newtown Castle, she thought.

'I offered Deirdre what it's worth.' He edged his queen's knight's pawn one place forward and Mara frowned. This was a strange move. She hesitated and then jumped her king's knight over the solid row of her own pawns.

'Make no mistake, Deirdre will be the one to run that business,' he said, watching her face and then slotting his bishop into the empty space in his pawn rank. 'But you can rely on me to save Cuan's pride,' he added.

Mara saw her opening. Courageously she moved out the queen, smiling at the little figure so like herself with scroll in hand. 'I saw you sent a boxful of silver over there today,' she said.

'You don't miss much,' said Toin, bringing his second knight over to protect his threatened pawn.

'Nor do you,' she replied ruefully. After a moment's hesitation she supported her central pawn with a second one. 'But, of course,' she continued casually, 'by the look of that box it held far too much to pay for a thousand chess sets, even one as valuable and as beautiful as this one.'

He did not reply. He frowned intently at the chessboard and when he did move eventually it was just an innocuous pawn.

'It was Ulick's debt, that you were repaying, on behalf of the king, wasn't it? I suppose Turlough has just taken it upon his own shoulders.' She cleared a space in the back row by moving out her second bishop.

He smiled. 'You play a courageous game,' he said with amusement. After some thought he moved another pawn, saying, 'Do you always rush at things like this?'

'I want you to do me a great favour, Toin,' said Mara, ignoring the question while rapidly castling. Now her king, with his huge moustaches and his amiable face, was well protected, snugly ensconced into the left-hand side of the board and flanked by the turreted castle on the right.

'So what's this favour then?' Toin sounded wary. His eyes were half closed and he was very still for some time. She wondered whether he had dozed off when his hand shot out and he carefully moved his queen to the back rank.

'I want you to allow me, instead of the king, to take over this debt,' said Mara bluntly. She moved the castle's pawn one step forward and then sat back. 'I can easily afford it; I have large savings; there is no problem there.'

He was taking a long time to think. He was a strange man to play against. Sometimes he moved very quickly and at other times he took a long time to decide. She had never played against someone like him before, she thought, and then tried to frame the words to convince him to grant the request that was foremost in her mind.

'Toin, do this thing for me,' Mara moved a pawn and then regretted it. There was no taking it back, though. The laws of chess, like the Brehon laws, allow for no erasure, just repentance and restitution. She had made a move and she would have to abide by it, as well as by other decisions

325

of hers. Neither in chess, nor in life, can a move, once made, be taken back.

'Toin,' she said gently and softly, looking into his hesitant face, 'I know this man, this king of ours. I know him heart and soul; I know his faults and his weaknesses, just as well as I know the warmth of his heart and the depth of his nobility. I know how important his friends are to him and how he suffers if one of them prove unworthy. I can't protect him from that; the truth has to be made clear to him. I just want to protect him from . . .'

'From people like me and Ulick and Sorley,' finished Toin, contemplating her pawn move with a dry smile.

'From moneylenders like Sorley, certainly,' she said steadily. She said no more; he was intelligent and sharp-witted; he would know, at least he would know part of, what was in her mind. How long could Toin last? And when he died who would inherit his goods, inherit the king's debt with them? And what would happen then as Turlough spiralled from one debt to another?

There was a very long silence after that as Toin stared intensely at the chessboard. Was he planning his strategy or thinking of what she said? Or was it some idiotic scruple about confidentiality that bothered him? Or possibly even a resentment that she, a woman, was interfering in an arrangement between two men.

Eventually he stirred, picked up his black bishop and decisively moved it across the board. Mara stared at it in dismay. Now both of his bishops were side by side, a formidable pair, and both were trained on the little cluster of pawns around her king on the other side of the board.

She glanced up at Toin to find that he was watching her with a glint of amusement. Irritated, she shut out everything from her mind. She would concentrate on this game, bring about a speedy checkmate and then force Toin to consider her request.

And then she would go back to Cahermacnaghten and talk to Turlough. He was her king; he had the right to know the truth before anyone else in the kingdom. Together they would make the decision.

Tomás, the reliable manservant, had slipped noiselessly in and out of the room twice, once to replenish the fire and then Nuala's bran bag, before Mara had worked out a winning combination.

'Check,' she said and then, as soon as he moved his king aside, she repeated, triumphantly, 'check.'

This time Toin countered by moving his castle in front of his king. An unexpected sacrifice, but still everything was possible, thought Mara as she picked up her queen intending to capture his castle. But then she stopped. No, her plans weren't going to work out. That last move of Toin's had revealed his whole carefully built defence structure.

❋

Toin was a brilliant chess player. That was the amazing thing. Mara had imagined a comfortable game such as she was accustomed to play with her scholars, where half her mind was on the game and the rest of it involved in conversation. Nothing like that happened with Toin. The next moves were a surprise: a daring sacrifice, then a rapid onslaught on Mara's queen; the old man began to play fast, so fast that Mara felt her pulse quicken and she had deliberately to slow herself down and to play at a more circumspect pace. It was almost impossible to guess what Toin was lthinking. Time after time, he leapt ahead of her step-by-step plan. Time after time, Mara thought to take advantage of an apparently careless move only to find that she had fallen into a carefully prepared trap and the final checkmate was a triumph of savagery and elegance that left Mara staring ruefully at the board, having racked her brains in a futile attempt to avoid the inevitable defeat.

'Well,' she said eventually, tipping over her king in acknowledgement of Toin's victory. 'I don't think I have ever had a better game. We must play more often.'

She continued staring at the board for a moment, trying to think how she could have changed her strategy and then looked up.

'Are you unwell?' she asked with alarm. Toin opened his eyes and gave a weak chuckle.

'Well, I am certainly not well,' he said drily, 'but don't worry about me. I haven't enjoyed anything as much as that game for a very long time. You're a good player, Mara, you just need to be a little less impulsive and rein in that optimism of yours a little, but you're about the best that I have ever played and I have played with many people. There was a time when this guesthouse used to be full of people: some of them brought by Cathal the sea captain, people from all over the world. I've played chess with them all, French, Spanish, English. Now pour me another cup of the Burgundy and take one for yourself. My little physician will soon be back and you have not had an answer to your question yet.'

Mara poured the wine and came back to her place. Putting the cup down, she carefully packed the finely modelled chessmen back into their box on top of the board of silver and of ivory.

'So, what is the answer to my question?' she said with a smile.

'You're very beautiful, you know, Mara,' Toin looked at her affectionately. 'You are beautiful, you are kind, you are clever. It's no wonder that the king is in love with you. But let an old man give you a little advice. Don't try to take the world on your shoulders. You're not responsible for everyone in the kingdom. You can't order everything. Just try to relax and let things take their course. Often things work out for the best in the end. Once I had an oak tree that fell down in the storm, completely uprooted with a gaping hole and half of its roots high in the air. Everyone wanted to cut it up for logs, but I said: *just leave it* and it was left, and do you know, that oak tree is living still, and no one, now, could tell that it was originally considered at the end of its life. Sometimes leaving things to settle is the best policy.'

'That's still not an answer to my question,' she said with a determined tilt of her chin, but his words had pleased her. 'Will you allow me to take over Ulick's debt – not for his sake but for the sake of the king? I don't want Turlough burdened by that. I know his feeling for Ulick – they were boys together and once Turlough gives his affection and trust, he gives it for life, no matter how unworthy the recipient.'

Toin smiled. 'I'd like to think about your question. Give

me one night. You will have your answer by tomorrow, or on Monday if I'm not well enough tomorrow.'

Mara looked at the greyness of his face and leaden colour of his lips and she did not have the heart to say any more. She would see him again.

Twenty

BRETHA NEMED TOÍSEC (JUDGEMENT TEXTS
CONCERNING PROFESSIONAL PEOPLE)

A briuga *should have a never-dry cauldron, a dwelling on
a public road and a welcome to every face.*

Uraicececht Becc (Small Primer)

It is expected that a briuga *should own at least a hundred
cows. He has equal status with the highest grade of poet
(a* file*). If he has land worth twice the land of his lord
then his status is equal to that lord.*

ॐ

TURLOUGH HAD ALREADY ARRIVED by the time that
Mara reached Cahermacnaghten. He was standing at
the gate to the law school, chatting to Brigid who had the
agonized, torn expression of one who, though overwhelmed

by the honour paid to her, is still conscious that there might be some problems arising with the supper cooking on the fires inside the kitchen. The two bodyguards were pacing the road and checking behind hedges anxious to discover and slay any enemy before tucking into one of Brigid's meals.

'My love.' Turlough left Brigid and strode over to lift Mara from her horse.

'My lord,' said Mara demurely, conscious of the amused expressions on the faces of the bodyguards.

'Guess where I've been!' said Turlough, holding her in his arms in a tight grip as Seán took the bridle of her mare and led it away into the stable.

'By the sea?' His high-bridged nose and prominent cheek-bones had a flush of summer sun about them. She disentangled herself gently, picking up an apple that had fallen from a small crab apple tree. Its leaves had all fallen during the couple of nights of heavy rain, but the clusters of small bright red apples on the tips of the branches glowed in the light from the setting sun. She smelled the apple and then offered it to Turlough's horse.

'That's right.' He beamed happily as he relinquished the reins into Cumhal's hand. 'I've been spending the day at Ballinalacken. You wouldn't believe the progress that they've made since you were there. Our bedroom is completely finished – it's right up next to the hall, everything is ready, the finest linen, a bedcover from Spain; I bought it from O'Malley of the ships; wait until you see it. And the hall; well, that's got the big window that you wanted already put in – no glass, yet – that has to come from France – why don't we make glass here in the west of Ireland?'

More expense, thought Mara, and what about that money borrowed by Ulick, but now guaranteed by Turlough. However, she said nothing. Tonight she would have to talk to him, but not yet, not until he had enjoyed his supper and shared his pleasure in his new residence with her. For now, she held tightly to his arm, hoping that he would always know the depth of her love and passion for him, no matter how much she was going to upset him when she revealed the identity of Sorley's murderer.

❋

Brigid was a wonderful cook, producing the most complicated dishes from her array of pots and pans over the kitchen fire, but the meal that Mara always enjoyed the most was a simple, thick slice of loin of beef. Tonight it was perfect, both pieces charred from contact with an iron plate heated to a red-hot point over a pinewood fire, Mara's slightly underdone and Turlough's almost raw.

'Try the sauce,' said Brigid eagerly. 'You've been so busy all the week, Brehon, that I haven't been able to ask you about it.'

The sauce was velvet smooth, almost black, rich with the musky scent of autumn woodlands. There was a hint of a sharper flavour underneath, but it was only when Mara chewed on a small, succulent piece that she knew what was the main ingredient.

'Mushroom,' she said in amazement. 'How on earth did you find mushrooms in November, Brigid?'

'It's very tasty,' said Turlough, lathering his meat with a plentiful supply.

'These are the mushrooms that I smoked over the pine

chips,' said Brigid beaming happily at her mistress. They shared a love of cooking. Now she looked expectantly at Mara.

'A little wine?' queried Mara tasting again.

Brigid nodded, but still looked expectant.

'Boiled boy,' said Turlough boisterously. 'I'm sure that I taste boiled boy. By the way, where are all those boys? I've not heard a sound from them since I arrived.'

'They are staying the weekend with Donogh O'Lochlainn and his lads – lads and lass,' amended Mara, thinking of Mairéad and her cloud of wild red curls. Hopefully Enda was occupied with chasing wolves only.

'So they are away for the weekend,' said Turlough with a meaningful gleam in his eye. 'Well that's very interesting!' He tried to catch Mara's eye and she avoided his glance, burying her nose in her cup of wine.

'It's a couple of juniper berries,' announced Brigid triumphantly.

'I'd never have guessed it,' said Mara, popping some beef in her mouth and trying not to giggle at Turlough's face. She felt a great love for him; he was like a child. Anything that he may have done was done as a child does things – the generous impulse of the moment, immediately acceded to without the weighing of consequences that she would have done. His upbringing would have been very different to the hard, disciplined study, which had formed her mind and character when she was a child. She would have to talk to him tonight and she knew that it would deeply wound him. Not yet, though, she thought, watching him enjoy his meal. Let him have a happy couple of hours with her first of all.

'Cumhal's bringing in some roasted roots,' said Brigid, watching with satisfaction the way that the Turlough's plate was being cleared. 'Would you like another slice of loin, my lord? It would only take me a minute to do one for you?'

'No, no,' said Turlough shaking his head vigorously. 'Ah Cumhal, yes, I'll have some of these. They look tasty.'

'Have some more wine,' said Mara pouring it from the flagon with a generous hand.

'Young Enda left this for you, Brehon,' said Cumhal. He put the small iron pot on the skillet by the fire and produced a scroll from his pouch.

'You don't want to be bothering with that tonight. You rest yourself. You've been working morning, noon and night this week,' scolded Brigid, so Mara, to please her, put the scroll in her pouch and continued with her meal.

'What is it?' asked Turlough. As soon as Brigid and Cumhal had disappeared, Mara had taken the scroll out and was unrolling it. She smiled as she scanned down the neatly written lines.

'Enda has made a case,' she said with amusement.

'Has he solved the murder, then?' said Turlough helping himself to some more mushroom sauce.

'He's a clever boy,' said Mara proudly, as she skimmed down through the list. 'He's arranged this very well; everything is very logical and very well set out. I'm lucky with my two eldest scholars. Enda has a mind as sharp as a well-honed knife and Fachtnan is a boy of great humanity with something very rare in a boy of his age: he has a sort of intuitive understanding of people.'

'How are he and little Nuala getting on?' asked Turlough,

going across to the hob by the fire and scraping the rest of the roasted parsnips on to his platter.

Mara smiled. 'I think they are still at the stage where he is very fond of her as a pretty child and she hero-worships him. The younger boys try to make more of it, but I'd say that is all there is to the affair at the moment. But Brigid and I are sure that there will be a wedding in the end.' Her mind went to Enda and the red-headed Mairéad once again. With luck, that would not be a match, at least until Enda was qualified and had a position. Mairéad, as the daughter of one of richest farmers on the Burren, would be considered a good match for Enda. However, at the moment, she appeared too empty-headed to make a suitable wife for a lawyer.

'Anything else, my lord?' Brigid stuck her head around the door after a perfunctory knock. 'Or for you, Brehon?'

'I think we have both had enough,' said Mara, 'thank you, Brigid, that was a wonderful meal.'

'I'll be dreaming of it when I go back to Thomond,' said Turlough heartily.

Brigid beamed. She would store up these words and everyone in the kitchen, every one of the farm workers and, within a few days, every one of the neighbours, would hear them.

'Well, what does the lad say, then?' asked Turlough, with a nod towards the scroll in her hand after Brigid and Cumhal had left.

'I can't fault his logic.' Mara read through the case notes again. 'Funnily enough a piece of evidence that I found out today and have not shared with the boys confirms what he says.' Her mind went briefly to the conversation with the porter at Newtown Castle and then she continued. 'Enda thinks that the murder was committed by Rory and Una, acting in unison. Una planned it; Rory executed. She could not have risked the verdict of *fingal* for herself, so she made sure to go into church in the company of her maidservant. She probably assured Rory that she would pay any fine if he were found out. He could always have pleaded that it was an accident, a prank that went wrong. Enda thinks that once the will was signed, then Una would have wanted to get rid of Sorley as soon as possible.'

'I guessed it,' said Turlough enthusiastically. 'I always did think that it was a woman's crime. I think . . .' There was the clang of the metal gate outside, the neigh of a horse, a loud knock at the door and then a quick rush of heavy, nailed boots outside in the passageway as Turlough's two bodyguards followed Brigid to the front door.

There was no alarm, though, no angry shouts, no clash of weapons, just a few words quietly spoken and then Brigid was at the door.

'It's a shame to trouble you, Brehon,' she said. 'But that's the manservant, Tomás, from Toin the *briuga*.'

'Send him in, Brigid,' said Mara quietly. She put aside an untouched glass of wine.

Tomás was pale with heavy dark circles around his eyes.

'He's not well, your master?' Turlough looked at the man with anxious concern.

'He's dying,' said Tomás. Suddenly his eyes filled with tears, but he blinked them away. 'The physician is with him and he says that he can't last more than a couple of hours.

He wants to see the Brehon. He asked for you. I know it's late, Brehon, but would you be able to come?' Tomás's voice was full of appeal.

'I'll come at once,' said Mara. This summons had come earlier than she had expected, but she was prepared for it.

Ṫwenṫy-one

GÚTHBRETHA CARATNIAD

(THE FALSE JUDGEMENTS OF CARATNIA)

There are seven witnesses whose testimony is always to be believed:

1. The evidence of a bishop given between the host and the chalice

2. The evidence of a woman in childbirth

3. The evidence of a man who walks seven times around the altar

4. The evidence of an honest person who has no interest in the case

5. The evidence of a person who swears an oath in three cemeteries

6. The evidence of a child who has not learned to lie

7. The evidence of a man on his deathbed

❦

NUALA WAS THERE IN the bedroom when Tomás brought in Mara. The fourteen-year-old's face was very white beneath her tanned skin, but she was holding Toin's wrist and counting his heartbeats with the assurance of a qualified physician.

'No more of that syrup for the moment,' she scolded, her tone of voice light-hearted and teasing. 'You're a terrible man for getting addicted to these drugs. First it was the poppy syrup and now it's that ivy berry mixture.'

'Just one sip,' said Toin with a smile. 'I want to be in good form to chat to the Brehon. I might even have another game of chess,' he added.

'No, you shouldn't,' said Nuala seriously. 'That last dose made your heart thud very fast. I could hear it. I don't think you should play chess, either. Just try to keep quiet and still.'

There would be no more chess for Toin; Mara could see that at a glance. The old man's face was livid and his lips were a strangely blue colour. Her own father had died when his heart failed and Toin resembled him at that moment.

'Just a chat, I think,' she said copying his own tone as she took a seat by the bed. 'I daren't play chess with you. You're too much of an expert for me.'

'Now, why don't you be a good girl, Nuala, and go and take a rest by the fire downstairs.' Toin's voice was quite strong; he almost seemed to have rallied since this afternoon, but the lips and the skin told its own story.

'You want to get rid of me.' Nuala smiled affectionately at her invalid. 'Do you want father to come? He's just gone for . . . gone for a little while,' she amended.

'Gone to fetch the priest,' said Toin. 'I asked him to do

that. You go down and entertain them both. The Brehon will come for you once I have finished talking to her.'

'I'll look after him, Nuala,' said Mara. Toin's strength was limited. Those few surges of power would be paid for with extreme weakness later on. She walked to the door with the girl, shut it carefully, drawing the heavy curtain across it and then returned to the bedside.

'I want you to write my will for me,' said Toin. 'I tried to do it myself but I was too weak to hold the quill. Will you do it?'

'Yes, of course, I have some vellum and a pen here in my satchel,' she added as she saw his eyes look fretfully around the room as if in search of writing materials.

'Just put down the usual stuff in the beginning,' he said.

So Mara dipped her quill in the ink horn and began to write, reading aloud as she formed the words on the vellum:

'*I, Toin the briuga, sometime physician, of Rathborney in the kingdom of the Burren, being of sound mind, though weak in body, do hereby bequeath . . .*' she stopped and looked enquiringly at him.

'*to my dear lord and king, Turlough Donn, Mac Teige,* . . . you can put the rest of it,' he broke off to say impatiently and she nodded, writing down Turlough's sonorous lineage.

'*. . . the sum of six hundred ounces of silver,*' he went on and her voice murmured the words after him and then she put down her pen and looked at him with astonishment. This was a huge sum.

'Go on,' he said with smile. 'You're just the scribe you know.'

And so she took up her pen again.

'. . . *in token of the very great favour that his patronage and friendship have paid to me during the years when I have been a* briuga *in this kingdom,*' he went on, his voice fluent and easy, and somehow regaining some of its former melodious power.

'*And I bequeath to Nuala, daughter of Malachy O'Davoren, physician in the kingdom of the Burren, my house at Rathborney and all the revenues from the farm situated in this place.*' A huge amount of pleasure now infused his voice and Mara wrote on, determined to say nothing. She was, as he said, just the scribe, taking his instructions.

'*This gift,*' continued Toin, '*is for her to have and to hold without conditions. However, this testator would like to express a hope that the gift will enable the said Nuala, daughter of Malachy O'Davoren, to fulfil her ambition to have a school of medicine and also to enable her to pursue her studies in that subject.*'

Mara found her eyes wet. It was an unbelievably kind and thoughtful gift.

'*I should like,*' continued Toin, but now his voice was weak and long gasps for breath punctuated every pause. There followed the usual simple bequests to faithful servants, money for Masses to be said for the eternal repose of the soul, so that Toin, the hospitaller, should find equal hospitality in the mansions of heaven.

And then with a slight smile on his face, Toin ended his last will and testament: '*I should like to leave to Mara, Brehon of the Burren, my silver and copper chess set and all of the Dutch bulbs in my garden and whatever flower or fruit bush or tree that she might wish to have.*'

Mara smiled. 'What a lovely gift,' she said appreciatively. But there was one more thing to be said and it had to be said. The truth had to be known.

'You leave nothing to your son,' she said mildly.

There was a silence for a minute and then, quite unexpectedly, he laughed, a full robust sound. 'How did you know?' he asked, and then stirring restlessly in the bed, he demanded, 'Give me some more of that potion of Malachy's. What does an hour more or less of life mean to me now?'

Without demur, Mara poured some of the inky black liquid from the phial into his open mouth. He gulped it down eagerly, shut his eyes and there seemed to be a sort of shudder that shook his whole body and lasted for a minute. For a moment Mara feared that she had killed him, but then his eyes opened again and she saw that the blue colour of his lips had softened to a light purple.

'I should have known you'd guess,' he said with amusement. 'I should have known once I had played a game of chess with you. You have that sort of mind. You make a quick leap of imagination; confirm the position and then move. I suppose this is checkmate to me. How did you guess that Cuan was my son? What led you to it?' He was alert and interested, his eyes shining with intelligence, his face was a better colour and Mara thought that she could proceed. She smiled at him and settled his pillow into a more comfortable position.

'You see,' said Mara, 'from the beginning this divorce puzzled me. When you told me the story first, I imagined Deirdre as a gentle, sweet-natured woman who could not stand up to her husband, but when I met her I found her to be tough, astute, intelligent; it seemed unlikely that a woman like that would be unaware of her rights, that she would allow herself to be divorced without a word in her defence, without an appeal to her powerful relations in Galway. But what if it was true? What if she had strayed from the marriage bed? Of course, you yourself made the point that there was no appearance of a lover afterwards, but that would not rule out a lover beforehand. If that were the case, she might have had a guilty conscience – you said that she was a very religious woman – so she might have felt that the divorce was a judgement on her. She might even have feared that her sin would be uncovered and her son's paternity questioned. By saying nothing, she left Cuan in his place as Sorley's son, and, under English law, his sole heir. And, of course, this is the reason why you have not left him anything in your will; you, no more than she, don't wish for any questions to be asked about the boy's parentage.'

She looked at him carefully, but he said nothing. His eyes betrayed interest, but nothing else, so she continued, 'And another thing also, Cuan did not look like either of his supposed parents. He is brown-eyed with good features. He probably looks quite like you when you were young.'

Toin smiled. 'I hope so,' he said. 'It would be good to think that something of me, though unacknowledged, lives on. I still wonder how you guessed.'

'The other thing was that the boy is musical. Sorley disliked music, according to you, yourself; and Deirdre, I noticed, seemed indifferent to it,' she continued. 'I knew that your father was a noted harpist in the service of Turlough's father and of his uncles and I wondered about why you didn't become a harp player; these positions are usually passed from father to son.'

'Not everyone inherits a talent,' said Toin drily.

'Ah, but you did inherit the talent.' Mara's reply was quick. 'The king has spoken of your beautiful singing voice and even to hear you speak is enough to tell that the talent is there. Turlough said something else too; he said that a physician cured you of some illness when you were young and then took you as an apprentice. Thinking of inheritance, I wondered if Cuan's problem with his hand had been inherited from you; that would explain why you could not become a harp player, with all the prestige and the high honour price that goes with the position. There is no deformity to be seen now, but I remember that you spoke of your mentor's cleverness as a surgeon.'

In answer, Toin stretched out his hand to her, turning it over so that she could examine it. The skin was sear, almost transparent, an old man's hand and there across the palm was a faint white scar, the track of a sixty-year-old knife incision.

'And what else brought you along the trail?' Toin seemed to be enjoying the talk. His brown eyes were alert and amused and his voice was strong with no trace of the breathlessness. In any case, Mara knew that she had to go on. The truth had to be established.

'Cuan's eyes were another clue.' Mara returned his smile. 'I've often noticed that a brown-eyed child always seems to have a brown-eyed parent, yet neither Deirdre nor Sorley had brown eyes. His were a light bright green and hers a blue grey. Cuan has your eyes.'

And then she was silent for a moment, thinking of Sorley's eyes swollen and protruding as she had seen them last. Had his murder been justified? Could anything justify murder? The deed was evil.

'I suppose,' she said aloud 'that you could not bring yourself to acknowledge the deed in case you shamed Deirdre and her son.' Mara's voice was gentle, but she knew that she had to establish the truth now. Toin had not much longer to live, she guessed. 'You were the last person into the church that morning,' she said aloud. 'You were sitting on a bench quite near the bees and you had a stick in your hand.'

'And you wove your case around these points? You couldn't prove anything from that in a law court, could you?' He sounded amused, almost as if she were the scholar and he the *ollamh*.

'I kept thinking that the person who has benefited from Sorley's death was Cuan,' Mara replied steadily and confidently, 'and yet, it was fairly obvious that he did not have the courage or the initiative for a quick spur-of-the-moment killing like that. But what if someone, someone else with a strong bond to Cuan, did it on his behalf? I thought of Deirdre, but nothing seemed to fit. And, of course, you, yourself, gave her an alibi; you said you saw her go into the church behind Cathal and that Sorley was still alive at that stage. This absolved both. In any case, I thought she was too cautious, too wary to do something like that. It was only when it flashed on me that Cuan was your son that everything fell into place.'

'Women's thinking!' There was a teasing smile on his face.

'That's the way I work; the solution comes and then I go step-by-step through the evidence. But I make no move until the logic is overwhelming.'

'Still no proof.' She hadn't seen Toin look so well for weeks. It was almost as if all of his energy had come back to him. Could that potion of ivy berries have had that effect? And, if so, how long would the over-stimulated heart keep beating?

'That's not quite right,' said Mara slowly, looking at him carefully. 'Yes, there was a piece of evidence which connects you, and you only, to the crime – not directly, perhaps, but certainly indicative of guilt.'

Toin surveyed her, a mixture of surprise and curiosity in his eyes.

'The plectrum,' she said. 'The silver plectrum belonging to Rory's zither. I noticed that zither the night that Turlough and I were at supper in Newtown Castle. It was of one piece with the surroundings, I observed that everything there was made from silver – and when Rory played that night he had a silver plectrum, but when he played for us on Wednesday night, after your supper party, he wore a gold plectrum on his thumb. And the silver plectrum had turned up, lying in the alcove where the hive had stood, on Sunday, the day of Sorley's burial, three days after his murder.'

'An indication of Rory's guilt, surely, rather than mine.' Toin cocked a bushy white eyebrow at her in an amused way.

'Possibly.' Mara's tone was non-committal, but then she added quickly, 'But only if it had been found straight after the murder. However, as a matter of fact, that place was searched very well by my scholars after Mass on All Saints' Day, on Friday and another boy, Marcan, searched the area immediately after Sorley's death on Thursday and I don't think that anything as noticeable as the plectrum would have been missed by any of them. This meant that I knew then that it was probably not Rory who murdered Sorley. It had to be the guilty person trying to lead me to think that Rory was the killer. I think what happened is that Rory mislaid it – probably it had vanished into your pouch – and you immediately offered the gold replacement. He took it, of course; he was always a greedy boy, and gold is better than silver. You kept the silver plectrum and you put it in the little alcove in the graveyard. I remember Tomás talking of you making too many visits to the church.'

He said nothing, just nodded, his expression amused and rueful, like that he wore when she took a piece of his during the chess game.

'And, of course, your name was mentioned in the evidence that we took at Poulnabrone. You were sitting on a bench outside the church, alone, while Tomás went back to fetch your medicine. I think that was the time that the beehive was overturned. By the time Tomás arrived, Sorley was dead and there was nothing to attract your servant's attention. He would not have been able to see the body from the wooden bench where you sat. We were all busy thinking about who came late into church, but of course your name did not arise because you did not attend the service after all.'

'I'm not denying anything.' Toin's voice was fainter now. The over-bright eyes had begun to dull. 'I'm just interested in seeing how your mind works. You're right, of course. I did kill him; I hadn't planned it, but when I saw the opportunity, I took it. I wanted to punish him; time after time, I saw him scream at my son and hit him, an innocent boy who had always given Sorley his love and his duty. I didn't care whether the man died.'

'And your collapse, was that feigned in order to give you a few minutes alone without Tomás?'

'No,' said Toin wryly. 'I don't need to feign weakness and pain; I live with both, they are my constant companions. I sat on the bench, sent Tomás for the poppy syrup, saw Sorley, wandering along with his eyes fixed on his wax tablets, saw the bees in the hive,' and the weak voice grew weaker, but then with tremendous effort of will, it strengthened. 'I suppose,' said Toin, 'I wished for him to be stung and the wish prompted the deed.'

'And, of course, you had your stick with you. It was when I saw Anluan's stick that the last piece of the puzzle fell into place.'

'It was done quickly,' said Toin. 'It was done, and I'm still not sure whether it was wrong or it was right.'

There was a silence after that. What would the judgement of heaven be upon Toin's deed? The root of the matter had all happened eighteen years ago. Did the love of man for his son justify that death? Toin lay with his eyes closed and Mara could not bring herself to say any word of reproof or of condemnation. Her place was to establish the truth and appoint restitution, not to condemn.

'So Sorley was correct after all.' Mara was suddenly struck by the thought and she smiled. 'Deirdre did have a lover.'

'No, he wasn't right.' Toin opened his eyes and spoke

vigorously. 'Deirdre and I were lovers on one occasion only. He never knew anything of the matter. Many years later, he just wanted to get rid of her and he bribed the Brehon of Kinvarra. Deirdre was shocked by it all. She was a very religious woman. She never even acknowledged that Cuan was my son; though I knew the truth once I saw his pitiable little hand. Poor lad,' added Toin compassionately. His face was reflective, thinking back over the past.

'There is only one thing more that I must ask you,' said Mara. 'I still am not certain what happened to Rory the bard.' There was a dread within her of asking this question, but she forced herself to do it. Would this man, so kind and so gentle, a man who was driven to do an evil thing on the spur of the moment, pushed by anxiety for his unfortunate son and anger at the terrible blight cast on so many lives by this evil silversmith – was Toin also responsible for the murder of a venal, but harmless young man in the first flower of his manhood? Or was her surmise correct?

'Rory,' Toin's voice strengthened. There was even a slight smile on the dry lips. 'I've known many "Rorys" in my life. You can do a lot with them by the application of a little silver. Don't worry about Rory. He's gone off to Brittany with Cathal; they'll like him over there; they enjoy the Irish music. I paid for his passage and gave him enough silver to keep him going for quite some time.'

'I see,' Mara nodded. Her lips curved in a cynical smile. 'He went to see Una first thing in the morning that he left; no doubt he extracted some silver from her, also. He should do well, that young man.'

And then a thought struck her and she asked: 'But what

was this business of leading everyone to believe that he was lost on the mountain?'

Toin chuckled, a weak, hoarse sound, but undeniably a chuckle. 'I planned that; I thought it would keep you busy and keep your mind away from Cuan. You would have found out sooner or later that Rory had walked across the mountain pass to the harbour at Fanore and gone in Cathal's ship. You would then have thought that he fled the country because of guilt. He would have been, in everyone's mind, the man that killed Sorley, the silversmith. And, of course, I would have protected Deirdre's secret and allowed my son to retain his inheritance.'

Mara smiled. 'Well, I sent Cumhal over to Drumcreehy and a man on the quayside told him that Cathal left early because he had to pick up a passenger at Fanore. I was fairly sure, though I could not be certain, that it was Rory. I suppose you sent the sea captain off early as a way of keeping me hunting after clues, also; you were a good customer of his, he would have done that for you. He would not have gone earlier than he planned for a nobody like Rory.'

'The truth is there for you now,' said Toin. He drew in a deep breath and made a visible effort to rally his strength. 'But it must now be confessed openly to all in the kingdom, once I am dead. No one else must be burdened by any breath of suspicion. I would just ask this one thing of you, Brehon, that you spare Deirdre and my son by not allowing my reasons to become public.'

Mara nodded silently. She could do that, she knew. No one on the Burren would question her; most would be sympathetic to Toin and saddened by his death. '*Marbhaid cach marbh a chinta'*, 'every dead man buries his offences', was a proverb well known to all.

'Let's get this will witnessed, then.' Toin's voice was brisk, but his lips told another story. He would not have much longer to set his affairs in order. 'Tomás will call two stablemen. I told him to have them ready. Once that is done, I want you to bring in the king and Malachy and Nuala. Tell them to come with the priest. Convince that young man that I want to make my last confession in public and before witnesses.'

✻

'I confess to Almighty God, to all the angels and saints, and to you, father.' The faint voice of the dying man lent a fearsome solemnity to the words uttered so perfunctorily at Mass every Sunday. Mara knelt down on the floor beside the bed and Turlough also dropped to his knees on the other side. Distressed, he stretched forward a hand and Toin took it and held it. After a minute he continued, with long pauses to gasp in enough air to keep his dying heart still beating, his brown eyes looking anxiously at Turlough. 'And I confess to you, my lord king, that I have sinned grievously in thought and deed.'

The young priest moved slightly, as if to focus the penitent's attention on himself, but Toin's eyes remained fixed on Turlough's compassionate face.

'I confess that on the eve of *Samhain*, I caused the death of Sorley the silversmith by overturning a bee hive with the intention of causing harm or death to him.'

Then the sick man's voice strengthened.

352

'I ask pardon for this deed of God Almighty; of you, father; and of my dear lord and king, Turlough Donn O'Brien.' The voice faded and the dark eyes closed. The young priest lifted his hand, but then Toin opened his eyes again. Now they had to strain to hear the feeble murmur.

'I also ask pardon of God, of my king and of the king's Brehon, that, to conceal my crime, I wove a tissue of lies and tried to put others under suspicion.' His voice broke. His mouth opened and closed as if the energy needed to form the words was too much for him. Beside her, Mara heard Nuala make a small moan. She put an arm around the girl and looked an appeal at Malachy.

But then Toin seemed to rally. In a surprisingly strong voice, he said, 'May the Lord have mercy on my soul.'

'Now may God bless you and forgive you your sins.' The priestly voice was loud and confident. 'May He bring you into everlasting life. In the name of the Father, the Son and the Holy Ghost.'

And as the November new moon reached its midnight place, high over the sacred mountain of Mullaghmore, Toin breathed his final breath.

❋

When the early morning bell for matins sounded from the abbey, Mara and Turlough rode home from Rathborney to Cahermacnaghten. It was a silent journey. She had read the will to him as well as to Malachy, Nuala and to those who had served Toin so faithfully. Only the servants had received their bequests with simple pleasure. Turlough had been overwhelmed by feelings of bewilderment, gratitude and sensations of unworthiness, and, strangely, Nuala had almost seemed to share those emotions, receiving the news with a passionate outbreak of weeping.

Mara and Turlough had left her there at Rathborney with her father. After a few hours' sleep, she and Malachy could inspect the house and farm which was to be hers. Nuala would need some time to recover from the emotions of the night and the shock of knowing that all of these possessions were to be hers. But recover she would, and she would make good use of Toin's legacy.

I'll leave her to her father today, thought Mara as she and Turlough rode through the valley. The morning was misty, but already there was a promise of a fine day in the pale gold of the sky over Mullaghmore. The mountains were now clear of fog, their outlines crisp in the dawn light, and the rounded heads of a line of oak trees glowed amber against their silver flanks.

And make the time to talk to her next week, her thoughts ran on ... *and I must go and see Cuan and try to put a bit of backbone into him ... and keep Toin's secret as a sacred confidence ... and give Deirdre some advice ... and make sure that Una gets her dues ... and force them into rebuilding that wretched village and caring for the mineworkers ... oh, and check that Finn O'Connor makes proper provision for Sheedy ... and have a word with Muiris about the budding romance between Aoife and Daire ... and make sure that everyone knows that Rory has gone to France so that no ugly rumours attach themselves to Cuan ... and talk to Turlough about Ulick ...*

Mara's mind was filled with that strange clarity that

comes sometimes after a sleepless night. She continued sorting out her tasks for the week ahead. But then she smiled to herself, remembering Toin's words: *'Don't try to take the world on your shoulders. You're not responsible for everyone in the kingdom. You can't order everything. Just try to relax and let things take their course.'*

The sun was just rising as their horses breasted the last hill before the law school. Smoke rose from the kitchen house: Brigid was preparing breakfast, shouting orders to Nessa. In the distance, Seán sauntered down the Kilcorney road driving the cattle towards the milking cabin and Cumhal briskly chopped wood in the yard. The sky to the east was now a glory of pale gold, streaked with the delicate blue of a fine autumn morning. The paved road was softened with piles of yellow hazel leaves and crisp brown nutshells and the sealing-wax red gloss on the rose hips blazed in the hedges above them. In a sheltered spot across the road, a spindle tree still kept its flame-coloured leaves and its berries glowed in the early morning sunlight like tiny flowers – the dull pink segments spread wide open to reveal the orange seed within their star-like shape.

Mara reined in her horse and turned to the man riding silently by her side.

'Turlough,' she said, 'it's going to be a lovely day. Let's go over to Ballinalacken Castle after breakfast: it's Sunday and there will be no workers there; we'll have the place to ourselves and you can show me that splendid bedchamber.'

And later on, at sunset, she thought, as she watched his face with a feeling of great tenderness, they would sit, just the two of them, by the new, three-mullioned window in the hall and look across the white-capped waves to watch a sky that flamed with banners of crimson, saffron and royal purple behind the misty blue outlines of the Aran Islands.

And they would talk of their future life together.